HALF DEAD

HALF
DEAD

A NOVEL

Brandon Graham

CROOKED
LANE

NEW YORK

Copyright © 2021 by Brandon Graham

Published in the United States by Crooked Lane Books, an imprint of The Quick Brown Fox & Company LLC.

Library of Congress Catalog-in-Publication data available upon request.

ISBN (hardcover): 978-1-64385-822-7
ISBN (ebook): 978-1-64385-823-4

Cover design by Patrick Sullivan

Printed in the United States.

www.crookedlanebooks.com

Crooked Lane Books
34 West 27th St., 10th Floor
New York, NY 10001

First Edition: August 2021

10 9 8 7 6 5 4 3 2 1

For Michelle—for every good thing.

Homing Instincts

Calvert waits inside. There is no other option. It's early, still dark out. He sees a thin transparency of himself reflected in the pane of glass. It's uncomfortable to look at what he's become. He wills his eyes to focus through his likeness to the circle drive out front. No car has arrived.

The main entrance of New Horizons is like an airlock: exterior doors open onto an alcove of glass and steel, and a second set of doors open into the facility. Calvert knows the exterior doors have to be closed tight before the interior doors can open, and vice versa. To use the doors, one must be buzzed in or possess a code.

The keypad next to him looks like a solar calculator screwed to the wall. Despite being officially discharged as a patient, he hasn't been trusted with the code. Nobody is at the front desk, no one to push the buzzer that unlocks the doors. He's as anxious as he is currently capable of being. He doesn't know how he'll leave when his ride arrives.

Worry is exhausting. It pushes his overtaxed intellect to the edge of failure. *My breaker could flip.*

The admissions area is not a place for loitering. There are no chairs for him to sit in. He uses his cheap suitcase as a stool. It is neither stable nor comfortable. The cushioning fat of his rump has atrophied since his accident. His bones grind against the hard edges of the suitcase. His body sends pain signals to his brain, a curious sensation. After a time he decides he prefers standing.

"Professor Greene. There you are. I, like, went by your room and couldn't find you. I thought you, like, made a run for it. Just kidding." Abbey touches his shoulder.

He's not certain of Abbey's job. She'd been assigned to him recently, and they'd been together daily to prepare him for independent living. The young lady has tendencies he finds difficult: she often edges in too close, and she's loud, speaks fast, and asks questions she answers before he can form a thought. *She's bewildering.* Her eyebrows are dishonest, like tadpoles bobbing over wide, black eyes, and they move around her forehead independent of the other parts of her face. As always, Calvert's gaze goes to her forehead.

"Are you, like, all set? Of course you are." Her hand brushes along his arm and takes his fingers where they dangle aimlessly. She pulls him to the doors. Her hand flutters over the keypad. The lock pops. She pushes the door and holds it open. He walks his suitcase out ahead of her. "You packed everything? I bet you did. Ready to start your new life? I know you are."

"Yes," he says. As an afterthought he takes issue with the term "new life." He knows from experience correcting her is pointless. She always misunderstands him.

"I, like, knew it," she says. She has her phone in one hand. She taps the screen and reads. "Your driver's name is Agatha. This is what she looks like." She tips an image in his direction, takes it away before his brain can process. "Looks like a nice person. Right? Yes. She really does." Abbey follows him into the airlock. The door catches firmly behind her. She taps a second keypad and they exit.

The wind hisses in Calvert's ear. He knows air can't make words. *I'm not crazy.* But this morning it carries voices with it. First he hears a wail of anguish, then an infant's laugh, and last an escalating squabble between lovers he can tell will end badly. The wind whisks the people away, and he notes the rattle of an engine coming closer. A car drives slowly in their direction, headlights pinning him in place.

"Like, right on time," Abbey says.

Calvert recognizes the make and model. "We owned a Vue," he says.

"Yes," Abbey says, glancing up at the moon. "It is a nice view."

"The car," he says. "A Saturn Vue—we had one like it."

"Wow, Professor! Your memory is coming back." Abbey isn't really paying attention to him. Her accolades are generated automatically.

The car pulls to the curb. Abbey waves and the driver rolls down the window. Agatha, the driver, is a granny with short white hair and a loose, crinkled face. "This New Horizon?"

"Yes," Abbey says. She opens the back door for Calvert.

Calvert pushes his suitcase in, settles, and buckles.

The two women talk through the front window.

Calvert pays no attention. The seat is soft. *More comfortable than the suitcase.*

Abbey raps on the window next to his head. He watches her eyebrows swim toward each other. There is no crank to turn. He can't find a button for the window. He gives up. Abbey flaps her hand so quickly it looks like she's holding a bird, like a magician manifesting a pigeon from nothingness. She is waving goodbye. He places his palm flat on the glass. The car rolls forward. His dry skin leaves no phantom print when he takes his hand away.

"All set back there?" Crinkled Agatha asks.

"All set."

"You like country music?"

He considers the question seriously. "I don't think so," he says.

Agatha doesn't turn on any music. She may be mad at him. Calvert isn't certain.

The sky glows a weak gray as sunrise approaches. He watches the half-familiar world out the window. They stop at a traffic light. A man with a green Mohawk and chewing an unlit cigar stands under a streetlight, holding a sign that reads "Homeless vet seeking human kindness." The vet extends a plastic coffee can and shakes it. Agatha rolls her window up.

How many servings of kindness fit in a coffee can? Calvert wants to know.

"I'll have you to your place in no time," Agatha says as the Vue gets back in motion.

Calvert speaks with no forethought. "Can we make a stop?"

"That girl from Horizon told me to take you to your apartment and be sure you make it in the door. You're supposed to get ready for something or the other."

He hadn't realized he was planning anything until now. "I remember my old address." He accesses it, repeats it in his mind so it won't slip away. His nose aims loosely in the direction of the building he and Mere had called home. "I need to get my things." Agatha doesn't reply, only watches him through the rearview mirror. "I have money. I can pay," he adds.

"I'd love to help." Agatha is persuaded.

He considers what he's about to do. "Will you wait while I go in?

"How long?"

"I'm not sure. I'll pay you for your time."

"I can wait. It's not a problem."

Eighteen minutes later, Agatha circles the block four times, trying to find a spot before parking at a CVS near the coroner of Huron and Wells. "I'll take that money now."

Calvert passes a folded bill to her.

"This is a dollar."

He passes another bill.

"That's more like it. I'll wait twenty-one minutes. That's a dollar a minute. It doesn't get fairer than that. If you're not back, I'm going. Sound good?"

He replays the verbal contract. "Yes." He opens the door and bumps the next car. He tries to slip out and finds he's still buckled. He can't work the button. "I'm stuck."

Agatha gets out, jostles sideways between vehicles, and reaches across Calvert to undo his seat belt. "Best take your stuff in case I have

4

to leave." Everything she says sounds like a threat. Calvert does as he's told.

He walks his suitcase to the front of the building marked with the address he remembered. It doesn't look familiar, not at all. He fears he made it up. He sees movement inside. Based on the expression of the doorman, he recognizes Calvert.

The doorman opens the door, already talking, "Professor Greene, what a surprise. How longs it been? Hadn't heard you'd be by."

"Picking up some things."

The doorman holds the door wide. Calvert stops short.

"Can I take your bag?" the doorman asks.

"Yes." Calvert passes the suitcase. "Also, I lost my key." He walks in.

In the elevator, Calvert hesitates over the array of buttons. The doorman reaches in and pushes "5." They stand side by side. Calvert doesn't trust his social assessments, but he thinks a tense silence develops.

The doorman eventually says, "I was sorry to hear about your wife."

"Thank you," Calvert answers reflexively. He's pleased with the response. He's also afraid to ask what about his wife makes the doorman feel sorry.

"So sad. I couldn't go on if I lost my Betty."

Calvert remembers "lost" is a euphemism for death. *Does he mean Meredith is dead?* He'd suspected it when she never came to visit during his recovery. The doors open and he's saved from formulating an emotion.

They walk past three apartments before the doorman unlocks a door and switches on lights. He gives Calvert the key and stands with one hand turned up. The hand makes a shallow reservoir. Calvert imagines if he dribbled water in the hollow place it would attract birds. *Abbey's flapping hand could fly over for a drink.* Calvert stares intently into the hand while thinking this over. The hand goes away.

"If you don't need anything else, I have to get back. Bring the key when you're done."

The door closes.

Calvert is alone, a dead man surrounded by ghosts.

Conflict Resolution

He feels immediately overwhelmed being in this place. Not by the moment he's standing in, but by a torrent of past sensations. He makes his feet move him to the kitchen. The second he sees the linoleum floor, a scene plays on the screen in his mind.

Young Calvert in a kitchen with an older boy. Not this kitchen. The two stand facing one another. Calvert doesn't know the older boy; he only knows he held a deck of cards when he said, "You want to play?" Calvert didn't answer. "Well? You know about cards or not?"

"Sure I do," Calvert said. "I know all about cards."

The bigger kid held the deck out, an offer. He pulled away the moment Calvert reached out. "You must know how to play canasta?"

"No. Not really."

"You ever hear of euchre?"

"No. Sounds made up. Is it real?"

"Hell yes, it's real. What about poker? You must play poker." The older boy let himself sound frustrated.

"Yes," Calvert said. "I heard of that one."

The older boy cut the deck, shuffled the two stacks together. Knocked the pile against the counter a few times. "You have to bet in poker. You got any money?"

Calvert went through a pantomime of checking his pockets before saying, "No."

"Then poker is out. What can we play? What can we play? Any ideas? I know. You ever hear of fifty-two-card pickup?"

"Yes. Of course," Calvert lied.

"You want to play that?"

"Okay. I'll play. You might have to tell me the rules."

"The rules are simple."

Calvert, watching the memory play, can clearly see the glee in the boy's expression. The kid thrust the cards at Calvert's face, bent the deck back, released his grip, and shot the cards against Calvert's head and chest. Calvert squeezed his eyes against the onslaught, against the deception, against the meanness. The older boy laughed the laugh of someone who'd fallen for the same trick. It was the joy of subjecting the next victim to the same injury. Decades ago, Calvert stood in a kitchen amid the scattered cards and started to cry. It had only made the other boy laugh harder.

In this place, besieged by a life now lost, Calvert feels much as he did back then, sharp shards of memories ricocheting off him, falling in a random, loose pile around his shoes. He feels wronged and robbed, attacked and confused. He can't make sense of it. *My memories are a jumble; everything is out of order.* He doesn't want to sort through the fragments, is afraid to remember what hand he'd been dealt and how he'd chosen to play it.

He blinks it all away and reaches for the refrigerator, as he would have any evening after work. It's nearly empty, only a pile of ketchup packets in the butter cubby. *If Meredith is dead, who cleaned the fridge?*

The digital clock on the microwave is flashing: 00:00. He deduces the power went out. *Or time has ended.* The thought of time reminds him that Crinkled Agatha is waiting.

He passes through a living room that used to be his and into the bedroom he shared with a woman only he was allowed to call Mere. The mattress is bare and has a brown stain near the foot. *Blood? No.* He knows it's from spilled wine.

7

The closet is mostly empty, the mirrored accordion doors left open, with plastic hangers strewn on the ground. *Someone took Meredith's clothes, the photos from the dresser, her shoes and purses and belts.*

In the bathroom, the medicine cabinet is empty except for a razor, shaving cream, and some tubes of ointment. He finds his toiletry bag under the sink. His drawer of deodorant, hair gel, and waxed cinnamon floss looks untouched. He takes the things he thinks he'll need. In the bedroom he finds a gym bag. He fills it with socks, underwear, and other clothes. From the side table drawer he takes a wristwatch, a wallet full of expired IDs, and a stash of twenty-dollar bills. He tucks the wallet in his pocket.

There's more room in the bag, so he throws in a suit and a fistful of neckties. He rummages in the dresser until he locates a certain photo of Meredith. She's in the sun, cheeks tan, on a ribbon of beach with the ocean behind her. *The Mediterranean.* He creases the photo and puts it in the wallet with the cash.

He throws the duffel's strap over his head and passes back through the apartment. He remembers to take his suitcase and hurries down the hall to the elevator. On the way down, he realizes he doesn't have the apartment key. He didn't lock up. By the time the elevator slows, he knows the doorman's name is Justus.

He finds three people in uniform when the doors open. There's a skinny man with buzzed blond hair and an older woman with hair combed close to her skull, both in Chicago Police Department uniforms, complete with too-short bulletproof vests over black cargo pants. The skinny man's name is sewn on the right side of his chest: "Becker." The third person in uniform is Justus, the doorman. He stands at the back but looks anxious to step closer. Realization dawns like a stab of light piercing his eye: *Justus's hand had been cupped to hold money.*

The two cops approach as Calvert steps out. Becker moves behind Calvert and takes his wrists, making him drop the suitcase. He yanks the duffel over Calvert's head, dragging the strap roughly across his ear.

The other officer says, "Are you Calvert Greene?"

"It's him," Justus says.

She turns to glare at Justus. "Let him answer." Calvert reads the word "Police" stitched across her back. *Redundant,* he thinks. She turns to Calvert again and asks, "Are you Greene?"

He feels he needs to answer quickly. "I'm Greene. I'm Calvert. Yes." Behind him, cold cuffs slap on one wrist. It startles him. He pulls away. Becker wrangles him.

"Mr. Greene," the female officer says, "are you aware you trespassed on property you have been prohibited from entering by restraining order?"

Justus says, "An injunction."

Behind Calvert, Becker asks, "What's the difference?" He ratchets the second cuff closed.

The woman says, "First you get a restraining order—"

Justus interrupts. "There was a restraining order issued around the time detectives came to search the apartment."

The officer gives Justus another withering look. Justus shuts his mouth with an audible *clop.* Calvert studies the Chicago flag on her sleeve. The six-pointed star is not in the symmetrical rhythm of a Star of David. The female cop says, "First a temporary restraining order, then the prosecutor's office can go to a judge. Based on the evidence before the court, an injunction may be issued."

"Yes," Justus says, determined to stay relevant. "That's what they said. An injunction. Call the police if Professor Greene shows up 'cause his wife's family filed an injunction."

Calvert's eyes are drawn from Justus's smug face to someone outside. Agatha is approaching fast. She barges in. "Are you coming or not?"

Calvert ignores her question. "I needed my clothes," he explains to the officer in charge. He steps forward.

Becker tugs up on the cuffs. Calvert feels the head of his right humerus torque out of socket. There's a lot pain. Despite being mostly numb to such things, a scream escapes Calvert.

Crinkled Agatha produces a phone and starts shooting video. "I'm documenting this. Police brutality. Police brutality. This is on the record."

Everyone talks at once.

"I said to be careful about that," the female officer yells at Becker. Then to Agatha, "You don't need to record this."

"You'll be on the nightly news. You are about to be famous. Not in a good way."

"Infamous," Justus adds.

"That's right," Agatha says. "About to be infamous."

"I barely tugged it," Becker says.

To Calvert, everything sounds far away, like listening from six feet underground.

"I was told to call," Justus says to Calvert. It might be an apology.

Despite the pain, Calvert keeps his feet under him.

"Police brutality," Agatha says again. She moves her phone closer to Calvert's anguished expression.

"You got to stay back," the senior officer warns.

That's when Calvert blacks out.

Moe's Fresh Ride

It's hazy out as Moe pedals down Cermak to grab the Pink Line at Cicero. She rolls past the Tastee Donuts on her left and the liquor store to her right before lifting her ass from the seat to bump over the tracks. She dismounts and ignores the bike parking.

She finds her usual spot tucked next to the fare card machine and uses it to shelter from the damp wind. Out of habit, she tries to unsnap the chinstrap of her helmet. *I forgot my helmet.* She makes a clucking sound with her tongue. *Need more sleep.*

Moe hates feeling sorry for herself. She looks for a distraction. She read somewhere it's seven miles from this platform to Union Station. She turns her eyes east to the place where the rails pinch into one line. Tall buildings, like the woody stalks of swamp plants rise around the vanishing point. She takes her phone from a side pocket on her messenger bag and checks the time. *Running late.*

She ignores the other people by sipping thin tea from an insulated thermos she takes from her bike's bottle rack. The grass-flavored water is no substitute for strong coffee, but the ritual half satisfies.

It's not long before she hears the train approach like a gathering storm. She stays put as the train's brakes grab and the doors open with a hydraulic exhale. She lets everyone board ahead of her. Finally she lifts her bike over the gap and stands it vertical as the doors close.

The ride to Clinton and Lake is short. Holding Bernstein, the bike she'd named after her favorite journalist, is no inconvenience. When the train reaches her stop, a number of seated commuters trade places with those standing and begin to bunch in a herd in front of the exit. She rests the bike against her left hip, her wide stance a brace against a sudden jolt. She and Bernstein will be the first to exit. She can feel the pent-up pressure of the crowd. Before the doors open, the mass edges ahead and someone knocks into her bike. It twists, grinding the narrow seat into her hip.

"So sorry," a woman's voice, very near, apologizes.

Moe turns and sees an angel with creamy skin in a dark suit, auburn hair in big rich waves, makeup luminous and flawless. Moe doesn't go for the business types, but she likes what she sees.

"So sorry," the woman says again, followed by an embarrassed smile.

Moe puts on her best James Dean and says, real cool, "No problem, ma'am." She doffs the brim of an imagined cowboy hat.

The doors crack open, and she and Bernstein turn the opposite direction from the crush of bodies heading for the ramp to the street. Once people quit pouring out, a wave of commuters washes into the train. The doors close, the train leaves, and the platform is deserted. Moe exits down the ramp, Bernstein rolling beside her until she hits the sidewalk. She checks her phone to make sure she's had no messages from Vivian, before throwing her leg over the bike and edging her way into traffic. Once she has her bearings, it's a short ride to her meeting with a guy named Ricky.

Ricky, she'd learned in correspondence the night before, owns a business called Grip Audio, installing after-market sound systems from a garage near Washington and Peoria. The spot is easy to find, and the overhead door is open as she coasts to a stop. She can see the Honda CB550 sitting inside. It looks better than the pictures she'd seen. A lanky guy with a saggy ass is knocking around at a workbench.

She walks Bernstein through the door and calls, "Ricky?"

Ricky drops what he's doing and reaches his lemur arms behind him to wipe his long fingers over the butt of his coveralls. He's all elbows and knees and seems to fold and refold as he moves. It's insectoid and it makes Moe's skin prickle. He extends his mostly clean hand for a shake. He towers over her diminutive frame. The poor quality of the handshake is repellent.

"You found me," he says, letting her hand slip from his feeble grasp. "You the one here about the motorcycle, right?"

"I've been looking for a while." She leans Bernstein against the nearest wall and eyes the Honda. It's her dream bike. She can afford what Ricky is asking. But she hopes to get a better deal. She puts on an unimpressed expression.

"Nice bike," Ricky says, looking at Bernstein.

"Cyclocross. A good all-around bike." She doesn't mention a cracked weld where the top tube joins the head tube, getting worse with every pothole. "I hate to sell him. He's a treasure."

"Looks good," Ricky says. As if she's a mother whose child has been called adorable, Moe decides Ricky isn't so bad.

"Tell me about the Honda?"

"Well, . . ." Ricky scruffs his chin stubble, considering where to begin. "Got the bike about two years ago as a gift for a girl I was dating." He fills the space between sentences with a sour look. "She never learned to ride it. When I found it, it was real grimy. It'd been sitting a while in an old chicken coop out in Kane County. I saw a "For Sale" sign when I went to catch a minor league game. The Cougars. Real fun, real fun. You ever been?"

"I never have."

"Real fun. Highly recommend. The bike was covered in dust and feathers and smelled like chicken shit. But the price was right. It had bad gas in the tank, you know."

Moe nods that she knows. She hunkers down to look over the engine.

"You can see I changed the exhaust to a high-performance setup." He waggles a long finger at the chrome pipes. "Mostly I gave it a good tune-up. Cleaned the carbs with Pine-Sol, boiled the jets in lemon juice. Replaced the plugs and wires. Got some fresh gas running through her. The inside of the tank was in good shape. What else?" he asks himself. "Charging system is strong. Battery is new. The body is in good shape. Really good. Long story short, when Crazy Vicky left she didn't take the bike."

"Ricky and Vicky huh?" Moe says. "Very cute."

"Shoulda known it was a bad omen when our names rhymed."

"Live and learn." Moe smiles at him to seem polite.

Ricky goes on, "After you said you were stopping by, I checked to make sure she was ready. She started straight away. I tooled around the block a few times, then rode out past the lot where Harpo used to sit. McDonald's built some giant complex on the lot. Seems strange, but what do I know? She rode great. I almost changed my mind about selling her. What else?"

Moe has ridden a little, mostly around warehouses in the Fulton River District. But she can see herself on the bike. "You said you wanted three for it?" Moe stands slowly, shoves her hands in the front pockets of her skinny jeans.

"Yes. I've got more than that in it. But it doesn't make sense to keep her."

Moe's body is buzzing. She wants the bike. She already has riding boots, and they look fucking tough. Vivian, her boss, told her to get a real vehicle if she wants to move up. Looked at the right way, the Honda is an investment.

Last night, in anticipation of this moment, she narrowed the bike's name down to two options: either Taibbi after the *Rolling Stones* contributor, or Fahrenthold after the *Washington Post* reporter. In person, the bike just doesn't look like a Fahrenthold. The moment she settles on a name, she knows she's going to buy it. "Think I can take him for a spin?" She pats Taibbi's seat.

Ricky talks her through the start-up procedure. Moe finds his instruction more helpful than insulting. The engine fires up. Ricky hands Moe a helmet the same forest green as the bike's tank, full face with a yellow bubble shield. She likes the look. On the back she finds a curly script that reads "Vicky." She gives it a long look.

"That will come off. I don't want the helmet," Ricky says.

She uses the chinstraps to tug the helmet on. It's perfect. Snug but not tight, and her field of vision is unobstructed. The yellow tint gives her artificial hope. For Ricky's amusement she says, "Vicky must have been a pumpkin head." Her voice is muffled, like talking into a pillow.

"Yeah. But it was mostly hair." Ricky replies.

Moe pulls out of the garage and rides toward Randolph. She takes it slow, keeping her head up and scanning side to side. The helmet is heavier than she's used to. *Neck is going to be sore.*

The streets are lined with cars along both sides, which makes the way narrow. She smells in the air a mix of heat coming off the Honda and greasy short-order food. The transmission shifts easily and she zips down the length of the block, slows to a stop, looks for cross traffic, then accelerates down the next block. Her fingers get cold in the wind. She can hear the traffic from the Eisenhower, cars honking, and a radio blaring a conservative talk show. She makes it to the main drag and works her way through a confusing traffic snarl before turning left. The West Loop has been transformed over the past couple decades, from a rugged series of warehouse loading docks into an epicenter of luxury lofts and retail boutiques, art galleries, repurposed architectural salvage, nightclubs, and one restaurant after another.

A Porsche Cayenne backs in front of Moe. Her reflexes save her. She leans the motorbike to turn it, has to drop a foot to keep from laying the bike down, rolls on the throttle and zips out of harm's way. *Now it's a test drive.* She reaches up and gives Taibbi a pat on the headlight before finding a place to make a U-turn and ride back to Grip Audio.

She has trouble finding the kickstand. Her legs are rubbery. She drags the helmet off and hangs it from the throttle grip.

"Pretty sweet ride, huh?" Ricky says.

Her phone buzzes. With one hand she combs her fingers through her hair, with the other she tugs her phone loose from the bag at her back.

Vivian: *Get your ass north of the river. There's a body. I'll send the exact location. First come, first serve.*

The message had been sent three minutes earlier. As she's looking, a follow-up text pops up, with an address. "First come, first serve" is Vivian's way of telling Moe to move it before another freelancer files the story. Especially before Jerome gets there. *Jerome is relentless.* Ricky waits. Moe taps a fast reply and tucks the phone away. She looks at Bernstein. It would be a hard pedal in morning traffic. She makes a decision.

"I'll give you twenty-three-fifty and the cyclocross in trade."

"Well," Ricky says slowly, rubbing his chin, "I'll do twenty-six, the trade, and you keep the helmet."

"Let's call it twenty-five." Moe crushes his hand to seal the deal before Ricky can decline.

She is out the door on Taibbi in four minutes flat.

Unmet Expectations

Whistler walks straight toward the desk sergeant. He plants his newly polished shoes firmly and stands so his shiny badge on his new belt clip can be easily observed. The desk sergeant doesn't look at him. Whistler clears his throat, feels his Adam's apple rub against his starched collar and fat tie. He draws a deep breath to confirm his airway is unobstructed, resists the urge to ease the knot. The sergeant's attention remains fixed elsewhere. *That's how it's going to be.*

Whistler worked hard for this. He grew up in Little Village, focused on school, and mostly stayed out of trouble. He was one of the first in his family to attend college. After his criminal justice degree, he excelled at the police academy. He did two years on patrol in North Lawndale, a stone's throw from his own neighborhood. He learned a lot, had a number of close calls. Mostly he mediated chaotic conflicts between ordinary people caught in bad moments. Some days he felt he was doing good work. He was also frequently embarrassed for the people he dealt with. They were poor, stressed, and in tough circumstances.

High divorce rate among police is blamed on stress. Whistler has come to believe the nature of the job causes a loss of faith in humanity. Exposure to too much meanness and ragged anger corrodes the soul. In the end, Whistler saw too many people destroy the lives of those they were supposed to love. He knew he couldn't be a patrolman long term, not if he hoped for a life outside the job.

He'd pursued detective the moment he'd met the minimum require-ments. Unlike most first-time applicants, he'd passed the exam. He'd spent the past several weeks daydreaming about walking up to the offi-cer on duty and announcing himself. Being welcomed: *"Detective Diaz, so excited to meet you. We've heard good things. Inspector Ruther is waiting."*

Instead, he finds himself staring at the desk sergeant's puckered, bald pate.

Whistler clears his throat loudly.

The sergeant glares through the top of his eyes, his half-glasses rid-ing the end of his plump nose. Gravity tugs on his jowls, exaggerating creases on either side of his mouth. He looks like a hound dog. "What?" he barks.

Whistler tucks his thumbs in his belt. He tips his chin toward his badge, angles it. The badge looks good. He'd spent a long time decid-ing if he should clip it on or wear it around his neck like he'd seen cinema cops do, like Serpico. Whistler has a fear of accidentally hang-ing himself—*the necktie is scary enough*—so he went with the belt clip. He stays his hand from loosening his tie again. "I'm Detective Diaz. Assigned to Inspector Ruther."

"What do you want me to do about it?" The sergeant is unimpressed.

"I don't know where to go," Whistler admits weakly.

The sergeant flicks a dismissive hand at the elevators. "Fourth floor. Ruther's not in yet. He'll find you when he needs you."

Whistler's broad shoulders roll forward in a defeated hunch. He swings his arms and taps his foot outside the closed elevator. He gets bored and strides into the stairway. *I'll always take the stairs so I don't turn into a fat bastard like that desk jockey.*

The stairway opens across from a room of disorganized industrial desks and roller chairs roaming free. There is no indication of the work done within. The place is abandoned. But the smell of coffee draws Whistler in. He finds an ancient Mr. Coffee machine in a small break room at the back.

He opens cabinets until he finds a mug. The phrase "Crafty Ass Bitch" is glazed brazenly in gold letters across a green mug that looks unclaimed. "Green is for the money, gold is for the honeys," Whistler says to himself, a nod to the infamous Chicago pimp known as The Archbishop Don Magic Juan.

Whistler pours half a cup of black coffee. He lets the faucet run, tests the temperature. When it's cold, he tops the mug off, nearly over-filling it. He likes his coffee weak and room temperature. It's a trick he picked up from his father. *Why wait for coffee to cool? Be smart, Whistler. God gave you a brain. Put it to work once in a while.* Whistler brings the mug to his lips. He takes a careful sip.

"The hell are you?" A gruff voice explodes behind him. He sloshes coffee down his shirtfront, jumps his hips back to avoid wetting his slacks, and holds the mug away.

"Did I startle you? So fucking sorry."

Whistler sets the mug aside and snatches a fistful of brown paper towels from a roll on the counter. He dabs at his shirt and faces the other man.

"Who. The hell. Are you?" the man asks again.

"Diaz," Whistler says. He wads the damp paper and tosses it at the trash can. He misses.

"You are using my mug," the man says. His dark mustache is streaked with shiny silver beneath each nostril, giving the impression his nose is running. The mustache bristles as if pointing its stiff whiskers at the pilfered mug. The man, a cop by his dress and demeanor, notices Whistler's eyes on his upper lip. He slips a plastic comb from his pocket and works it through his expressive 'stache. He tucks the comb away. "My mug," he repeats, making his left hand into a pistol aimed at the mug. "I'm a crafty ass bitch. Everybody says so."

Whistler thinks it's a joke, wants to smirk. But he gives in to his healthy fear of authority and says, "Sorry. I didn't know."

"I'm fucking with you. It's not mine. I'm Inspector Ruther, but you can call me "sir." Grab your shit. We got a crime scene." Ruther walks away and yells back, "Grab one of the fucking digital tablets from the dock by the door."

"Yes, sir." Whistler slurps more coffee and leaves the mug in the sink. He hustles to catch up to Ruther.

"Tablet," Ruther says.

"Yes, sir." Whistler turns back and finds the tablet dock, takes the last one. At the elevator, Whistler remembers his resolution about the stairs. He's not brave enough to say anything. When the elevator arrives, the two men ride down in silence.

As they pass the front desk, Ruther calls over, "Hey, Wendigo, this is Diaz. We're out on a call. Radio if you need me."

"You bet, Inspector." Then to Whistler the desk sergeant calls, "Diaz," waits a beat, then says, "You got a little something," and wipes his hand over the front of his own uniform. Whistler looks down at his stained shirt and tie, catches a malicious glint in the sergeant's cloudy eyes.

Crossing the street, Ruther talks over his shoulder, "That's Wendell."

"You call him Wendigo?"

"Yeah. I do. You can't. I'm the nickname guy. It's a perk of being in charge. No one can say shit when I give them stupid nicknames."

"Isn't the Wendigo from a Native American story about a man who turned into a monster after tasting human flesh?"

"Fuck if I know. You're the one with an education. I thought it sounded funny. Say it. Wendigo. It's a fun name. Speaking of which, listen up: Wendell doesn't suffer fools, so don't be a fool and you'll get along. Trust me, your life will be easier if you get along with Wendell."

When they reach the car, Ruther stops to face the young detective, looks him square in the eyes. He brushes his hand down the length of his own tie and lets his mustache bristle at Whistler's shirtfront. "You got a little something." He lets the dig sink in. Whistler can't stop from looking at his stained shirt again. Ruther adds, "From now on at least try to look professional."

As Whistler's lap belt pushes his damp shirt against his stomach, the lines of movie detective Frank Serpico sound in his mind: *"The reality is that we do not wash our own laundry—it just gets dirtier."*

Death Is No Picnic

Calvert drifts in a still pool of absolute black. It's peaceful until it's shot through with a beam of shocking bright light. *This is it.* He's sure he's finally completely dead. He believes it only for an instant. He gradually understands that he is flat on his back in the lobby of his old building. Rubber gloves hold one of his eyes wide. A penlight sweeps his pupil and blasts his optic nerve. The eye is let loose. He closes it tight, can still see a massive white spot. His other eye is given the same rough treatment. He blinks his eyes to clear them. It doesn't help.

"Ah. You're back among the living," a glowing orb says. "Do you know your name?"

"Yes."

"That's a good start. Mind telling me what it is?"

"Calvert."

"Good, Calvert. Do you know what day it is?"

"Is it Friday?"

"Ding ding ding. Correct. Friday it is. I'm going to touch your shoulder. You tell me if it hurts."

"It hurts!"

"Sorry about that. Give me a minute and I'll get you taken care of. Stay still, okay?"

Calvert nods ever so slightly. He has no idea if the man behind the orb sees the gesture. He lets his eyes close.

"You fainted." It's Agatha. She speaks quietly. "The one cop radioed for an ambulance when you fell over. The one that had your arms looked plenty scared. It didn't help that I got the whole thing on my phone." She's gone. Her vacancy is filled with a slow and steady, wet clapping sound.

He opens his eyes. He can mostly see now. A man with a stethoscope kneels beside him, chewing gum loudly. "Ready to get your shoulder in working order?"

"Yes."

"It's going to hurt." The man puts both his hands on Calvert, one on his shoulder and one around his wrist. He moves the arm. Calvert tries to help and winces with the effort.

"You let me do it. Pretend it's not even your arm."

That makes sense to Calvert. The arm that isn't his is rotated through a series of positions. Each time the pressure becomes nearly unbearable, it is eased to a less stressed orientation. Overhead Calvert sees the vintage fixture in the center of the ceiling. *I never noticed that.* It's fuzzy with dust and has a bulb out. The arm is forced up. Pain rushes in. He sucks air to scream. The pain recedes. He holds his breath. The man carefully lays the arm at Calvert's side. "There," the man says. He packs his supplies and goes.

Agatha is back. "Let's get you on your feet." She helps him stand. "You dizzy?"

"No."

She watches that he can stand on his own before she says, "The police asked what I was doing here and what business it is of mine. I said I was your big sister. Play along."

"Okay."

"That EMT was worried because of that scar on your head. Your pupils were even and dilated like they oughta. That means you didn't whack your noggin. I told the lady cop that maybe I didn't need to show anyone my video. She said maybe there is no need to press charges. Pretty good, huh?"

"Yes." Calvert looks around. Doorman Justus and Officer Becker are watching him with identical sullen expressions.

"You ready to get out of here?" Agatha asks. "That Abbey person said something about an appointment. Better make sure you keep it." She gathers his duffel and suitcase. "Oh," she says. "The EMT guy said you should take some Tylenol and wear this." She hands over a plastic bag with a sling in it. Agatha marches out the door and Calvert follows.

When the Vue is on the road, Agatha says, "We're getting into the morning rush. Might as well take Lake Shore to get south." Calvert doesn't reply. "That scar of yours is recent. I told the EMT you'd been at that Horizons place." Her eyes look at him from the mirror. "You still alive back there?"

The best answer to her question is complicated. He says, "Somewhat," which he thinks is accurate. Truth is, death is different than he'd imagined. He'd always assumed a dichotomous relationship between life and death. Either one was alive or one ceased living and entered a state of nonlife commonly termed death. Like a light switch: either on or off. Binary. His recent experience tells him life and death happen on a sliding scale. For reasons he doesn't understand—though he suspects it has something to do with penance—months ago he slipped into nonlife without quite reaching definitive death. He's stuck like this for as long as it lasts. It's all very confusing.

He'd been assured by numerous sober doctors of psychiatry at New Horizons that he was not, in fact, dead. Officially, a head injury from a violent collision and related emotional trauma led to a rare condition known as Cotard's syndrome, sometimes labeled less charitably as Cotard's delusion. It's basically a wrinkle of human reasoning in which one believes they are dead, a piece of them has died, or that they are rotting away as they go about their business. Calvert knows all this.

While still under medical care, with his body recovering and his neck in a puffy brace, he was subjected to extensive blood work, a CT scan, an MRI, and some kind of photon gun called a SPECT test. A large lesion to the frontal and temporal regions of the right hemisphere of his busted brain confirmed his primary physician's giddy suspicions: Calvert may be a rare freak, one that could lead to research grants and publications in multiple prestigious journals.

Calvert does not feel that slipping between the laws of existence makes him special. It wasn't his doing. All he knows is he once lived a charmed life with an esteemed career and a beautiful wife. He was in a crash and woke in this half-dead state, a piece of his skull missing, shaved bald and with an ugly scar hidden under a gauze turban. He'd lost the knowledge he'd spent a lifetime accumulating. It seems clear now: Mere is dead. Which he guesses would be devastating if his emotions were functioning normally. His health is failing fast. He's no longer qualified for the job that defined him. While in treatment, he overheard that a student of his died in the accident. He can't fathom a way to reconcile that. Although his memories are returning in larger chunks each day, firsthand details of the crash remain hidden from him.

All he can say for certain is he's no longer alive in the ways he once was, despite his brain still rippling with memories that once belonged to a man known as Professor Greene. The body that moves him around is a loaner, and when the stubborn electrical current in his system is expended, he will mercifully drop like a sack of gooey compost. Until then, Abbey has explained he needs a job to pay for the maintenance of his shriveling allotment of conscious agency.

Agatha keeps glancing in the mirror, concern making her crow's feet even deeper. "You sure you're okay? If you're going to be sick, let me know. I can pull over."

"I'm not going to be sick."

"If you say so. But if it sneaks up on you, hold it. Don't you dare vomit in my car." She sounds like her old self.

Out the window, the sun shines off bent metal forms floating on a grid of crisscrossed poles. He knows he and Mere once spread a blanket in the grass under those shapes. That place has a name he can't recall. A word is attached to that scrap of memory. He says, "Frank Gehry."

"What?"

"Is Frank Gehry anything?"

"Not to me," Agatha says.

That disappoints Calvert.

They stop at the next two traffic lights along a long stretch of green space. Agatha turns the car west. "Not far now," she says.

"Thanks for taking me home earlier. It was a bad idea. But thank you."

"All's well that ends well."

That assumes that things end well.

A few minutes later, Agatha pulls into a parking place reserved for the Best Friends Veterinary Clinic. Calvert shifts his haunches to get at his wallet. He passes her a number of bills.

"It's okay," Agatha tells him. She pushes his hand away. "I don't want to take more of your money. You've been through enough for one morning. Besides, that Abbey paid me and tipped me already."

Calvert puts his money back. "Good. Bye." He works the seat belt by himself and steps onto the sidewalk with his bags. He has to wait for a small man with a huge mastiff to take his dog in the veterinary clinic. Agatha toots her horn as she drives away. When the path is clear, Calvert crosses to the unobtrusive entrance to his second-floor apartment. His shoulder throbs. His grip fails. He drops the suitcase. *I left my sling in the car.* He lifts the suitcase with his good hand. A *USA Today* is on the ground. He takes it and tucks it under his damaged arm before trudging up a very long flight of stairs.

The place is as he remembers when Abbey first brought him here: a small room with a twin bed, dresser, kitchen table, two wooden chairs, and a little kitchenette along one wall. A closet and bathroom are opposite the entrance. Calvert hadn't thought the place was bleak when he first saw it. But knowing how he used to live, this place is a letdown. *Or would be if I were living.* He drops his bags and searches until he finds his wristwatch. *I have lots of time.*

He takes a seat and thumbs through the newspaper. He reads several articles from the Chicago section. The first is about how most crime occurs in only a few neighborhoods. Then he learns about the crowd size and route of a march to protest the shooting of an unarmed black man by police. Next is about the shocking break-up of Hollywood sweethearts, complete with full-color relationship time-line photos. He closes the paper and looks around.

He hasn't eaten, but he has no appetite. Abbey stocked the kitchen with a few basics. He decides to make coffee. He uses four heaping tablespoons in the one-cup coffee maker. The coffee comes out black and thick. When he drinks, it makes no taste in his mouth. He tips two pills commonly prescribed for schizophrenia into his palm. They are intended to trick him into believing he is a living person. *They will have no effect.* Still, he gulps them with the remainder of the coffee and leaves the mug on the table.

He does certain things, like reading the paper, because it will make it easier to be among the living if he shares their schedule and habits. Plus his caregivers at New Horizons were comforted when he behaved in not-dead ways. With Abbey's help, he'd practiced phrases such as "I know I am actually alive," "Thank you for helping me conquer my delusional thinking," and "Gosh, I am famished; may I have a sandwich of meat?"

He's aware the timing of his departure from the facility was not about his getting the best treatment. His insurance would only pay for a certain amount of care. After failing to procure grant money, it became important for Dr. Shaw to declare Calvert a success simultaneous with the last of the insurance payments. That is the impression Calvert has based on overheard conversations.

With the help of an occupational therapist, a man who spoke in breathy whispers because of a throat condition, Calvert learned to keep his body clean, to feed it and water it and rest it. It was never explained to him explicitly, but he believes his flesh must be rotting, and so he is extra conscientious about cleanliness.

In the bathroom, he runs water in the chipped sink. He swishes his newly retrieved razor under the stream. *Fingernails and whiskers continue to grow after death.* He looks at the face in the mirror. They lock eyes. He doesn't like what he sees. He logically knows his other self is not a separate entity with hidden motivations. But he can't quite commit to the belief that his likeness is not a malicious doppelgänger come to witness his slow-speed demise and report back to an omnipotent judge. But being dead, he feels little cause for concern. He ignores his own gaze and drags the razor over his face until smooth. The scraping sound reverberates in the loosening folds of his cerebral cortex like the lingering thrum from a slapped chord on a stand-up bass.

He has no towels. *I should have remembered towels.* He dries his face with toilet paper. Layers of tissue pull apart and leave wet bits on his chin and cheeks. He balls most of the damp pulp into a lump and throws it in the toilet. He pinches the remaining pieces from his face. His skin is pale, perhaps turning green. He imagines it's cold, though his sense of touch becomes less sensitive with every passing day.

He showers with a bar of Irish Spring supplied by Abbey. He holds the bar to his nose and takes a whiff. Something fires in his brain. He knows scents can trigger memories, but none come. He uses the soap to scour his hair, careful over the uneven scar. Not because it's painful, but because he worries it might be. He's careful with his shoulder, though it seems to operate normally.

He lets his body drip before using his New Horizon's robe to scrub away the remaining water. He liberally applies deodorant. He brushes his teeth gently, afraid too much pressure will make his gums let loose.

Thinking of loose teeth reminds Calvert of an essay he'd written in graduate school about *War and Peace.* A French soldier named Johann had trudged across Europe behind Napoleon after his defeat in Russia in 1812. One winter night, after freezing and starving for months, Johann lost a tooth while trying to whistle at a stray dog he hoped to coax into his coat to help him keep warm. As a graduate student, Calvert posited Johann had hoped to eat the dog but was too ashamed to be honest about it in his diary. He used the story to buttress the notion that Tolstoy's description of postwar Russia was a well-researched historical document in the guise of fiction; that it was more historical record than literature. He'd received a ninety-six percent on the assignment.

Since then, Calvert has harbored a worry that he'll swallow a loose tooth in his sleep, feel it grinding against his ribs every waking moment, like something sinister gnawing its way out. He ignores his reflection's silent observation and swishes with antiseptic mouthwash, spits, and leaves the bathroom.

He dresses in clothes from his gym bag. He pulls on a T-shirt with writing across the chest. He buttons a dress shirt over it. He reads through the pale fabric: "Czech Me Out." He doesn't remember having owned the T-shirt.

The suit is serviceable: chocolate brown with matching shoes. Probably dated. He wraps a tie around the back of his neck and flips up his collar. He takes the fabric in his hands but can't tie it. His dead fingers don't remember how. He attempts to twist it like a bread tie. It unwinds. The same procedure yields the same result each time he tries. He leaves the tie on the bed and turns down his collar as he exits. He doesn't bother locking up. It is a thing he finds unimportant.

He turns his wrist to check the time. He forgot the watch. Staying on schedule is valued by the living, so he will need to be certain to wear the watch next time. *Living is harder than I remember.* He's glad to have put it behind him.

Calvert only has to walk a block. A week ago he'd gone to a job service appointment Abbey arranged. They had been sitting side by side in two of eight folding chairs arranged in a circle for group counseling. He leaned his body away so his mouth wouldn't blow bad breath on her. "I have no reason to work. I don't need to make purchases."

She ignored him. "Haven't you worked hard in rehab and therapy? Of course you have. Your recovery has been, like, so steady. No one would know you'd suffered a head trauma since your hair has grown out." He touched the horseshoe-shaped weal of flesh under his hairline. The texture of the new skin was smooth and soft. "You've done, like, so well you're being discharged." She tried to hold his gaze, but her eyes on his made him self-conscious. He looked over at the clock on the wall. The orange second hand was frozen at thirty-one seconds.

She placed her hand on his knee to regain his attention. "You'll continue to get, like, financial help from the state and from the arrangements made with your credit union."

"Didn't I have a home? Don't I have savings?"

"We've talked about this. Because of the nature of the accident, it's gotten complicated. Legal issues need to be resolved." She stopped there, looked around, and added quietly, "Legal issues regarding the cause of your collision and other details. Your wife's family has your assets tied up until it's settled." She took a breath, her tone lightening. "You're still young, aren't you? You are. The routine of work will be good. You're capable of being a contributing member of society. Aren't you, like, looking forward to that?"

He shrugged. The old Calvert was moved by abstract concepts like collective society and civic duty. Current Calvert is less impressed by those ideas.

"Good news though: the U of C has said you will be, like, welcome to return if your memory improves," Abbey continued in a soothing voice. "But there were lingering unanswered ethical questions that may need to be addressed. For now, no need to worry. You've been here long enough. It's time to go."

Calvert didn't respond. He'd forgotten the rules of conversational ebb and flow. He sat quietly, considering why her hair was honey at the roots and white at the tips.

Abbey cleared her throat. He didn't recognize it as an attempt to prompt a reply. "Do you understand?" she finally asked.

"No," he said. He'd forgotten what they'd been discussing.

Abbey gently persisted. Taking his cold fingers in her warm hands, she said, "Meet Bill. Look at what opportunities might be available. I will drive you."

He enjoyed the heat that came from her body: it felt like an emotion he once knew. Her eyes were shiny and sincere. Most significantly, they were the greenest green, similar to Meredith's eyes. "I will meet with Bill," he said. For no reason at all his eyes had started to leak.

Days later, in Bill's waiting room, he had looked over a series of job postings written on three-by-five cards and pinned to a corkboard. One card read: "Want to be a real hero? Work to rid Chicago of the scourge of pestilence." There was a name, Kaz Gladsky, and a cell number. There was also a promise of "good pay, full-time hours, and transportation provided." Ten minutes later, Bill made the call and arranged an interview in the neighborhood where Abbey had found Calvert's Section 8 housing.

Now, Calvert pushes open the door marked "Grand Opening" and is greeted by a friendly voice from behind the counter: "Welcome to Coffee Girl. What can I get you?" The room is narrow, with a counter down one wall and café tables spread around. The floors are worn pine planks. The woman is white teeth and round cheeks over a sparkling espresso machine.

"I'm meeting someone," Calvert explains.

"You're my first customer. That calls for a drink." She has a warm, inviting way.

"This is your first day?" he asks.

"Yes. We were supposed to open weeks ago, but there was a plumbing issue. Stressful! Better late than never, right? What can I make for you?"

Calvert moves to the counter. His brown suit gives his wilting body needed structure. His mouth hangs open as he reads the list of options. Time passes. He rubs his sore shoulder. He reads each description like he's interpreting an unfamiliar language.

The woman leans her hands on the counter. "Can I tell you about our coffee?"

"Yes, please."

"Our espresso is Coffee Girl. It's roasted in small batches at Candy Skull. They're local. Humboldt Park. You know Candy Skull?"

"No. I've been away. Espresso sounds good. I'll have that." He nods once.

"Can I recommend a cortado? It's my specialty." Her smile lights her face.

Calvert can't remember if he's ever heard the term. He's forgotten a lifetime of information. "'Cortado' is like a word from a poem. I'll have that."

Coffee Girl makes her smile a little bigger. Calvert watches her grind beans and pack grounds. She twists the coffee into the machine. There is a churning sound and a rumbling noise. Streams of rich, dark coffee fill two shot glasses.

"Meeting someone special?" Coffee Girl asks.

Calvert doesn't understand.

She adds, "You said you're meeting someone. You're in a suit. Must want to make a good impression. You didn't have any papers and things to write with. I'm guessing it might be, you know, a meeting with someone special."

He touches his suit. "Job interview." He worries he needs paper and things to write with.

"This should help." She sets a short glass of espresso and frothy milk on the counter. He lifts it and sips. His dying taste buds fire. "Very good," he says. "I taste it."

Her smile beams. "I'm Rosa."

"Rosa," he says. He likes the round way it fills his mouth. "I'm Calvert." Her eyes glance over his outfit. "Is my suit okay? It's the only one I packed. My tie was broken." His fingers fiddle his open collar.

"You look nice."

He asks, "Do you have paper and a pen?"

She holds up a finger to indicate he should wait. She steps through a swinging door and comes back with a yellow pad and a pencil.

"I'll return it," Calvert says.

At the table he makes a list: *Make list. Paper and pencil.* Some of the money Abbey had provided was intended for a phone of some kind. He writes, *Phone.* Next to it he writes, *Cheap.* He also writes, *Mouthwash. Toothbrush with soft bristles. Clip tie. Towels and washcloths.* He recalls clothes smell good with the use of dryer sheets, scented candles cover odors, and baking soda draws smells from the air. He adds those to the list. He crosses the first two items off. He folds the first page over.

On a new page he writes *Rosa* to help him remember. He thinks of her bright smile, her care with her coffee. He has no interest in women. Not since his death. Not since Mere must have died in an accident he may have caused.

There's a line from a dead comedian: *"I refuse to join any club that would have me as a member."* Calvert feels the same about women. He wouldn't want a woman who would have a dead man. *If only I could meet a nice dead woman.*

Next to Rosa's name he writes, *cortado*. He writes, *brown eyes* and *not dead*. He underlines the last part. His pencil hovers over the down stoke of a capital "K" for "Kati," but he doesn't write his former student's name, a name that came to him out of nowhere. *More fallout from my visit home.* Kati's eyes may have been brown too. He can't recall. His focus had often lingered elsewhere when they were together.

He taps the pencil, thinking of half-buried details. No words materialize. He flips to a blank page and waits to see what strikes him.

Road Rage

Whistler's day is off to a fast start. Not a good start, but a start nonetheless.

Inspector Ruther jams the brakes. Whistler's sticky shirtfront is cold where the seat belt crosses his torso. His preference for tepid coffee saved him a burn. He's pushed into the seat as the unmarked cruiser accelerates. His stomach doesn't like the way his new boss drives. Ruther casts a long shadow in the department, has worked in the city his whole career, and has a reputation as Chicago's best detective. Several of his major cases are taught in the Academy. But so far, Whistler is not impressed.

Whistler would not call himself introverted. In fact, he likes to think he's plenty outgoing. However, he does prefer to ease into new situations, get the lay of the land. This chaotic race toward a crime scene, with no preamble, is not what he'd wanted.

Much of his training as a cadet was geared toward making fast assessments and taking definitive action to interject control into any scenario. He was taught that snap decisions guided by tactical muscle memory, rather than careful deliberation, might save his life. He understood the value of the strategy, though it was contrary to his personal preference. He imagined, with no evidence to support it, he would be more comfortable working as an investigator than he had as a beat cop because he'd have more time to consider the facts, gather evidence, understand the truth.

Beside him Ruther is talking. "So, as I was saying," he hears Ruther say. But Whistler is preoccupied with how clammy his chest is.

Traffic is heavy and every other street is partially blocked for road repairs. The ride is the most stressful of his life. Ruther's driving makes Whistler nervous. He wonders if that's the point. *It has to be newbie hazing.*

"Your job is simple," Ruther says, gaining Whistler's attention. "Solve the cases I assign. I answer to the chief of detectives, he answers to the chief superintendent. But there's a catch. This department is the way the mayor directs resources to situations that threaten to spin out politically." As Ruther talks, he accelerates up to the taxi in front of him, riding as close as possible without touching the other car. The cab's brake lights flash red; Ruther smashes his brake pedal. The sedan stands on its nose. Whistler stomps the floor on the passenger side where a brake pedal should be. The digital tablet slides across the seat. He slaps his right forearm against the edge of the dash and stops the tablet with his left hand.

Ruther doesn't speak as they wait at the light. He drums his fingers on the steering wheel. The light changes. The cab moves forward. Ruther starts talking as the squad car rushes within inches of the cab's bumper. "The mayor's chief of staff sometimes has directives from the mayor. Or the mayor talks to the superintendent. If the superintendent is under pressure, the chief of Ds gets his ass chewed. As you know, shit runs downhill. In other words." Ruther slams the brakes. Whistler's seat belt presses painfully into his chest. He saves the tablet again.

The cab runs the red light and makes it across the intersection before pedestrians fill the crosswalk. Ruther is aggravated. He drums his fingers harder than before. He radiates irritation. He glares as if his heat vision might blast the cab. He chews his lower lip; his mustache crawls under his nose with the motion.

The light turns green. Ruther guns the engine despite people in the street. He honks. Pedestrians make a hole. "In other words," he repeats, "we work for the superintendent, the chief of Ds, and the mayor's office simultaneously. We are always under pressure. You understand? I give you a pile of problems, and you find solutions fast as you can. Easy peasy motherfucker!" A businessman in a trench coat the same color as the shadow from the overhead tracks steps in front of the car. Brakes grab. Whistler jams one hand against the headliner. The department-issued tablet flies, and he barely saves it.

Ruther mashes his palm into the horn. Business Man looks up from his smartphone and steps quickly across the street. The light turns red. Ruther rolls down his window and yells, "I will run your ass over!" The man doesn't turn to look. Whistler has no doubt of Ruther's commitment to vehicular homicide.

The car starts rolling before the light goes green, "Easy peasy, slick and greasy. You do all the work and I take all the credit. If we can't clear a case, you get the blame. I try to give you the resources and time you need. The good news is, we get significant resources compared to other departments. That's the job. Got it, Diaz? You're not saying much. You follow me?"

"Yes. I follow. What about today?"

"Dead white female in the mayor's favorite part of the city. The mayor called the superintendent, and his chief of staff called me before my corn-flakes could get soggy." Ruther cranks the wheel and jams the car down a one-way alley. He drives on the sidewalk and parks. "Come on." A twitch of his lip and his mustache flicks toward the back of the car.

Whistler meets Ruther as the trunk comes open. Ruther pulls a paper bag over, takes out a folded white dress shirt and a black tie. "Here. Get yourself together and meet me up there." He points toward the crime scene. "Sorry about the coffee gag. I didn't know you'd be so jumpy. Your file made me think you were made of sterner stuff. Come up when you're ready. I'll introduce you, and you can get to work."

"Sure, Inspector," Whistler says, thinking maybe Ruther's not so bad.

"Oh, Diaz. I'm going to keep calling you Diaz, okay. Whistler is a stupid fucking name. I hate it. It's embarrassing. You may not be embarrassed, but you should be. Because it's fucking stupid." Ruther turns and goes.

Whistler looks around to be certain no one is easing up on him. He sets his tablet in the trunk. He removes his holster and badge. Next he unbuttons his shirt, removes his tie.

Once Ruther's loaner shirt is buttoned and tucked, with the sleeves rolled up, Whistler finds it baggy but acceptable. He gets the tie knotted and the collar turned down. His badge and gun go back on his belt, his tablet goes under one wing. He takes a look in the side window. *I'm no Serpico.*

Ruther is at the center of a gaggle of men when Whistler approaches. "What time does Sean Connery arrive at Wimbledon?" There is an expectant pause. Ruther delivers the punch line in his best Connery. "Tennish." The men standing around laugh. Whistler joins in. Ruther has a solid Connery. When he's sopped up the adulation, Ruther says, "This is Detective Diaz. He drew the short straw this morning. Be nice to him." The other men acknowledge Diaz with chin nods and shuffling feet.

"Hi," Diaz says.

"This," Ruther says, indicating a patrolman to his left, "is Chief. He was first on the scene." Diaz wrinkles his brow, confused by the title, but shakes Chief's hand. Chief's skin is dark and glossy, and his head looks like it's been waxed and buffed.

"This is Champ. He's with Chief." Champ is pale, with a face full of freckles and an orange flattop. His hand is cold, hard, and dry.

"Over there we have Hoss and Tiny." Hoss is a patrolman, medium brown skin and fit. The one called Tiny is in dark jeans and a tight, tan blazer. He dwarfs Whistler. He looks like a linebacker moonlighting at Banana Republic. "Tiny is on a diplomatic mission from Homicide. It's our case, but Homicide is a good resource. So lean on him as much as you can." Tiny nods in Whistler's direction. "Last, to your right, you've got Doc." Doc has receding silver hair and glasses. The combination of high forehead and spectacles give him a thoughtful look.

"The name is actually Ted Majors, I'm on crime scene for the medical examiner's office. Don't mind Ruther. We'll get you up to speed."

"Wow. I'm going to choose not to be offended," Ruther says, "Introductions made. My work here is done. Diaz, do what you need to. Catch a ride back to the house with Hoss. Find me and let me know where things stand. I promised the superintendent a briefing at the end of the day. Let's hope the press stays away. Did you finish the media training?"

"Yes. How to prepare a statement, strategies for taking questions, how to behave in front of a camera, always assume the mic is hot. We broke into working groups and filmed ourselves, took critiques, went again. It was—"

Ruther dramatically throws his hands up, "Jesus Diaz. Let me stop you there. Fuck. Save it for your diary. We have work to do. Point is, fuck that training. You don't know what you're doing, no matter how rich the feedback in your breakout group. The press will eat you up. Reporters are slippery animals. If reporters show up, ignore them and skulk away. Don't say dick. Got it? You follow me?"

"I follow. But what about the public's right to know? It is one of the things—"

Ruther's mustache is irate. "The public has a right to know my balls. Listen. Someone will decide when to speak to the press. That person will not have a made-up name and a brand new big-boy badge. Got it?"

"Got it." Whistler is thankful his complexion mostly hides his flushed cheeks.

The mustache seems soothed. "To recap, what do you do if the press shows up?"

"Skulk."

"That's right. You skulk. You skulk, you skulk the fuck away. Enjoy your weekend. I don't know about you, but I'm working. Actually I do know about you. I'm authorizing overtime until this is put to bed. So everyone is working. And break!" Ruther slaps his big mitts together and leaves Diaz to sink or swim on his own.

Wrong Place, Wrong Time

Earlier, Anna Beth had stood shifting from foot to foot as the elevator dropped, getting some blood moving in her tired legs, giving her stiff hip flexors a stretch. She yawned so wide she snorted. Something tickled the back of her neck. She reached behind to capture an errant sprig and retighten her ponytail. A bell pinged and the elevator doors parted before her. Her bodyweight settled into the deep pile of lush, ornate carpet. She had no idea which way to go. There must have been signs, but they were so discrete she couldn't spot them.

It had been almost five in the morning, local time. That made it nearly three, her time. She'd yawned again at the thought. She'd lost track of days. *Is it Friday?*

The hotel felt abandoned. The air was chill on her bare shoulders. She crossed her arms over her tank top and vigorously rubbed her dry palms over her upper arms. She felt exposed in her fitted getup, wanted to avoid anyone from the conference, anyone at all.

She picked a direction at random and moved down a long hallway of floral wallpaper and oddly formal sconces. Under a chandelier that marked a crossing of hallways, she spotted a sign that pointed down an identical stretch of guestrooms. Her feet moved fast. She swerved around a cluster of three silver ice buckets with an empty wine bottle upended in each. *Someone had a good night.*

The last door on the left was glass and leaked the distinctive scent of chlorine. She waved her room key and the door opened itself.

Anna Beth's job was not fulfilling. She was, in fact, not much more than a glorified assistant. Although her boss, Greg Kidd, was one of the foremost consultants in the burgeoning autonomous car sector of the transportation market, she primarily spent her days coordinating travel and meetings. Attending this conference had been her idea. She believed it would demonstrate she could do more. After a successful professional conference, she'd planned to ask Greg for a raise and a change of title, new responsibilities. After all, she had a degree in computer engineering from Carnegie Mellon. Not a doctorate from MIT like Greg, but nothing to sneeze at.

The whole scheme had turned out to be an unmitigated disaster. Her flight from San Francisco was delayed by a thunderstorm. She'd slept in a chair in the terminal, hoping to grab a standby seat that never materialized. She landed at O'Hare on the second day of the conference, only a few hours before her panel discussion. She had at least had the clarity of mind to make certain the hotel didn't let her room go. She checked in, took a spit bath at the sink, changed clothes, and made it in time for the tech meeting.

It turned out her laptop didn't play well with the projector, and Buddy, a self-proclaimed problem solver, didn't have the dongle to solve the problem. Buddy had smirked when he said "dongle." Anna Beth was careful to ignore him. Nothing undermined a woman's capacity to be taken seriously more than the slightest hint of seeming sexually available. Smirking at dick jokes was all the encouragement some men needed. Besides, Buddy was gross.

Admittedly it had been a long drought, sexually speaking. Despite that, she was not the least bit confused about how uninterested she was in Buddy. Someone named Buddy was not to be taken seriously. *Buddy is a dog's name.*

The panel started on time, and she couldn't use the slides she'd spent a week perfecting. The talk was poorly attended. She counted fifteen heads in an auditorium that seated three hundred. It took place late morning, nearly the lunch hour, and most attendees were already sucking down cocktails. The moderator introduced her as "an associate of the very influential Dr. Kidd," but failed to share her name or credentials. The other panelists were older, more experienced, and acquiesced to one another's technical expertise like only longtime peers in a small industry could. The dance they did, talking back and forth, joking lightly, nodding significantly at one another's contributions, was exactly what she had intended when she formed the panel. They each gave examples of recent advances that led to measurable increases in driver safety.

Despite the fact they'd coordinated the discussion via teleconference twice the previous week, the old men stepped all over her prepared points. Anna Beth was left with little to add. She fumbled pathetically for a couple minutes, restating points already made. During the Q and A she was directly asked one question: *Why isn't Dr. Kidd in attendance?* To top it off, when she chucked her heavy workbag over her shoulder to make a fast exit, her hips gave an involuntary twist, and she'd broken one of the heels of her favorite pumps.

With that behind her, all she wanted was to sweat it out, an honest purge. She had a plan to ditch the conference once stores opened so she could replace her heels with something too expensive. She would put it on the company card. *Because fuck it. That's why.*

She had been pleased to find the gym empty and that the treadmills faced a wall of glass overlooking the Chicago River. It was a gray morning and foggy over the water. The sun was only an orange coal warming the horizon. The river below was a glossy black ribbon. Her forehead bumped the glass when she leaned to take in the view and her fingers squelched when she rubbed the greasy spot away.

She picked out the newest treadmill and started her warm-up. She ignored her reflection as she pounded out four miles in half an hour. When she'd finished, she found a stack of hand towels and dried her face. In a mini-fridge were complimentary bottles of water. Once her heart had quit rattling her ribs, she started a half-ass circuit of the Nautilus machines. Her head wasn't in it. She was still demoralized about her presentation.

After the failed panel, she'd removed her damaged heels and pitched them. She'd gone to her room and flopped face-first on the bed, intending to cry her eyes out. A good cry could be cathartic, and she'd earned a complete breakdown. But she couldn't work up enough feeling and fell asleep instead.

Sometime after dark, she'd wandered groggily to the bathroom and sat on the toilet, removed her makeup, showered, and raided the minibar for an eight-dollar jar of almonds and a five-dollar sparkling water. She'd rummaged through her suitcase until she found her favorite oversized sweatshirt. Outside her room, a couple giggled as they drunkenly knocked along the corridor, on their way to a shared bed, she had assumed.

"Good for you," she called. She'd belched, laughed, and had fallen asleep with almond crumbs dusting her chest and stuck in her teeth.

In the gym, she stared at the shoulder-shrug machine and chose to give up on the weight circuit. She could feel the cry she intended the night before, and she didn't want it to hit her in a public place.

She walked to the indoor pool and took a stroll around the perimeter. She kicked off her running shoes and sat with her legs dangling in the water, up to her knees. The water was neither cool enough to refresh nor warm enough to relax. She swirled her feet, stirring the pool for a while.

The sun was mostly up and illuminated the vast sky over Lake Michigan. The view out the floor-to-ceiling window worked a powerful spell, persuading her that drifting in the pool could heal what ailed her. She thought briefly of stripping and slipping her naked body in the lukewarm water. She could almost feel the buoyant water lifting her, cradling and rocking her, comforting her. But she'd slammed the brakes on the daydream at the thought of her bloated panel participants blundering in and finding her. Her skin had crawled. She stood, dried her feet, and hustled out.

She exited the way she'd come, out the same doors, up the same halls, to wait in front of the same bank of elevators. Once inside, on a whim, she'd jabbed the button for the lobby.

On the first floor, she marched across the grand entry, ignored the people who watched her pass, and went out the revolving doors. She approached a man in a maroon uniform with gold epaulets.

"I need coffee. Bad. Is there a good place within walking distance?" She folded her arms over her chest to shield herself from the chill. Doing so made her compressed cleavage swell.

The bellhop gawked. To compose himself, he pulled off his cap. "Complimentary coffee is available in the restaurant over there." He aimed his cap into the hotel.

"I'd like to get some air. Make an outing of it."

"Nice morning for it," he said. He kept his eyes far away from her chest as he scanned the world around them. "I don't do fancy coffee. But there's probably someplace good thataway." He nodded toward some distant buildings.

"Thanks so much." Anna Beth walked in the direction he'd indicated.

She crossed a covered drive where cabs waited to snatch tourists and whisk them to one of the airports or some popular destination in the loop. The driver in front of the line, a Sikh by the look of his head wrap, was leaning on the hood of his car and smoking. He pitched his cigarette to the ground, stopped short of grinding it out when he realized she didn't want a ride. He snatched the cigarette, inspected it, blew on it, and returned it to the groove in his lip.

Anna Beth tightened her ponytail and looked both ways before crossing the street. A man in a work van waited for her to cross. She found a winding path that cut through a green space along the lakeshore. The fog was lifting and a breeze came off the lake. The sheen of perspiration on her forehead dried and pulled her skin taut. She breathed deeply, felt satisfied. She was enjoying herself despite the conference debacle and her personal history with the city.

It had been her senior year of college the last time she'd visited. She and Ramon had taken a trip over Thanksgiving. They'd left Pittsburgh and skirted Lake Erie, stopping in Toledo the first night. At an aquarium they walked through a glass tunnel, surrounded by dark water and sea creatures. While Anna Beth was pointing out a graceful ray, a shark surged and startled a yelp from her. She'd felt embarrassed and claustrophobic, and they'd left. Throughout the evening Ramon had ridiculed her by repeatedly humming the theme to *Jaws*. She'd laughed it off the first few times. But he'd pushed it, and she hadn't been in the mood for sex at the shitty roadside motel they'd found.

The next day, they'd arrived in Chicago around lunchtime. It was blowing wet snow. The sidewalks were crowded, the streets damp with dark slush. They hadn't packed clothes for the weather. Ramon bought her a coat with matching insulated gumboots at a thrift store in Edgewater. They'd eaten as much deep-dish pizza as they could stand and gone to the Museum of Contemporary Art to see a traveling exhibition of Wayne Thiebaud paintings. The lush colors and repetitive shapes of desserts were delightful, but it was the rolling hills, warped perspectives, and vivid blue shadows of San Francisco street scenes that had enticed her.

After the exhibition, Ramon had suggested they find another cheap motel. Instead, Anna Beth got a room at the Blackstone. During her pre-trip research, she discovered the hotel had once been associated with Al Capone, and that the Maharishi Mahesh Yogi used money from his lucrative Transcendental Meditation empire to buy the building in a failed attempt to convert it into condos. After sitting vacant for years, it was renovated and back in business.

On the walking trail, a yellow Labrador pulled a jogger around the bend of the path ahead of Anna Beth. She sidestepped and let them pass. The man, who wore extra-short shorts, wheezed and nodded and tried to smile. Anna Beth smiled in return. But her head was still elsewhere.

That night at the Blackstone, they'd sat in the bar, drinking Cuba libres and eating fresh-cut potato chips hot from the fryer. They talked about the future: they agreed that children were not in the cards, they would definitely buy investment property, and international travel was a priority. She laughed at his bad quips, grinning until her cheeks ached.

Back in the room, after sex that was more athletic than usual, she'd been compelled to ask for Ramon's hand in marriage. He was hesitant, but he accepted. They showered together, which led to more sex. She'd fallen asleep in his arms. Spent. Content. Safe.

The pathway ahead of her forked in two directions. One trail continued along the lake, where she could see a woman removing a baby from a stroller. The mother hoisted the infant, threw him in the air, and caught him, smiling into his ecstatic, flushed face. The infant's overexcited laughter did not delight Anna Beth. She turned her eyes away. That path was not for her.

The other way led down a pedestrian tunnel, under a road congested with morning commuters. She followed the path with her eyes. It appeared to come up in a neighborhood of high-rise apartments. This is where the bellhop had directed her.

Her intuition told her the tunnel was not a safe place. Her body told her she was tired and needed caffeine, or her shopping excursion would be interrupted by migraine-level stimulant withdrawals. She fast-walked toward the tunnel.

She hadn't thought of that asshat Ramon in years. Or that's what she always told herself each time her mind wandered back to the man she'd once wanted to marry. The engagement had been short because of the inconvenient fact that Ramon was already engaged. He'd broken it off with Anna Beth in a tearful confession, in which he offered to pay for half the hotel bill. *Only half.*

The breakup had led to a long depression. The depression, and the paintings of Wayne Thiebaud, had eventually persuaded her to move to San Francisco. For her, the idea of a real relationship was dead. *Ramon had killed it.*

Her mother used to tell her, *"Be careful whom you choose to care for. Because they hold the keys to your heart."* Her mother had been talking about motherhood, to make Anna Beth feel guilty about something.

Anna Beth had felt the emotional jab but had also tucked the advice away.

Her footsteps echoed as the path dipped under the road. Her legs felt heavy and her shoes registered every stone. Her early morning had caught up to her. Ahead, the path exited on a narrow street with a sidewalk down one side, loading docks along the other. She put her hands on her thighs, letting her slender arms pump her tired legs. She wanted to be buff. She wanted a round butt, but she hated squats. She wanted to have defined arms and cut shoulders like those fitness freaks she followed on Instagram. She wanted tattoos and a Jet Ski and house on a lake so she could use her Jet Ski. She wanted a man, if only temporarily.

She exited the tunnel; her feet moved steadily under her.

She jerked her arms in a defensive seizure before her mind knew why. The violent collision jarred all thoughts from her head. An unstoppable force had her throat. The impact stole her control, knocked her off balance. Whiplash momentum carried her across the street and crushed her to the pavement between dumpsters.

Her ribcage lost its shape. Her air was gone.

She dug at the vise clamped to her throat, scratched with her nails. Tried to scream but had no wind. Tried to inhale, but no oxygen got to her lungs, no room in her body for her burning air sacs to inflate.

She bucked and arced. Her head scraped the ground. Something gouged her scalp.

Her legs scrambled, her feet kicked. Her toe struck something so hard it sent a flash of white pain shuddering through her system. Her adrenal glands did their best. It wasn't enough. She shoved with weak arms. She had no strength.

Through the corner of her eye, she watched a strip of sky slowly eclipsed by a face. Her loose hair obscured the view, but his eyes didn't look angry. His breathing slowed as she stopped struggling. He made sounds, like comforting a baby. "Shh. Shh, shh now. That's it. That's it. Shh."

She watched a drop of perspiration form on his temple. Saw how gravity pulled it down his cheek to the edge of his jaw, where it hung over her without falling.

The pressure in her skull grew. Her eyes bulged. She gagged, a raw sound. She smelled flowers. When blood traced a hot line down the back of her neck, it felt like a caress. Then there was only letting go before she burst.

A last tiny pop of static fired her brain. For a sliver of a moment, she believed Ramon was there. He was killing her. Killing her all over again.

Competitive Rivalry

Moe turns Taibbi down a one-way street and has to squeeze the brake and clutch immediately. An unmarked patrol car backs directly at her. She fumbles her thumb for the horn button; when it sounds, it's a goat with laryngitis. *Shit!* She straddle-walks the bike backward as fast as she can.

The patrol car stops hard, the red glare of taillights bright in Moe's face. The transmission grabs, and the car races ahead and bounces through the center of a few potholes before leaving the block and a fog of exhaust fumes behind.

Moe settles her rump on the seat. She taps the bike into first and lets her feet drag the crumbling pavement. Her hands ache from the drive over. *I need smaller hand controls.* She bumps onto the curb and knocks down the kickstand. The drive was more harrowing than expected. Her thighs hurt from pinching the bike as she swiveled and shifted and held on for dear life. Her body feels battered from maneuvering the weight of her new transportation. *Still, I made good time.*

She pats the side of the bike's gas tank before dismounting, pleased with the decision to buy something with a motor. She hangs her Vicky helmet on the handlebar and tries to read the situation, automatically composing possible phrases for her impending article. She sees a couple police milling behind a flapping piece of yellow tape. Further away, three plainclothes cops are working, one silver-haired, a short guy in a stark white dress shirt, and a gargantuan man in a horrible khaki blazer. They focus on the space between two dumpsters. Moe can see one more cop at what must be the far end of the crime scene.

She starts to pull her press credentials, stops as her attention is drawn down the street where the unmarked police car exited. A white news van is angling into the one-way block from the wrong direction. The driver has second thoughts. The van backs out and takes the long way around. The van reads: "TV13 *Chicago News in Action!*"

Moe's expression curdles. She puts her press pass away and adjusts her bag strap. *Maybe ten minutes in this traffic.* That's her most optimistic window of time before she's overrun by a production crew angling for gruesome video for the midday broadcast.

Moe approaches the tape barrier and makes a show of rubbernecking. She recognizes the silver-haired man; his wire-framed glasses and sweptback hair mark him as Dr. Majors from the medical examiner's office.

"You'll have to stay back," a broad man with a smooth head says authoritatively.

"What's going on?" Moe addresses the younger officer, a fit and freckled ginger with a flattop he clearly takes seriously.

"It's a crime scene," Flattop explains uselessly, but not unkindly.

"Oh really? How long? I gotta get to work," she lies.

"Might take a while. You best find a way around," says Flattop.

"Sorry for the trouble," the short Michael Jordan puts in. He doesn't actually sound sorry.

Moe slips her phone from her bag and checks it, giving the impression she's worried about getting to work. There's a clock ticking in the back of her mind, one that ends with the fucking Action News team elbowing her out of the way.

She casts her gaze between the two officers. Beside the distant dumpsters, she can see shoulders and backs, gloved hands, and maybe a pair of bright running shoes on a prone body. The colors indicate women's shoes.

She puts her phone away and turns as if to leave, lets the men relax their guard. She calls this move "The Columbo." She turns back, "Oh, is that the pathologist down there? I've seen him on the news. Must be a body. Right? Oh my god, what happened? Should I be concerned? Am I in danger?"

"Hey, listen, we can't tell you about the body," Flattop says, flustered. *That's confirmation.* The bald officer scowls.

"So there's a body." Moe says. "A woman? I'm a woman. Should I be worried to walk alone? You have to tell me. For my safety."

"You need to go," says irritated Michael Jordan.

"I can stand here. Besides, the public has a right to know." She hears the news van's door slide open behind her. She peeps over her shoulder and sees what she feared: her nemesis, Sophia Garcia, in a dress like a sausage casing, a mic clasped in a hand tipped with manicured fingernails, primping her curls in the van's side mirror. Moe knows the cameraman by sight, but not by name. He is, like most of his professional tribe, of formidable height and mass, an asset when jostling for a shot. He's busily organizing equipment and throwing a battery pack over his shoulder. The officers spot the news van too.

While the cops brace for the coming onslaught, Moe pulls out her credentials.

"Ruther is not going to like this," Michael Jordan says.

Moe knows Inspector Ruther is head of a special task force. She'd shouted questions to him at several crime scenes and press conferences. He'd never given her a printable response.

"Can I quote you on that?" Moe asks. "Detective Ruther doesn't want the press to get wind of this case. A body was found, but homicide isn't in charge. Last I heard, Ruther was focused on sex trafficking. Is this related?" She waits for an answer. *Nothing.* "What makes this death more important than the seven shooting deaths in the past forty-eight hours?" *Nothing.* "Listen," Moe says, "these TV13 assholes are the worst." She makes an educated guess and says with conviction, "From chatter on the police scanner, you got a white female, DOA." She throws it out to see if they will deny it. They don't. *Figures.* If the Special Crimes Unit is involved, it's because the mayor smells trouble. "This thing is about to go public. You might as well give me something . . ."

Sophia is suddenly there. She backs her round ass toward the officers while holding the mic. "How's my light?" she asks.

The cameraman snaps a light on his rig. "Better now. Turn a little left. Other left."

"How's that?"

"You're good."

"Let's shoot the intro, then some interview tape. You have the body in the shot?"

"As much as we're going to get. Let's try one. You're ready to rock in *five, four, three* . . ." The patrolmen scatter. The cameraman finishes his countdown by holding his fingers in front of him: two fingers, one finger, and a finger pointing at Sophia.

"This is Sophia Garcia reporting for TV13 *News in Action!* I'm at the scene of a vicious, early morning attack that ended in the death of a woman. We are only blocks from Chicago's historic Water Tower Place in a popular shopping district. We will share the details of this tragedy as they develop, exclusively on TV13 *News in Action!*" She holds a big smile for a count of two, lets the mic fall away like it's too heavy. "How was it?"

"It's good. Let's move on."

Sophia takes four steps and puts the mic in Moe's face. "Sir, how do you feel knowing a murder took place here this morning?"

"Fuck off, Sophia. That's how I feel. Fucking fuck off."

Sophia looks at Moe. Cameraman quits filming, busies himself with turning knobs on his battery pack. "Monica," Sophia says with mock enthusiasm. "I thought you were a boy. You beat us here. Well done. Did you get anything?" She gives Cameraman a look to make it clear whose fault it is she didn't arrive sooner. "Never mind. I don't care. Excuse me. I have to get back to making news."

"Journalists report news. Not make it."

Sophia flips Moe off, showing that her long polished nails are encrusted with tiny fake jewels. She struts her fat ass away.

Cameraman gives Moe a nod and counts it down again as Sophia puts the mic in Michael Jordan's face. "Officer, what can you share about the attack?"

He glances over his shoulder to the men near the dumpsters. "No. Comment."

Moe follows his gaze. *Oh my fuck!* She knows the shorter detective. She hadn't realized who he was before. While Michael Jordan is occupied, she scoots over to Flattop. "Officer," Moe says. "What's your name? Off the record."

"Chapman. Patrick."

"Thanks, Patrick. I'm Moe. I work for *Text Block*. Can you do me a favor and tell Whistler that Moe wants to say hello?"

"What's a Whistler?"

"Down there. Whistler Diaz. He's my cousin."

Officer Chapman looks confused but says, "I'll let him know."

Geometry of the Learning Curve

The first thing Whistler learned as Ruther walked away was that the big man in the small jacket was not named Tiny. "I'm Ezekiel. Don't call me Zeke." He'd said it as he and Whistler followed Ted toward a half-hidden body left to rot between dumpsters.

Whistler was nervous about the reality he was walking into. His mind looked for a distraction and noted that despite Ezekiel's size, he moved with a light step. He said, "I've never met an Ezekiel. It's distinctive. I notice distinctive names. My name's Whistler." Ted and Ezekiel both stopped and turned. He knew the look. They expected an explanation. "Don't ask," he said. Neither of them asked. They had all started walking again.

Ted lugs an oversized wheeled duffel behind him. It has an enormous Blackhawks patch on the central compartment. The small wheels vibrate over the asphalt, and the sound moves through the frame and is magnified by the hollow of the bag, turning the soft rectangle into a resonant amplifier. The whirring sound surges and recedes in rhythm with Ted's long strides. It swells as they near the corpse. The sound makes Whistler a little crazy. His forehead starts to sweat. His armpits feel wet. He mops the sheen from his face with the rolled sleeve of Ruther's shirt. Whistler realizes he'll need to get it dry-cleaned before he returns it. The duffel stops.

Ted unzips the bag and passes out blue booties. Ezekiel forces the average-size booty over his above-average shoe. Ted hands around a box of latex gloves. Whistler snaps one on his right hand. His left he leaves free for working his tablet.

They approach the body. A woman. She is bruised and scraped flesh with matted hair. She is deadweight in the early stages of rot. She's the meat that remains when the soul leaves. The way she lies looks uncomfortable. The rumpled and crushed shrub of her hair causes Whistler to brush his own hair down. She had soiled and wet herself. To witness a body so nearly lifelike but clearly dead causes activity in the less-evolved corners of Whistler's brain. He takes a step back.

The woman looks young. Fit. Dressed in athletic gear with expensive running shoes. Her throat is mottled with dark marks. At a casual glance, Whistler might think she wears a scarf. Her body is on its left side. Hair hides her face. There's a pool of blood on the pavement under her head, a congealed brown halo.

Whistler doesn't know what to do; he stands and gawps. He shuts his mouth and looks to the other men. They wear neutral expressions. He tries to emulate them, tries to be professional. *I'm not fooling anyone.*

Ted squats; his bony knees make sharp angles. He eyes the body. He shifts his center of gravity to fish in his duffel and get out evidence baggies.

Whistler backs further away. He powers on the tablet. He swipes and taps and starts taking photos with the pad. He types notes with one hand, capturing as many details as possible.

"Do we know who the victim is?" Whistler asks.

"Not yet," Ted says.

Whistler tries to suss it out by the numbers. Given the victim's outfit, she was likely going to or coming from the park along the lakeshore. He looks toward the lake. Twenty yards away, Hoss has the tunnel taped off and is standing guard.

Ezekiel is done with his initial assessment. He says respectfully, "This is where it happened. She may have been dragged this way." He draws a pretend line from the tunnel to the body. "The killing happened here."

Ted takes a digital recorder from his bag and starts it. He moves between the dumpsters. A breeze comes off the lake, rushes through the tunnel and stirs the scene. A rancid smell swirls from one of the dumpsters, sour, like food waste sharp with rat piss.

Ted places two fingers on the woman's carotid artery. "No pulse," he says. "It never hurts to check." Ted talks as he carefully examines the body, starting at the head, working his way down. He is slow, meticulous. "The victim is a white female. Early thirties. Cause of death appears to be manual strangulation. These contusions are excessive." He gently slips his hand under her neck and lifts lightly. "Based on rigor around the neck and jaw, but absent in the limbs, I estimate time of death two to four hours."

Whistler looks at his watch and makes a note. He hears a commotion. Chief and Champ are keeping a few people away. He sees a tall man with a camera on his shoulder. He turns from the news crew.

Ted's attention is on the dead woman's head, walking his fingers carefully over her scalp. "Brown hair of medium length. Recent cut and style. Expensive. Its rumpled, but no split ends, tasteful, conservative. She has product in here, maybe some kind of paste. It's crispy near the roots. Dried perspiration. I'd guess white-collar job. She may have been exercising recently, or the sweat could be from the struggle. Based on damage to her throat I'd guess she died quickly. Maybe too fast for this much perspiration. I'll do a rape kit at the shop. Maybe we'll find DNA. But her clothes look undisturbed. A laceration under her head. I'll look when we move her."

Whistler asks, "Is it possible a blow to the head was cause of death?"

"This amount of blood . . ." Ted leans back to let Whistler see the puddle. It looks like take-out duck sauce left in the fridge. "It's not a major wound. Likely happened during the struggle. Even minor scalp wounds bleed a lot." He folds himself back over the woman. "Her right ear is pierced, but no earring. I'll check her left in a moment."

Ted takes a light from his pocket and holds her nearest eye open. He passes the light across her pupil. "Blue eyes. I'll get a height measurement, but I'd say five—five and a hundred and forty pounds. As expected, pete-chial hemorrhage in the eye indicates asphyxia caused by pressure from strangulation. Or more accurately, in this case, throttled with prejudice."

Whistler taps notes. He walks closer, curiosity assuaging his primal need for distance.

"If someone took her earrings, we could have a motive," Ezekiel suggests calmly, not an assertion so much as a collaborative guess. "Mugging gone too far. Maybe she fought back or lipped off? Things got out of control."

"Not that likely to get mugged in this neighborhood. She probably wasn't carrying a bag. Not if she was out for a run." Whistler says.

"Maybe," Ezekiel concedes. "But you're more likely to be mugged than choked to death over here."

Whistler types *Mugging? Robbery? Earrings? Purse?* "Do you see a phone?"

"Not yet," Ted says. He continues moving down the body. Periodically Ezekiel asks a question. Whistler takes notes.

Whistler edges in, leans to see the gouge of flesh missing from the underside of the scalp. He reaches his gloved hand forward to smooth her hair and get a clear view. "Look here," he points. "See how her hair is crimped like it was pulled back. You find a hair tie?"

"No. Not yet."

"You smell that? Like lilacs and Windex? Only a whiff."

"No, I don't smell it. But I caught a scent of chlorine. Maybe she went for a swim," Ted says. "The smell of the dumpsters makes it hard to be sure. I'll swab for compounds at the shop."

Whistler takes a hard look at the woman's throat. "I've never seen bruising like this."

"Someone clamped on her so hard he crushed her trachea and probably fractured vertebrae. Her neck was squeezed out of shape. She never had a chance."

"Someone she knew or someone out of control," Ezekiel says.

"You said *he*. Did you mean to say *he*?" Whistler asks.

"Most likely a man. On the large side," Ted says.

"Statistically, a female victim choked to death, a man did it."

The redheaded patrolman approaches. "Detective Diaz. There's a woman. A reporter."

"Hold on," Whistler says. He watches Ted pat the corpse around the hips. At the small of her back, he locates a zip-pocket in the waistband of her stretch pants. He produces a blank magnetic key card and a mashed roll of five-dollar bills.

Ted says, "No ID. Just this."

Ezekiel says, "Well, shit."

Whistler turns to Champ, "You heard Ruther. Don't say a word to the reporter. Skulk."

"Yeah. I know. She says she knows you. She wants to say hello."

Whistler looks west. He sees Moe. She's cut her hair even shorter, but there's no question it's his cousin. "Okay. I'll get there when I get there." He continues watching as Ted zip-ties clear bread bags around the dead woman's hands.

"Excuse me, Detective," Champ says.

"Yeah?"

"She called you Whistler." Champ squares his body in preparation to ask a follow-up question.

Before he can form the words, Ezekiel and Ted say, "Don't ask."

Like a Boss

The hanging supplies slap against the insides of the panel van when Kaz breaks hard at the intersection of State and Congress. The light turns green, and he leans hard on the horn in a rage at the cars that clog the intersection.

"The light is red. You drive like fuck. Stop going. Come on!"

He edges his way between cars that blare their own horns. It takes three minutes to reach his destination and ten minutes to find parking. He backs into a spot reserved for compact cars, next to a tiny park.

The park has cast cement benches encrusted with oversized backward and upside-down letters that spell illegible words. The benches rest at perfect angles for watching dogs shit in dead grass. Kaz hates those benches. Kaz is no fan of city dogs or their owners dangling plastic bags of turds like opaque scrotums. Nor is he impressed with the abandoned lot converted into a disgusting open-air toilet with seating for perverted voyeurs.

When he rams the gearshift into park, he knows he's blocking the car behind him. He imagines his bride's loving encouragement: "Quit acting like a bitch." Svetlana would approve of his ruthless parking.

Kaz jumps out, nearly dooring a bike messenger.

"Open your eyes, asshole," the messenger calls as he swerves, standing on his pedals and pumping his legs to get up to speed.

"Fuck you," Kaz says, flipping off the biker's back as it moves into the distance. He jogs across the street and onto the sidewalk, checking the clock on his phone. *Made good time.*

He takes a moment to get focused on the task ahead. He assesses his image in the plate glass of a storefront. *I look good.* He uses his palms to stroke his pale hair against both sides of his head: right side, left side. *I'm the boss. I'm in charge. I've worked hard, made moves. I'm a machine.* He thinks of Svetlana again. *She is a hard woman.* But he believes she wants what's best for him, what's best for their growing family.

"Showtime," he says under his breath.

He walks into Coffee Girl and approaches the only customer in the place. He ignores the greeting from the woman behind the counter. He sticks his hand out and forcefully pumps the little man's hand before he can rise. He looms above the older man.

"You must be Greene. Pleased to meet you," he says, taking charge. He chooses not to call him "Doctor Greene"—the title elevates the other man. Kaz doesn't want that.

"Yes," the smaller man says. Greene is not much to look at, not particularly professorial despite his credentials; not tall, neither fit nor out of shape, not young but not too old. An average, unremarkable man in a crappy brown suit and no tie, a collared shirt with the top two buttons undone over a black T-shirt with writing on it.

Kaz looks at the face of his phone and says, "Let's get started."

"Yes," Greene says again. The man's awkwardness makes Kaz feel in control.

"I'm Kazimierz Gladsky. Named after Casimir Pulaski. You know Pulaski: American Revolutionary hero, father of American cavalry, was the first to introduce the fruit-filled paczki to North America. Very famous." He waits for a response and is disappointed. "Kazimierz was his true Polish name. That is my name too. Kaz for short or Mr. Gladsky if you'd prefer."

Greene nods, a gesture so slight it's more like a tic. The man's eyes are dead.

"Did you know this city has the largest population of Poles outside of Krakow?" Kaz adds the tidbit to prove he's no dummy. "It's true. Believe me."

Greene moves his head in an indefinite manner that is neither negative nor affirmative, drawing a tiny shape with the tip of his nose. Something about this Greene is off. He's stiff and shabby like a sun-faded mannequin in a tailor shop window. Kaz sets his bag in an empty chair but doesn't sit. "Is the coffee good?"

"This is a cortado. It is Rosa's specialty. It is strong enough to taste. The espresso is local." It's not a recommendation, just a list of facts with no particular emphasis.

Kaz turns his eyes on Rosa. She's petite and curvy with black hair. She's so excited she bounces slightly, like she might launch through the ceiling. He approaches, raps his knuckles on the counter and smiles. "You must be Rosa. My friend says to try the cortado. Make it two."

"I could add simple syrup if you like it sweet."

"I do like it sweet," he says, not talking about coffee. "Your cortado, is it full-bodied?"

"The espresso is nutty, and the milk gives it a velvety feel." Rosa gives him a sales pitch as she works, talks about the quality of the beans and the rarity of the espresso machine. He doesn't listen, keeps his eyes on her body as she moves it around behind the counter. When she's done he asks, "Are you *the* coffee girl?"

"The one and only."

"I didn't expect to meet a celebrity today." He smiles it up.

She seems to take his flattery as an unwelcome pickup line, because her only response is a polite smile. She slides the drinks across the counter. "Enjoy," she says.

Back at the table, Kaz plunks the drinks down and takes some papers from his bag. He sips the coffee. It's strong and, despite the syrup, bitter. He doesn't like it. *Worse than Polish coffee.* The scrawny professor gulps his like it's cold milk. Kaz doesn't want to lose the upper hand, so he says, "Mmm, good," and sets his drink to the side. *Four dollars I'll never get back.*

"That girl seems nice," Kaz says leadingly. He cocks his thumb at Rosa.

Greene says, "Yes."

Kaz squares the pages of Greene's CV loudly against the tabletop. "Mr. Greene. Associate Professor of Literature at the University of Chicago. BA, MA, PhD." He flips the pages of the document, "Published papers, keynote speaker. Three years' teaching in Moscow. You are impressive," Kaz says. He scrutinizes Greene and qualifies the statement, "On paper."

The little man doesn't react to the insult. Kaz tries again. "A lot of letters after your name. I never went to school. What matters is horse sense. You agree, don't you?"

Again the man draws some infinitesimally small shape in the air with his nose, his expression blank.

Kaz goes on, "Why are you looking for work?" He sets the pages down and leans back in a display of his intention to pass judgment.

"I was in a crash. I hit my head and died. But I got better. I don't remember the things I used to know, so I can't teach. I'm in a new phase and I need a job." Greene talks like he's repeating a mathematical proof.

Kaz taps the pages against the table again. "What do you know about Bug Off?"

"What's Bug Off?"

"The job you applied for."

"Oh. The card said 'Heroic work to rid the city of the scourge of pestilence. Good pay. Full-time hours. Benefits with transportation provided.' That's what I know." His monotone makes Kaz want to punch this Greene in the throat.

"What most interested you in a job with Bug Off?"

"Transportation provided. I'm not supposed to drive." Greene doesn't gesture when he speaks. His fingers are interlocked on the tabletop with his cortado resting between his hinged palms. He must notice Kaz looking, because he lifts the drink to his lips and gulps the remainder.

"It would be better if you could drive."

"I used to."

Kaz takes that as confirmation Greene can drive and moves on. "Bug Off is a family company. My father-in-law started it. I took over when he recently passed." Kaz pauses to allow Calvert to offer his sympathies. Calvert stares, unblinking. "We provide inspections and remedies for bed bug infestations. Once we worked for individual customers. One house, one room, one couch, bed, or drape at a time. But I changed it." He takes credit for Svetlana's business acumen because bosses project confidence and she told him to do so. "Now we contract with luxury hotels. We check and treat rooms with discretion." "With discretion" is a phrase Svetlana told him to use when selling Bug Off's services. "We're the leading Cimex lectularius remediation experts in the greater Chicago area. You are familiar with the Cimex lectularius?"

"No."

Kaz is getting angry. This guy is ruining his delivery. "Would it be hard for you to work around parasitic insects that feed exclusively on blood?"

"No," Greene says with an unsatisfying lack of animation.

"Okay. Well, we have three vans. I drive one. Jackson drives the second. The third is Allen's. You'd train with Allen. Allen is a convicted criminal." Kaz slows down. "He's rough around the edges, but a good worker. Loyal. Could you work with someone who's been in jail?"

"I could do that."

"Even if he killed someone?"

"Yes," Greene says firmly.

"You could let someone who doesn't have a bunch of degrees tell you what to do?"

"Yes."

"We use dogs that can smell an infestation. If needed, we use heat and natural, nonchemical sprays to address the problem. We check and treat every room. Every crew checks a set of rooms every day. If there's an outbreak, we take care of it. If word gets out that a hotel has bed bugs, it kills business. You see? We do vital work for the economy. Very important."

"I see."

Kaz is sick of this guy and wants to move it along. "That's basically it. But there is a lot to learn. Do you think bed bug abatement is the right career for you?"

"Yes. Thank you so much for sharing this information." With that, the little freak tips his lifeless gaze on Kaz for the first time and says, "When do I start?"

A True Friend

When his interview with Kaz is over Calvert has nowhere to go. He starts his career in bedbug abatement in a few days. Until then, he only has to eat and sleep and take his medicine as a living person might do. He lifts the empty tumbler to his lips and tries to slurp the wet foam that clings to the side. Gravity is too weak to overcome the surface tension. He looks sadly at the reluctant remnant of his cortado.

Two women push the door open and tap their high heels toward the counter, where Rosa greets them. While they order, a round, young man with an overstuffed backpack holds the door for a bent old lady pushing a dog in a wire cart. They queue up behind the others.

The women in heels leave with drinks, heads together, talking in happy, hushed tones about a concert that night. As they go, a short, dark man enters with a miniature version of himself riding on his shoulders. The old woman's cart dog grabs the toddler's attention; the boy lunges for the dog and comes sideways off his father. The father reaches out his arms to scoop the boy before he hits the floor. The round man with the bulging backpack applauds the father's quick catch. They exchange pleasantries about Bear's football. The little boy is hoisted back on his dad's shoulders, unaware of the trauma he nearly suffered.

The old lady slow walks her coffee, her movements labored. She leans heavily on her cart. Her expression is pained as she sits with her furry friend. Calvert considers the woman's need for companionship in her last years. *Should I have a companion?*

A luxury of death is that Calvert has no reason to be hasty. Living Calvert was forever trying to accomplish something. Dead Calvert enjoys watching people come and go. He especially likes seeing Rosa do the work of three people: taking orders, making drinks, and counting change. Every customer gets a genuine smile as she gracefully crafts complicated drinks. *Rosa is doing what she was made to do.*

Calvert has a sense being a professor was like that for him. He relished preparing a talk, he'd become excited discussing a specific passage, and in return a few students would get equally excited. *A good life while it lasted.*

The old woman totters back to the front counter and asks for a spoon. Three men in dark suits order blender drinks. They are tall and speak in loud, deep voices. The worried dog, left at the table shivering, whimpers for fear of abandonment, agitated by the self-important men. Rosa passes a plastic spoon across the counter. The old woman's drawn shoulders don't want to extend that far. Rosa stretches until the aged hand can grasp the utensil. Looking at the men's clothes, Calvert realizes how shabby his suit is, how coarse the weave and how slick the slacks are worn at the knees.

At her table the old woman scoops froth from her cappuccino and holds the spoon for the dog to lap. Spoon after spoon, the dog makes a snuffling sound and a snarly smile with sharp teeth poking from the side of his muzzle. Flecks of foam speckle the dog's dark nose. The woman's face is content and relaxed, as if her pain is gone.

Two of the men in suits argue the relative merits of a potential property acquisition. The third man sticks his hands in his front pockets and surreptitiously fiddles his genitals. Three frilly drinks piled with whipped cream and sprinkles are set on the counter. The genital fiddler puts a five-dollar tip on the counter. The old woman struggles with the door. Calvert begins to rise to her aid. A passerby on the sidewalk takes a moment to help her. On the way through the door, the cart dog looks drunk on dairy fat, his expression sleepy-eyed and satisfied.

Being deceased was easy enough while institutionalized. At New Horizons many of the patients inhabited alternate realities. Christopher, a bearded man in his fifties, snickered incessantly at dirty jokes whispered in his ear by an invisible Benny Hill. A woman named Edie proclaimed herself the secret Queen of America and demanded people kneel as she passed on her way to the communal shower. King Reo, so named because Queen Edie believed they had been married, often wept, explaining in desperate gasps, "My hair screams when they cut it. But they cut it anyway." When Reo wasn't worried about his screaming hair, he liked to eat things that were inedible—for instance, all the vowels from a box of foam letters kept in the common room. Among the coterie of diversely afflicted at New Horizons, Calvert's slow-speed death felt rather mild.

Sitting at Coffee Girl, watching seemingly emotionally healthy people, makes Calvert fret about exactly what happened to him. It's becoming important to him that he discover his past before his mind loses function. He does not view these thoughts as either good or bad. Still, the emotional complexity of the associated feelings challenges his limited capacities.

Rosa hurries into the café to wipe the front table. Back behind the counter, she organizes and cleans. She hustles to the backroom and comes out with a couple gallons of milk. Calvert approaches the counter.

"You got the job," she says with certainty.

"I got the job," he confirms.

"I had a good feeling." Calvert sees Rosa has foam splashed on the side of her nose. "When do you start?"

"Monday morning." Calvert lifts a napkin from a stack on the counter and puts it in Rosa's hand. "You have something on your nose."

"Do I?" She opens the napkin and tucks her nose in its folds. She turns away to blow her nose. Turning back she asks, "Did I get it?"

"You got it. It's gone. It was only a speck of foam."

"That's embarrassing. You are a true good friend. Thank you." She gives a shy smile, then washes her hands and dries them on her apron.

He likes being called "a true good friend." He knows friendship is important. To connect with someone is one of life's few joys. Before he loved Mere, they had been friends. *I did love her. She loved me. She must have.*

A memory of his past life comes to him, as vivid as if it just happened.

He stood next to the bed, pleased to see the comforter, pillows, and sheets shoved on the floor during the vigorous encounter. Mere's flushed body was crosswise on the mattress. She was oblivious to the two corners of the fitted sheet creeping toward her with each exhale. She smacked her damp abdomen saying, "If that didn't impregnate me it wasn't for lack of trying."

"I aim to please." Calvert kicked a pillow out of the way, looking for his clothes. He couldn't stop grinning. "Give me a few minutes. Let's go again. For medical reasons." He slipped his T-shirt on and stood there with no pants.

She turned over and tugged at his damp penis. "Lookie there. It didn't even take a few minutes."

That had been in the early days of the relationship, Calvert remembers. After the frustration and expense of a decade of failed fertility treatments, their love morphed into a dependable thing, static and strong with the passage of time. Their relationship was as reliable as a German engine, running smoothly with little need for attention, all the parts of their life continuing to churn while giving off little heat.

What he feels with Rosa is different from that. There is an electric charge that tingles through his mind when she smiles. *My dead brain is still receptive to certain inputs.*

Rosa's voice brings him back, "Let me make you another cortado and some food."

She wants to care for him. Like the old woman cared for her little dog. *Does a dead man make a good pet?* Looking into Rosa's kind face, he doesn't mind the idea. He thinks again of how only a dead woman would be fit to love him.

"I'm going to make you a bagel. Do you want it toasted?

"Yes. Please toast my bagel."

Rosa looks amused at his phraseology. She gets to work grinding fresh coffee. After a few moments, she says, "My day started badly. How can I explain? I have a little boy, Thomas. He's in second grade. He keeps getting notes home. They say, 'Dear Mrs. Zhang, Today Thomas made it clear you don't know how to parent.' Just kidding. But that's how it feels. He came home with a new note yesterday." She fishes in her pocket, pulls out a folded piece of paper, and hands it to him. He opens it and reads:

Dear Mrs. Zhang,

Your son has been recruiting for a club for children of mixed ethnic backgrounds. He called it Patchwork Kids. We have a strict policy of not allowing clubs based on race, ethnicity, or belief. Some children may feel excluded, which can damage self-esteem and lead to conflict. We can't allow this. We fully expect your support enforcing these rules.

"How stupid is that?," Rosa asks as he finishes the note. "He got in trouble for trying to find people like him. Trust me, there are no other Chinese-Mexican Americans in his class. The other kids say things like, 'What are you?' It makes him feel bad." She pats her hand over her heart as if to tamp down pain. "That was yesterday. Last night I tried to talk to him. Thomas didn't understand. He felt picked on. He cried. Not a little cry—a big cry. It broke me. He finally wore himself out and fell asleep. I stayed up most of the night, sad for him. Worried for him. Mad and wanting to do something but unsure what I could possibly do.

"I worry I'm messing up. I do my best. Lots of kids grow up without a dad. I didn't have a dad at home. But Thomas is a boy, and maybe that makes it different. Thomas's father was not a good man. His attitude about women—I want Thomas to have more respect."

"I never met my dad," Calvert volunteers. He's pleased with the natural way older memories have started percolating from his dry synapse. "He was deployed to Vietnam when my mother was pregnant with me. Missing in action by the time I was born."

"Your mom made it work. You turned out okay."

"My mother went swimming in Lake Michigan when I was in kindergarten. They never found her body. Her father, Harry, raised me."

Rosa looks pained by the news. "Oh no. I had no idea. I'm sorry."

"People make their way as best they can. There is no right way." He shares the rote wisdom with no idea of its source.

She seems saddened by the turn of conversation.

Calvert says, "You were talking about your son."

"This morning Thomas was angry and exhausted and pretended to be sick so he could stay home. I was tired too, but the grand opening. I practically had to drag him to my mother's. Bless Consuela. I couldn't do this without her. I needed a hug or a smile from him. But he wouldn't cut me any slack. What a mess. It's a cruel trick how easily loved ones crush us. Don't you think?"

Calvert wants to squeeze Rosa until her worries are gone.

Rosa puts a toasted cream cheese bagel and a fresh cortado on the counter. "This morning I was afraid no one would like my coffee. You eased my mind. Thank you."

"You're welcome." He hadn't thought of his parents since his death. In high school, Calvert learned the paradox of Schrodinger's cat, had determined his father was both alive and dead until proven otherwise. His mother, he imagined, was adrift in a vast cold void, her existence suspended. *Perhaps my undead status is hereditary, I'm genetically predisposed to linger after life in a poorly defined state.*

A pack of customers walk through the door. He takes his items and returns to his table. His injured shoulder throbs but doesn't really hurt anymore. He nibbles food he can't taste and chews carefully with teeth he can't feel. The cortado, once again, fires his numb taste buds as nothing else can. He wonders if Rosa is a sorceress. He doesn't know how else to explain why she's able to give him sensations he thought his body was dead to.

Relative Diplomacy

Moe lingers out of the way as Sophia and the cameraman try to elicit any usable response from Michael Jordan. They give up and take a few long shots of the scene. Finally Sophia struts back to the van. Moe watches surreptitiously when Sophia takes off her heels and slides into the passenger seat, waiting impatiently to be chauffeured to the next location.

Moe texts so Vivian knows she's working the story. She lets her know Channel 13 is at the scene and promises to get in touch soon.

It takes a while for Officer Chapman to return from speaking with Whistler. He lifts the yellow tape and allows Moe to walk a few yards closer to the victim.

"Wait there," short Michael Jordan orders.

It's not long before Whistler trudges toward her. "Hey, cuz. What do you want?" He gives her a quick hug.

"When'd you get out of uniform?" Whistler looks suspicious, doesn't answer. "Off the record, Whistler. No joke. Two cousins chittin' the chat. What could be more innocent?"

Whistler looks skeptical, but he relents. "I've been doing mandatory bullshit for weeks. I started today. It's a bad time for chitchat. I gotta get back."

"They threw you in the deep end, huh? Puttin' a lot of faith in you." She ignores his attempt to end the conversation quickly.

"It's a bunch of stuff. The squad is putting a big case to bed. The boss wants to test me. Maybe a little faith, though Inspector Ruther doesn't strike me as religious."

Moe grins. "Still, this is what you wanted, right?"

"Listen, it's good to see you, but seriously, I need to go."

"I understand. But what if I had information? Something solid? Could you give me background, off the record? Anonymous source. I'd protect you."

He opens his mouth but doesn't speak. Shuts his mouth. Checks to see how closely the two patrolmen are watching.

Moe voices the things he must be thinking. "Detectives develop sources. Why not your cousin? You know me. You can trust me. Plus, I have connections all over the city. If I don't know someone, I know someone who knows someone. Theoretically, some people might not want to talk to a man with a badge, but they will talk to me. I could be a vital go-between."

"You have something?" Whistler allows himself to be interested.

"I'm not sure yet. Let me get back to you."

"I'm not saying yes. Depends what you have. If it's real, I'll share what I can. Off the record. Right? That's the only way."

"Of course. Isn't that what I just said? We have a deal, then. Let me buy you a cerveza to celebrate your promotion. Tonight? It's Friday night. RJ's Hot Shrimps?"

"If you have something on my case, don't be shy. I have to report to Inspector Ruther when I get back. I'd like to have something worth saying."

Moe can't help but smile. Whistler wants to impress Ruther. She can work that. "That's fair. As soon as I have something, I'll call. But see you tonight either way?"

"Okay," he says, stepping away. "If I have time."

"TV13 claims the woman's death was the result of a vicious attack. They're running it on the noon broadcast. Is that accurate? Can you tell me how she died?"

Whistler gets close to Moe's face, "A woman was murdered. Cause of death was manual strangulation." Whistler looks shaken. He loosens his already loose tie. "Finger-shaped bruising." He unbuttons another button on his baggy shirt. His complexion goes gray.

She's pushed as much as she can. She doesn't want to take advantage of Whistler's big-heartedness. *Not yet.* She doesn't want to ruin a potential source. Uncharacteristically, she holds her tongue. She thanks Whistler and lets him lead her away.

No Accidents

After leaving Coffee Girl, Calvert can't remember where he's going and finds himself standing in a cluster of strangers anxious to traverse Congress Avenue. He's preoccupied. His body is trying to tell him something important. After careful consideration, he recognizes the nagging pressure under his waistband as the need to urinate. *Too many cortados.* He would've refused anyone else's generosity, but not Rosa's.

The pressure is becoming urgent. But urgency is in the eye of the beholder. Calvert is not overly concerned. Death has taught him you can get used to anything. Sometimes giving up leads to answers faster than making an effort. Take, for instance, his desire to know the circumstances of his accident. The doctors and staff at New Horizons would never give him details, no matter how often he asked. He stopped asking. In the relaxed state that followed, memories of his life with Meredith began to surface. His theory is, not dwelling on his full bladder may eliminate the necessity to pee.

People around him begin to cross the busy intersection. His feet move automatically. The short woman with high hair directly in front of him dictates his pace. After a dozen jostling strides, he knows his attempt to ignore his bursting bladder is futile. He needs to find a place to relieve himself. High Hair turns east at the next corner. Calvert continues to follow her.

A kid with fat headphones and downcast eyes walks a collision course for Calvert. Calvert steps wide to avoid catastrophe. Light flashes off the lake from blocks away. He squints against the glare. Thinking of all that water makes him desperate to piss. He hustles to catch up to Big Hair. When he closes the gap, she alters her stride to avoid what appears to be a frozen green smoothie dumped on the sidewalk. Calvert steps on the back of her sensible flats. She glares over her shoulder and mumbles an angry monologue. She and her hair hobble-walk across the flow of foot traffic so she can shelter in a doorway and slip out of her shoe. Calvert is preoccupied with the pressure in his middle; he follows her and stops walking when she stops.

She wields the shoe, swats it in the air near his right ear. "Look at it. Look what you did." Calvert tries to look, but she lashes her footwear too wildly. "Why? Why would you do that?"

"It was an accident," he explains as reasonably as he is able while dodging her attack.

"There are no accidents." She slips her shoe on and bumps him out of the way. He nearly wets himself. He focuses on clenching the muscles that control his fluid sac. His neurons spark, his nerves respond, his body follows orders.

Her voice bounces around his vacant skull: *There are no accidents. If one backtracks, is there always a tipping-point when a poor choice led to a domino of consequences that only seem unintentional?* He chose to follow the woman, which led to the kid with the headphones nearly hitting him. Because of that he saw the lake, thought of water, and his bladder. His acute discomfort distracted him. He scuffed High Hair's shoe. *I'm responsible.* He looks for High Hair to deliver a mea culpa. Dead Calvert has no ego. He only wants to do what's right. But the woman is long gone.

He has no time for guilt. He charts his own course amid the bustle. He hunts for anyplace to pee. Halfway between Van Buren and Jackson, he ducks down a narrow alley. He walks around a man leaning one shoulder against the bricks to suck on a cigarette. The space between the buildings is a haze of burnt tobacco. Despite his absent sense of smell, the thick air catches in his throat. Calvert wills himself not to cough; his bladder would let go. He walks toward the deeper shadows, steps behind a dumpster, and fumbles with the old zipper. He barely fishes himself out in time. Once he starts to pee, he can't stop.

The smoker avoids looking in Calvert's direction, stubs his butt on the wall and sprays a few puffs of Binacca in his mouth, looks both ways before he's pulled out of sight by the stream of humanity.

Still Calvert's bladder drains. The pressure lets up. He tucks himself away and struggles to zip his fly. He gets it half closed and gives up.

He hears a rustling and a smattering of high-pitched cries. He's drawn deeper into the alley. Calvert knows walking toward unknown noises in a dark alley is the opposite of what he should do. *What have I got to lose?* He edges around another dumpster. On the ground, he finds a grubby man asleep on a nest of crushed boxes. In the curl of his body, a skinny cat nurses three mewling kittens.

The mother turns wild yellow eyes on Calvert. She begins to stand, but the kittens keep pressing their paws into her exposed pink belly, making emphatic, tiny sounds, soft claws too new to retract. She settles for lifting her head and lets a rumbling growl slowly build.

The sleeping man scratches his beard but doesn't wake.

The cat lets go of a feral hiss, afraid and dangerous; sharp teeth and sinew. *Motherhood makes her capable of any degree of violence.* Calvert backs away.

On the sidewalk, his empty bladder has made room in his body for a thought. He remembers how much Meredith wanted to be a mother, how much of their life focused on remedies for the perceived absence of child, and just how badly he had handled it. He also remembers his intention to shop for the things written on the list tucked in his wallet.

Shoe Leather

Whistler lifts the yellow tape and lets Moe out of the cordon. *He's a gentleman, even though I ticked him off. He can't help it.*

"Maybe I'll see you tonight." His tone makes it clear he doesn't want to get together.

Moe knows her cousin keeps commitments, even the ones he'd rather avoid. *He'll show if I push him. Besides, he has a weakness for hot shrimps.* She says, "I won't quote you, Whistler. I mean it. You're safe."

His taught jaw relaxes.

"Good luck with the case."

Whistler nods.

Moe watches his broad shoulders roll forward in the overlarge shirt. His head hangs. *Built like a bulldog.* He's under a lot of pressure, always out to prove something. She truly would like her reporting to help his case. *I'll report the hell out of this.*

Short Michael Jordan hovers near by, keeping an eye on her. She notices the crime scene tape is wrinkled.

"Answer me one question. Nothing to do with the case. I promise." She crosses her heart. "Nothing at all to do with the case."

"Ask your question. Doesn't mean I'll answer." Short MJ leaves his arms crossed, showing his biceps.

"The tape is mangled. I've seen a lot of crime scenes, and I've never seen it like that." She leaves the question unasked; the indirect-question strategy pays with reluctant sources.

"We're reusing it. Cost savings."

She clucks her tongue, shakes her head sympathetically.

MJ goes on, "Been told to make the cordon area small as possible. We went two years without a state budget. Thank god Springfield finally had the cojones to override the governor's veto. Some budget is better than no budget."

She clucks her tongue at that too. "More crime, smaller budgets."

"Don't have to tell me," he tells her.

Detective Chapman talks to a mic on his shoulder, moves to the far end of the crime scene.

Where's he going? She decides she needs to find out. "Thanks, officer."

"Don't let me see my name in print."

"I didn't get your name."

"Even better. The same rules apply."

She crosses her heart again. Moe's fatigued legs won't lift when she turns to jog away. She stumbles and kicks crumbled pavement before righting herself.

At Taibbi she pulls her helmet on, turns the key, and presses the ignition. He fires up. She pats his tank lovingly as the engine rumbles. The exhaust pipe is warm against her ankle. She taps the shifter into neutral and backs the bike, eases into first and shifts her body to swerve around potholes. Traffic is what one would expect in the Loop. Wind comes off the lake and strikes her at every intersection as she spirals through a series of one-way streets until she finds the shore-side path.

Parking Taibbi is challenging. She finds a metered spot and reluctantly jams her debit card into the slot. She punches a few buttons, waits for the parking receipt to print. She peels the backing away and slaps the sticker on the bike's front headlight. It only takes a couple minutes to find Officer Chapman's wedge of red hair cutting up the footpath. She shadows him to the massive Echelon Hotel, where he enters with purpose.

She nods to the bellhop while waiting for the revolving door to spin to an opening. The helmet is clumsy and draws attention.

"Can you hold on to this?" she asks.

"Sure thing." He rips a ticket and hands it over; the other half he tucks in the helmet.

She follows Chapman's trail into the grand lobby and spots him at the reception desk. He passes an evidence bag over the counter. A young lady in a dark blazer clacks at a keyboard and relays some information. Chapman returns the evidence to his pocket. The young lady picks up a phone and makes a call. Chapman mills around while he waits, chewing his thumbnail.

Moe keeps her distance, helps herself to a complimentary bottle of water and inconspicuously settles into a comfy chair. From her seat she reads a sign set on a collapsible easel: "Welcome to the (1) National Athletic Trainers Association; (2) The Autonomous Vehicle and Smart Road Technology Annual Summit; (3) College Book Arts Association."

The victim was here for a conference. Based on her shoes, the trainer thingy. Out-of-towner. That's why the mayor's pet detective squad is involved. The death could ding tourism. She slips her phone out and snaps a quick image of the conference sign board for reference.

Chapman is still pacing. She texts: *Viv: Think I'm onto something big. I'll drop in and hash it out.*

A lanky man in his fifties with a mane of sandy hair approaches Chapman. The new guy has a lot of muscle stacked neatly into a fitted suit. They shake hands like men, talk in low tones. The fit guy gestures to a door and escorts Chapman that way.

Moe walks to the reception counter, smiling at the young lady, "Hope Officer Chapman won't have trouble getting what he needs." She makes it a friendly warning.

"Mr. Windisch took him to the security office. They can put whatever camera feeds he needs on a thumb drive. You need to go back?"

"No. Chapman's a good man. I trust him. He will handle it. So the victim was here for the Athletic Trainer Conference?" Moe reaches for her phone, looks at the screen, swipes her finger over it a few times and pretends to read.

"No. She was here for the driverless cars."

Confirmation of being a guest. "Where'd she fly in from? Do you know?"

The woman looks at Moe's street clothes. The ruse is crumbling. But she replies cautiously, "No. I don't know. Do you have some ID?"

"You bet. I didn't do that?" Moe returns her phone and twists her bag around, rips the Velcro loose and digs through the contents. "Don't tell me I left my badge in my car again." She mumbles it under her breath, but pitched for the benefit of the attendant. When her performance has run its course, she says, "I can't find it. I better go get it. I'll be right back." She walks briskly away, takes four steps, turns and asks, "Oh, one more thing. Can you confirm the victim's name?"

"Let me get you someone from security." The young woman picks up the phone.

I had to try. "Okay. That is perfect. Have security wait here."

She hustles out the revolving door and waves her half ticket at the doorman. He takes her helmet from the cabinet beneath his workstation. Moe grasps it and slips him a folded dollar bill. She puts the helmet over her head to shield her face from cameras. She hurries across the circular drive and forces her legs to jog the half block to her bike.

The Napping Canadian

Moe sits at the Ainsworth Diner in South Chicago perfecting her ritual of using the string attached to the tea bag to wring the liquid from her alfalfa peppermint tea. She stirs in honey and brings the heavy mug to her face. It smells good: earthy and floral, but weak. She shuts her eyes on the tiny laptop in front of her. She feels the third draft of her article watching her. She dismisses the computer's malicious Cyclops gaze.

She gulps too much of the scalding tea, burning her tongue. She lets the hot liquid spill out, run down her chin to drip back in the mug. "Thamn it!" She snatches at napkins to cover her mess. She'd told herself she wouldn't do that again. A fresh cup between drafts is part of her process, but her wandering mind loses track of the fact that a fresh cup is hotter than the dregs of the previous one.

"Thamn mith," she says, gripping the scorched tip of her tongue. She allows herself a laugh, sets the mug aside and reads the article again. It takes only a few minutes. She makes a single change, preferring "strangled" over "choked." She considers reading the article one last time. Decides against it. *Good enough.* She sends it to Vivian. She takes out her phone and texts:

Viv—be there soon. Want to talk about a follow-up article I have in mind.

She carefully sips the tea. Her tender tongue regains some feeling. Now that she has Taibbi, she's under less pressure to rush. Freelancing for a digital paper is different from working in traditional print journalism. Moe needs to generate eight stories a week for her finances to work out, but there are no hard deadlines. Vivian has yet to employ anyone on staff, but she keeps dangling the possibility. *Now that Whistler is a detective, my potential for bigger stories is huge.*

She's not above using someone to get what she needs. She can be calculating and cold. She knows that about herself. It's not something she's proud of. It's ruthless to have a transactional relationship with her cousin. In her defense, making it as a journalist is nearly impossible. Most of her classmates went into broadcast news, which she barely considers news. Some have moved to regional papers where they remain journalistically insignificant, reporting local Girl Scout bake sales and high school sports. Not her. She's willing to bend some rules in the service of real reporting. Perhaps one day she'll be privileged enough to travel the moral high ground. It seems like a luxury reserved for established journalists. Still, when it comes to Whistler, she wants to play nice. *Within reason.*

Sitting here, watching Momma putter behind the counter, Moe has time to fully grasp what an opportunity she's stumbled into. If she can partner with Whistler, they could both build their careers. Not necessarily on this murder, but with a series of hard-won articles over years. She finishes her victory beverage, staring out the window.

Across the street is a two-story brick building with three storefront shops. One is a barbershop that specializes in tight clipper fades. The middle space is empty. The other is a used bookstore with a hand-lettered sign that reads "Ramshackle Books." Beside the bookshop is a community garden in what used to be a derelict lot.

A fat man in a broad-brimmed sun hat is harvesting produce from a raised bed. He walks over to a spigot to rinse a carrot. He rubs the firm orange skin clean under the flow of water, shakes off the excess wet, and chomps the tip from the fresh vegetable. His big jaw works the food around. The carrot greens wave in the wind as he chews and chews. *I love this neighborhood.*

South Chicago is one of over seventy-five neighborhoods within the city limit. It sits along the lakefront and covers an area of around three and a half square miles shaped like a chevron that fell over drunk and chose not to right itself. Moe knows this because she wrote her first published article about this diner, this neighborhood. The abandoned diner had reopened in a wave of optimism that followed Barack Obama's inauguration. The area was once known as Ainsworth, thus the throwback name of the diner. Though in truth, most people call it Momma's Place.

"You need any food today, honey?" Momma is there.

"No, Momma. I'm about to go."

"You need to eat. The pie is fresh."

"Not today, Momma. Thank you."

"Okay then, honey." Momma fishes in her apron and passes a fold of paper across the table. "You pay when you're ready." She shuffles away. *Getting old.* Across the street, Fat Man takes a last bite of carrot and throws the spray of greens onto a compost pile, his jaw still working mightily.

Moe wrote that article about the diner sitting in this very booth. A snapshot of a spry Momma appeared on the top of the day's feed. A story with her name attached: *M. Diaz.* It wasn't hard-hitting journalism—more of a human-interest piece. But the place she wrote about would have been completely ignored by the mainstream press. The act of writing it was political. She'd been proud. She'd highlighted the depressed local economy and the hopeful surge of Mom and Pop retail cropping up. She'd found her voice. She takes a last sip of tea. *Time to go.*

Six minutes later, Taibbi rumbles under her as she rolls in front of *Text Block*. The gate is open. She shoves down her kickstand. Her thighs are hot after the short ride. Her ass is sweaty and her jeans have slipped down, showing the top of her butt to the world. She hitches her pants as she walks.

Her Vicky helmet dangles from one hand as she raps on Vivian's office door.

"Come in." Vivian closes her laptop.

Moe exhibits the helmet.

"You got the motorcycle. That's good." Vivian leaves it at that and moves on to business. "I uploaded your story. The part about the crime scene tape gets at the funding crisis perfectly. Nice hook."

"Glad you liked it."

"You used personal observation. I haven't seen you do that before."

"Too much Hunter S. Thompson in my formative years," Moe explains, half sincere.

"It worked. You've built this place as much as I have. On that note, take a seat; I've got something to tell you."

Moe sits across the tidy desk from Vivian. "It's time to put someone on staff. For real this time. You and Jerome are my top writers. Jerome has an idea for a big story. I'm going to have him come in and pitch his idea. You need to have a pitch too. I'm going to decide who gets the staff position based on the pitch. You understand?"

"I guess."

"I know I'm dropping this on you. That's why I'm telling you now. I wanted to let you know, this dumpster girl you wrote about—there were three other women choked to death in the city in the past month; two Latinas and one black. Practically no press. I'm not saying there is a pattern here. I am saying there is a potential pattern here." Vivian digs in her desk drawer and hands a piece of paper to Moe. "Those are names, dates, places."

Moe glances at the list.

"I'm getting Jerome. This is about to happen." Vivian walks out.

Moe knows the broad strokes of Jerome's personal history. He isn't a Chicago guy. That's good for Moe. The city has a Midwest openness, but that ends where city politics begins. There's a turn of phrase, "We don't want nobody nobody sent." It's about Chicago's history of cronyism and a fundamental mistrust of outsiders. That gives Moe a leg up over Jerome. He moved here from one of those "C" cities in Ohio. Columbus or Cleveland or Cincinnati. She can never keep them straight. Won an award for reporting on chronically over-chlorinated public pools lead-ing to a painful rash that scarred dozens of kids. The city cut corners on pump equipment for pools in poor neighborhoods. That led to dan-gerous levels of irritants. Parents reported the odor, burning eyes and rashes for weeks before anyone took them seriously. It made national news, led to a class action lawsuit. After that Jerome decided to move to a bigger market. He arrived in Chicago and strategically took a job as a bartender at the Dearborn, one of those restaurants where City Hall employees go to drink. Before long he was on a first-name basis with dozens of city employees. He knew aldermen by their cocktail. After six months, he wrote a story about abuse of environmental oversight rules related to dumping in Lake Michigan. The uneven application of regulation was causing dangerous toxic algae blooms. He sold the story straight to *The Atlantic*. The article led to a book deal. The book sold well. Somehow, Vivian convinced Jerome to start writing for *Text Block*.

Vivian walks back in her office. Jerome takes a seat next to Moe.

"Hiya, Moe." As always, his presence brings with it a strong whiff of nicotine.

"Hey, Jerome. How's it going?"

"Good. I was reading your article. Good stuff. You put yourself in that story. Hunter S. Thompson fan?"

"You got me," she says.

He's gaunt, in his late thirties, bald spot at the back of his head. His tenor rings around the room like a bell. "You dropped that pinch of first person in the right spot. My hat's off to you."

"Thanks. Good work on that story about those rooftop wind tur-bines in Pilsen."

Jerome nods back. "A guy in permitting tipped me. The story wrote itself." He's humble like that. He's a talented writer. Not full of flour-ishes and melodrama, but workmanlike and honest.

Vivian clears her throat and props her chin on her fist. "You've both earned the right to be staff writer. The catch is I can only afford one right now. Whoever gets the job will have some management and editorial responsibilities. Nothing major. Wrangling a couple freelancers so I can focus more of my energies on sales."

Moe hates the idea of editorial work. She wants to write and be left alone. She certainly doesn't want to deal with the revolving door of self-righteous twenty-two-year-olds that produce much of the filler *Text Block* requires.

Vivian shifts in her chair. "Jerome, you don't live in the city. You take the train from Hinsdale, right?"

"My fiancé grew up there." Moe and Vivian have heard the explanation before. Moe smirks slyly for Vivian's benefit.

Vivian turns to Moe. "You're born and raised here, a woman of color and gay to boot. It gives you a diverse perspective. I'm not saying better. I'm saying diversity is part of the project of *Text Block*." Swiveling back to Jerome: "No offense, but there are a million straight white men journalists."

"True fact. I get it," he says.

"Ultimately, Jerome, you've got a hell of a knack for making complicated, bureaucratic malfeasance comprehensible. You don't dumb it down. You clarify. What're you working on?"

His voice rings. "It's all over the news: the country is divided. Urban blue areas and rural red areas. Right? But why? What does that mean for Chicago? What does it mean for a divided Illinois? What does it mean for the future of democracy? There's research from Loyola that suggests psychological underpinnings for this national self-sorting. My idea is to interview research participants, bring these issues to the fore, and explore policy remedies. I see this as an ongoing series that could run through the next election. It would involve discussions around specific policy as seen from opposing perspectives. For instance, gerrymandering. But not as sound bites—as reasonable people making informed decisions from radically different circumstances. My connections at the elections board are willing to share sociological data to help bolster the story. Also, my publisher has been encouraging. There could be a book down the road." He spreads his hands as if to say, *The ball is in your court.*

"Interesting," Vivian says. "Might get national traction." Vivian gets a faraway look, seeing a future in which she's recognized as an internet-era news maven, a world where *Text Block* is the new *Huffington Post* but with a focus on news about historically marginalized people.

Moe is ready to concede defeat.

Vivian comes back to reality. "Moe, what do you have for me?"

Moe barely knows what to say. "Nothing really. My idea is to juxtapose the attention the attack of a white woman in the North Loop is getting with the lack of coverage of similar crimes in predominantly black and brown neighborhoods. I have here"—she waves the paper Vivian gave her—"three similar attacks that took place in the past month within miles of the site of this morning's murder. Violent crimes against women are underreported. When they are reported, most often the victim is white, young, pretty and well-to-do. Under the current immigration umbrella, women with precarious citizenship are unlikely to report crimes. In black communities, there's little trust for the police, I'd argue for good reason. I see this series as a critique of corporate so-called journalism. I don't want to reveal my source, but I have a highly placed detective who's willing to work with me." Moe doesn't notice how loud she's gotten until she stops talking. She's worked her body to the edge of her seat.

Vivian looks thoughtful but doesn't speak. Moe flops back in her chair. Her pitch was thin compared to Jerome's.

"Wow," Jerome says. "That settles it. Moe deserves the staff position."

Moe's wants to object but she has no words.

"Jerome," Vivian says, "I'll give you what help I can, time off for travel and research. Your pitch is an important story. I'll publish parts of it as a continuing exploration. How's an elevated title like senior contributing writer strike you? I don't want to bog you down too much. Books are long projects. I can afford a slight increase in scale along with the title."

"Good," Jerome says. He stands and shakes Moe's hand. "Go get 'em. If I can help, let me know." Jerome has a big stupid grin on his face. He leaves so fast Moe can't reply.

Viv wears an identical smile. "Congratulations *executive feature writer.* Has a nice ring don't you think?" Vivian leans back in her chair, tucks her hands behind her head, clearly satisfied she orchestrated a good outcome.

Moe was steamrolled. The fix was in. She's no longer a freelance stone-thrower. She's part of the establishment. She has to manage young journalists, a subgroup who are deeply offended by being managed. She'll have to be supportive. Being supportive is not her skill set. *I've been conned. The game they ran must be called The Napping Canadian or some vague title like all of those historical cons.*

Her internal rant is going off the rails. She errs on the side of a pat reply. "Thanks for the opportunity. It means a lot." Her forehead feels hot.

Vivian won't stop grinning.

Varying Degrees of Rapport

It's been a long day already, but Whistler feels responsible for the dead woman's remains and refuses to leave until the body is transported to the morgue. Thanks to his hunch, and Chapman's hustle, the body has a name: Anna Beth Harpole. *That should make Ruther happy.*

Once her body has pulled away, Whistler hits up Hoss for a ride. In the car, he keeps his head down, his mind conjuring the shadowy impression of the monster that murdered a woman visiting his city. The mental exercise depresses him.

At a stoplight, he watches people heading home. *So many people. So oblivious.* It's hard to believe only this morning he'd survived his car ride with Inspector Ruther. The squad car drives on.

He considers the box of personal effects he'd gathered and the portrait they paint of Anna Beth's life. He's interrupted by a vision of her mottled throat and blue lips hidden by the slow zip of a body bag. He dreads calling the next of kin, hopes Ruther will take that task from him.

Hoss leaves Whistler alone with his thoughts. The patrolman is in his late thirties, similar build to Whistler but taller. They drive in silence most of the trip. Finally Hoss says, "Detective, you're from around here, right?"

"Little Village." Whistler welcomes the interruption.

"I'm from Lawndale. I would have gone to Little Village Lawndale High School, but we moved to Sugar Grove. You hear of Sugar Grove?"

"Never heard of it."

"Close to Aurora. I never heard of it till we moved there. Dad was okay with me going through the Chicago Public Schools. But his daughters, that was harder for him. Too many girls getting into gangs. This guy who owned the corner shop, he gave me free squeeze pops every summer. An eleven-year-old girl on the next block shot him dead when he was sweeping out front. Lupe, my baby sister, had been friends with this girl, been to her house to play. They watched Pixar DVDs and ate cupcakes with *Monster's Inc.* characters. Can you believe it? Sugar Grove was safe with nice parks and good schools. My uncle had a job set up for my dad. Best thing for us kids."

"I get it," Whistler says. "When I was coming up it felt like a full-time job to stay out of trouble."

Hoss pulls into the station and rolls along until he finds an empty spot. "Look at you now: Detective Diaz."

"Thanks for the ride," Whistler stops himself from saying "Hoss." "I didn't catch your name."

"Oh yeah. Ruther's a dick. Willy Ramirez." They knock fists and Whistler slips out of the car. He takes the file box of personal effects and walks across the lot.

Inside, Wendell isn't at the desk. That suits Whistler fine. He remembers his oversized shirt and alien tie. He retucks with one hand, maneuvers the box, tucks with the opposite hand. He pushes the knot of his tie up, not too tight. When he feels put together, he takes the stairs.

He passes through the squad room. A few older guys are slumped over desks, talking on phones, hunting and pecking a key at a time on old, chunky computer keyboards. One guy in light slacks and a red polo shirt smiles all of his teeth at Whistler. Whistler gives him a crisp nod. He knocks on Ruther's doorframe.

"Tell me you solved this son of a bitch."

"Can't do that."

Ruther's mustache droops. "I guess that was too much to hope for. But I can't help it. I'm an optimist. Ask any of these sad motherfuckers and they'll tell you *'Inspector Ruther keeps it on the sunny side.'* I'm known for it."

"Yes sir," Whistler's too exhausted for banter. He drops into a chair in front of the cluttered desk. He looks around. The office is big, with a wall of windows at Ruther's back, the view completely blocked by a line of file cabinets.

Ruther stares. "Did I invite you to take a seat?"

"No. Sorry. I . . ."

"I . . . I . . . I. I'm fucking with you. You're welcome to take a load off. My door is always open. Not really. Sometimes it's closed, and don't fucking bother me if it's closed. But I want to hear what you've got. First, speaking of sad motherfuckers . . ."

Willy Ramirez was right: Ruther is a dick.

Ruther yells, "Suzuki, get your ass in here."

"Right away," someone replies.

Ruther settles heavily into his leather throne. "That Channel 13 bitch didn't waste any time stirring this shit right up, did she?"

"No, sir."

"The mayor is not happy. I've been on the phone all day with the chief of Ds. The mayor has apparently used strong language to underscore how seriously he wants this wrapped up. Though the mayor uses strong language to invite his mother to fucking Sunday brunch."

A short man in his fifties, with floppy salt and pepper hair, shuffles into the room. It's the smiley cop with the red polo shirt.

Ruther says, "Suzuki, this is Diaz. You two are partners, my two ethnics working together. It's like the fucking United Nations all of a sudden. I'm a regular Boutros Boutros-Ghali."

"You're the boss," says Suzuki. "That's what I was telling my wife just the other day." He glances Whistler's way. "Good to meet ya." He's got a heavy North Side accent. Whistler shifts around to shake his hand, starts to move the box so Suzuki can sit. Suzuki ignores Whistler and keeps his hands in the pockets of his baggy pants. Suzuki says to Ruther, "I'm pretty excited about this weather." Whistler leaves the carton where it sits.

"Oh yeah? Why's that?" Ruther asks, playing along.

"The first warm snap means it's bush trimming season. You know how I love a trimmed bush." He slaps Whistler's shoulder. "If you know what I mean?"

"I think I know what you mean," Whistler says.

"Everyone knows," Ruther says. "It's not at all subtle." Ruther is amused. "Enough pretending you have a sex life, Suzuki. We know you wear the kimono in the family. Diaz, tell us about our dead girl."

Whistler pulls the digital pad onto his lap and taps the screen.

"Based on an initial examination Ted says the attack happened after five thirty this morning. The victim was strangled. No signs of sexual assault. Ezekiel is certain the attack took place where the victim was found. Ted concurred. She had no ID, no phone or purse. But Ted found a magnetic keycard, and she smelled a bit like chlorine. So I sent one of the patrolmen over with the keycard to check the Echelon. Sure enough, she was in town for a conference. Her name was Anna Beth Harpole. An itinerary of events shows she was part of a panel discussion yesterday and was scheduled to check out tomorrow morning. I'm going to confirm her return flight, but her baggage tag shows she flew out of San Francisco. The head of security was helpful and asked that we keep the name of the hotel out of the press. He provided copies of pertinent security feeds. We have her in the elevator before five this morning, entering the gym and pool area alone and leaving again almost an hour later. No one else entered or exited. No one was following her. Elevator again. In the lobby after six. Talking to the doorman and walking across the motor court. That narrows the time of the attack to after six. That's good because the one you called Chief—"

"Officer Harris," Ruther says.

"Yes. Officer Harris. Reggie, correct?"

Ruther nods.

"He had patrolmen canvas the area, knock on doors, and look for security cameras in the area. No witnesses. No reports of strangers hanging around. Nothing at the scene other than the victim."

"Who called in the body?"

"An old woman named Greta Hovarth who walks her wiener dog through the tunnel every morning to do his business in the park. Reggie took her statement."

"Did he tell you he was named after Reggie Jackson?" Suzuki asks.

"It didn't come up," Whistler says. "Mrs. Hovarth walked past the spot where the body was found and didn't notice a thing. She thinks it was six twenty. Came back about fifteen minutes later, sees the shoes, finds our victim. Goes home to call the police like a good citizen. If she was paying attention, that means our victim was killed in that fifteen-minute window. Which fits with Ted's time of death."

"What else?" Ruther asks.

"The exterior video at the Echelon shows the bottom half of a white panel van passing after Anna Beth crosses. So far, that's all we have."

"That's exactly what the mayor won't want to hear." Ruther is serious.

Suzuki asks, "When can we expect the ME's report? Toxicology? Rape kit? Stomach contents? What are next steps? This is your case, am I right, Boss?"

"You're not wrong."

Whistler loosens his tie, rests his arm over the box of personal effects. "Like I said, Ted says no signs of sex. Ezekiel and I secured the victim's room. It's being dusted for prints. It's a hotel room, so it'll be covered in latent partials. Maybe we'll get lucky. Nothing to indicate anyone was in the room except Anna Beth. We found her phone and a laptop she left charging next to the bed. It was sent to Tech. They'll pull recent e-mails, texts, calendars, etcetera. Ted expects the ME report in a few days."

"A few days. Bullshit. I'll call over and rattle his cage. You'll have that report in the morning. I'd stake my life on it," Ruther says.

"Full autopsy is required for homicides. Ezekiel said that adds days," Whistler says.

"They always say it takes days. The mayor wants it yesterday. They'll get it done."

Suzuki chimes in unhelpfully, "You want me to fly to San Fran to interview her lovers, coworkers, friends, neighbors, family, more lovers? Shit, could take weeks to run down leads."

"Shut up, Suzuki," Ruther says. "Diaz. What's your gut tell you?"

"It was violent. My first guess was she knew the assailant. Jealousy, revenge, that kind of thing. But the odds are low given she flew in for a couple days alone. It's starting to look like a crime of opportunity. The rage involved, this guy may be volatile, dangerous, mentally deranged. Likely has a record of assault or domestic battery. Doesn't look like it was sexual, and that bothers me. There was no robbery, no sex. That makes the motive to strangle this girl. More accurately crush her throat. She was left between dumpsters like a sack of trash. Suzuki is right. Once we get the data off her devices, we'll run down any leads back home, see what her life looked like. Did she have a boyfriend? An ex? A stalker? Workplace affair? Any connections with Chicago? Maybe she travels here regularly? She was at a hotel conference; might have met someone in the bar, hooked up. I'll pull video from the bar. Unless forensics comes back with something from the room or the ME finds something unexpected, all we have is a potentially missing ponytail holder, perhaps stolen earrings, and a panel van we can't identify and was likely not involved."

"Shit," Ruther says. "What about the dumpsters?"

"Ezekiel coordinated with Officer Harris and had a few patrolmen crawl in every dumpster for a two block radius. They found nothing. I've got this box of stuff: a purse, a workbag, some clothes and toiletries. Her luggage. But as of now, not much to go on."

"Shit," Ruther says again. "Okay." He combs his mustache to compose himself. "Suzuki, you take Diaz to conference room two. Start getting things set up. Diaz, when you get the phone dump, make the notifications. Do as much as you can over the phone. Once you know exactly where she lived and worked, I'll make calls through official channels to get any potential records. Let's talk in the morning. I know it's Saturday, but I'll be in by eight. Now get the hell out of here while I try to put lipstick on this pig." Ruther reaches for the phone. "Oh, and Diaz?"

"Yes."

"Welcome to the unit."

Suzuki slaps Whistler on the shoulder. "Come on. I'll order some food. We'll be here late. You like soosh?"

Whistler snatches the box, follows Suzuki. "No," he says. "I hate sushi."

"That's because you never had good soosh. Trust me. The soosh is on me. I'll order hot sake too. Enough hot sake and any soosh tastes good."

Whistler bumps along behind his new partner, resigned to an unpleasant few hours stuck in a confined space with Suzuki talking and the smell of raw fish. *Hopefully he will stop saying "soosh."* Whistler has never had sake, but the idea of hot booze makes his stomach roll. He sincerely wishes he were about to share a plate of hot shrimps and cold beer with Moe.

Baby Talk

It's after midnight and Calvert lies atop his covers in the dark, like a corpse spread out at a wake. He's unable to sleep. His brain spins like a gyroscope yanked into motion by his day. The first several hours had been deeply challenging: leaving New Horizons, visiting his old home where he was accosted emotionally by fragments of his past life, and physically by an overzealous patrolman. He moved to a new place, had a job interview, got lost, and navigated an exhausting shopping trip. An unexpected highlight had been meeting Rosa. Since arriving home, he'd had nothing but unstructured time alone with his centrifugal thoughts. In the end, all he could do was let things spin and stare at the ceiling.

Despite being off, one halo-shaped fluorescent bulb glows slightly over his kitchen sink. The mercury vapor housed in the fragile glass retains a weak charge. This is much the same as his busted biochemistry. His system is turned off but has juice to fuel a fraction of a life. A term springs unbidden to Calvert's mind—"bioluminescence." A free-floating artifact of the lost knowledge of his former life.

His brown suit was soaked through when he returned from shopping. He hung it on its hanger. He was unsure how to purge the scent of his corpse sweat from the material. He knows suits are meant to be dry-cleaned. The concept of cleaning without water is absurd, though he thinks chemicals are used. *Perhaps it's like embalming.* He doubts it as soon as he thinks it.

Recalled knowledge rushes in. When bodies are embalmed, an incision is made, and arteries are filled with a mixture of formalde-hyde, water, and other mystical chemicals. Simultaneously, all blood is drained from the circulatory system. To embalm the average adult requires two gallons of fluid. This proves his skepticism about dry cleaning. *How could clothes remain dry with so much fluid?* He knows his logic is faulty. *Perhaps dry cleaners blast clothes with baby powder.* The memory of baby powder tickles his nose. The imagined sensation summons a wave of personal history crashing into him, as real as when he first experienced it.

* * *

Mere had a sister, Franny, who was pregnant with her first child. Calvert and Mere were traveling in Eastern Europe. They'd had sex before going down to breakfast. They watched a matinee of Les Misérables *at the Prague Opera House. After a late lunch, they strolled along the Charles Bridge.*

"If we have a boy," Mere said, "We should name him Charles." She browsed a stall of acrylic cityscapes, lazily passing the beautiful afternoon.

"I always hoped to name my first son Anton, after Chekhov," Calvert said.

"What about Calvert Junior?" Mere teased.

"God no. Well, depends if we like him. If he's a horrible human, he may deserve to be Calvert Junior."

"How will we know if he's horrible when he's the size of a sack of sugar?"

"A tiny Hitler mustache is a good indication."

Mere laughed at the joke. Mere had a warm, full laugh that made him content in his core. She took his hand and led him across the bridge, between milling tourists. She looked at a rack of hand-dyed silk scarves. "It doesn't really matter," she said. "I'll have a girl. My mother cursed me. One day you'll have a girl as selfish and mean as you've been to me."

"That's good parenting."

"Yeah," Mere said. "She set a high bar. How will I ever live up to it?"

"You'll be a great mom." He pecked her cheek. While browsing he picked up a silk tie, more flamboyant than he would normally go for. He held it under his chin. Mere made a disapproving face and put it back. "So if we have a girl . . .?" he said leadingly.

"If we have a girl, we will name her Olga, after Chekhov's heroine." She said it in her Professor Calvert voice. "Little Olga Greene."

"I prefer Meredith," he said. "After the loveliest person I know." She moved into the circle of his arms. Then he added, "Or Bubbles. The stripper from my bachelor party." She punched his shoulder. "Bubbles could be the middle name." She punched him again. "Actually, she prefers to be called an exotic dancer. It's an art form." She had punched him a third time, and he knew it would leave a mark.

Minutes later, in their hotel lobby, only yards away from the banks of the Vitava River, Mere's sister called from a hospital on another continent—her water had broken, she was going into labor a month early. She was scared.

"We'll be there as soon as we can," Mere had promised.

They cut their trip short, made a series of pricey arrangements, and arrived at the maternity ward forty-four hours later. There were complications; the baby was delivered by caesarian and was in an incubator, but stable. Mere began consoling her sister, comforting her and reassuring her that the baby would be fine. Calvert walked the hall, dead with exhaustion, the scent of baby powder irritating his nose.

*   *   *

One last splinter of knowledge flies into the reminiscence: the day Franny was discharged, she named the baby girl Meredith.

The memory abandons him as quickly as it appeared, leaving him to stare forlornly at his ceiling and consider what tumbledown dominoes may have led to his well-deserved death. A lingering sense of loss settles cold on his prone body like morning dew, but he has no inkling where the feeling originates.

Deceitful Furnishings

When Whistler arrives, he grabs his tablet on the way to his desk. He walks through to see who else is around and checks the conference room. He's thankful it aired out from the previous night, the trash can emptied.

Despite Ruther's insistence he would apply enough pressure to make short work of the ME's report, the report isn't around and neither is Ruther. Ruther had bet his life on his ability to get the report expedited. *I hope he's not dead.* "Ha," Whistler says aloud at his own silent sass.

He gets coffee brewing before turning on his tablet. When he logs in, he finds a link from the digital forensics department. He clicks it and is rewarded with a clone of Anna Beth Harpole's phone data. He makes a cup of lukewarm coffee and sits at his desk to learn about her life.

It's boring reading and exclusively work related. The most frequent correspondence is with her boss, Greg Kidd. After picking through the four most recent months of tedious exchanges, Whistler is convinced they maintained a professional relationship. He finds nothing suspicious, no veiled innuendo to sets off alarms in his suspicious mind.

There are confirmations of travel arrangements, notifications from American Express, and a great many reservation notices for lunch and dinner for Mr. Kidd, arranged through her phone. Even though Suzuki had warned him that supplies are tight and he should be frugal about the laser printer, he sends everything to the printer. It's easier for him to have something he can get his hands on.

Whistler shifts his rump in the office chair. He drinks coffee for the first time since beginning to read. It's gone completely cold. He doesn't mind. He sets the "Crafty Ass Bitch" mug aside and grabs the tablet, leaning back. He throws one foot up to the edge of his desk, and the chair goes over backward. He's pitched so fast he does a back roll and finds himself belly down on the slick, smelly carpet.

"Jesus!" Whistler says.

He gets to his feet fast. He checks that the tablet's screen isn't damaged. It's fine. *Thank God for small miracles.* He sets the tablet carefully on his desk. He moves slowly, expecting some other catastrophe. He sets his chair up, inspects it, and finds nothing obviously wrong, but he will never trust that piece of furniture again. He abandons the chair and moves into the conference room to continue working.

Anna Beth's contacts are all business related. Each entry is accompanied by a job title and the name of an organization or company: *Joseph Dunn, Executive Director of Futurist infrastructure at the Marconi Group.* Whistler doesn't understand what any of these people do. There are no plumbers, teachers, or roofers. No cops or firemen or factory foremen. The number of contacts isn't too daunting—over a hundred but less than one fifty. There are no Harpoles to call, no obvious family members. Kidd's cell number is there, of course, and he is the next most likely avenue of contact.

Whistler puts off calling Kidd for several hours. Time zone differences are as good an excuse as any. He returns to nosing through the dead woman's e-mails. He still finds nothing suspicious or noteworthy. According to the techies, the laptop is new, activated in the past few months, and contains nothing not available on her phone other than a PowerPoint presentation and a web browser history of virtual shopping: shoes, twelve-dollar deodorant, three tank tops, and a room humidifier that looks like a frog on a lily pad base.

He searches social media and finds Anna Beth tagged in a high school photo with bushy, overprocessed hair, eyebrows that look like they were badly drawn with a fat Sharpie, and a large hoop-style septum piercing like a doorknocker for her face. He also finds her at Carnegie Mellon on stage in a production of *Steel Magnolias*, her blonde wig pushed back, revealing her dark hairline underneath. He finds a headshot on LinkedIn. *Beautiful.* Her position is listed as assistant to Mr. Kidd and his consulting group, Kingfisher. He also finds a long list of impressive professional bullet points. He sends some images to the printer and hears it start to spit out pages.

I can't put off calling her boss.

He dials and the phone rings and rings. Finally a canned voice says: "You've reached the phone of Greg Kidd. I'm away for the weekend, hopefully doing something pointless, but I doubt I'm so fortunate. You can reach me on Monday during business hours. If it's an emergency, please contact my assistant, Anna Beth." The affable Greg Kidd gives the number of Anna Beth's cell phone, which currently sits in a plastic bag in an empty office one floor above Whistler. He's relieved to have dodged the conversation.

He's hungry. He takes the stairs down to the canteen, which is what they call the room in the basement with three vending machines: one for soda, one for snacks, and one for coffee. He feeds the dollar slot and punches up some salty peanuts in a cellophane sleeve. He tears it along the marked line; it rips down the long side and spills its innards. He catches the majority of the nuts in his palm and kicks the others under the machine with the side of his foot.

Back upstairs, Ruther still hasn't arrived. *Maybe he really is dead.* He wonders who would take over the unit. *Oh please, not Suzuki.*

He picks up a stack of laser prints and goes to the conference room to sort through the boxes of potential evidence he hadn't yet touched. He sets up two tables so he can spread out, inspect, and label the items Ezekiel sent the previous evening. He snaps on gloves. He unzips her sleek wheelie suitcase. He removes a pair of slacks and searches the pockets, finds petite silver earrings, and bags them. *The missing earrings? Looks even less like a mugging.* He methodically moves to the next item.

It's early afternoon when he hears someone rattling around in the front office. Whistler folds one of Anna Beth's tops and slips it into a bag. The label reads "Eileen Fisher." A quick search of the internet reveals the item is a Cashmere Boucle Bliss Box-Top in light gray and sells for full retail at four hundred and sixty-eight dollars. It's a nice top, feels great, clearly of high quality. Whistler's entire wardrobe might cost less. He's beginning to suspect Anna Beth was somewhat high maintenance.

Suzuki arrives like he's making an entrance at a comedy showcase and dressed like he's ready for a drunken round of golf: bright plaid pants, orange Polo shirt, boat shoes with no socks. Whistler is momentarily happy to have company. Then Suzuki says, "Hey, partner, did I mention my wife's sausage-only diet?"

Whistler stops mid-reach for the next item.

"You get it?"

"You mean because sausage is slang for penis?"

"Yeah. You get it." Suzuki turns as if including an imagined audience. "This guy gets it."

"I wish I didn't."

Whistler hands Suzuki the stack of printouts: lists of contacts and other text-based documents, and images of Anna Beth from his digital surfing. "Start arranging those on the board. When you're done, call the airline and get a list of passengers for both of her flights, confirm she was flying alone. Cross-check her contacts with passenger manifests and the conference attendees."

"What for?"

"Look for connections. Also, we got the list of conference participants, but that wasn't the only conference at the Echelon. We need those other participants and every guest. Plus a list of all employees. Everything needs to be checked—run names through the database to look for criminal records. Who knows? We could get lucky."

"She obviously didn't fly home with anyone. Because, you know, she didn't fly anywhere." When Whistler doesn't respond, Suzuki adds, "Because she's dead."

"Doesn't mean someone she knows wasn't booked to fly out with her."

"Fair enough," Suzuki concedes. "Odds are good, people leaving the conference could be flying back on the same flight. Doesn't mean they are stalking her."

"We're trying to make whatever connections we can. Find someone to talk to, whoever might have spoken to her."

"I suppose so. What are you doing?"

"Going through her personal effects."

"I'd be happy to go through her lingerie. Anything lacey or leather." Suzuki grins.

Whistler finds Suzuki extremely not funny. "No, thanks. It needs to be handled with care. That's why you are using Scotch tape and push pins to stick things on a wall. That's why you get the data entry."

"You catch on fast," Suzuki says. He seems to relish being an object of scorn.

They turn their backs on one another and settle in for more long hours of drudgery.

The Inevitability
of Death and Taxes

It is full-on daytime when Calvert rolls off his bed. The crepitus of his desiccating joints announces his body's ongoing protest. *Perhaps post-mortem lividity has begun.* He rattles his skull to shake out the feeling of dread that seeped in during his sporadic slumber. His exhaustion is due to a combination of his unconscious mind burning itself out and yesterday's activities.

In the bathroom, he rolls his damaged shoulder. It makes crunchy sounds but doesn't hurt. He can't feel it at all. He empties his excess fluids in the commode. On the back of the toilet is the newspaper he found when Wrinkled Agatha dropped him off. Seeing the paper gives him an idea. He gets his robe from the floor.

He leaves his apartment open, tromps down the stairs, and shoves open the door that leads to the street. On the sidewalk he finds another paper with a sticker addressed to the previous tenant. His body idles in neutral while he contemplates his new address. It reads "201½." The half feels right. That is how he is: about halfway between what he once was and where he will end up.

He doesn't know when the *USA Today* subscription will run out, but he's pleased to have the paper. He puts it under his arm, as is his habit, and lumbers back upstairs. There are two apartments above the veterinary hospital: his studio and a sprawling warren of patrician walls that make up an unauthorized artist's co-op. Or so the owner told him when he and Abbey had met her to look at the place.

"Please let me know if the neighbor gives you any trouble," she had whispered conspiratorially, leaning toward Calvert. Her hair was tied into a cascading fountain on top of her head, and it whipped about as she checked both directions. "The self-proclaimed artist who lives next door has a long-term lease. But I'd love to get him out of there. When I heard he was holding art exhibitions, performances, and whatnot, I mailed him a stern letter. He replied through Lawyers for the Creative Arts or something like that. For now my hands are tied."

Calvert hadn't known what to say. He was confused by the word "whatnot." He'd looked to Abbey for guidance. She was on the landing, staring at her phone, either attempting to look like she wasn't listening, or actually not listening.

The plumage on the woman's head flicked Calvert's face as she glanced around. "If you see any illegal things going on, let me know. I'll make it worth your while."

"What things?" he asked.

"Illegal drugs, deviant behavior, proof of a business being run on the premises, pets, anyone not on the lease living in the space." She slipped a business card into his hand. The card told him her name was Megan Ranch. *What do they raise on a megan ranch?* He didn't give voice to the question. She had a presence that even his stunted perception had easily decoded as "not fond of speculative musings ."

The door to the co-op opens as Calvert tops the flight of stairs. A bear of a man in his sixties steps out, lighting a doobie. He sparks the wheel of a disposable lighter until the flame licks the point of the fat joint. He sips the other end and holds the lighter's chrome band near the hot tip to watch the cherry of heat swell. Satisfied, he draws on it and holds the smoke in his chest. When he exhales, his face floats in a cloud. He winks at Calvert.

The big man's oversized hands work nimbly returning the lighter to the small pocket on the front of his overalls. The joint bobs between his lips. He pats the pocket reassuringly and winks at Calvert a second time.

Calvert makes his mouth in the shape of a smile.

"Wake and bake?" the man-bear asks and tries to pass the weed.

"No thank you. I can't get high anymore," Calvert explains.

"That's too bad," the man-bear says, but he doesn't offer twice. He holds the smoldering twist of paper close to his heart. Smoke burrows into his bushy white beard. "I heard you coming up the stairs and thought I'd introduce myself. You the new neighbor?"

"Yes. I'm new."

"Hmm. From around here?"

"I was at a transitional mental health facility until yesterday."

The man squints his eyes and holds in more smoke. He speaks with a tight voice, "You know you should probably close your robe." He points toward Calvert's exposed briefs.

Calvert looks, finds his robe wide open. "I forgot to belt it. To be honest, since I died I don't know what I'm doing half the time."

The big man scrutinizes Calvert, "You're saying you're dead?"

"For a while now. Months."

"You look good, though. You pull it off. Not everyone could. Besides, it happens to the best of us."

This strikes Calvert as unassailably true. "May I ask a question?"

"Knock yourself out," the big man says kindly.

"Should I cover myself?" He glances down his body again.

"Up to you. I don't mind."

Calvert leaves his robe open. He feels good about the decision. "I got a new job. I start Monday."

"Gotta pay the tax man," Man-bear says around a mouth full of smoke.

Calvert believes the conversation has ended so he waves, takes the newspaper, and shakes it open. He begins reading, walks through his door, and knocks it closed behind him.

The Lord's Day

It's Sunday. The sun is out, the sky clear. Moe is parked across the street from Pilgrim Baptist, waiting for services to end. The church is white clapboard. The grounds are lush green and immaculate. Moe has her helmet off and sips tea from the screw-top cap of her thermos. She stands next to Taibbi, biker boots crossed at the ankle, leaning her butt on the Honda's seat. Her face is warm in the sun. *Not a bad way to kill a little time.*

She spent the previous day researching the list of homicides Vivian provided. Jerome was helpful with contacts in police records. It was slow going as her process was stymied by irregular interruptions from Loni and Dale, the two ankle biters Vivian had recently recruited to the *Text Block*'s cause.

Loni seemed bright but wouldn't listen. Moe gave her suggestions and notes on an article about the link between kids living in urban food deserts and poor academic performance. An hour later, Loni returned with the same copy, along with a long argument about why it was best to keep her writing structured as is.

Dale was overambitious and wrote a frantic, scattered article that lacked any clear point and was far too long. She wondered exactly what he'd been taught in J-school. Moe sat with him and patiently chipped away two-thirds of his initial story. What they discovered was a solid, well-researched narrative on aggressive application of fines for traffic infractions caught on red-light cameras, and how that abuse was leading to a modern-day debtor's prison. It was time-consuming, and every red mark of Moe's pen seemed to eat away at Dale's brittle, idealistic soul. Dale's feelings were something Moe tried not to be concerned with. But the empathy trap was inescapable. In the end, both articles were published to the website. It felt like the longest day she'd spent as a journalist.

Now, she hopes to interview the mother of one of the victims for her own article. When Moe called Loretta Sharpe, the grieving mother had been receptive, even grateful.

"Mrs. Sharpe, I know this is a hard time for you. I'm truly sorry for your loss. My name's Moe Diaz, and I'm the executive feature writer for *Text Block*." It was the first time she'd used her new title. She wasn't yet convinced she liked it. "It's a digital newspaper. You may have heard of it."

"Oh, honey. Thank you for calling. I've never heard of your paper. I don't read newspapers, so don't take it personal. When I find time to read, I spend it with my scriptures."

"Yes, ma'am. I understand. I'm calling because I'm writing about your daughter, Precious. Not only about her death but about her life too. Could we meet?"

"Oh now, honey, I'd like that. Precious was a blessing. She's in a better place."

"Yes, ma'am. Is there a time that would be best for you?"

Loretta Sharpe had asked Moe if she'd accepted Jesus Christ as her Lord and savior, and invited her to attend services. Moe pretended she would be attending church elsewhere. When Loretta asked for specifics, Moe said, "Nondenominational." Loretta seemed to find that disappointing but minimally acceptable. Meeting after services was Loretta's idea.

Moe wants to start writing. She hadn't written anything yesterday. Her initial article about the woman strangled north of the river was her most viewed story so far. She wanted to build on it. The police had issued a basic statement giving the name of the victim and her age, and had confirmed several details that bolstered Moe's reporting.

She and Whistler were playing text tag. He sent a note late Friday night, after filling his guts with hot sake and sushi. He complained about the aftertaste of raw fish. Or "Soosh." Apparently Whistler's new partner refused to stop calling it "soosh."

> Whistler: *31 times. Now 32 times he has said the word soosh! He'll be Chicago's next homicide if he says it again. At least hot sake goes down pretty easy after the initial shock.*
> Moe: *Have you gotten the preliminary report from the ME? Any witnesses? Which way are you leaning on this? Can you give me any background on the victim?*

Even in his drunken state Whistler didn't respond to her questions. After her third not-so-subtle inquiry, he wrote that he was heading home. That didn't bother her much, nor did it surprise her. *Had to give it a shot.*

What's starting to get under her skin is developing a long story. The notion of digging deep and researching, nurturing witnesses over time, and breaking uncharted journalistic ground is all very romantic. In practice, it goes against the pattern she'd developed freelancing.

As she waits in the warm sun, Moe knows Precious Sharpe had no criminal record. She had finished her first year pursuing an associate degree in applied sciences in respiratory therapy at Malcolm X College. She had been choked to death in the stall of a spray-it-yourself carwash. No one was arrested. There was no press coverage other than a three-line mention in the *Sun-Times* and a paid notification for the memorial service.

Officially, as far as the CPD was concerned, there was nothing to go on. After learning the little she now knows, Moe wants to paint a portrait of a girl with a close family and a bright future who died too young. But she's holding back on presuming too much until she speaks to the person who knew Precious best. Yesterday she found a Facebook page that seemed little used. Precious's profile picture was of a pretty girl making an ugly face. Searching Instagram she found images of

Precious at parties, drinking, dancing in crowded small rooms teeming with bodies and hormones. Moe had found nothing shocking about a teen being wilder than her family might approve of. She sips a bit more tea, shakes the dregs into the weeds growing through cracks in the pavement, and twists the cup lid in place.

In recent years, Moe had come to terms with her career. Yes, there were negatives associated with working as a freelance journalist: low pay, no benefits, no stability, no real opportunity for advancement. But she had time to perfect her craft.

In truth, she was an adult with a college degree, living with her father, and making only minimum payments on her student loan. Moe often claimed she needed to be home for her aging parent. That was at best convenient shorthand and at worst a blatant lie. Francis always made her feel welcome, but he didn't need her around. She did cook for him some evenings, and they'd watch a game or an old rerun, share a beer or three. The reality was she couldn't afford a place of her own. His continued understanding allowed her to attempt to make a living doing the thing she loved. *Or enables me to continue living a pipe dream.*

If she believed in metaphysical hoodoo, she'd say she was called to be a journalist. Writing had chosen her, not the other way around. But she prefers practical concepts. She tells herself that her innate skills and the demands of investigative reporting are a good fit. Nothing more.

She liked the flexible schedule, autonomy, personal freedom, sovereignty, and independence of freelancing. She knows her list is a string of synonyms, but they carry more weight than the negatives. Her articles give her a place in this world. On a good day, she writes things she cares about for a publication whose goals she shares. She holds the powerful accountable and shines a light on corruption and hypocrisy. Sure she works ten hours a day, sometimes seven days a week. She wears freelance like a comfortable pair of jeans; freelance fits her just right.

The new title Vivian had thrust at her turns everything on its head. She has less flexibility, has to spend her time reading and editing Lola and Dan's insipid attempts to write. *Or whatever their fucking names are.*

She suddenly has a salary and benefits, and will soon be able to afford her own place. May have the cash to pay down her student loan; could even help her dad with his medical bills. Potentially she will get the privacy and space needed to pursue a relationship. *At the very least, a sex life.* But none of it is sitting well with her. She's worried she sold out. *I'm Sophia without the mass-market sex appeal.*

The church doors swing open, and a dark-skinned man in white robes steps out and takes a prominent position at the top of the steps. Moe straightens up and stows her thermos. She puts her bag over her head and strolls across the street, keeping an eye out for Loretta.

A line of well-dressed men in bow ties and sweater vests, and women in hats and matching summer dresses, files out of the church. Some of the younger women have sleeveless dresses and sport elaborate shoulder tattoos. Moe feels underdressed. What she thought was a cool biker look may actually scream "young queer."

Loretta told Moe she'd be in a pink dress and a white hat with pink flowers. She isn't too hard to spot. She lingers with the preacher as she exits, exchanges a few words, perhaps condolences, perhaps a discussion of the day's sermon. She nods at his parting message. He hugs her. Loretta waves at Moe as she walks down the steps, one step at a time, as if she doesn't trust her balance.

"Mrs. Sharpe. Thanks for meeting. Do you mind if I record our conversation?"

"Oh now, I don't know why I would."

They walk slowly around the block. Loretta tells Moe about her deceased daughter singing in the church choir, about a childhood illness that "might have killed a baby that wasn't so strong." About what a good student Precious was. "She placed fourth in a citywide spelling bee. Not enough for a trophy. But praise be to Jesus, it was enough to help her get an academic scholarship." She put her palms up to heaven when she said, "Praise be to Jesus."

"Precious sounds like a wonderful daughter."

"Oh now, she was. For the most part. She had her moments."

"Anything in particular?"

"Well, I think she didn't make the best choices with boys."

"I see. Why do you say that?"

"Well, look how it turned out."

"You're saying a boyfriend was responsible?"

"I told the police Ronnie was the one that did it. They broke up. She wouldn't tell me why. People say he was dogging around on her. He warned her she best not break up with him, but she went on ahead and did it. Not ten days later, well . . ."

"You know Ronnie's last name?"

"I don't know. But it doesn't matter. If he gets caught it won't bring her back, will it? It'd be another black boy in prison, and I don't want any part of that. Romans 12:19: 'Vengeance is mine; I will repay, saith the Lord.' The pastor spoke on it at the funeral service. Another reason I know it was Ronnie is he left town right away. Went out West with his brother. I told the police the whole story."

They talk the rest of the way around the block. Finally Loretta says, "Now if you ever want to come to a service, Pastor Jenkins is about as good a preacher as you'll ever find. You can feel the Lord come right down among the congregation when he gets after it. And the choir will have you dancing in the aisles."

"Yes, ma'am. I'll remember that. Here you go," Moe passes over her old business card on which she's written her embarrassingly long title. "You can read the article on that website later this week. Spread the word. You can call me anytime if you think of something. And if you don't like what I write, if you feel I got it wrong, you can send me a note. I will work with you to write a correction. I want to pay respect to your daughter. She deserves that much."

Moe is surprised when Loretta traps her in a warm hug. "I know you'll do right by my Precious baby. But she'll get her reward in heaven. She is blessed not to grow old, not to toil on this earth a day longer than she needed to. And you. You gotta get yourself right with the Lord."

"Believe me," Moe says, "I'm doing my best."

Working Man

The morning is foggy. Calvert doesn't feel the damp seep into his clothes. It doesn't make him involuntarily shiver the way he assumes a living person might. He is oblivious to most sensations of the body. Death has made him a stoic.

He woke to the alarm on the watch he took from the home he once lived in. Upon opening his eyes, he wanted to close them again. He doesn't know if the term "fatigue" applies to the dead. So he calls it "entropic degradation" and blames it on being active past his expiration date.

Upon deeper consideration, he also attributes it to the fitful dreams he had after spending all of Sunday observing his mind's efforts to make sense of his disorganized past. *Perhaps I do need rest in order to optimally exist.* He'd also forgotten to eat for most of the weekend until this morning, when he crunched a few pinches of dry Grape-Nuts from his palm and washed it down with black coffee, and a dose of antipsychotics as a chaser.

Now, he stands with his back to Coffee Girl. He considers the watch on his wrist. He's second-guessing his decision to wear it. The watch is big. It feels heavy. He worries it will stretch his shoulder tendons until his arm falls out of the socket again or comes completely loose.

The watch has five buttons and a numbered ring around its face. He has no idea what most of the buttons do. He gives the ring a turn.

Nothing changes other than the orientation of numbers. He squeezes buttons; the harsh edges bite his finger pads. He's not bothered. After his best analysis, all he knows is the time is 5:50 AM; if he squeezes the watch randomly, the alarm will turn off; and if he pinches certain buttons, the entire face lights up bright enough to leave a ghost image on his retina.

The door to the shop opens beside him.

"Good morning, working man. Long time no see." Rosa is a few feet from him, smiling her smile. It looks especially radiant on this bleak morning.

His mouth smiles in response; the first high-quality smile he's managed in ages. "I've got ten minutes before I meet my trainer, Allen." He taps his big watch.

"Nice watch. You want coffee?"

"Yes." His uncertainty over the timepiece evaporates.

"The espresso machine is all warmed up." She holds the door and Calvert walks in.

Rosa ties her apron in place before starting her elegant coffee choreography. Calvert is in awe. A few moments later, she slides a drink across the counter in a paper cup. "I made it to go. Though it tastes better in glassware. Nice new T-shirt," she says. She pinches the fabric of her own shirt. "We look like twins." Calvert doubts the resemblance. Rosa is younger than him, darker complexion, longer hair, with a feminine physique, and is living. He is past middle years, graying, unremarkably built, and mostly dead. She reads his confusion and adds, "Matching white T-shirts."

Her attention pleases him. Calvert takes out sixty-two dollars and hands it to her. "For all the coffee," he says. "Including Friday."

"That's too much." She leaves the cash on the counter as she rings him up. She puts fifty-some dollars back in Calvert's palm. When she turns her back, he stuffs the cash in her tip jar.

By the time the Bug Off van pulls up, Calvert is on the sidewalk, sipping his cortado. A wiry man with a scraggly blond beard and matching shoulder-length hair cranks down the driver's-side window and yells. "You Calvert?"

"Yes," Calvert replies quietly. He adds a vigorous head nod.

"Well, hurry the hell up," the man calls with a broad beckoning wave.

Calvert holds his coffee steady and tries to make his legs and arms work smoothly as he moves to the passenger door. He climbs in and looks for a place to set his cup. The footwell is littered with crumpled fast-food bags. One cup holder is full of change and a pair of toenail clippers. The other has a half-full travel mug that reads "Hillary sucks but not like Monica;" its lid is missing, and mold has formed a cap over the liquid inside. Calvert holds his cortado between his knees and fumbles with the seat belt.

"Don't leave me hanging," the other man says.

Calvert sees a hand extended his direction. He grasps it.

"Allen," the man says. There is a whimpering from the rear of the van. Allen jerks his thumb and adds, "That's Daisy. Coffee smells good."

Calvert lifts the cup and breathes the aroma.

"You're not banging that tasty senorita are you?"

Calvert sees Rosa wiping down tables near the front window.

"No," Calvert says.

"Great. 'Cause I suddenly got a hankerin' for something hot and Mexican spiced. You stay put. I'll be back." With that, Allen slides out of the van and into Coffee Girl. Calvert watches the two disappear into the recesses of the store.

His body works up the emotional equivalent of heartburn, and it lodges in his chest. *Perhaps it's rage.* He feels he could do great violence. He can't pinpoint what he has to be enraged about. A sound behind him demands his attention.

Daisy is a small beagle with a tan spot around one dark eye. She wiggles in her crate, her nails pattering as she walks in a tight circle and flops down.

Calvert looks back at Coffee Girl. He sees Allen return to the front door. Calvert slams the rest of his drink. After he swallows, he regrets not tasting it.

Back in the driver's seat, Allen says, "The senorita was not receptive to my advances. It'll take more than one visit." He puts the van in drive and goes.

Calvert watches the city and makes no comment.

Ten minutes of driving takes the van to the back of the International, a luxury hotel within walking distance of the Art Institute and Millennium Park. There are a few parking spots near the loading docks in the back. Allen parks badly, taking one and a quarter spots. Calvert shifts around in the bucket seat.

Allen says, "Kaz probably told you how I was in the joint. He loves giving the impression he would give an ex-con a leg up. But that's bullshit. Kaz didn't hire me. The old man did. I bet you want to know the whole story." Calvert doesn't answer. He holds his paper cup stiffly, uncertain where to put it. Allen instructs him, "Chuck it on the floor. I'll clean it out sometime."

Calvert leans down to place the cup between his loafers. His movement is hindered by either the seat belt or creeping rigor mortis. He flicks the cup the rest of the distance.

Allen continues talking, "Everyone wants to know two things: why I was inside and did I get raped in prison. Let me clear that up right now. No. I didn't get raped. Believe me. I see you doubt it. I'm not a big guy and I'm kind of pretty. Long hair. Lean. Nice proportions. But I'm stronger than I look. I never had sex with a man and I never will. Nobody made me do anything. Okay?"

"Okay," Calvert replies solemnly. It seems important to Allen.

"Glad we got that straight. Now quit gabbing and let's get to work." Allen steps out of the van. Calvert adjusts where his watch rides his wrist, slides out, and walks to the back of the van.

"Put this on," Allen has the doors open and hands Calvert some branded coveralls.

Allen slips his uniform over his dirty jeans and pokes his shoes out the leg holes. Calvert unfolds his new outfit and kicks off his shoes. There is a lengthy struggle to put his inflexible body into the unyielding uniform. At one point, his watch gets caught in the sleeve, and Allen has to help free his wrist. Before Calvert forgets, he takes his prepaid phone from his pants pocket and secures it in his uniform pocket before zipping up from crotch to throat and awaiting further instructions.

Meanwhile, Allen has dragged a dolly onto the pavement and started stacking it with items: a heavy five-gallon bucket, a lighter five-gallon bucket, a pile of plastic sheeting, and an industrial blower of some kind. "Hop up and let Daisy out."

Calvert doesn't hop. Instead, he walks to the side door, leans in, and squeezes the latch so the wire door swings free. Daisy bursts out, all wiggles and happy licking. She snuffles Calvert's hand and his coveralls, and licks his chin. She stands stiff and gives a haunting howl.

"That's strange," Allen says. "That's the sound she makes when she finds bugs. You don't feel itchy do you?"

Calvert assesses his body's dull receptors. "I don't think I'm infested."

"I'm just shittin' ya. She's excited, that's all. Clip that leash to her harness."

Inside the service elevator, Allen positions the dolly and hits the button for the eighth floor. Daisy lies down on top of Calvert's feet. Allen pinches his nose.

"Shoo-weee! What the hell is that smell?"

Calvert takes a big sniff. "I don't smell anything."

"Is your nose broke? It's about to knock me over. Look." He points down at Daisy. "Daisy couldn't take it. She passed clean out." At the mention of her name, Daisy lifts her head and wags her tail. "You really can't smell that stench?" Allen's voice is as pinched as his nose.

Calvert sniffs again. "I can't smell that well since . . ." He considers saying "my death" but knows it makes people uncomfortable. He says, "my accident."

"Well, that's fucked up. Consider yourself lucky 'cause it smells like they've been hauling bodies in this box. Wonder if they had to get rid of a dead hooker?" Allen waits for Calvert to laugh. He's still waiting when the elevator doors open.

Allen pushes the dolly ahead of him. Calvert and Daisy follow down a stretch of carpeted hallway. The guestrooms are open, the beds stripped.

"Here we go." Allen says. He parks the dolly. "How was your week-end? You do anyone interesting?"

Calvert says, "I took two showers, added contacts to my phone, and read old newspapers."

Allen nods. "You're my kind of party animal." Then he gets down to business. "So let me teach you the system." He takes hold of the leash. Daisy shakes her floppy ears, the tags on her collar rattle. Calvert stands attentively.

"You get to the block of rooms you're supposed to check. You try not to cross paths with any guests. The management doesn't want people getting the impression there's a problem. If a bunch of guests get itchy at the thought of bed bugs, start calling the front desk, it equals more work for us." Allen pauses, misreading the blank look on Calvert's face. "I know what you're thinking, Cal; you're thinking more work, more money. I like the way you think. It used to be a good panic meant more money. But with these contracts Svetlana writes, it means more work with no more money. So it's best to avoid guests. Okay?"

"Yes."

"I start with the lowest room number and work my way along one side, then stop for lunch. After that, come back along the other side. Kaz likes to zigzag this side of the hall, that side of the hall, this side, that side." He makes a zigging and zagging motion. "It's stupid. You have to keep track of rooms to know when to take lunch. Jackson trained me to do one side, then the other. That's what I'm teaching you. Got it? I don't want to catch you zigging."

"I will not zig."

"Or?"

"Nor will I zag."

"Good. The beds have been stripped by housekeeping. See?" He points in the first room. Calvert sees the bare mattress and nods. "This clipboard here"—he takes up a clipboard hooked to the dolly—"has the job number, room numbers, the date, this box here, and a place for notes." He angles the clipboard to show Calvert. "We go to the first room: eight thirty-six. Lowest number. See?" He points to the number on the page, then the matching room number on the open door.

"Yes."

"You say to Daisy, 'Daisy. Sit.'" Daisy sits. Allen unclips her leash. "Daisy. Go." Daisy's head drops and her haunch sticks in the air. She puts her nose on the carpet, sniffling and maneuvering, smelling a spot here, a bit of paper there.

"It takes ten minutes per room. If she's on to something, she may linger. If there is food on the floor or stinkin' foot odor in the closet, it might take longer. Let her work. But if it runs past fifteen minutes and she hasn't sounded the alarm, get her to the next room." Allen looks at his watch. Calvert turns his watch up too.

After a long silence Allen says, "So you was a professor?"

"Yes, I was a doctor of Russian literature."

"Go on and say something smart."

Calvert has forgotten most of what he once knew. Allen insists. Calvert searches his memory. The name Pushkin comes to mind and crosses his lips: "Pushkin."

"What's a Pushkin?"

"Often called the father of Russian literature, Pushkin was best known as a poet early in his career. But I'm especially fond of a collection of stories titled . . ." Calvert can feel the thought slipping away. He finishes quickly, "*The Tales of the Late Ivan Petrovich Belkin.*"

Allen flicks a tendril of scraggly hair from his field of vision. Then he says, "Well. Okay. What use is that to me?"

"None that I know of," Calvert says. If standing in front of a classroom, he would have argued the value of literature, the arts, the historical context, understanding the human condition. But in this hallway, being interrogated by an ex-con while waiting for a hound to sniff for blood-sucking insects, he feels the argument might fail to find purchase.

"No wonder you had to get honest work," Allen says.

"No wonder," Calvert replies.

Daisy, having finished her inspection, returns to the doorway, walks in three circles and lies with her side on Calvert's right shoe. He looks at her fondly, leans over to scratch her head, and gives her side a few firm pats.

"Well, lookie there," Allen says. "She likes you." Allen hands the leash over. "Clip her up so she knows she's still working." Calvert reattaches Daisy's leash. "When Daisy finds evidence of infestation, she'll yowl like she did in the van. If she does that, you gotta clip her up fast to let her know to stop. Got it?" Calvert nods. "Once you finish a room you find it on the clipboard, see?" He traces his finger under the number 836.

"Yes."

"You check the box to show the inspection was completed. In the notes, you jot the time." Allen passes the clipboard to Calvert. Calvert stares at the spreadsheet. Allen produces a pen from behind his ear. "Go on."

Calvert checks the appropriate box and turns his watch and writes the time.

"Good," Allen says. "You did good. Now what, Professor?"

"Go to the next room?"

"Good. And which room is next?"

"Eight thirty-eight. No zigging or zagging."

"Damn, you catch on quick."

With that, the three move slowly down the hall, one room at a time. It takes three hours to check half the rooms on the list. Allen walks away for a time. Just before they stop for lunch, he comes out of a room, tippling a tiny bottle of vodka. When the last even numbered room is cleared by Daisy, Allen says, "Cop a squat and let's have some grub."

Calvert sits on the thick carpet with his back to the wall, his legs stretched in front of him. He feels the warmth of Daisy as she rests her chin in his lap. He rustles her ears in a way she seems to appreciate.

"Grab your lunch, Professor. It's mandatory break time."

Allen takes a Walmart bag from the dolly and pulls out two plastic butter tubs. Daisy perks up, trains her attention on Allen. He shakes one of the tubs. It sounds half full of something small and hard. Daisy stands, focused. She yips.

Allen peels the lid and sets the tub on the carpet near Calvert. Daisy yips again.

"Stay," Allen says, a playful warning. "Staaay. Stay. Staaay. *Go.*" Daisy has her nose in the tub, crunching kibble before Calvert sees her move.

"If she gets hungry, she gets distracted." He twists the top off a bottle of water and dumps it in the other butter tub. Daisy lifts her head from the kibble. "Go on," Allen tells her. She sticks her face in the water and laps loudly.

Allen sits catty-corner, his back along the opposite wall. He pulls food from a wadded brown paper bag. He looks at Calvert. "Eat," he says.

"I didn't bring food. But it's not a problem. I don't need sustenance."

"Bullshit. I thought you might forget, so I made you a cheese sammich. You like mayo on your cheese sammich?" He tosses a wax paper square at Calvert. It falls in his lap. Daisy looks excitedly at the sandwich. "Daisy," Allen warns. She goes back at her kibble.

"Thank you." Calvert doesn't know if he likes mayo on his cheese sammich. He can't remember ever having tasted such a sammich. He imagines it must be similar to a cheese sandwich, which he can only remember having eaten grilled and with tomato soup.

"Like I was saying," Allen says, as if they were in the middle of a conversation, "everyone wants to know why I was in prison. Well, I'll tell you." Allen takes a mouthful of food. Calvert peels back the wax paper to expose a block of white bread.

Allen talks with his mouth full, pointing his food for emphasis. "I killed a woman. Broke her neck. It was an accident of course—manslaughter they call it. Funny, right? Because it wasn't a man at all."

Calvert bites down and soft bread sticks to the roof of his mouth.

"The woman was a mean old biddy. My Aunt Agnes. My father's sister. I called her Aunt Anus because she was an A-number-one asshole." He laughs.

Calvert digs a finger at the wet dough suctioned to his soft pallet.

"When my mom died, my aunt moved in. Apparently I was running wild for lack of a strong hand. She intended to be the disciplinarian I needed. 'Spare the whip and spoil the child' was the thing she said when she beat me. I took the beatings until I got bigger than her. One day I said, 'I'm taking the car. There's a girl who wants me to fuck her. I need that back seat. You understand? Give me the keys.' We was standin' in the upstairs hall, and I said it to her face. Can you believe it? I was sick of her ridin' my ass every goddamned day and raisin' her hand to me like it was for my own good. Bullshit is what it was. You can imagine the whole thing provoked her. Can you imagine the balls I had? Can you?"

"I cannot imagine the balls."

"Well, I said it. We started to tussle over the car keys. I nearly broke her brittle old fingers gettin' the keys out of her claws. I held them high where she couldn't reach. I laughed right at her. You know what she did?"

"What?" Calvert asks. He holds his sammich, one bite missing. Daisy finishes her kibble and seems to be listening too.

Allen puts the last half of his lunch in his face and talks around it. "She couldn't reach the keys, but she could reach my face, and she hauled back and smacked me so hard it rattled my teeth. I bit my tongue and my cheek swoll right up. I don't mind tellin' you, it came as a shock. I forgot the keys and she snatched 'em right quick.

"Lordy, I was mad. You know that sayin' about seein' red? Well, I did. My blood got up and I didn't think about it. I shoved her hard as I could. That old bitch come off her feet and flew straight down the steps. She didn't hit one stair on the way down. A swirl of housedress, slippers come off her feet, she landed on her big Irish head. Neck snapped like a dry twig. Dead as a doornail. The end. It's easy to kill a person. That's a thing I learned. Sometimes it's harder not to kill someone than it is to kill 'em. I mean it."

Calvert knows how suddenly a person can die. He tries not to imagine Mere after her life left her body. Doing so brings the image to him immediately. Then he sees his student Kati with her head bashed open and blood leaking from her ears. And he knows, too, there was someone called Bump who never made it into the world. His synapses snap and pop and fire in a déjà vu loop as real as the moment of the actual tragedy. He's distressed. *If I were alive, this would be unbearable.* The vision recedes, and he tries to forget what he's seen.

Allen says, "It's a real conversation stopper I know. But on the plus side, I met my wife while I was on the inside. She read about me in the paper and wrote to me. We married while I had three years left. Very romantic. We got conjugal visits. You know what that means?"

"Yes," Calvert says. Though he can't remember what the term entails, he's certain he doesn't want to hear about it.

"It means we got to fuck in a trailer in the prison yard. If you've never been a convict fuckin' in a trailer, then it's hard to explain," Allen says knowingly. He cranks the lid off a Yoo-hoo chocolate drink and washes down his sammich. "You know what, though? I have regrets. I wish I'd fucked that high school girl before I went away. The one I needed the keys for. She had a body for sinning. I should look her up. A man has to have somethin' on the side. You know?"

"Yes." Again, Calvert hopes not to hear about it.

"A piece of ass on the side is different than a mistress. A piece of ass is a piece of ass. But a mistress is a commitment. It requires an investment of time. There's a woman who works here I'd be willing to take as a mistress." Allen looks up the hall as if the woman might materialize. She does not.

Calvert remembers a moment when Meredith's eyes locked on his from a distance, the exact instant that she cared more about hurting him than about self-preservation. He knows he deserved what he got, even if Meredith didn't. He doesn't want to remember any more.

He sets the rest of his cheese sammich on the carpet. Daisy snaps it up and swallows it whole. She shows her teeth in a canine smile, her tongue slipping out the side of her mouth.

Allen screws the cap back on his Yoo-hoo and says, "Anyway, let's get back to work."

Notification

Monday is officially a day off, and although the Harpole case is his baby, Whistler's plan is to move at his own pace this morning and work late into the night. He makes coffee and takes it on the iron balcony lashed to the side of his building. He doesn't keep furniture out there, so he drags a couch cushion and sits with his knobby spine between two thin rails. It's uncomfortable, but he makes the best of it.

He listens to pigeons cooing on the balcony above. It's a pleasant enough sound, but increasingly obscured by angry traffic from below.

Relaxation is never easy for him. Once it slips away, there's no point trying to claw it back. His boxer shorts are uncomfortable around his crotch, his neck hurts, his shoulders ache, and his gut is distended. He pats his middle and recommits to some kind of exercise. *I'm stalling.* He dumps the last half of his weak coffee into a hanging pot of dead flowers the previous tenant hadn't bothered to take. "You know what they say, don't you?" he asks the pigeons above, who *coo coo* quizzically. "If you love a man's garden, you gotta love the man!" The birds don't seem to mind his mediocre Pacino.

He changes into running clothes, walks outside, and plods at an uncomfortable jog until he can't take it anymore. He turns around, sweaty and winded, and walks home.

It's after ten by the time he's dressed and sitting in his sporty Honda Civic Type R. He's convinced it's the most attractive four-door on the market and the cheapest sports car he could find. The zippy engine and stiff suspension do him absolutely no good as he drives to work in constant congestion.

At the station, he finds a fresh door ding in his rear quarter panel. The impact took some paint and left a gash of raw metal. Nothing gets him pissed like others' carelessness. "You stupid fuck!" he says loudly. "You didn't know me? You fired without a warning, without a fucking brain in your head? Oh, shit. If I buy one, motherfucker, I ain't buyin' it from you." It's his favorite Serpico scene and cussing lets him vent. He's immediately in a good mood. "You know, you're a pretty fuckin' weird cop," he tells himself, still in character. "Yeah," he admits as Whistler.

He's happy until he sees Wendell. "Good morning, Wendell," Whistler says with medium cheer.

Wendell doesn't look up. "What's good about it?"

"You raise a legitimate point." Whistler keeps walking.

Upstairs he takes a tablet and nods to a few of the guys whose names he hasn't learned. Suzuki isn't in the squad room, so that's good. Ruther is in. He walks straight to the inspector's office. "Knock-knock," he says.

"Diaz, I just got off the phone with the ME. The report will be here tomorrow. Wednesday morning at the latest."

It was originally promised by today. *So much for Ruther's clout,* Whistler thinks, but is careful to keep his expression neutral. "The sooner the better," he says flatly.

"Where are things? You get notifications made?"

"Not yet. Couldn't find next of kin. Her boss was off grid all weekend. I'm about to call."

"Well, goddamn!" Ruther's mustache stands up. "What're you waiting for? Get to gettin'. When you're done, drag Suzuki in here. We need to discuss next steps."

"Yes, sir."

In the conference room Whistler looks over the evidence they've sorted. An incomplete picture of Anna Beth's last few days is developing.

There's no indication of who might have wanted to hurt her or why. His phone calls to her co-presenters at the conference yielded absolutely nothing. The techie for the presentation, Buddy Teutul, sounded sad to hear of Anna Beth's death. "She was so much fun to work with," he said. Despite long hours spent, Whistler feels like he's getting nowhere, pushing paper around. He dials Greg Kidd.

"Kingfisher Consulting. Greg speaking." He sounds like a man who never had a bad day. *That's about to change.* "Mr. Kidd, this is Detective Diaz with Special Crimes here in Chicago. I'm calling about your employee Anna Beth Harpole." Whistler plows straight into it. "I have some bad news. Anna Beth was found dead Friday morning." He has the urge to apologize. Instead, he listens closely, trying to glean anything at all.

"Oh no. Oh my God. Wait. Friday morning? Why am I just hearing this? Oh God, it doesn't matter. I'm sorry. How could this happen? I spoke to her just a few days ago." He's upset, says Anna Beth was like a daughter, that she had no family and he had no children, he and his wife had adopted her and the other way around. "Not legally, but in all the ways that matter. Oh my God. Elizabeth will be crushed."

"Who will be crushed?"

"My wife, Elizabeth."

"She and Anna Beth were close?"

"Very. They had lunches and went shopping. That type of thing. Elizabeth always wanted a daughter. We couldn't have children. Low motility. Not Elizabeth's fault. Bless her for sticking with me. She wanted a little girl. You see what I mean? Do you have a wife, Detective?" Whistler hesitates, decides to answer, but doesn't get the chance before Mr. Kidd continues. "If you find a good woman hold on to her."

The call goes downhill from there. Mr. Kidd is progressively more emotional and unfocused. Whistler asks questions and doesn't give any answers. He learns what he can and makes arrangements to call again once Mr. Kidd has calmed down and gathered documents to better answer Whistler's questions; once Greg has spoken to his wife.

When the call ends, Whistler is exhausted. Mr. Kidd's vulnerability has left Whistler feeling exposed. He forgot to eat breakfast. It's nearly lunchtime. *I need food.* He wants a drink. Not hot sake. Something cold. Something to take the edge off.

Beloved Racist Kitsch

Tuesday Moe rides Taibbi to a joint in West Lawn a block from the old Capitol Cigar Store with its saluting American Indian mascot reigning above the intersection. The cigar store closed years ago. From her booth by the window, Moe can see the fiberglass Indian wears black retro acrylic eyeglasses. The blue sign affixed to the statue's chest reads "Eye Can See Now," a repurposing of the statue into an ad for the ophthalmologist who leases the original space.

She orders a turkey club and hot water for her tea. She doubts the man she spoke to will show, but it's worth a shot.

She pulls her laptop from her bag and starts typing. Her food comes. She eats and types. She sips and types. She finishes a third draft about Precious and makes a third cup of tea, stirs in honey, takes a deep breath. She's careful not to scald her mouth.

A man approaches. "You are the reporter?"

"Yes, Mr. Reyes?"

"*Si.* Yes."

"Please, sit."

Mr. Reyes sits. "You don't look like a reporter." Moe would normally ask what he thinks a reporter looks like, but she doesn't.

The man pulls the trucker cap from his head and wrings it with blocky hands. "You want to know about Maria. To write a story."

"I'm sorry for your loss, Mr. Reyes." Moe shakes the man's hand; it's rough as a brick. "I want to tell her story," Moe says, reaching into her bag. "I'm going to record this if you don't mind." Moe knows Maria was a sophomore at Hubbard High. A custodian had discovered her body in the parking lot three days after school closed for summer vacation. She'd been strangled. Moe read a brief description of the crime on the Tribune's digital site. It wasn't deemed worthy of the print edition. The police report had few details. No one was charged. Moe wasn't able to get her hands on crime scene images. But the sparse details in the incident report sounded similar to what happened to the woman from San Francisco.

"What was Maria doing at school that day?"

"Forgot her piccolo in the music room. We rent it. I told her to get in the school so I could return it. You see. She didn't want to play piccolo anymore. She was bad at it. I needed to give it back to the store, you see?" He keeps his hands working in front of him, twisting the brim of his cap, rolling it tighter and tighter.

"I understand, Mr. Reyes. You told the police?"

"*Si*. Yes. Of course. The custodian who found her, he let her into the school. She got her piccolo. He walked her out and she left. He found her body at quitting time. She was dead. Someone stole her backpack, piccolo, and everything. Her phone. Whatever she had. A necklace from her mother. You see? What kind of person does that?" Mr. Reyes doesn't expect an answer.

"Do you have any idea why she was killed?"

"The police called it a bad mugging."

"You don't suspect anyone? A boyfriend? The custodian?"

"No. No. She was not cute. You understand? She looked like me. She was not a girl that got attention. She was a girl who was ignored. She dressed in sweatshirts and baggy pants. She didn't wear makeup. She never had a boyfriend."

His description could have applied to high school Moe. She tries not to judge. Although he seems unfeeling, he also looks ready to shatter. She knows this kind of man. His pride won't allow him to weep in public. She will follow up with the police. The story will serve as another example of how little coverage crimes against minorities get, but it won't help her cousin's case. *Vivian's leads suck.* "Is there anything else?" she asks.

"*Si.* Yes. The store wants me to pay for the piccolo. They hired a collection agency. Maria is dead. The funeral was expensive. You have to help them understand." He looks at her pleadingly.

"Mr. Reyes, I don't know how much help I can be." His eyes well with tears and he turns away. She relents. "You give me the name of the store and I'll do what I can."

"*Si.* Yes," he says. He quits wringing his cap and puts it on. He wipes his eye and gives Moe some specifics. When he's done talking, he leaves without saying goodbye, bumps the table hard, and her tea spills. She scoops up her recorder and laptop and scoots over so tea won't run on her pants.

Moe juggles her equipment and plucks napkins from the dispenser to soak up the tea. She's depressed and stares outside. The sinking sun projects the cigar store Indian's forlorn shadow on a building across the intersection. Its upraised hand waves a sad goodbye.

A Piccolo's Worth

On Wednesday, Vivian greets Moe as she walks in to *Text Block*. "Good morning. Right this way." Moe follows Vivian until they arrive at a closed door with a plaque that reads "Moe Diaz/Executive Feature Writer." Vivian turns the knob and lets the door swing open. Inside the windowless six-by-eight room sits a desk, a few mismatched chairs, and a lamp. "Well?" Vivian asks.

"Whoa," Moe says.

"There's my wordsmith. Welcome to your new office. From here you will wage a mission of journalistic world conquest. In the name of all that is good, of course."

"Of course," Moe agrees.

"Take a seat. Put your feet up. Plug in your laptop. I'll call a newbie you can boss around."

"No. No newbie. I'm trying to enjoy the moment."

Vivian's tone shifts to something more genuine, "It's not much, but it's a start. Took me days to make space. I'm sorry. I should have thought of it sooner. I hope you like it."

"'Like' is not the word. I love it." She hugs Vivian. Not until this moment did Moe know if she was going to live with this promotion or try to buck it. Standing in her own office, she's in.

"Where are you on the follow-up to the Magnificent Mile Strangler?'

"That has a very yellow journalistic ring."

"Your friend at Channel 13 coined it this morning. She interviewed an old woman and her long-haired dachshund. The woman lives in the neighborhood and was the one who called the police. There was no news, but she got fresh video. The strangler title is catching on."

"Fucking Sophia," Moe says.

"Fucking Sophia indeed. But where are we?"

"The story of Precious is done. I was about to send it. She was strangled. Seems she knew the killer. Crime of passion. Her momma, Loretta, believes it was the ex, Ronnie. He's got a history of assault and possession. He left the state, and the police let it drop. No resources. Compared to the money being thrown at Miss Magnificent Mile, there's the beginning of a story about resource discrepancies. Nothing to tie it to the other case, though."

"No substantial media coverage of Precious," Vivian says.

"Except us," Moe adds.

"Except for us," Vivian agrees. "Send it to me. And the other people on the list?"

"Maria Reyes was strangled and robbed. It smells fishy. But there's an angle about the shop that rents school instruments being too heartless to waive the cost of a stolen piccolo."

"What's a piccolo?"

"It's about a half a flute."

"That's what I thought. What's the street value of a used piccolo?"

"I'd say almost nothing. I'd bet it was someone who knew her. I'm going to keep digging. I want to look into the father and the man who found her."

"No connections to our strangler?"

"Not other than superficial circumstances. Two tips down, one to go. But I wouldn't hold my breath."

"With an office like this, you're destined to work wonders." With that, Vivian leaves.

"But no pressure, right?" Moe calls.

Vivian laughs from down the hall, as if it were a joke.

The Cold Cold Trail

Whistler arrives early, anxious for an infusion of details that might resuscitate his dying case. He's first in the squad room. He opens the door and flips on the lights, watches the array of fluorescent tubes flash on around the room. *Looked better in the dark.*

He finds no report from the ME's office, and it's too early to make calls. He does some simple math in his head. *Five days since Anna Beth died on a hard patch of pavement.* Whistler feels he's letting the young woman down. He's beginning to like her. At least the version he's reconstructed. Smart. Driven. Seemingly setting aside a personal life in favor of building a career. More likely making it up as she goes. *Not so different from me.*

From Elizabeth Kidd, he'd learned that Anna Beth was an only child of Dutch immigrants. The couple had moved to the United States to take jobs in finance. Shortly after arriving on American soil, there was an unexpected pregnancy, and Anna Beth was born. Anna Beth's father passed away when she was a junior in college. Her mother, heartsick, traveled home to be with family and never returned. She died a few years later.

"Was Anna Beth left an inheritance?" Whistler smelled motive.

"Not really. She got a small monthly payment from an estate her parents arranged. It wasn't a fortune. For financiers, they were not particularly wealthy. But they left her a safety net. Enough to help out until her career took off. If she lived that long." Elizabeth's voice broke.

"Take your time."

After a long pause: "I'm fine. My point is, cost of living in San Francisco is brutal. Anna Beth had a better lifestyle than she could afford, in a better building than she should be able to swing. She had expensive taste in clothes. That kind of thing. The money from her parents subsidized her spending habit. I think splurging was a way of feeling cared for by her parents. As if they were still alive and doing things for her."

Whistler could hear her set the phone down and blow her nose. He waited. When she was more composed, he said, "I know it's difficult. Unreal. But you were about to say something."

"Nothing really. She always let me pick up the tab when we went out. She knew I liked to mother her. She took advantage a little. It was a playful thing. I never got too offended."

"What about her social life? Was she seeing anyone? Any bad breakups?"

"She didn't date. Didn't seem particularly interested. I tried to set her up more than once. She never went for it. When I was her age, I dated. Not Anna Beth. Men were not her thing."

"Is it possible she was gay or bisexual and afraid she'd be discriminated against?"

"In San Francisco?"

"I take your point. Perhaps dating older men? Married men? Into open relationships or something kinky she might feel people would judge her for?"

"Anna Beth? I know these questions need to be asked, but you're barking up the wrong tree. She had boyfriends in the past. She was engaged once. She was idealistic about love. She wanted it to work a certain way. When reality didn't meet her halfway, she gave up on it. That's all. Got her heart broken and decided it wasn't for her."

"Do you have the name of this fiancé?"

"I'm sorry, no. It was years ago. Before grad school. I don't think she ever told me his name."

"What about jewelry? Perfume? She wasn't wearing earrings or rings. No watch."

"I feel naked without my jewelry, but Anna Beth rarely wore any. Though, as part of an outfit she might have worn something. Small and silver usually. Something elegant, simple, and too expensive for what it was."

"And perfume?"

"She was sensitive to scents. She used unscented deodorant and detergent. When we shopped, we'd avoid the perfume counter."

"I noticed something odd. I found suits, skirts, tops—that kind of thing. Plus some casual wear. Sweatshirt. She was in workout gear when she was attacked. What I never found was a pair of dress shoes."

"That is odd. Shoes were her main accessories. And bags. She liked a good bag."

Whistler made a note of that. Underlined it. Asked, "Can you think of any reason she wouldn't have dress shoes with her?"

"She would have rather gone topless than without her heels. I don't know what to tell you."

Whistler asked more questions. Elizabeth Kidd was conversational and forthcoming. She was upset but wanted to be of use. She seemed relieved to have someone to talk with. The last thing she asked was, "You saw her after. She didn't suffer, did she?"

He thought of Anna Beth, the thin skin of her neck dark with trauma, the curve of her crushed windpipe lumpy and wrong. He said, "She didn't suffer. It happened very quickly." Though she was a smart woman, and he wasn't a talented liar, Elizabeth Kidd had seemed grateful for his effort, desperate to accept a fictional version of events.

He'd also spoken again to Mr. Kidd. Anna Beth's boss explained a bit about his work, about the role Anna Beth played. "She was a real go-getter. She wanted to do more and didn't want to wait. I was considering giving her a bigger role. Either that, or I was going to lose her. She was too good and too smart to stay here forever. She would have been gone within a year if this hadn't happened. Sorry." He had gotten progressively apologetic for being upset. He'd provided Anna Beth's home address and other personal details. None of it likely to be of use.

Whistler gets coffee going and walks to the conference room while it brews. He wanders deeper into the building, looks into the empty interview rooms. This is where Ruther's reputation for greatness really stems. Getting a suspect cornered with circumstantial evidence and working it to get a confession, or at least self-incrimination. *That is something I'd like to see.*

In the break room, he makes his coffee the way he likes it. He hears someone approaching and sets his coffee aside to avoid a spill.

"Diaz. You're here early. Very industrious. I've got good news and I've got bad news. Which one do you want?" Ruther waves a large envelope.

"The ME's report? Thank God."

"Not so fast. I guess I'll give you both barrels in one blast: the report is done and thorough. Clean rape kit. Clean toxicology. No surprises on cause of death. No useful DNA from her attacker. Her nails had nothing under them except a sliver of black Latex. The attacker likely used gloves. That shows intent and planning. Two broken toes. Probably occurred during the scuffle. The cut on her head was from the ground, not a weapon. It was full of gravel. Her stomach was mostly empty, hadn't eaten that morning."

"Where does that leave us?"

"Short of a miracle witness or a spontaneous confession, it's time to take it to the public. Set up a tip line. The mayor wants to have a press conference. The superintendent will give a statement. I've been promised bodies to man the phones."

"Should I wear a suit?"

"Shit, Hollywood," Ruther chides. "You won't be on stage. This will be high level and political. Got it?"

"Got it."

"What next, Diaz?" Ruther asks.

"I'm going to talk to Ted, see if he can give me anything at all to go on. There was a smell on the victim's body; something other than chlorine. A scent like floral perfume. It was faint. I mentioned it to Ted. I want to follow up. She was close to her boss's wife. Mrs. Kidd said Anna Beth was sensitive to scents. So that smell came from somewhere. I'm hoping it's from our killer." Ruther's mustache registers doubt. Whistler keeps going. "I'll update Ezekiel—maybe he has some ideas. Suzuki is still churning names through the database. He keeps kidding about heading to California, but the only reason would be to search her apartment. I don't believe the killer followed her from there. This was homegrown. I'm going back through all the video. Reggie identified some ATMs I have to run down this morning. Like I said, the search of the dumpster came up with nothing. But that tells me we could have a missing hair tie."

"That's not much."

"Also, I sorted her clothes into likely outfits as I bagged and tagged them. It looked to me like she had three suits to choose from for the conference. One had been worn and was wrinkled. But there were no dress shoes, which is strange. All the suits were similar in color so I think she may have only had one pair of heels for the conference, But they were probably her favorite, and expensive. Mrs. Kidd said Anna Beth was a shoe horse. She would have definitely brought heels with her. Perhaps she left them somewhere. Wherever that is, we haven't accounted for her being there. I hate to be clichéd, but perhaps she slept with someone in the hotel and forgot her shoes? I mean, it is a conference in a hotel. These are the kinds of things that happen. So I've been told. By Suzuki. But given what I have, leaving her heels in another guest room at least makes sense."

"That's thin. Without evidence it's just a story. You could send Zeke back to the hotel to scour video."

"He hates to be called Zeke."

"I know. But I'm the boss. And do that. Get Zeke on the video from the previous night."

"I will."

"Anything else?"

"I checked the sex offender registry for perpetrators in the immediate vicinity. There were twenty-eight within three square blocks."

"I'm not surprised."

"I had Suzuki run them. None of them were violent, none were rapists; mostly peeping Toms, flashers, public masturbators, and numerous old men who'd been in possession of kiddy porn. Old wannabe kiddy diddlers always get my attention. Far as I'm concerned, they're recidivists-in-waiting. But not one had a record of actually touching kids or anyone else—definitely never strangled anyone. The closest thing I found was a guy with a restraining order. Looked into it. Contentious divorce. No violence. Heated words about throttling his wife."

"The world is full of every kind of creep," Ruther says.

"I'm learning that lesson. You know, I keep going back to this missing hair tie."

"Lack of a thing is not evidence. It's at best a theory of evidence."

"Her hair had been pulled back. You could see the mark clear as day. I can show you in the photos."

"I saw."

"The hair tie is nowhere. That may tell us something. He brought gloves. That shows premeditation. If he is taking trophies . . ."

Ruther's mustache leaps to attention. "This is not a serial killer. Don't say the words. This is already a big enough shit storm. Don't add more crap. When you find yourself at the bottom of a deep hole of feces, stop digging. Do you take my point?"

"Point taken."

"Good. Now make something happen before I get a stress headache. I've been told I'm unpleasant when I have a stress headache."

Whistler takes up his "Crafty Ass Bitch" mug. "That's hard to believe," Whistler says. Then he takes a quick swig to hide his smart-ass grin.

Ashes to Ashes

Allen materializes as Calvert and Daisy exit another hotel room. He announces, "In my professional assessment, you got a handle on the basics. You can't be expected to use training wheels forever. You see what I mean, Professor? You're a smart guy. You pickin' up what I'm puttin' down?"

Calvert is confused. He'd slept badly again, woke feeling freshly abandoned by the loss of his mother and father, and thinking of Grandpa Harry's funeral. He's dead on his feet. He slowly focuses his awareness and tries to grasp what Allen is saying.

"Well?" Allen asks.

"I am picking what you are putting."

"Good. You fly solo for a while. I'll meet you in the van around six." Allen turns and jogs away. He calls over his shoulder, "If you got questions, figure it out." A few yards farther away he yells, "Ask Daisy."

Calvert watches Allen go, sees him turn into a stairwell at the end of the hall. Daisy shakes her head, clapping her ears against her skull and rattling her harness. She looks puzzled.

He pats her head. "Don't ask me. I just work here."

Satisfied, Daisy drops on top of Calvert's feet until her next olfactory inspection begins.

Calvert could not attend the funerals of either of his parents. Neither of their bodies were recovered. For his father, who was MIA, there was eventually a military event. Calvert had only been a child. "Money was an issue," Harry had once explained to young Calvert. But Calvert suspected his mother didn't have the strength to both grieve and parent. She had chosen mourning her husband over comforting her son.

The impetus for last night's round of nightmares had been his acceptance of culpability in his own death, the death of his wife, and his student. The wakes for the women whose deaths he'd caused had taken place during his coma. The only funeral he'd ever attended was Harry's.

In his last days, Harry's old bones had begun to ache, and his hips had quit working. He'd spoken with Calvert on the phone, saying, "I'm no spring chicken."

"I could come this weekend. Take you for a steak dinner."

"Don't trouble yourself. You're busy with school. I'm getting along. Besides, my teeth don't fit good enough to chew steak."

It was the last time he'd spoken to Harry. Ten days later, Harry chose to stay on the downstairs couch near a roaring wood stove. It was easier than getting up the stairs. He'd fallen asleep with a copy of *A Hero of Our Time* open on his chest. The novel, by Mikhail Lermontov, had been a birthday gift from Calvert. The inscription read simply, *For Harry. My hero. As always, thanks for everything.* Harry never woke. His body was found the next morning by a woman who came to cook him a hot breakfast and take away his dirty laundry, the fire having burned itself down to ash.

Calvert had mixed feelings upon hearing of Harry passing quietly in the night with an unfinished book over his heart. It was a good way to die, peaceful and definitive. But it was tragic to leave a good book half finished. *Harry would have liked it.*

He recalls seeing Harry at the wake, snug in his tight, silk-upholstered casket. Relieved to no longer have the complicated task of daily life to contend with, finally able to leave regret behind, nothing but a nice long death ahead of him. *That's the life,* thought Calvert longingly.

Daisy yawns, wags her tail against the carpet. Calvert snaps on her leash so she knows she's still working. They walk the dolly of supplies to room 724. He takes up the clipboard and makes check marks and notations. He reads the time on his heavy watch. He writes that too. He unhooks Daisy and says, "Daisy, go."

His voice is weak. She turns her brown eyes over her shoulder, to see if he means it. He makes a minimal shooing gesture and flicks his chin toward the room. She casually begins to search for unseen bloodsuckers.

Sixty old friends had attended Harry's funeral, many of whom had known Calvert as a boy. He recognized none of them. They shared stories he'd never heard about his grandfather—about his humor, his humanity, his adventures. It was as if they'd known a man he'd never met.

Harry had deserved his easy death. He'd deserved the attention friends paid at his passing. Conversely, Calvert had earned a death that lingered and taunted. He deserved to be tortured for the pain he'd caused. It is apt there's no one left to attend his funeral, no one to share his stories or mourn his passing. He imagines a generic student saying, "I remember that time he wrote a vocabulary word on the board. Classic Professor Greene."

He likes to believe that after Harry's casket closed, after it was hoisted and pushed into the furnace, after the ashes were swept into a pile and gathered in a brass urn, that somehow Harry found himself swimming out in Lake Michigan with his daughter. That Harry was the young man his friends remembered. He likes to think the water was warm.

Third Time's a Charm

It's after four, Friday afternoon, when Moe's phone rings. "Hello," she says.

"Moe Diaz?" It's a woman's voice, heavily accented. To Moe it sounds Honduran.

"Moe speaking. Who is this?"

"I got a note that Moe called. He had questions. Moe is a man's name."

"It usually is." Moe pulls paper and pen over. "Mrs. Flores?"

"Yes. I am Brina Flores."

"Could we meet? I'm available now. I need an address and I'll come to you."

"No, thank you."

"It doesn't have to be today. Whenever you'd like. I'll work around your schedule."

"I don't want to meet. I can talk now. You have questions about Ginny?"

"Yes. I'm sorry for your loss, Mrs. Flores. This really would be easier in person."

"Not for me. What's your question?"

"What happened the day Ginny was killed?"

"Ginny is a Dreamer. You understand? Legally speaking they call her a Dreamer."

"Development, Relief, and Education for Alien Minors."

"*Si*. Ginny is a Dreamer. Was. She was nine when I brought her here ten years ago. She was my oldest. I have other children here now. You

142

understand? I didn't want to talk to the police because I could be sent away. My children would have no one. You see?"

"I understand. What about Ginny?" Moe makes notes in a short-hand of her own invention.

"After high school she took a job at the laundry where I work. That day, the one she died, she came to work sick to her stomach. The work is too hot if you don't feel well. She took a bus home before the shift was over. Neighbors found her in the alley next to the dumpsters. She'd been choked. Her lips were blue." Mrs. Flores exhales raggedly.

"I'm so sorry, Mrs. Flores." Moe pauses, guilty for upsetting this woman. Her heart beats faster at the thought of finding a lead. She forces herself to sound calm and asks, "Can you think of anyone who would want to hurt her?"

"Everyone loved Ginny."

"Did she have a boyfriend?"

"She met an older man. He gave her gifts. She got pregnant. They stopped talking."

Older than nineteen is every adult male in the city. "Do you have his name or a description? Did you meet him? Did he have silver hair? Facial hair? Glasses? Balding? Tattoos? Anything to go on? Big? Small?"

"No. No. I never met him. Ginny didn't say his name. Older is all she said. I didn't know about him until he left her. She was so upset she couldn't hide it from me. She kept him secret until it was over."

"You think he was married? Is that why she kept it secret?"

"She was a good girl. But the heart has a mind of its own."

Moe can hear Mrs. Flores getting more upset and knows she's running out of time. Mrs. Flores will end the call any second. "How did they meet?"

"At work."

"At the laundry?"

"In the building. The laundry is in the basement."

"I see. Can you give me the name of the building, the address?"

"The International Hotel."

The Coffee Girl

The polite chirp of Rosa's phone barely wakes her at five in the morning. She stretches from beneath the covers and pats the nightstand until she finds the cold touch screen. She's back to sleep as soon as she tucks her arm under her pillow.

Fifteen minutes later, a frightening clatter rumbles from the top of her dresser. She lurches across the room for the wind-up alarm clock: her backup system. She works a micro-switch with tired fingers. When the alarm stops, she exhales. *I'm up, I'm up.* It's what she said every morning of high school when her mother yanked the blankets off her.

She scrubs her face with her hands to get the blood pumping. She yawns. Her morning breath is hard to take, even for her. She shuffles to the bathroom to pee and sits all the way in the bowl, her ass wet and cold. Her torso clenches at the shock; she jumps up and knocks the seat down. When she's done her business, she's too tired to stand. She reaches across the sink for toothpaste and a toothbrush. She loads the bristles and tucks them in the side of her mouth. She brushes with her underwear around her knees. Reluctantly she stands, pulls her drawers up while clinching the toothbrush in her mouth, spits in the sink. There is blood in the foam. Her gums are inflamed. She needs to get to the dentist. *There's no time. No money. Thomas needs shoes.* She finishes brushing, willing her concerns of dental hygiene down the drain.

She planned to forgo the shower, pull her hair back, and take an extra few minutes to make Thomas a hot breakfast. One look at herself in the mirror and she dismisses the plan. Her fingernails are too long. *I need to do my nails.* "Ha." She laughs at herself. Some women get manicures, but she only hopes to find her clippers.

In the hall she knocks on Thomas's door and enters. She sits on the edge of the bed and looks at his face. "Thomas," she says quietly, smoothing his hair across his forehead. "Thomas, time to get up." He rolls away, burrows deeper, and puts a pillow over his head. "Thomas, listen. I'm hopping in the shower. Come in if you need the bathroom. It's fine. We have to get moving. Okay?" In reply, he curls his knees tighter to his body and bumps her off the bed with his rump. She turns on his bedroom light and leaves his door open.

The water from the shower is brown with rust. She washes so quickly it doesn't have a chance to run clear. She reaches for a towel and wraps it around her back, tucks it over her chest. She whips her hair over and twists another towel around her head. "Thomas," she calls, "are you up?" No reply. No movement.

Thomas's bedroom door is closed. She bangs on it and enters. His light is off, and he's in bed with all the pillows on his face. He got out of bed, turned off the light, shut the door, and ignored her suggestion to get moving. Her mother calls Thomas "willful," but Rosa fears he's becoming an asshole like his father. The door knocks against the wall as she snaps the light on and rips the comforter away, taking the pillows with it. Thomas's scrawny limbs convulse at the insult; he flips face down, desperate to escape the glare.

"Mom! Are you kidding me right now?" Thomas's muffled voice is indignant.

"It's the circle of life," she says angrily.

"That doesn't even make sense." He sounds as mad as an eight-year-old can.

"Get up," Rosa commands. "Don't make me say it again."

She scowls because she's becoming her mother. Next to her bedroom door is a folding chair where she throws all the clothes she's worn but that aren't dirty enough to wash. The third shirt down looks good. The jeans from yesterday make the cut. She dresses. Thomas has a similar system. He calls it The Pile. *How will he learn if I don't do better?*

She untwists her hair from the towel, pats it, scrunches it with her hands, and lets it air dry. The cussing stage of morning cajoling is about to commence, when she hears her son take his morning piss. *He's moving.* It's a relief. She hates to start the morning screaming at him. She slips on socks and shoes. In the bathroom, the toilet flushes and water runs. On her way past the open bathroom, she says, "Waffles in five minutes. Put down the toilet seat. Wet that hair down!" Thomas turns his hot-chocolate eyes on her and frowns as best he can with a Transformers toothbrush in his mouth.

In the kitchen, she drops frozen waffles in the toaster. She needs coffee, but it'll keep until she gets to Coffee Girl. She checks the time. *Fuck.*

"Thomas. Hurry. We'll take breakfast to go. Don't forget your backpack." Thomas walks smugly into the kitchen, dressed for school, his hair wet and raked with comb marks, his backpack over his shoulders. "Thanks, baby," she says, kissing his forehead.

Thomas loudly drags a chair from under the table and sits heavily. Rosa pops the toaster prematurely, smears peanut butter over one wholegrain disk and smashes a second on top. "Here," she says. "Why are you sitting? Let's go." She takes a bite of the remaining dry waffle, expecting it to be frozen in the center. She's surprised to find it warmed through. *I'm a great mom,* she says to make light of her tiny victory. She throws her bag over her shoulder and ushers Thomas out the door.

They twist down two flights of steps and knock on her mother's apartment. The door opens right away. Thomas walks inside.

"Rosa, you need to dry your hair." *"When will you grow up?"* is perpetually left unsaid. "You'll catch cold if you go out with a wet head. How will you work?"

Rosa is mildly wounded but has no time for an emotional break. She says, "Thanks for taking him. He needs lunch for school. Sorry. Ran out of time." Her mother's lips go tight. Rosa keeps talking, "He has a spelling test. Try to go over his words. Okay? We made flashcards." Inside, Thomas turns on *Clifford the Big Red Dog*.

They won't go over the flashcards.

At the bus stop a boy who once had a crush on Rosa is on his way to work. He glances up from his phone to say, "Bus is late." He doesn't give her a second look.

"If it was on time, I'd have missed it." The boy, whose name she can never remember, gives her a minimally courteous smile while watching his phone screen. She's disappointed. She would never date him, doesn't have time to date anyone. Still, it would be nice to know she could turn his head.

The Chicago Transit Authority bus makes a slow turn two blocks up. The familiar slash of red over the front bumper reminds Rosa of badly applied lipstick. Fifteen minutes later, she steps off the bus and walks down the alley to the back door of Coffee Girl.

She pats her pockets for keys. Can't find them. Panics. She remembers her bag. After a frantic rummage, she finds her keys covered by a stack of loose napkins. She huffs out a breath, works the keys, and uses her hip to knock the stubborn door open. She quickly types the code to turn off the alarm: Thomas's birthday. She kicks the back door shut, snaps on lights, bumps up the AC, and sticks her purse on a shelf amid cleaning supplies. The mop and broom handles slide sideways. She catches them before they can fall, props them back in place.

She pulls her slightly damp hair into a ponytail and ties it with a band she wears around her wrist. There is a small mirror on the wall next to the swinging door. She checks her hair and picks a piece of lint from her shirt. She slips some ChapStick from her front pocket and uses it. There's dry skin under her nose and she greases that with a swipe of ChapStick as well. Lastly, she takes her apron from its hook and ties it. *Here we go.*

She pushes the swinging door open and twists on the espresso machine. She turns on the drip coffee machine, pries the lid from a container, and scoops beans into the grinder, letting it rumble. When the coffee is ground, she whacks the grinder to knock the last sticky bits into the waiting filter. She drops the filter in a metal basket and slides it in place. She assembles a pump thermos from clean parts on the drying rack, pushes it under the grounds, and repeats the process twice more, once for medium roast and once for dark.

While she waits for the machines to heat up, she stocks milk from the refrigerator in the back. She charges the stainless steel cylinders with CO_2 so they are ready to express whipped cream. Finally she gets the first pot of coffee brewing. In the café, she straightens chairs and stocks sugar, napkins, and wooden stirrers. She brews the next batch. At the front window, she looks into the dark, the horizon blocked by tall buildings, no sign of Calvert coming for his prework coffee. She snaps the neon sign to "Open" and unlocks the door.

Behind the counter, she empties the used grounds and drops the last filter into the basket, gets the last pump pot brewing. She opens the espresso container, sticks her face over the oily beans and smells. *I'll feel better after coffee.* The beans seem different from usual. *A floral note. Maybe the ChapStick on my nose.*

A sound draws her attention to the back room, a scrape of something hard sliding over metal. She imagines the wooden handles of the mop and broom shifting along the shelf's edge again. She listens for the handles to hit the floor. Hears nothing. *Must have caught on something.*

She packs espresso into a firm puck. She toggles the button that forces hot water through the grounds. Her mouth waters. She grabs the shot glasses and places them carefully to catch every dribble of the creamy espresso.

There's a loud sound and a rush of movement. She yelps. Flinches. Tries to turn. She's struck from the side before she can see what's coming. An unstoppable force has her by the throat. She crumples behind the counter. Her body bounces like a ball, but only once. Her temple grinds against the floor mat. Her ribcage loses shape under the body weight of her attacker. All the air goes out of her. She scratches at the hands clamped to her throat, digs her overlong nails into gummy-feeling fingers. Her nails bend painfully. She sees his calm face, recognizes him. She tries to scream. Tries to inhale, no room in her body for her burning lungs to expand. Over the staccato pounding of her heart, she hears the espresso machine running. She has a desperate urge to turn it off. She thinks of Thomas. Her eyes bulge wet in their sockets. Everything turns black.

* * *

Sunlight strikes the espresso machine and illuminates the warm depression at the notch of her collarbones. It's damp. The man takes his thumb and rubs the perspiration. The Latex of his glove slides smoothly. He rubs, back and forth. He longs to feel more of her. Instead, he pulls her hair loose, lets the elastic band roll over his hand and onto his wrist.

The Heroic Dead

Whistler walks on careful cat feet from the break room, again, having overfilled his "Crafty Ass Bitch" mug with a touch too much tap water. He settles at his desk and rests his shoes on the edge of his city-issued trash can. He sips coffee. He'll need the caffeine to comb through the pile on his desk. So far, the hotline tips have been plentiful, but not helpful. The phrase "comb through" makes him think of Ruther's mustache. He smirks and sips more coffee.

The desk phone sounds loudly: RING-BRINNG. *There must be a way to turn that thing down.* His cell phone gives a muted chirp in his front pants pocket: *vzzzzt-vzzt.* He's careful not to move abruptly because he's been given a trick chair as part of his hazing. He learned the hard way that if he leans too far, too fast, the chair will tip him on his head. RING-BRINNG. *Vzzzzt-vzzt.* He'd taken a tumble twice in four days. Ruther claimed to have requisitioned a new chair, but his mustache looked shifty when he said it.

Whistler sets his perfect coffee between stacks of tip-line leads. He shifts his weight forward, spreads his stance as wide as possible until his shoes reach the floor. RING-BRINNG. Only then does he grab for the desk phone. *Vzzzzt-vzzt.*

"Detective Diaz," he says.

"Detective. This may sound strange, but I think I have information on the girl killed near the lakeshore a week ago. The one in the news. The Magnificent Mile victim."

Vzzzt-vzzt. Whistler fumbles his cell phone from his pants. "Uh-huh. Yes. That's my case. Hold on, please." He checks the screen of his cell, the desk phone clamped between his jaw and shoulder. The incoming call on his cell is from Ruther. *Vzzzt.* The ring stops midway. Ruther has hung up. Whistler sets that aside and grabs a pen. "Let's start with your name." There's silence through the receiver. He readjusts the phone. "You still there?"

"Yes. Still here." She sounds young, cautious, a hint of an accent he can't place, but solemn and sincere.

"Okay. What's your name and a number where I can reach you if the call is dropped."

"Mimi. But this is anonymous. No last name. Is that okay? Please? I've never done this. I'm sorry. I want to tell you what I know. That's it. Can I tell you and go?" Whistler's cell blips to tell him he has a voice message. The screen reads "Ruther."

"Go ahead. Tell me what you have." He'll track Mimi through the incoming number. He wonders what Ruther wants. Maybe there's been a break. He could use a break. The case has gone fully cold. Ezekiel found security footage of Anna Beth walking into the conference hall in heels; riding the elevator with the overhead camera at a poor angle to catch her feet; and, later, walking to her room barefoot minutes after her panel discussion ended. No explanation. But no real leads. There wasn't enough time for a romantic tryst in the few minutes she wasn't on camera. Fortunately, the news outlets have started to move on, with the exception of Moe's digital paper, which no one reads. The mayor's office is slightly less agitated about immediate results. Ruther is starting to lighten up. The tip hotline was manned for a few days. He and Suzuki have slowly been sorting through hundreds of bogus tips.

"The killer has an agenda," Mimi says. Her voice sounds distant. "There is a plan. Maybe instructions."

"What do you mean? Like a how-to guide? Like *Strangulation for Dummies*? Something on the internet? A dark web chat room, or 8chan, or some kind of angry incel manifesto?"

"I know it's strange. I don't know the answer. They are telling me he will kill again. I see a white van. I see black latex over white skin. Strong hands. He's leaving bodies in a trail. But the trail is to mislead. They are showing me the card game with three cards. What's it called?"

"Three-card Monte." Whistler stops taking notes. He was hopeful about the call. Mimi's voice has a devout quality, like the few remaining sisters teaching at Dominican. There is an authority that comes with commitment to a belief, and this girl has it. *Saints and the insane.* At the mention of the white van, he was momentarily convinced Mimi had a real tip. But that detail had been in the press. *Another waste of time.*

"That's it," Mimi confirms. "That's the card game I'm seeing. I'm not sure why I'm seeing it, but my sense is of the killer shuffling for misdirection. That's all I know."

"When you say you see a white van, do you mean you are an eyewitness? Are you looking at the van? Can you give me a license plate? Even a partial plate may be helpful." Whistler's internal bullshit-o-meter points to the red zone. He suspects another gag from his coworkers. They're a bunch of immature kids. *A woman is dead. My first case!* "Or do you mean something else?" he asks, letting anger and exhaustion color his tone. "Like you have a crystal ball or can read tea leaves or sheep entrails? Is it entrails?"

"Spirits show me things. This morning I saw an attack that hasn't happened or was about to happen." His phone on the desktop lights up and displays a text from Ruther: an address.

"Mimi-who-spirits-show-things? I'll write that down. Thanks for the call." Whistler drops the receiver in its cradle and takes up his cell. He taps and swipes and plays the voicemail: *God damn it, Diaz. There was another attack. You caught a break. We may have a witness or two. Our guy was caught in the act. I'll text you the address. Get there and call me as soon as you assess the situation. And goddamned pick up your fucking phone when I call.*

Whistler can hear Ruther's 'stache rubbing against the phone's mouthpiece. He gathers his things, leans too far, and goes over in the chair. He rolls with it, leaves it where it lies, and keeps moving.

It doesn't take long to reach the crime scene. Whistler swings the car around a double-parked news van and creeps down the block, honks at three lookie-loos edging out to survey the commotion. They move back. He parks behind two angled patrol cars that cordon off the end of the block. Whistler slips out and walks to his trunk.

He pops it and stares at a picture taped to the underside of the trunk lid. The image is of him from last Thursday. He's on his back on the floor, stuck like a turtle in his chair, wearing a frightened expression. He found others like it this morning, one inside his desk and another rolled into a scroll to greet him in his coffee mug. He remembers Wendell pitching him the key on his way out the door, "Take number six." He had been not abrasive. Whistler had attributed it to Wendell warming to him. *I should've known better.*

He removes his coat and lays it in the trunk. He rolls his shirtsleeves and plucks a couple rubber gloves from the top of a box. The white gloves remind him of what Mimi said: "Black latex over white skin." They had found evidence of black latex. Ted Majors suggested the killer wore gloves. The public statement hadn't mentioned the gloves or the color. *Could Mimi know something?* He dismisses it. *Gloves are an obvious guess.*

He closes the trunk and retucks his shirt as he walks. He doesn't know the beefy patrolman who eyes him as he ducks under the yellow tape, but he has his badge and a purposeful stroll. The patrolman nods respectfully.

"What's the situation?" Whistler asks, looking into the larger man's face.

"Woman from that coffee shop was attacked." He points over cars to a storefront four doors down. "She's alive but unconscious. They say it might be the Strangler. That guy over there"—he points toward a

crowd of cameramen and reporters pressing toward one glum figure—
"chased the attacker off and carried the woman out of the building.
When I pulled up, he was rocking her in his lap, sitting on the sidewalk. Looked like he was trying to get her to wake up. He was making
this croaking sound—*crawk crawk*."

"I get it," Whistler says.

"He was making that sound, but no tears. Like he was all dried up."

"You were first on the scene?"

"Two units pulled in about the same time."

"And the suspect?"

"Bolted out the back. We got a description. But it's generic. White
male. Medium height. Medium build. Nothing to go on. You could be
the killer—I could. Practically anyone could. The guy could have driven
away, caught the L, or grabbed an Uber. Who the hell knows? He could
be sitting at that breakfast joint on the corner, eating a honeybun."

Whistler looks at the upscale retro breakfast place down the block.
The plate glass window is lined with customers eating giant artisan
short-order fare and watching the crime scene like an episode of Chicago PD. "Okay. Thanks."

"I'm Officer Mann."

"Detective Diaz. Who gave the description? We have another witness?"

"Yes, sir. Apparently a guy saw part of it go down." Officer Mann
scans around. "That guy with the hair," he says, nodding at a scraggly
character with lank blond hair, thinning on top.

Whistler cranes around until he spots a van. *White.* Vinyl letters read "Bug Off" down the side. His wheels start to turn. He sees
the crowd around the primary witness begin to shuffle. "That's a big
help, Officer. See ya around." He walks toward the press scrum, gets
close enough to hear a curvy woman from Action 13 frame the pitch.
She looks good. He immediately forms a small crush. He doubts Moe
knows her, but he intends to ask.

The TV reporter says, "We are in Printer's Row, where Calvert
Greene is being hailed as a hero for his quick action thwarting an early

morning attack on a local woman," She turns to the sickly-looking man in stiff coveralls. Whistler sees the "Bug Off" logo sewn over the heart of the man's uniform. "Mr. Greene, can you describe what happened?"

The sad man looks at the microphone pushed in his face, confused. He speaks softly and plainly. "This is where I meet my ride. Rosa makes me coffee." The reporter rips the microphone away. The man looks worried, as if he's done something wrong.

"Rosa is the woman who was attacked?" The reporter shoves the mic back at Greene. He looks at it uncertainly. The reporter shakes the microphone to speed his response. "Yes," he says.

"And Rosa is a friend of yours?"

Again the microphone is shoved at Greene and waggled. He's beginning to understand his role. He speaks more quickly this time. "I walked in. I didn't see Rosa. I called for her. A man stood from behind the counter. I said, 'Hey.' He ran out the back. I found Rosa. I thought she was dead, but she was breathing. I carried her. Allen called the police. I should go to work."

"Did you get a good look at the attacker?"

A head waggle. "No. Not very good. He moved fast."

"The authorities have been unable to apprehend the person who strangled Anna Beth Harpole ten days ago. Do you think you stopped the Magnificent Mile Strangler from killing another victim? Do you think you did more than the CPD has managed?"

Another head waggle. "I don't know about that. Should I know that?"

"People are calling you a hero for your quick action. What do you say?"

"I'm not a hero."

The reporter faces the camera, leaving Greene's mouth moving mutely in mid-thought "There you have it," she says. "A humble hero." She throws it back to the channel 13 news desk. The cameraman turns off his spotlight, and the duo walk away without thanking Mr. Greene.

Whistler gets his tablet working and searches until he finds the initial crime scene reports just posted to the system. He gives them a quick scan. He's halfway through when Moe appears beside him.

"You believe that shit?" she asks. "They don't even know if he's a suspect. That guy is off." She nods toward Greene, who is now answering questions from several print reporters. "I don't like him."

"Hey, cuz." Moe's comment puts him in action. He doesn't ask about the channel 13 reporter; he's less interested after the manipulative performance. Besides, he has work to do.

"You got anything to tell me? On the record?" Moe asks.

"No."

"Anything off the record?"

"No, Moe. Shit. I just got here." He stretches himself tall to look for Ezekiel. Spots him down the block, arms crossed over his chest, big biceps straining the parameters of his sleeves.

"Sorry," Moe says, not sounding sorry. "Listen. I found something you need to look at. I texted you."

"I've been swamped."

"Remember our deal? I find something concrete, you give me an inside lane. I found a connection."

"What are you talking about?"

"I'm publishing my fourth strangling story. The vic was working a fancy hotel. A hotel like the one your Harpole woman was a guest in. And my victim, she died only a month ago. Her body was found on its side next to a dumpster."

Whistler gives her all his attention. "What hotel? Are you serious?"

"Meet me for lunch if you're ready to trade. You've got my number."

"I've got my hands full. Don't jerk me around."

"I'm not." She walks away, clearly enjoying the moment.

Whistler wants to avoid the lingering reporters, so he ignores Calvert Greene for the moment. He can see Ezekiel is busy giving assignments to the patrolmen. He looks for the other witness, who has moved from the spot where he stood a few minutes ago.

Whistler finally finds the guy lying in the back of the open Bug Off van, looking impatient and chewing his fingernails.

"I'm Detective Diaz." Whistler coaxes his tablet back to life, ready to take notes.

"Allen Schmidt."

Schmidt seems startled. The little man immediately slides out of the van and knocks the doors closed. Whistler wonders if he's hiding something. Whistler schemes about how to get a look through the van. Allen doesn't offer a hand in greeting. His bony fingers hold each other like he's afraid what they'll do if left unchaperoned. He avoids looking in Whistler's eyes. "I read the statement you gave the patrolman. Thanks for your cooperation."

"Sure thing, boss." Still glancing everywhere but at Whistler.

Whistler taps on the digital keyboard: *Prison record?* "I know this is inconvenient. We'll get you through this and on your way as soon as we can."

"No problem." Allen lets his rump knock into the van's door. The sheet metal gives and rebounds, making a hollow two-part sound, *clunk-clunk*. "We all got a job to do, right? Nothing personal."

"That's right, Mr. Schmidt."

"Call me Allen."

"That's right, Allen. Nothing personal."

"Never is," Allen says, a slight swell of judgment in his tone.

"Tell me what you saw this morning. In your own words."

Allen exhales heavily, fatigued by the repetition of the process. He relents without squabbling. "I went by the Bug Off yard, supplied up the van, and got gas at the Shell where we have an account, you know. Svetlana set that up so we don't have to spend money and wait on reimbursements. That's why I don't have a receipt, if that's what you want."

"I have no reason to doubt you." Allen's knee-jerk defensiveness makes Whistler doubt him.

Allen knocks his butt into the van a few times. *Clunk-clunk. Clunk-clunk. Clunk-clunk.* He casts a skeptical look into the overcast sky and continues. "I drove straight here. I been picking up the professor since he started. He lives pretty close. He comes here for his morning coffee."

"You pick up Mr. Greene, you mean?"

"Yeah."

"You work together?"

"I'm his manager, you might say."

"What do you think of him?"

"He's kind of a squirrel, but I like him. It's the last week of his training. I'll miss hanging out with him when it's over. It's been kinda nice having another human to talk to. I'm a people person. Not the professor. But he's a hell of a good listener. Greene, I mean. He doesn't interrupt much. But don't let that fool you. He's got a lot of information in that head of his, loads of stuff rolling around up there. His brain might be in a low gear, but it keeps chugging."

"So you like him?"

"I just said so. I prefer working with Calvert to working with Kaz."

"Kaz?"

"Kaz Gladsky. The boss. He used to be a solid enough guy. We had some good times, shootin' the shit and telling lies about women we were banging. You know." Allen shows Whistler his stained teeth.

Whistler doesn't want to get roped into a conversation about the fairer sex with Allen Schmidt. But the job is to make him feel at ease, keep him talking. So he says, "I know exactly."

Allen smiles wider, revealing more bad teeth, and talks faster. "That's how it was with employee Kaz. Not now that he's the big boss. *Mr. Gladsky*, if you please. Over the last six months, Kaz has changed. He's more interested in status than friendship. Chalk that up to Svetlana." Before Whistler can ask, Allen adds, "That's Kaz's bride. She was the daughter of the man that owned Bug Off. Back when Kaz was only another employee, we made residential house calls. Honest work. Then Kaz got his hook in the old man's pretty daughter. There was a wedding. The old man dropped dead. Next thing you know, Kaz is wearing expensive watches and driving fast cars, giving everyone orders and throwing his weight around like a big shot. He wears gold necklaces and bracelets. He and Svetlana started changing to these big hotel contracts, switched from chemical sprays to natural stuff that hardly works, and once Calvert is trained, Kaz will never drive a van again."

"You don't think the changes are for the better?"

"Kaz has become the kind of guy I hate. Let me tell you this story. I'm going to be honest because you'll find out soon enough. I was in prison."

"I had no idea," Whistler underscores his note to check for Allen's record.

"Well, in the joint I read *People* magazine if I got the chance. I read one story about that Irish singer Bono. You know Bono?"

"I know who you mean." Whistler is impatient. But he keeps his expression neutral, knows to let Allen keep talking as long as he's in the talking mood.

"Bono was sucking up to Americans by saying in Dublin people would gather at the pub and say, *'You see that bastard up on the hill in that big house? We hate that bastard. Let's finish our pints and go kill him and take what's his.'* But in America, people gather in bars and they say, *'Did you see that big house up on the hill? One day I'm going to have a house like that. One day I'll be that guy.'* Bono was sayin' Americans don't resent people who make it. Americans are dreamers. Which may be true, but I think it's mostly bullshit. I guess I got too much Irish in me 'cause I can't be happy for Kaz. I want what he has. I'll be honest, I'm bitter about it. Why him and not me? Huh? You know that feeling?" Allen smiles. Whistler figures the ex-con is thinking of driving fast cars and screwing younger women, owning his own business. Essentially becoming exactly what he hates about Kaz.

Allen says, "In the joint I knew an accountant who poisoned his wife for the insurance money. Real nice guy named Gary. He never seemed like he belonged in prison. Even when he told me how he killed his wife and why he did it, I didn't believe him. Too good at talking to be a killer. Too smart to be in prison. He's one of the guys I've missed most since I was paroled. Calvert is like Gary."

Whistler tries to redirect. "Let's get back to this morning. You got gas at the Shell station, but with no receipt because of Svetlana's new system of bookkeeping. You came here to pick up Mr. Greene, same as other days. Then what?"

"That's right. I backed the van in here."

"What time was that?"

"It was three minutes to six."

"You are certain of the time."

"Well, there's a fucking clock right on the dash isn't there? Besides, after being inside, I like to keep a routine. The structure helps hold my day together. You understand me?"

"Go on."

"It was kinda miserable out here. Calvert wasn't in front of Coffee Girl. The 'Open' sign was turned on, spilling red light out on the sidewalk. But the lights were off inside. I started thinking that Calvert was going to be late, that he'd gone and gotten cocky about things now that his training is almost over. I killed the engine to save gas, you know, for the environment. I hadn't eaten yet, so I took out my pepper and egg sammich and ate it up. I gave Daisy the last bite."

"Who's Daisy?"

"She's a bitch we use to find bedbugs." Allen enjoys the confusion his statement makes, before adding, "We use dogs to sniff out infestations. You know, like a truffle pig."

"Daisy is in the van right now?"

"Where the hell else would she be?"

"Go on."

"So I turn around to shove a bite of food through the door of Daisy's cage. She gets all stupid and starts thumpin' her fuckin' tail. She won't let up and it's makin' me crazy. I'm about to get pissed off at all the noise and Calvert being late, when I catch something moving. Over there across that little dog park, I see a man go running past. Next thing, the door to Coffee Girl knocks open, and Calvert comes out big as life, with that woman's body in his arms. Her ass was startin' to sag because the professor's grip was slipping. He was about to dump her on the sidewalk. I sat there, stunned at first. I couldn't make any sense of it."

"What did Greene do?"

"I'll never forget it. Calvert's eyes were big and shiny as saucer plates. He was lookin' for help, I guess. Or checkin' for witnesses. It would be hard to say for sure because I don't live in his head. He saw the van, sank down on the spot, and held that woman's body to him like he would never let her go. He started yowlin'. That's when I snapped out of it and got my ass in gear to call nine-one-one."

While the Iron Is Hot

Whistler forgets about Moe's possible lead. During the interview, Allen Schmidt managed to be both forthright and shady as hell. Whistler is suspicious but decides the best move is to keep from tipping his hand to Schmidt and gather all the information he can before passing any judgments. He walks away from the Bug Off van and moves around the crime scene to delegate assignments. He scans the witness statements some more and talks to the officers who took them.

He puts Ezekiel in charge of evidence and asks him to continue organizing a canvas of the area. "Listen, Ezekiel, I don't know how the press got here so fast. I don't like it. It's too late to change it. But I need to get our hero Calvert Greene and his creepy coworker to the station in separate cars. They gave statements but I need to ask follow-up questions where I will have their undivided attention. I'm going to see about a warrant for that van. If I can't get it, I'll try and get permission from the owner. Let's have it gone over before they get back from the station."

"White van. I get it. But a warrant may be a stretch. What's probable cause?"

"I'll put Ruther on it. That's what he's there for. Be ready for the go-ahead. Schmidt said they use a dog to find bedbugs. With Schmidt and Greene being interviewed, somebody ought to check on that dog. I mean heat and what not. Dehydration. We are talking about a living creature. What other choice do we have?"

"I get it. We'll see how it shakes out. The witness the press got to, Greene, has already asked about the dog. I wouldn't bet on having that excuse. Besides, I love dogs. It wouldn't be right to do an animal that way."

"You're right."

"Meanwhile, I'll work the scene. I'll call once we finish. You try for the warrant."

"Have the dumpsters up and down the alley searched for latex gloves. Schmidt says the suspect ran down the block behind that park. If this is the same guy, we are looking for black gloves. I'm going to ask Ted to at least go over the medical files. He's familiar with Anna Beth and will know what to look for. He may catch something. If he's willing, I'll have him actually go look at Rosa Zhang's bruising. If we don't get the warrant, if the dog doesn't do it for you, maybe we can find another reason to take a look in the van. Something suspicious in plain sight."

"Try for the warrant. A warrant would be best. I'm telling you, a high-profile case you want to play by the books." Ezekiel says. "Don't ruin the conviction before it even starts."

"Of course," Whistler says. He walks away and calls Ruther. "The victim's name is Rosa Zhang. She was opening her business for the day when she was attacked. I'm sending a couple witnesses to the house, and I want to do the interview. Calvert Greene is the one who stopped the attack. I haven't been able to talk to him. The press was all over. The other guy is Allen Schmidt. He's got a record of some kind. He's slimy. Cool them in different rooms."

"I can do that."

Whistler remembers Ruther's reputation for being the best interrogator in the city. He's on a roll, doesn't want to lose his train of thought. He plows ahead, "From an initial walk-around, it looks like the assailant came from the storage room. The back door wasn't bolted. Alarm was switched off. Two cold shots of espresso and freshly brewed coffee on the back counter. I'd guess Zhang was busy. Never saw it coming. Greene walked in, the attacker had her on the floor behind the counter, the lights still off."

"Seem strange Greene walks in like that?"

"He's a regular customer. It's worth a conversation. The "Open" sign was on, the front unlocked. It happened at opening time. According to his statement, Greene walked in, the perp bolted and got clean away. Greene is a little off. Either shaken or hiding something. I'm not sure. We need to look into him. He works for an extermination company, Bug Off. He and his partner, this Schmidt, drive a white van."

"I'll get their records. What's the victim say?"

"Nothing. She's unconscious and on her way to Rush Medical. I sent Suzuki to get a statement when she comes around, get the low-down from the doctors. In the meantime, Ezekiel is at the scene, and I'm getting Ted to compare Anna Beth's injuries to Zhang's. He'll cross all the "Ts." I'm going to talk to the rest of the first responders before I leave. I need to get a copy of the video channel 13 aired. Can you have that sent to the house?"

"I'll make the call," Ruther says.

"Also, about the van. That makes two attacks with a white van at the scene. You think we can rush a warrant?"

"On what grounds? What are you looking for? What do you mean 'on the scene'?"

"On the scene. Driven by witness number two to pick up witness number one. Black gloves, a pair of heels, and an elastic hair band from Anna Beth. If it's the same van, we could find her DNA and have our killer. Case suddenly closed."

"It'll take time to run it up the flagpole. I'm likely to get my ass chewed for asking. But I'll make the ask. I'll try to sell it."

"Do what you can. I'll be there to talk to Greene and Schmidt."

"It's your baby."

"Thanks, Boss."

"Don't thank me yet."

Indigestion for Lunch

It's three o'clock and Moe is waiting on Whistler. Being kept waiting is one of her pet peeves. Since she arrived, she's been working on her laptop, swigging suds, and ignoring the time. Now she's run out of work to occupy her overactive mind. She's getting increasingly irritated. To relax, she attempts to enjoy the dark interior of Legends. The blues bar sits a few blocks north of its previous location along South Wabash. The new iteration is sanitized and tourist friendly, less authentic than it once was. Moe is careful how she thinks about things. She reframes her judgments about the bar. *The new location is less broken-in than the place I first visited.* She's comfortable with the reassessment. Truth is, she's avoided stopping in since they moved, a silent protest against creeping gentrification. The spot was Whistler's choice because it's not far from his office and not a cop bar.

She and Whistler played together at family barbecues from the time they could walk, wearing nothing but saggy diapers and sporting matching toddler tummies. Now, because of their chosen careers, they are at odds. She believes the police feel entitled to act with impunity and box out the press in an attempt to hide nefarious actions. Conversely, she knows Whistler worries that the press, and by extension Moe, second-guess events after the fact and intentionally make cops look bad. Despite that, she hopes they can come to terms. She tries not to take it personally when he treats her as a necessary evil. *He acts like his job is important and mine is just frivolous. As if a free press isn't the cornerstone of any healthy democracy.* Her irritation wins out. She finishes her second bottle of Blues Brew and slams it on the table, preparing to leave.

Whistler rushes in the front door. She settles back in her seat. *At least he has the sense to look like he's in a hurry.*

There is no cover charge to listen to local musicians tinker on stage in the afternoon. Neither is there a bouncer on duty. The metal detector sounds, and Whistler shows his badge. The woman at the front counter waves him in, gun and all. Moe stands so he can find her at the far end of the long, dark room. It was the least conspicuous spot she could find. He jogs a little to get to her.

"Sorry I'm late. Can't stay long. I've got a meeting with the squad. Thanks for texting. I was so scrambled I forgot about your lead."

"No worries," she says, attempting to sound casual. "I made use of the time, finished my article, drank a couple beers. Want one?"

"I shouldn't. Yes. One beer. When I finish, I gotta get back."

Moe waves to the server, watches her swivel her hips in time to the walking bass of the two-piece on stage. The server is named Molly. Moe thinks she's straight, but she's been flirting with Moe: complimenting Moe's boots, her hair, her cheekbones, and lingering for conversation each time she was near the table. Moe understands it's to run up a tip. She'd done her time as a server during college. Moe has enjoyed the mock flirtation. Now that Whistler is here, Molly isn't sure who to flirt with. She keeps it basic. "Need another beer?"

"Make it two, please." Whistler takes charge, seems unaware that the server wasn't addressing him. "And a burger. You do burgers, right?"

"How do you want it?" Molly asks.

"Medium well. Cheddar. That's all. No tomato or onion."

"It comes with fries. You can substitute onion rings for two dollars."

"Fries are fine. How long will it take?"

"Not long." Molly struts away.

"Moe. If you have something on the case, just tell me."

In reply, she opens her laptop and passes it across the table. "Read this. If you see problems, let me know. I want to get it right."

He's bothered, but he reads.

About halfway through the article, the beers come. He swigs and reads for a few minutes longer. He sits back. "Is this right?"

"I spoke with neighbors and coworkers. Read the reports and what little press there was. Made a few calls. Brina Flores has worked at the laundry of the International for a decade. After her daughter, Virginia, finished high school, her mom found her a job there too. Sometime in the past six months, Ginny met an older man. She started seeing him. He gave her gifts, including a gold necklace. She got pregnant. He ghosted her completely. She goes home early from work one morning, probably with morning sickness—"

"And is attacked in the alley behind her home, left strangled next to a dumpster," Whistler finishes in disbelief.

"Homicide moved on for lack of evidence. It's still open. But my source says no one's chasing it down. The mother's legal status is iffy, and she didn't want to draw attention. With no leads, no pressure, and plenty of squeakier wheels—"

"Holy hell, Moe. The similarities are hard to ignore." He takes a long pull of his beer; it foams in his mouth, and he chokes, coughs, and wipes his chin. "This is great. I can't believe it. Well written, Moe."

"It's what I do? I told you I had something." She plays it tough but relishes the compliment. The respect of her cousin means more than she expected.

The server shows up with a burger, greasy fries falling off the sides of the plate. "There you go. Anything else?"

"No," Moe says.

"I'll take another beer," Whistler says. "You want one, Moe?"

"Mine's still full."

Whistler knocks the mouth of his brown bottle against the neck of Moe's. He drinks the bottle dry. He manhandles the burger, shoves a giant bite in his face, and his eyes roll back in his head, practically orgasmic. "Oh mah glod"—his mouth full of food—"thith ith tho good." He finishes chewing. "Help yourself to fries."

Moe nibbles a fry. It's fresh and too hot, but she eats it anyway. "The details connecting Anna Beth to Ginny are legit, right?"

"Sure. It's circumstantial. But convincing."

"You think the point about resources being allotted to a dead white girl while none being spent on the dead brown girl is a reach?"

"I mean . . . it's more complicated than you make it out. First, it wasn't a white girl. She was a woman. So that's something that doesn't fit. Right? Age difference."

"I thought of that. But it doesn't have anything to do with the point I'm making. Does it?"

"No. Not directly. It's just the implication is intentional racism. That's not fair. I mean . . ." he takes another bite of burger, with less enthusiasm.

Moe tosses another fry in her mouth, rubs her palms together to brush away the salt and oil. "What do you mean? No, wait. I see what you mean. You mean you're a sellout. A shiny badge so important to you? A pat on the head by Inspector Ruther and you roll right over to have your tummy scratched. Now that you're on the payroll you can't criticize the system you're beholden to."

"Come on, Moe," Whistler says plaintively.

"*You* come on. Look at this." She brings up her previous article. "Maria Reyes, strangled same as Anna Beth. I barely looked into the case and can guess it was someone she knew, probably the custodian who called it in. But there was no follow-through." She pulls her computer back, taps and scrolls. "This girl, Precious Sharpe, spelling bee champ and sings in the church choir. It's an open secret that people think her ex, Ronnie, killed her and left town. The case was dropped. Not for lack of leads—for lack of resources. You read these and tell me it's not a race thing. Read the statistics. It's right there. Numbers don't lie. Politicians lie. Police lie. Statistics are statistics." She points to her screen.

Whistler pushes the remainder of his food away. "Right now I'm trying to find one killer. Not close every similar case from across the whole city. You make some good points about a broken system. I'm trying to make it work better. What do you want from me? Tell me. What do you want?" He's getting mad, his stomach churning. He pounds his chest with his fist and works up a belch.

"I want you to be different. I expect it."

Molly is back with his second beer. He says, "Cheers, Moe," but he doesn't mean it. He takes a long pull, sets it aside unfinished. "I gotta go."

"Whistler, goddamnit. Damn, Whistler. Come on—we had a fucking deal. I gave you something. Give me something in return."

"What?"

"Something about the woman in Printer's Row. I need to keep the narrative going."

"Glad it's about the victims. You sure you can trust a sellout like me? I don't even care about justice." He burps again, looks uncomfortable.

"Don't be a baby."

Whistler puts both fists on the tabletop and leans across. His voice is a whisper with a warning growl. He says, "The Mexican American woman attacked today, Rosa Zhang, is a brown person the department is spending time and resources on. The newest detective in CPD is Mexican American, he's busting his ass, and he's your fucking cousin. Publish that."

"You think you scare me? You don't scare me, Mister Big Time. I don't scare."

"What scares me is you think you're the arbiter of right and wrong. You think you know the answers before you even know the right questions."

Moe can't form a response. She closes her laptop.

He takes her silence as his cue to leave. After three long steps, he stops to gain his composure. He sits down again. The growl is gone when he says, "We brought in the man who found Zhang. You're right.

He's a strange one. Used to be a doctor of something academic at U of Chicago. Had some kind of head injury. Now he does bed bug remediation. Guess where?" He answers his own question: "The International."

"No way."

"Problem is, he hasn't been with the company long enough to connect to Anna Beth's attack. Also, I'd say he doesn't have it in him."

"Everyone has it in them."

Whistler ignores her, his voice rising above the blues shuffle coming from stage. "His partner, Allen Schmidt, has a record, spent time in the pen. I'd put my money on him. He's shifty. He's tied loosely to three attacks."

"Something's not right with this Greene," Moe says, not buying Whistler's insistence on Allen's guilt. "Sophia pronounced him a hero. All the other outlets ran similar stories. But he's off. I don't like him."

"You're not listening. I'm giving you information. We have the perp in our sights. We are building a case."

"Maybe they're both in on it? You said they were partners."

He frowns. "Listen, Moe. You're the authority on truth and ethics. Write whatever you want. The future of our democracy depends on it. I'm trying to follow the law so we can convict a killer. That's all. I'm not single-handedly saving the American way of life. I'm not a crusader." He stands, throws a twenty on the table. "We should really do this again sometime. Really." He stalks away.

On stage, the song ends, and the singer says, "Thank you. I'm Reverend Raven and this is one of the Chain-Smoking Alter Boys. We're going to take five, but we'll be back with a whole lot of blues."

Moe watches the bright flash of afternoon sun strike Whistler when he steps outside.

"Shit," Moe says. "Shit shit shit."

Whistler Center Stage

"**Y**ou are one CH away from missing your own briefing," Wendell says from his raised perch behind the counter. He holds up a leathery finger and thumb with a tiny fraction of space between to demonstrate how small a measurement one CH must be. His jowls dangle. He expects Whistler to take the bait, but he's disappointed.

"No time for your bullshit," Whistler says and hoofs it up the stairs.

The accusations Moe made weigh on him. *I'm a good guy. I mean well. I do my best.* But he can feel the pressure of the institution, of its history, and his peers in opposition to the pressure he puts on himself to prove his loyalty to his neighborhood—two sides crushing him into something harder and meaner than he wants to be. His expectations of detective life don't match his day-to-day experiences so far. *I may not be cut out for detective any more than I was for patrolman.*

Being around Moe always makes him existential. He hates that. She has a real knack for needling his most tender spots.

He strides through the squad room, ignores the eyes on him. He gets to conference room two in time to get an update from Suzuki before the rest of the crew follow Ruther in for the scheduled briefing.

Whistler waits while people settle. Ruther takes a seat up front. Suzuki leans half his ass on the corner of a table. There are two detectives that Whistler still hasn't met. He expects Ruther to say a few words, introduce him, and give him some guidance; he doesn't.

Whistler takes a deep breath and steps forward. "Thanks, everyone. For those of you who don't know, I'm Detective Diaz. I'm new to the squad. Detective Suzuki and I caught what the press is calling the Magnificent Mile Strangler case."

One of the men Whistler doesn't know, a blocky man in a short sleeved shirt a size too small, is leaning his back on the doorframe. At the mention of Suzuki, he cups his hand and booms, "Zucchini!"

Suzuki flips off the detective to general chuckling.

Whistler keeps talking. He lays out the attack that morning at Coffee Girl. He talks about how it relates to Anna Beth Harpole's murder. Ruther seems to pay no attention. He gets to the new developments. "I've discovered a third case. Ginny Flores, an employee at the International, found strangled next to a dumpster over a month ago."

Ruther is suddenly alert. The guy at the back quits leaning against the wall. Suzuki lifts his whole ass off the table.

"This establishes a pattern of increasing frequency. There was nearly a month between Ginny Flores and Anna Beth. Ten days between Anna Beth and the Rosa Zhang attack. One thing they have in common, besides the nature of the attack, is a possible association with Allen Schmidt. Allen is an employee of Bug Off pest control under contract with both the Echelon and the International. He's training Calvert Greene, the press's hero of the day. Schmidt has a record: he broke his aunt's neck by shoving her down a staircase. Convicted of manslaughter. We have a potential missing trophy from the Harpole case. We may find a personal item was taken from Ginny." There is grumbling and shifting from the squad. "If so, we have a textbook serial strangler."

"Hold the fucking phone," Ruther says. He stands. "Listen up, hotshot. We don't need to turn this into more of a mess. Please, for the love of God in heaven above, no one utter the words 'serial strangler' to anyone outside this room. Or inside this room. Don't mumble it in your sleep. Don't have cereal for breakfast until this case is closed. I'm going to take the lead, Diaz. You and Suzuki can step back. I'm running this now. Sit the fuck down."

Whistler's whole head goes hot, his forehead starts to perspire, and he clenches his jaw and balls his hands into fists. He sees his mistake. He sprang the Ginny situation on Ruther. He wanted to impress the squad, maybe get some respect, at least get Ruther to pay attention. He wanted to prove something to Moe. He looks into Ruther's red face. His mustache is out of control. Any lingering intention to defend himself, to speak at all, evaporates absolutely. He exhales heavily and sinks into an empty seat.

Ruther steps up front. "I'll give assignments. We'll build the case. I'll consult the district attorney. We'll make an arrest when we have enough to convict. Until then, no press. None. Diaz, I heard from a bald blackbird that you had a tête-à-tête with a certain dyke reporter."

"She's my cousin," he tries to explain. His voice is quiet and hoarse. His throat has started to close up. "She wanted to congratulate me."

"Well, congratu-fucking-lations. Don't talk to any of your thousand cousins or second cousins or grandparents or your priest until this case is in the win column. Okay?"

Whistler loosens his tie and can only manage a stiff nod in response.

Private Exhibition

Calvert uses a tiny key to unlock the door of his mailbox. His fingers fumble the fine motor movement. He drops the key. His fast-twitch muscles grudgingly engage, and he snatches the key before it can hit the floor. The mailbox opens. It is empty. He hinges it closed and methodically walks the long flight of steps to the second floor. His legs are dead. The toe end of his loafers brush the worn bullnose of each tread as he steps up. The day had been a trial for a man with truncated emotional capacity. His meager reserves of energy have boiled off, leaving him dried out and empty. He uses a larger key to unlock the door to his apartment, finds he didn't lock it again. Once inside, he slumps onto his oversoft mattress, certain that merciful, absolute death is about to take him.

After finding Rosa's body, and his subsequent painful attempt to work up a single tear, he spent hours being shuttled around and asked questions. Finally he, a confused Daisy in her crate, and an edgy Allen were dropped back at the van and allowed to go to work. He exhales to push the bitter air from his lungs. There is knocking at his door. He draws the old air back in, stands on his dying feet, and shuffles to the door. His neighbor the man-bear is there, holding a smoldering joint and taking up most of the doorway.

"Saw you on the news. You're a regular savior." His easy beatific grin seeps smoke into the claustrophobic hallway.

"I was on the news?"

"You were the main story the whole livelong day. You remember talking to that loud reporter? The one with the cleavage."

Calvert recalls the bright light in his eyes, the microphone pushed under his chin. He remembers letting words spill out. He gives a nod.

"I'm getting off track. That's not why I'm here. The co-op kids put together an exhibition, and we could have a crowd later tonight. Maybe you've seen the fliers?"

"I have not."

Man-bear puts a flier in Calvert's hand. It reads "Fluxus Flotsam Studio Happening. Things Believed." The flier is photocopied in black on goldenrod paper. The text is formed from random letters cut from magazines, like a ransom note in a B movie. The words are strewn higgledy-piggledy over a snapshot of a woman dressed in black rubber, holding a Bible across her chest and a flashlight above her head, a pose reminiscent of the Statue of Liberty. Under the image, the address, date, and time are listed.

"I see," Calvert says, not certain what the flier means or how to respond.

"It's a fundraiser for our trip to the Far Afield Fest—the Great Lake's Burning Man. The thing is, I hope you'll be cool. I'll try to keep it down. The kids are into nineties hip-hop, and they can only play it loud. Sorry."

"I'm not bothered by things, really. Death lends perspective."

"I bet it does. Forgot you were dead. I'm Barney, if I didn't say so last time." He waits for Calvert to share his name. Calvert does not share. "I forgot your name."

"Calvert," he says it like his tongue isn't used to the feel of it.

"Right. I heard on the news. I'd forget my own head if it wasn't sewn on. Maybe. I should lay off the weed. Screwing up my memory." He gazes at the joint, waves it in the air, leaving a pale wisp that quickly curls into nothing. "Nah. Who am I kidding?" He chuckles and smokes a little more weed. "Okay, then. Thanks again. I'll see you." He turns halfway. "Hey, Calvert. You wouldn't want to see the stuff we made, would you?"

There's something about Barney that reminds Calvert of his grandfather Harry. Calvert misses Harry. "Yes," he says. "I want that."

"Right this way," Barney says.

The hall into the co-op is narrow with low light. Barney leads him around a corner and into an eight-foot-square room. A series of clip lights are aimed at a raised platform that resembles a screened porch attached to a gray clapboard house. A dark-skinned man stands next to them as they enter; his head is a mass of bouncing dreadlocks threaded with thick strands of multicolored yarn.

"This is Andrew," Barney says. "Andrew, my new neighbor, Calvert. I'm giving him a preview."

"Cool," Andrew says, his voice soft and high. "I've got to make a run to Loco Taco and put a burrito in my body. Cool meeting you, Calvert. See you around." He sniffs and catches sight of the joint in Barney's hand. "Oh man, can I get a hit off that spliff?"

Barney passes it over. Andrew draws three short sips and holds it tight, his chin tucked against his chest. Andrew tries to pass the joint to Calvert; Calvert shakes his head no. Andrew mouths, "Cool." Smoke leaks around the edges of the word. Barney takes the joint and smokes a bit more. "Before you go, you should tell Calvert about your installation."

Andrew exhales a personal fogbank. He begins to speak but is interrupted by a hacking cough followed by sputtering aftershocks. Eventually he says, "It's called Night Time Revival. Let me know what you think. Sorry, I gotta jet." Andrew lopes away.

Calvert and Barney listen to the apartment door open and close, the quick steps of Andrew's unlaced boots beating down the stairs. These sounds dissipate and subtler noises rise. Night sounds: crickets on a breeze, a shallow creek babbling over water-worn rocks, and the periodic punctuation of a dog's distant baying.

Barney watches Calvert and smiles a jolly smile. "So, take a look around," he says with a wink.

The installation is not like any art Calvert remembers. But his brain has lost knowledge like water through a colander. He notes a cognitive dislocation caused by the scene, by the sounds that transport him out of the city. Making sense of art is an exercise in futility. He opts to take it as it comes.

Barney pulls the porch door open, a long spring screeches as it's stretched. Calvert's feet are loud on the aged-looking porch steps. Barney lets the door smack closed. Small objects, hundreds of them, are strewn haphazardly over low church-pews that circle the perimeter of the porch. Calvert takes a closer look. The objects are religious figurines, crosses, household items, small booklets, and Bibles.

"Andrew collected these," Barney explains. He lifts a white plastic church with a tall steeple, a coin slot cut in the roof's ridge. Barney places it in Calvert's hand.

Calvert turns it and reads the inscription along one side: "Luke 12:15: Then he said to them, 'Watch out! Be on your guard against all kinds of greed; a man's life does not consist in the abundance of his possessions.'" He finds the scripture a confusing thing to print on a bank. He turns it over, looking for an answer.

"The Bible is full of stuff about the evils of money and the quiet dignity of being poor and meek," Barney explains. "But congregations run on money, and some preachers get wealthy spreading the good word. Capitalism holding hands with Christianity makes for a complicated relationship. Some might call it irony. Others might see it as hypocrisy."

Calvert puts the plastic church in its spot and picks up a bar of soap. "Have clean hands and a pure heart. Psalm 24:4" is pressed into its oblong side. He runs his fingers over the words, feels the deep relief, the dry surface pulling the moisture from the tips of his dying skin. It feels like his fingerprints might peel away, leaving him smooth as a newborn. Reborn.

He slowly moves counterclockwise along the pews, reading some things, skipping others. A few minutes later he returns to where he entered.

Barney waits, finishing his joint. He pinches the last bit of black-ened paper between his fingers and slips it into the front pocket of his overalls. He clears his throat and asks, "You think these things elevate faith, or you think they cheapen it?"

Calvert feels a reverence for the space. He doesn't want to speak for fear he'll break the spell. Very quietly he replies, "It may do both."

Barney nods and walks out the door, and the spring screeches; Calvert's footsteps resonate across the make-believe geography of a south-ern night. Calvert lets the door slap when he follows Barney out.

They turn into a similarly sized space where the walls are covered in evenly spaced color photos. In the center of the room is a collection of headless dress forms set at different heights. Each is costumed in elaborate black rubber outfits. There's a red vinyl couch along the far wall where two women sleep, legs entwined, one of them snoring softly. Barney places a shushing finger over his lips, and Calvert understands he shouldn't wake the couple.

"That's Lyla and Sandra. They were up all night getting the exhi-bition ready," Barney says quietly. "Lyla is the photographer. Sandra makes the clothes." Calvert nods. He recognizes Sandra from the gold-enrod flier.

Calvert moves around the room. He studies the first few pho-tos at length, attempting to decode the meaning. They are overhead shots of people on a sidewalk below a building, this building, probably taken out the window of this apartment. By the third piece, realization dawns: they capture people hunching over their smartphones, ignoring the people they walk beside, their children, their pets, their lovers. They are arranged chronologically, taken over the course of one day, start-ing in the early morning and moving until the sun has set. He finds himself watching the evolution of one particular shadow cast by one particular tree. The shape, direction, and scale of the shadow changes only slightly between some images, drastically between others.

When he reaches the couch, out of consideration he only takes a glance at the photos over the sleeping couple. He turns his attention to the display in the middle of the room. Each dress form has rubber clothing: a shirt, a jacket, vest, belt, or skirt. They are paired with backpacks, fanny packs, and messenger bags. Every item is fabricated from woven bike inner tubes, complete with strategically placed clusters of valve stems.

Barney gestures and Calvert follows him to the next room, where he finds a long table made of old doors dropped in a roughly welded angle iron frame, surrounded by mismatched chairs, no two alike. Dangling over the table is a cluster chandelier of oversized, side-mounted headlights, mostly rust pitted and dented, but rewired and working well. Against one wall sits a fifties-era juke box with most of the lights glowing. Further into the apartment is a kitchen with mismatched appliances.

Barney points to the table. "We'll have wine if you want to come have a drink later?"

"I can't get drunk since I died."

"I see. Well, we got a couple more rooms."

They pass the kitchen, move down a hall past a bathroom, and enter a space that's part bedroom and part art studio. "This," says Barney, "is my room."

Calvert nods.

"I don't make art. I make things. Those things are an extension of who I am. They are a record of my life, a creative document. There's no division between my living space and my working space. I don't exhibit. I invite people into my life."

Calvert likes what Barney has to say. He doesn't think he could be an artist, but perhaps he could make things. *If I weren't dead, I might like to try.* "What kinds of things do you make?"

"Let me show you." Barney walks to a chest of drawers that has a top that's a workbench. He takes a round tin from a shelf and pulls off the lid. "This," he says, holding it for Calvert to see, "is textile ink. Pantone Silver. Smell it?" Barney smells the ink to demonstrate. "I love that smell."

"I can't really smell things," Calvert says.

"Too bad." Barney takes up a putty knife and carefully sticks it into the open tin. He turns the tin while holding the knife still and scrapes an even portion from the entire surface of the ink. "Never gouge the ink, Calvert. Don't be that guy. Promise me you won't be an ink gouger."

"I promise."

"Do you know what happens when you gouge ink?"

"It hurts the ink?"

"Maybe its feelings. I'm kidding." He winks. "It lets in air and you get hard spots. Next thing, you've wasted a can of ink. It's tragic to waste supplies. Tragic."

Barney shows Calvert the shiny glob of smooth ink on the end of the metal blade. He works without speaking for long minutes. He wipes ink onto a thick slab of glass and begins spreading it out and scraping it up, over and over in a steady, hypnotic rhythm. When he's happy with the consistency, he takes a hand roller from a hook and spreads the ink flat. The roller runs over the viscous ink making a sticky hiss. Barney carries the roller to a waist-high surface filled with wood block letters. He lets the roller kiss the top of each letter, first in a series of vertical strokes, then a series of horizontal motions. He sets the roller aside. "What size T-shirt do you wear?"

"Medium," Calvert says.

Barney reaches under the worktable and pulls out a black tee stretched over a shirt-shaped board. "One medium shirt," Barney says. He slides the shirt and board into a slot. "Come pull this handle, nice and firm." Calvert steps beside Barney. Barney explains, "I made this press. I made the letters. A hardwood called holly wood works best. It's a clamshell press. You pull this handle, the letters tip up, the shirt tips up, they meet flat in the middle. Clap!" He claps his meaty palms with a loud crack. "Okay. So, pull this."

Calvert pulls the long lever, and the two halves clap together. He lets the handle return to its resting position, and the shirt has a phrase printed in silver over black: "The wages of sin beats minimum wage."

"There," Barney says, and he places a big hand on Calvert's back. "We made a shirt. How's that feel?"

"Like a magic trick," Calvert replies.

"Exactly," Barney agrees.

The Point

Moe slips into the bench seat across from Whistler. Her cousin is drinking Goose Island Honkers and eating chips with guac. "I wasn't sure what you'd want to drink. I went ahead and got chips." Whistler gives a wave to the server, points at Moe.

"Thanks for meeting again," Moe says. "Sorry how lunch went down. Besides, I promised you a meal." She digs through the chips until she spots the kind she likes: a little brown, still warm, folded over on itself in the fryer, and extra salty. *Asymmetrical beauty.* With great satisfaction, she scrapes the singularly irregular chip through her favorite chunky guacamole.

"Listen," Whistler says, "you were right. I'm sick. Literally my guts are in knots with this case. I want to do good. That's why I became a cop. But my new job is ostensibly to keep the mayor's office happy. Our mayor, being a politician, is mostly concerned with appearances. Don't get me wrong. I like the guy. But working people, real people, always get the short end of the stick in the game of politics. Whose city is it? High-rise citizens and out-of-towners? Or real fucking people?"

Moe clucks her tongue in solidarity.

The server approaches the table.

Whistler takes an angry swig of beer.

The server has a dapper waxed mustache twisted into a turned-up fishhook over each end of his thin lips. "What can I get you?" he asks Moe.

She avoids gazing directly at him. "I'll have a Golden Margarita. Rocks and salt. In a mug. And we'll take two shots of tequila with a plate of limes. Got all that?"

"Got it. Will you be sticking with chips?"

Whistler swigs more beer.

Moe says, "We'll decide on food later."

A lady at a nearby table taps her plastic menu and calls to their server. "This says the special is tacos de lengua. I don't know how to say it. What is that?"

"Excuse me a second," the server says.

Moe watches him leave and says, "Too bad."

"What?" Whistler asks.

"Too bad we gotta find a new Mexican joint."

"What for?"

"Hipster infestation."

"And suburban moms," he adds, cracking a smile.

The server comes back, "Another Honkers?"

"Why the hell not," Whistler says. "We're getting drunk."

"So look," Moe says, "I was tough on you. I'm upset. We have so much violent crime. Highest it's been since 1998. I'm a journalist, you know. I want to write about the problem, report solutions, and make a difference. You know, change things.

The dandy server comes back with drinks. "Wave me down when you're ready for food."

"You bet," Whistler replies.

Moe realizes Fancy Lad didn't bring limes. *That fucking mustache and poor service.* "Where was I?" She licks salt from the rim of her glass and takes a gulp of margarita, spills a bit down her chin and onto her chest. She pats her T-shirt dry with a napkin. "Mmm. That's good. The answer to our problems may be more booze."

"I'm coming around to that," Whistler says.

"What I was saying, though," Moe says. "As if it matters, no one wants to read those stories. Nothing I do matters one damn bit. The name of the game is quick sensationalism. The thing is to be first. If you're first to print, you win. I'm fucking tired of it."

Whistler nods. He shovels in a chip piled high with guacamole.

Moe goes on. "Aggregated social media news silos and a national piss-poor attitude about the free press. It's a terrible time to do what I do.

Whistler speaks while he chews, "Maybe it's exactly the right time to do what you do. Bad times are when journalists have the most impact."

Moe gulps half her margarita. "Maybe. In school I got romantic ideas about social crusades. That kind of journalism doesn't take place in the real world. It's academic bullshit so professors can have some-thing aspirational to talk about. But it's a big lie. In the real world, con-tent is secondary. Truth is rarely discussed."

"You were full of idealism at lunch." He points a loaded chip at her.

"I was full of something." The grin in her voice doesn't reach her lips.

He crunches a chip and part of it falls. He catches the errant bit in his palm and pops it back in his mouth. "You were about to lead a revolution earlier. What the hell? If you've given up, what chance do us mortals have?"

Moe looks bashful, smiles fully, and pushes a shot glass in Whis-tler's direction. He doesn't go for it right away. She tries to explain. "Two things: one is I got a raise. I'm on staff now."

"Way to go," Whistler slaps her a loud high-five.

"Yay me," she says with no enthusiasm. "Thing of it is, I'm helping these two kids right out of school. They are a pain in my ass. But the issue is, I'm starting to doubt journalism. Every time I help them, I feel like I'm perpetuating the same lie I fell for."

Whistler starts to object. She plows ahead. "And two: a few weeks ago, I got a text from Vivian about a shooting. Two people shot in a drive-by."

Whistler is starting to feel loose. He opens his yap to ask something silly. He sees by the look on Moe's face he's missing the point. He keeps quiet.

"One of those people was Candice Flores. She was the first girl I had a crush on. She never knew. Anyway, after high school she got married, had a baby, and was shot in a parking lot while dropping her boy at day care. Stray bullet. No reason. Random as fuck. A little boy's mom is dead. Candy is dead. I showed up cold. Found out who it was. Completely lost my shit. Here's the thing. I'm not going to write about it. Not because of our connection; because I'm spending my time convincing you to help me so I can build a story about a white man who saved a Chicana. Why? It supports stories I already wrote about the attack on the Harpole woman north of the river. In other words, white woman killed in the North Loop equals story. White man is a hero in the South Loop—there's a story. Mother shot in Little Village dropping off her toddler—not worth the ink."

Suburban Mom glances her way.

Moe lowers her voice, "Worst of all, it's me. I want to write stories other outlets will circulate. I'm invested in making *Text Block* a success. It's me. I'm selling out. What's happening to me? I didn't even have the balls to write a tribute about Candy."

"You've got balls, Moe. You've got giant girl balls." He holds out both hands and hefts imaginary oversized girl balls. She gives a polite smile. "Lookit, cuz, I feel you." He slams his shot of tequila, wipes his lips with the back of his hand, and washes it down with a swig of beer. "Last week I met this girl. First thing she asked: What do you do? I hate that because I know soon as I tell her I'm a cop, she won't see me anymore. Everyone has an opinion on cops."

Moe licks salt from the edge of her margarita, lifts her shot glass in a salute to a shared sense of hopelessness.

Whistler tips his beer. "So I told her. Then she asks, 'Why would you want to be a cop?' I gave her some lame answer to keep it light. But later I thought about it."

"Was she cute?"

"Pretty cute. She smelled good."

"Was she into you?'

"Not really. I won't call her back."

"You think she might be into me? I can be very charming." Moe winks badly.

"Really? You should be charming sometime so I know what it's like."

"Sorry I interrupted."

"It's okay. Listen though, that reminds me: the victim next to the dumpsters. There was a perfume smell. It was flowery, and a little chemical. Her boss's wife said Anna Beth was sensitive to smells. Allergic or something."

"I guess dying next to a dumpster was especially insulting."

"I guess so. Where was I? I ever tell you the worst thing I had to do on patrol? Man versus car homicide. The victim's girlfriend took his PlayStation controllers and drove off while he was in the bathroom. She threw the game controls out the car at an intersection. The boyfriend ran after her, dodged traffic, and snatched his gear. The girlfriend turned her car around and drove down the sidewalk after him. She hit a homeless woman digging in the trash and a dad wearing an infant in a sling. My job was to sort body parts into evidence bags. That's when I realized patrolman was not for me. That's why I started studying for detective.

"You never told me."

"It wasn't noble. I couldn't stand the job I went to school for. I was desperate. I was afraid." Whistler scrapes the remnants of guacamole from the bowl with his finger.

They drink in silence for a while, watch a couple of men in ball caps take up space in the next booth.

Moe digs for another folded chip among the boring average chips.

"Oh," Whistler adds. "Guess what?"

"What?"

"You got a raise, I got demoted. The case isn't mine anymore. Ruther is lead. I told the whole squad about Ginny Flores and her tie to the first murder. They think I want to be a superstar."

"Shit, shit, and shit," Moe says.

"That about sums it up."

"Okay," Moe says. She waves to the server. "Where does that leave us? You thought you got an important job, and it turns out you're keeping the city's image spotless for the mayor. I'm a queer idealist, in a non-ideal world for a queer on a crusade. What's the fucking point? Careful what you wish for, I guess. Francis and Sebastian are so proud of us. They think you get a degree and you're on Easy Street. They worked hard to give us this chance. What the fuck do we do? I'm really asking you. I'm lost. I don't know what to do. Just tell me."

Whistler shrugs. But he keeps turning the question over in his head.

They order tacos and another round of shots.

They crunch on more chips and guac. Finally Whistler says, "If we don't do what's right, no one else will. We make a stand. We fight the good fight."

"How do we do that?" Moe asks.

"We solve this case. We find this killer before he kills anyone else."

Surreal Confessional

Calvert steps away from the homemade printing press and watches Barney work.

"We can dry this shirt right now. That way you can take it with you," Barney says. He grabs the freshly made letterpress tee, board and all, and slides it into a waiting cabinet. He closes doors and turns on mismatched hair dryers mounted along the cabinet's base. "There," he says. "Ten minutes and the ink should be set. Want a drink?"

"Water is fine."

Barney flips the lid of a steel Coleman cooler, its retro-red paint worn nearly away. He pulls a wet bottle out and plunges his arm back in, stirring the contents and fishing for a bottle of water. "No water," he says. "I've got pale ale."

"I can't get drunk."

"So you said. Have a beer with me. It'll wet your whistle as good as a water. And you won't get a bit drunk."

Calvert considers Barney, and not for the first time, he finds the big artist's words full of uncommon sense. "Okay."

Barney rattles through a drawer of tools, digging for something. "So, this whole dead thing? What's that about? You're the first dead guy I've spent much time with."

Since the visit to his old apartment, Calvert has slowly managed to reassemble the pieces of his spotty past. He considers how much he's willing to admit to a stranger. How much he's willing to admit to himself. Not knowing Barney makes it easier. He says, "I was hurt because of something foolish I did. There was an incident. I died and never recovered. My doctors tell me it happens now and then. Though rarely."

"So you are special?" Barney finds a pair of needle-nose pliers and pries the crimped edges of the bottle's cap.

"I'm a biological anomaly. No big deal. It will run its course."

"I see." Barney passes Calvert an open bottle, knocks the mouth of his bottle into the side of Calvert's. "'May God grant you the desires of your heart and make all your plans succeed.' Psalms 20:4." He slumps on his mattress with a heavy sigh and drinks.

Calvert sits on an ink-speckled library chair. "You know a lot of scripture. I wouldn't have thought you were religious. I don't know why. Maybe all the marijuana?"

"Yes. There is the marijuana." Barney chuckles kindly. "Well, psalms is more like poetry than scripture. I love me some psalms. But—complete disclosure—I grew up very devout. I still believe we have a soul. When I was young, I planned on becoming a preacher. My father was a traveling preacher for The Church of God of Prophecy and Evangelism. You heard of it?"

"Not that I recall." Calvert drinks some beer. It has no taste, but it's cold like well water and makes his teeth throb.

"I'm not surprised. Not many that aren't members have heard of it. But there used to be a lot of us." The big man drinks beer and gets a far-off look.

"I wasn't a bad preacher's kid, like you hear about. I carried a Bible with me everywhere I went. I prayed when I woke. I prayed at every meal. I prayed before bed. If I passed someone coughing, I'd ask if I could pray for them to have a fast recovery. If I met somebody that seemed sad, I'd kneel with them and ask for God to lift the burden from their shoulders. I was a true believer. But it all came apart. I was shunned by my father, my family, and my church." Barney peeks to see if he's got Calvert's attention. Calvert swigs his beer and waits.

Barney picks at the damp edge of the label on his beer. "When I was fourteen, my family landed in North Carolina, Burlington area. We were staying with people from the local congregation, and one night we watched a news show from a nearby town called Graham. There was a disco club on the outskirts where a man got jazzed on drugs and shot another man to death. Shot him lots of times: once in his hand, his side, his foot, and finally in the side of the head."

Calvert scoots his chair closer to Barney.

"My father was transfixed by the news. That night he stood with the TV flashing behind him, and he touched his palms in the center of each hand, he touched his side, he touched his temple. He said, 'That dead man was marked as Christ on the cross. The crucifixion marks in his hands and feet, the spear in the side, the crown of thorns at his temple.' He declared it a message from the Holy Spirit. Three months later, my father had scraped together enough money to rent that disco and started to build a permanent congregation. To his mind, it was a miraculous happening to preach where people used to drink and deal drugs. It was proof of God's goodness to pray where people once came to fornicate. He liked to say it was a sinful place of vice and violence, and the transformative power of the blood of Christ washed away all evil.

"Sunday mornings, he tore it up from behind a section of the old bar that he'd cut into a pulpit. There was a spinning disco ball in the center of the ceiling, and my dad was happy to leave it as a reminder of the mystery of God's power." Barney peels the label from his beer in one wide, damp sheet, holds it crumpled in a curl of his fingers, and tips the bottle to his lips.

"You said you were shunned? What happened?" Again, Calvert scoots a bit closer to the big man, the chair legs stutter across the cupped floorboards.

"The honest answer is sex. Sex with Trina May."

"Trina May was my father's favorite kind of congregant. She grew up a church girl, went away to evil Boston, got mixed up in drinking, and bad relationships. Then she came back to the Lord, confessed, was baptized, and was born again, *praise be to God.* I barely noticed her the first few months. Until, one Sunday service when my father asked her to share her testimony. She rose and that exact moment the sun caught the disco ball. She began talking about how empty all her sins left her, how only the lord could fill her. Her face was marked by slowly spinning colored flecks sliding over her mouth, moving across her throat, slipping down her chest over her blouse buttoned up to her collarbone. I watched her every movement, and I wanted her so hard.

"In a few weeks, we were fucking every which way in her granny's basement. I don't mean to be crass, but that's how it was. It was nothing but naked lust. Next thing I know, she's pregnant. I'm scared to death. I stole money from the offering so she could get an abortion. But she goes to my father and confesses. He lets her keep the money so she can move. That night at home, he came at me in a rage, hit me with the family Bible, beat me until I couldn't stand. He disowned me. He told me to pack a bag. He wouldn't even let me say goodbye to my mother."

"Did Trina May have your baby?"

"I just don't know. I never found her again, never heard what happened. I have this feeling I have a baby girl somewhere in the great wide world. A girl like Lyla in there on the couch, curled up with someone she loves. Someone creative. I like to think she gets that from me. Someone wild and brave and passionate, who doesn't take any shit from any living soul. That she would've gotten from Trina May. But it's all in my head."

Calvert imagines the baby he nearly had. The unborn baby they called Bump. He always believed Bump was a little girl. *My little girl. What kind of person would she have been?*

His beer slips from his lax grip and strikes the floor, rolls in an arc, spreading a crescent of froth. He stands and his chair teeters. He rights it. He snatches up the bottle and looks for something to soak up the mess.

"Don't worry," Barney says, shoving off the bed. He throws a shop rag on the beer puddle. "It'll be fine." He takes the bottle from Calvert and sets it aside. "Let's check on this shirt of yours." He opens the drying cabinet and tests the ink with his fingers, pats it with his whole hand. "It's ready. Try that on for size." He pulls the shirt from the board.

Calvert holds it out and reads to himself: "The wages of sin beats minimum wage." He pulls it on over his coveralls.

Barney helps him straighten the shirt. "Consider it a gift."

"Thank you." Calvert looks down at the upside-down letters. "You think sin pays?"

"It's funny with a smidgeon of truth. That's about my speed. But if I still carry a version of my church learning with me, it's people's choices that create their circumstances. A person full of hate and meanness can outrun retribution for years. But eventually they pay. Psalm 7:16: 'The trouble they cause recoils on them; their violence comes down on their own heads.' Is karma evidence of God? I don't have an answer." He rubs his white whiskers thoughtfully, pulls a rolled joint from behind his left ear, and holds it with the side of his mouth as he goes on. "I'll tell you one thing though: I'm celibate. Have been since I was fifty. I figured Trina May didn't want me. She wanted to feel safe, loved, accepted. She wanted from sex what people want from belief, to be full of love. Don't get me wrong—we all know there are juicy hormones and physical drives at play. But spiritual fulfillment was what she wanted. Sex did that for me for a while. But it never lasted. I wanted something real and permanent from something fleeting. I thought sex was love. It's not. You know what a fetish is? It's when you worship one thing and imbue it with meanings that should be attributed elsewhere. For most of us, sex is a fetish in which we feel its love. I struggled with that for decades. Eventually I stopped expecting happiness from sex. Women were an unhealthy obsession. Giving up sex has made the past decade the most satisfying of my life."

Calvert stays quiet, letting the big man's words knock around in his brain.

Barney lights the joint bobbing in the corner of his mouth, draws on it, holds the twist of paper out, and assesses it at arm's length. He exhales and says, "No sex and lots of weed: that's my path to enlightenment. Now, let me show you one last thing."

Calvert travels in a slipstream of marijuana smoke down a narrow hall. He feels muzzy-headed. After the beer and weed smoke, he's reconsidering his assertion he can't get drunk or high.

Barney knocks on a closed door. "Christian. It's Barney. You all set?" In the pause that follows, Barney speaks to Calvert in low tones. "Christian calls this the Blake Machine. It's a trip. Do you know William Blake?"

"Sounds familiar." Calvert's mouth is dry, and he feels nervous and paranoid.

"Transcendence through transformation is the main theme of Christian's work. He's been transitioning for years." Calvert wants to ask from what Christian has been transitioning, and into what. But before he can form the question, a voice calls, "I'm ready." The voice has a quality Calvert would call "theatrical."

"This is Calvert," Barney calls. Then to Calvert: "Go on in. You won't see Christian. He'll give instructions. I'll be in my studio when you're done." He shoves his big body by Calvert, leaving a thick trail of smoke like a passing locomotive.

"You may enter," comes Christian's command. The cadence is exaggerated and dramatic.

Calvert reads a sign nailed to the door: "In the universe, there are things that are known, and things that are unknown, and in between, there are doors." He takes the cold knob in his fingers and twists. The hinges squeak and he enters a dimly lit room.

"Close the door," Christian calls.

The room has three black walls and one red. There is a waist-high contraption sitting toward the back of the room—an oversized erector set in the shape of a fireplug, surrounded by a rickety scaffold, peppered in light bulbs and draped in a jumble of wires and extension cords. A thick black electrical cord winds its way from the odd object to the center of the space, where it ends in a round, thick rubber pad. The way the cord meanders reminds Calvert of a fuse in a Loony Tunes cartoon.

"Step to the center of the room and face the red wall." The voice comes from the back corner. Near the contraption, a partition has been made from a shower curtain.

Calvert doesn't like the anxiety that comes with anticipation of the unknown. *I'm dead already. What's the worst that can happen?* He moves near the pad and faces the red wall, the contraption at his back.

"Stomp the foot switch."

Calvert steps on the pad with no effect.

"Press harder."

He leans his weight into it. Something gives under his foot. He hears a click. Lights come on behind him. A speaker he can't locate plays a quiet loop of a distressed infant's angry cry. Over his shoulder, the contraption comes to life, seems to unfold, lengthen, and stand tall. Small engines whir, gears and cogs spin, counterweights begin to swing, and long arms wave in the air. There is knocking and clacking. A building rhythm of random clatter converges into a syncopated chugging pattern. *As if Rube Goldberg designed a semaphore robot,* Calvert thinks. Though he can't recall who Rube Goldberg is or the purpose of semaphore flag waving.

"Don't watch the machine. Watch the red wall."

Calvert turns his eyes ahead. Initially, he notices nothing. Then he sees his shadow swell, surge up the wall, and wash back down. Moments later, again, his silhouette rushes into his field of vision, clearer this time, larger than life and dark as the sea rolling on a moonless night: Black figure on red wall. The swinging lights and waving arms behind him cause his likeness to dance in and out of focus, to leap and collapse, to materialize dense and firm, then dissolve into an ephemeral nonentity. The lurching lights are disorienting. The writhing of his intoxicated shadow-self is unnerving. His likeness has been hijacked and manipulated by a schizophrenic puppeteer. Calvert feels nauseous, motion sick. He doesn't trust he's on solid ground and rocks on his legs, trying to stay upright. The sounds of the machine fill the space and press like cupped hands over his ears. He tries to look back but can't turn away from the grotesque spectacle. Now his image swings across the wall with demonic horns. And now with wings of white. Those two incarnations of his body alternate—horned devil, winged angel, horned devil, winged angel—the frequency increasing, the metallic cacophony overwhelming his senses. His devil form bursts from one corner, and his angel self bursts from the other in broad violent movements, colliding and crashing in the center of the red wall. His eyes swing from side to side, following the personified battle of his internal intentions forever raging at cross-purposes. When he can take it no longer, the mechanical rhythm slows. The machine stops. Only one light remains, a bright spotlight capturing Calvert in its heart, displaying his isolated image on the red wall, static. The bulb turns off. Calvert glances nervously to see the device fold back on itself and slump into a stumpy automaton with poor posture.

"Come sit on the stool," Christian's dislocated voice demands. The melodramatic phrasing feels appropriate now. Calvert wants to sit. He walks to the corner and straddles a black stool, his left side to the shower curtain.

Christian's voice comes through the curtain, quieter now and very close to Calvert. "Blake said, 'Enlightenment means taking full responsibility for your life.' Transformation takes work. Share something good you've done but never shared, and something evil you've done but never uttered."

Calvert feels raw in the middle. His emotions have been scraped into a gooey mound with the hard edge of a spoon. He's aggravated. Scrubbed too hard from the inside out. Overstimulated. His innards are in an uproar, as if blasted with radiation. He wants to make the ache stop. He thinks of Rosa, of finding her nearly dead, of how little courage it takes to be brave when one is no longer alive. He's guilty for the attention he received. But there are other secrets that weigh on him.

He says, "I killed four people because I put my needs above everything else. I can't think of a good thing right now." In the pause after his confession, Calvert notices the sound of the screaming infant is still playing low from a speaker over the door where he entered.

Christian's affected voices proclaims, as if he were the judge at an inquisition, "You have met the requirement for bearing witness to the Blake Machine. You may go."

Calvert stands quickly, tipping the stool and letting it fall. He bolts from the room as fast as his dead feet will go.

Interview With an Exterminator

After conspiring over shots and tacos, Whistler and Moe agreed it was best to walk a few blocks and buy a dessert of churros and hot chocolate. As they walked back, Whistler decided Moe was sober enough to ride her new motorcycle.

"You're so cool," he called as she drove away. Then, as he read the script on the back of her helmet, "Who is Vicky?" But it was too late. She'd gone.

He got home and parked before admitting he shouldn't be driving.

He slept in his shirt and necktie, boxer briefs, and one black sock. The thought of unbuttoning buttons had simply been too much.

His phone's alarm penetrates his dream like a sharp pin pushing into the soft belly of a balloon until the moment it bursts. The tail of his tie is twisted around his wrist, and when he moves, he chokes. Awake, frightened, and sputtering, he falls out of bed, landing hard on his tailbone, one knee knocking into the bed frame. He rips the tie over his head and flings it away, convinced it intended to constrict his airway. His hangover manifests as a series of aches and a throbbing pressure under his eyes. "Oh hell." His breath is rank. The ebb and flow of pain in his skull is in time to his incredibly loud alarm. He taps it off, slaps it on his mattress, and gets to his feet.

He doesn't remember much about getting home. "My gun. Where's my gun?" He limps around the apartment, past his galley kitchen and into his tiny sitting room. No gun on the table next to his keys, wallet, and clip badge. No gun on the kitchen counter. No gun when he searches his pants bunched in the hall, only an empty holster. He can't find his phone either. *I had it a minute ago.* He locates the phone in a twist of bed sheets. He starts to call Moe to ask if she has any idea about his gun, but his bladder is about to burst. He limps into the bathroom and spots his pistol in the sink. Never did a morning piss bring such relief.

A shower, clean teeth, fresh clothes, three aspirin, and two fried eggs go a long way to making his life right. He'd made big plans while sitting over empty shot glasses the night before. He and Moe agreed that the same killer was responsible for two murders and one attempted murder. The interval between attacks was shrinking, and another attack could come any day. *"We need to move like our life depends on it,"* he'd said. *"Because someone's does."* He had felt pretty bad-ass when he said it.

This morning, though, the rough start has curtailed his ambitions. *First, get coffee. Second, handle Ruther. Third, get enough to bring Allen Schmidt back in for questioning.* He holsters his firearm and leaves with purpose, if not vigor.

Traffic is worse than anticipated. Wendell is bent over, pointing his scalp at Whistler when he bangs open the door. "Heard Ruther took over your case," Wendall says.

"My only concern is finding a killer," Whistler says without stopping.

"Don't let me catch you lying down on the job," Wendell calls.

There's no doubt Wendell is the one distributing the pictures of Whistler stuck in his chair.

"Ass," Whistler says to himself. He takes the steps two at a time. His knee hurts from falling out of bed, but the knock was superficial, no permanent damage. He crosses the squad room, noting that the lights are on and Ruther's door is open. Coffee is brewing, so he finds his "Crafty Ass Bitch" mug and pulls the pot out long enough to tip his cup half full. He runs cold water to cool it down.

He knocks at Ruther's door. "Any news from the hospital?"

"Good morning, bright eyes," Ruther says. "As of last night, Zhang was still unconscious. Suzuki made it clear we are to be contacted the moment she wakes. They will call. The hospital sent over a full blood workup for Ted to read. After finding nothing to add to his direct observations, he concluded the wounds on Zhang were consistent with the attack on Harpole. Including a knot on the side of her head in the same spot Harpole had a laceration. But the strangulation was far more restrained. Otherwise, Zhang would be dead and not unconscious."

Whistler hadn't thought of that. *The attacker is changing his MO. Wants to make it last.* He files that away and says, "I'd like to take Suzuki to check Schmidt's weak-ass alibi."

Ruther takes a file from the center of a pile and tosses it to the far side of his desk. "That's Schmidt's record. It took a minute to dig it up. The name of his parole officer is there."

"Thanks."

"Listen, Diaz," Ruther says. "You gotta pace yourself. This job will burn you up."

"Yes, sir."

"'Yes, sir,'" Ruther mocks. "Don't *'yes, sir'* me. You could be onto something with this Flores case." He pulls another file from the stack, pitches it over. Whistler flips it open. It consists of three pages: the initial report on Ginny Flores, a mandatory autopsy, and a few notes from a homicide detective. "You see that? I listened to you yesterday. I'm looking into it. But the rule is: keep it simple. Solve the part you can solve. Worry about the vast web of related deaths later. You see?"

"Yes, sir."

"For future reference, run developments past me before broadcasting them to the squad. That was dirty pool."

"Yes, sir."

Ruther's mustache goes wild. "You are one CH away from pissing me off and riding a desk permanently. My intention was to put you on hotline leads. You understand? I'm letting you check this alibi as a favor. I had to come down hard yesterday to keep you on task. Chasing endless sidetracks distracts from a case. I need you a hundred percent focused where I aim you."

"Yes, sir," Whistler says. He realizes his reply may further irritate Ruther and adds, "I understand. Thanks."

"That's more like it," Ruther says.

At his desk, Whistler rolls his trick chair out of the way and takes a folding chair from the conference room to replace it. He drinks his coffee and looks through case notes until Suzuki wanders in.

"Oh man," Suzuki says, "guess what my wife surprised me with last night?"

"Stop," Whistler says. "I don't want to know." Suzuki looks injured. "But I do have a question."

"Shoot," Suzuki says.

Whistler lowers his voice, "What exactly is a CH?"

"It's a technical term used in law enforcement. I can't believe you don't know it, Diaz. I thought you were smart." Suzuki grins with pointed little teeth and holds up a finger and thumb with a tiny fraction of space between to demonstrate how small a measurement one CH is. "It's the width of exactly one cunt hair."

"God damn it," Whistler says. "Grab your shit. Ruther is putting us to work."

Whistler sends Suzuki to check the alibis Schmidt gave for the times of both known attacks. He implies it was Ruther's idea. "When you're finished, go talk to the parole officer. Here." Whistler hands over Schmidt's file. "Explain our suspicions and get whatever insights the guy wants to share. I'll see you after lunch. If things go smoothly, we'll pick up Schmidt before dinner." Suzuki doesn't seem bothered taking orders from Diaz.

Fifteen minutes later Whistler is driving along I-90 to talk to Schmidt's boss, Gladsky. Driving his own car is not standard procedure, but no one has told him not to. This way he avoided asking Wendell to requisition a cruiser and having to explain why he's such a delicate prima donna he can't stand to ride in the same car as his partner.

Whistler tells himself it's a way to cover more ground. Partners are for backup when making an arrest, but not needed for legwork. *Divide and conquer,* he tells himself. In truth, his head is pounding, and he'd give even odds on committing murder if confined in a tight space with Suzuki and his incessant lowbrow humor.

The drive takes less than half an hour. His GPS leads him to a gravel lot next to a pole barn compound surrounded by twelve-foot-high cyclone fence. The gate is open and the main building has a few cars parked around it and a two-story overhead door rolled open. Whistler parks, slips into his blazer, and walks through the open door. Inside he finds a white panel van with the words "Bug Off" printed large across one side. It's identical to the one Allen drives. Near the back is an office with a couple windows looking onto the garage. Whistler can see a slender man with pale hair watching him. The man pushes open a door and stomps out to meet Whistler.

He has a severe look, sharp features, and a forceful presence. He advances fast, reminding Whistler of a shark slicing through dark water. His wrist sparkles as it swings, a flashy watch announcing his importance. The man extends his hand like a blade and cranks down hard on the bones in Whistler's fingers before he can make a grip. "I'm Kaz Gladsky." He steps a little too close, trying to intimidate. He doesn't release his grasp for a long moment.

"I'm Detective Diaz. We spoke on the phone," Whistler takes a step back, shows his badge. Gladsky wears a superior, smug expression, pleased to have forced Whistler to retreat. Whistler brushes his blazer open to reveal his firearm. Gladsky's expression sobers. "As I said last time, your employees Allen Schmidt and Calvert Greene are witnesses to a crime."

"Yes. I hope they were cooperative. Mr. Greene is in training. I hired him recently. We are growing here at Bug Off. Staffing is the most challenging thing running a small business. You wouldn't know about that, working for the city, but running a small company is the hardest thing a man can do. Contracts and suppliers. Payroll, regulations, taxes. So much to deal with."

"I'm sure. I'm here to get some background if I can. Friday the ninth, did you have a van over at the Echelon?"

"We contract with the Echelon. As of yesterday we have ongoing contracts with six hotels. We are growing almost too fast. If you decide to leave law enforcement, I'm looking to buy two new vans and staff up. Competitive wages."

"Is there a way to check your records regarding the ninth?"

"Let's go in here and ask my wife. She's office manager." He walks ahead of Whistler. "What exactly are you looking for?"

"Curious if Allen Schmidt was at the Echelon on or around the ninth?"

"Why would you think that?"

"A Bug Off van was spotted near a crime scene." Whistler says it to apply pressure and see what oozes out. Then he adds, "He may be an unwitting witness to a crime."

"Really? Well, I don't know if Allen was there, but he has worked there. It was our second contract. He spent a couple months there earlier this year. Here we go," he says, and opens the office door.

A young woman, tall and slender, turns. Her smile is radiant, her skin glows, and her hand rests protectively on a belly swollen with child.

"My wife," says Gladsky. "Svetlana."

Dead Man Dreaming

The Bronco was purchased in the first year it was offered and one month before Calvert was born. Harry bought it for the winters up north, but it had also been the car that drove Calvert home from the hospital after his birth, two weeks past his due date. It was said infant Calvert had been reluctant to start living.

The years and the salted roads had done what one would expect to the boxy utility vehicle. By the time it was Calvert's first car, it had seen some hard use. Though it'd been decades since Calvert owned it, while asleep in his small apartment, he finds himself driving it again.

The sky is black, no stars or moon. The damp, oppressive void presses hard on the windscreen. His hand knows where the wiper knob is, and when he engages it, rickety chrome arms lurch from the top of the windscreen, taking feeble, herky-jerky swipes at the increasing precipitation. Each time they pull back, the perished rubber blades stutter over the glass, setting his teeth on edge.

Visibility is bad and Calvert runs the defroster. The air that vents against the underside of the glass smells metallic and pushes a haze across his entire field of vision. He leans down and around the steering wheel to find a clear view of the road. He snaps off the heater and cracks the window beside him. The fog slowly dissolves.

His headlights are absorbed by the darkness. He stomps the floor switch for the high beams and the light gets weaker. He stomps to change them back and the lights dim again.

No white lines mark the road's edge, no dividing line runs down the center. He doesn't know the road's name or where it goes. He's lost. But feeling lost is not a new sensation and not, on its own, cause for panic.

Since his death, he's been defined by a single-minded plodding toward basic understanding of what he lost and how he lost it while enduring a swirling storm of people living their lives around him. Despite having made peace with the general pointlessness of the passage of time, he doesn't want to crash the ghost Bronco. He edges toward the center of the empty road, where the pavement is drier.

Great spans of asphalt pass under his tires. With each mile traveled, he becomes more anxious. Intuition tells him some unwanted event is imminent, something more vital to him than life or death. A reckoning. Perhaps he will be taken wherever one goes when one has finished walking the plane of existence called life. He eases his foot off the accelerator. A spring tip pokes through the seat and scratches at his back pocket.

He snaps on the AM radio, and a screech of static gives way to a reading of *The Overcoat*. The voice is speaking Russian with a Ukrainian accent, as if Nikolai Gogol himself is breathing through the brittle speakers, talking directly to Calvert. Though he no longer remembers a word of Russian, Calvert understands the story perfectly. It makes complete illogical sense. His knowledge of literature must not reside in his jumbled brain, but instead be protected in the hollow of his torso.

He tops a slight rise and sees the glow of a lone traffic light a long way ahead. He loses time and crosses a considerable distance in a blink, finding himself at an intersection. The light turns yellow, then red. He grips the column shift and lugs the engine down, afraid of jamming the brakes on the wet pavement. When the ramshackle tub rattles to a stop, a loose piece of the rust-ravaged floor shudders free and gets stuck under the heel of Calvert's clutch foot.

With the car resting in neutral, the air in the cab throbs in time to both his breathing and the monotone thrum of Gogol's raspy description of the bleak, brown meal of a low-level bureaucrat in historic St. Petersburg. *Or is it Leningrad?*

He turns to ask the young woman if she knows which incarnation of the city the famous story is set in. Such a simple detail, a hard fact he carried for so long it has become soft around the edges. "Do you know?" However, when he glances, he finds the passenger seat empty. *Too bad,* he thinks. *She is very bright.* Her absence underscores his isolation.

There are no other cars, no buildings, strip malls, or distant houses. He can hear no night sounds: insects, dogs barking, wind. There is only the Bronco's interior, the bludgeoning rain, the stuttering wipers, whatever his dying headlights capture, and a slick X of road lit by the overhead traffic lights. In his side mirror, he finds no sign of his own brake lights cast into the night behind him, as if he can't plumb the depths of the moments he's already lived.

The Bronco's presence is a comfort. It is the last earthly remnant of Harry, his grandfather, who ended up raising Calvert. The Judge, as Harry was widely known, believed in the order of books on shelves, text in straight lines organized in columns, page after page, one meaning stacking on the next until a perfect complexity is achieved. Despite Harry's sharp mind he'd never been good with his hands. The Bronco was not well cared for. It was, however, the car Calvert learned to drive. A fragment of his mind knows the car had rotted away in a dilapidated outbuilding behind a fishing cabin near Two Rivers, Wisconsin, an age ago. The shed had slowly curled in on the shell of the car, like a clenching fist crushing a beer can. In his dreamtime logic, and knowing he is a dead man, Calvert finds driving a dead car perfectly appropriate.

The signal light is long, practically eternal. He considers running it but finds himself in no particular hurry. He turns to the dilapidated bench seat between the rear wheels to make silly faces at Bump in her car seat. Bump isn't there. There is no car seat. The absence is an infant-sized hole where vital organs should be.

Before he can ponder the vacant back seat, a set of headlights approach from behind, the high beams painful and momentarily blinding as they flash across his rearview mirror. He squeezes his eyes completely closed.

When they open, the car has pulled along his right side. He recognizes Meredith's profile, as if he'd rolled over to find her looking at her phone before leaving the warmth of their bed. Her car is a black, shiny, European sedan—cold and hard like the husk of a water beetle, a car to take to a funeral.

His numb heart fires like he's been resuscitated, as if injected with pure adrenaline. He draws a gust of air deep into the dusty back corners of his lungs. He waves and yells.

"Hey, Mere! Over here. I'm here. Next to you."

She remains focused on the traffic light, revving her engine in anticipation. He reaches across the cab for the window crank, but his lap belt holds him away. He cranes his body, stretching his torso, fingers fiddling the air a fraction from the handle. He can't reach. He mashes the button on his lap belt, but the latch has no give.

The rain comes hard. His left side gets wet from the gap in the window. The wipers continue to scrape ineffectually in front of him, and his engine ticks and rattles. The overhead traffic signal winks to green. Through runnels of water sheeting his windows, he watches Mere, sees her fail to look his way when her car accelerates across the intersection. He hears her tires shushing him as they roll, as he screams for her, as he dry sobs.

"I'm sorry," he barks. Her taillights are evil red eyes, staring as she abandons him, smashes him, and leaves him a broken version of his former self.

He pounds the meat of his palm into the center cap of his steering wheel, over and over. It makes a *clack clack clack* noise, but the horn doesn't sound. He presses the clutch so hard the deteriorated metal cracks. He shoves the shifter into first gear, but the transmission pushes back.

A blast of wind joins the downpour outside, and water lashes the car, inky waves washing down the windows. His shoulder is soaked. Wind gusts under the car, threatening to lift it from the ground. The road is a puddle, now a pond. Wet flecks come through the floor and get the back of Calvert's ankles damp. The eerie green signal light goes sickly yellow. Gogol's monologue gets louder, trying to be heard over the ruckus. The author's accent gets thicker as his conviction pours into the old words, a literary conjuration.

Frantically, Calvert grinds the transmission until he finds a gear and pops the clutch. The light turns red, the intersection bathed in blood. The engine torques hard on its motor mounts, wringing the vehicle like a damp dishtowel. The Bronco jerks backward. He smacks his forehead into the steering wheel as the car yanks him away. He tries to focus on the vanishing taillights of the woman he planned a family with, shared a life with, but something hot and sticky runs over his forehead and into his eyes. Before he can blink it away, she's gone.

The Cure for an Existential Hangover

After falling in bed the previous night, Calvert slept like the dead. Something wakes him before the sun is up. He can feel it coming, a pressure behind his eyes, a painful burrowing under his forehead. *This is death*. His ripe lesion is spreading and engulfing his remaining soft tissue. His dark room is a padded coffin, and the lid is coming down. He finds he can't move his limbs. He's afraid, which he hadn't expected. His mind plays a scene from his past, not a whole life flashing, but a specific hurtful flicker he'd rather not see. He watches as if it's projected against the gray ceiling. He stares, unable to blink, unable to turn away.

Doctor Greene is there, the Calvert he once was. He's in the driver's seat of a car he would die in six months later. His likeness is initially soft around the edges, a plasma shadow gradually condensing into a solid. The Calvert cast on the ceiling turns the wheel and pulls to a curb. A young woman walks over and opens the passenger door. Her name is Kati. He's excited to see her. She's a Hungarian exchange student and one of his brightest pupils. He nominated her for an award. His letter of recommendation, and especially her excellent essay, persuaded the committee to honor Kati at an annual banquet. She asked Calvert to introduce her, to be a familiar face. He knows this as he watches her hips slide into the seat, as he sees her twist to find the seat belt.

"You look nice," he says politely. Professionally.

She touches her dark hair. It's in soft curls that bounce on her shoulders. He's never seen her hair curled. He likes it. She smiles for him, a nervous smile. "Thank you." Her accent draws his attention to the way her glossy lips work the words.

He is not the kind of professor who would sleep with a student. He is not that kind of husband to Mere. He long ago outgrew that kind of impetuousness. Maybe when he was younger. Young like the beautiful Kati sitting so near. He is afraid to speak. He nods and checks his rear-view mirror, moves it out of place, catches a flash of Kati's legs, fumbles the mirror back to its original position. "Here we go," he says. He leans forward to watch the sky. "Hope we beat the storm."

He begins the drive from her dormitory to the Reva and David Logan Center. As soon as the car begins to move, black clouds blow in. Within blocks, rain comes so hard the wipers can't keep up; everything goes dark, he can't see the side of the road, the wind picks up. Trash blows across the street; followed by a wire café chair, then two more chairs and a tumbling table. A red umbrella smacks the windshield and is whipped into the thrashing black night. At an intersection, they watch a parked car lift, roll, and settle on its side, tipped by the savage, elemental will of the storm.

Calvert can feel his car coming off the ground; the weight of the chassis lifting from the shocks, the tire tread of his spinning wheels barely brushing the slick pavement. Neither of them talk. Kati makes a worried chirp like a woodland creature.

Calvert drives into the nearest parking lot and stops. They leap out for fear they will be carried away. The rain dies. The wind changes direction. The water from the parking lot lifts and stands on edge like a dark, rippling wall. It holds that shape. His breath catches in his body. Then the water slams into them like the smack of a hand. They are drenched and disoriented. The wind comes back, more fierce for its momentary rest. Kati makes a run for the nearest building. She's blown so hard her straight path becomes a parabola. She abandoned her car door, leaving it wide open. Calvert runs around and forces it shut before the wind can rip it off. He aims himself at the restaurant Kati entered as a power line tears loose and falls across his path. It's live and throwing sparks. It cracks and spits at him, an angry living thing. He withdraws three steps in preparation to leap over it. He stops short, reconsiders, changes course, runs the long way around, makes it through the restaurant doors.

The lights are off. The employees and customers huddle in the dark, listening. The windows rattle to bust their frames. Kati finds Calvert's hands. He's drenched, his shoes filled with water, his eyelashes heavy with it. She hugs him, desperate. She presses her check to his chest. She's wild with fear. Calvert holds her close. He cradles her wet hair, her curls pulled strait. There is no thought in it. Her mouth is on his, she is happy and excited and crying and grateful, and they kiss long and deep. The wind shakes the building. There is a baby wailing somewhere. They kiss until the storm rolls away.

Calvert wakes again, still staring at the ceiling. The sun has risen. He doesn't recall finding his way to the bed after rushing from Christian's confessional. He's still in his Bug Off coveralls with the shirt he helped print pulled over the top half.

He draws a ragged breath. He doesn't want to remember his affair with Kati. Doesn't want to feel the empty place that used to be a life.

He hears a noise, casts his eyes toward the strip of light at the bottom edge of his apartment door. A shadow passes. A few beats later, it passes in the other direction.

Barney. Calvert is anxious to leave the place where he dreamed of Kati, anxious to put distance between his conscious self and the source of guilt. He turns on his lamp, slips his bare feet into shoes, and walks onto the landing.

Barney is drinking coffee. He lifts his mug in greeting. "Morning. Hope the hoopla last night didn't keep you up."

"I slept through it. I was exhausted."

"No doubt. Quite a day." Barney switches the coffee to his opposite hand.

"Thanks for the shirt." Calvert pats his chest. "Sorry I left so quickly."

Barney can see Calvert is upset. "Don't worry," he says, trying to be comforting. "Like I said, long day. I figured you needed some space."

"The Blake Machine was, um, I don't know. I don't have the words," Calvert admits.

"Unsettling?"

"It was. I confessed. To something I hadn't remembered clearly before last night. I dreamed it, and the dream was more real than memories should be."

Barney slurps a bit of coffee. "That's good. Christian will be happy it hit the mark."

Calvert feels Barney doesn't get his point.

"By the way," Barney goes on talking, "we did well last night. Everyone sold work. Donations were good. Lyla's photos sold well. Did I tell you she took photos for one whole day for the show? She printed them and framed them and displayed them all in one go. We made more than enough money for the Far Afield Fest."

"You don't understand." Calvert is focused on the Blake Machine. "I've sinned. Taken lives. I'd forgotten. But now a door in my brain is open, and it's all I can think of."

Barney turns his eyes down the long flight of steps to the front door. He says, "Hmm." He drinks coffee.

Calvert stamps in place, trying to get feeling in his numb feet.

Barney finally says. "I like being in a city like this. In small towns, everyone knows your business and has an opinion about it. In a city, you can reinvent yourself. Memories aren't so long. In a place like this, you can move past things. Start fresh. It's a place big enough to get lost in. Lost in a good way. It's why I've stayed."

Calvert tries to cast being lost in a good light. He'd never considered it that way, isn't certain of the logic even now. He says, "This city is where I've done horrible things."

"You can let go of the past. No one around here will tie you to it. You're the one who makes it an issue. Not this place. Not me. Honestly, people don't care about the things other people have done. People are too self-centered for that."

Barney is right. But the taste of Kati's kiss lingers in Calvert's mouth, and the dirty blue color of the wall over Barney's shoulder looks remarkably like the shade of Kati's broken neck the last time he laid his eyes on her.

Barney keeps talking. "I've had too much coffee. Not good for the blood pressure. Besides, Calvert," the big man says, "What the hell does any of it matter? You're dead anyway."

"I'm having concerns I'm not as dead as I'd thought."

The Old College Try

Jerome helped Moe make a connection with Assistant Professor Cynthia Regan, the U of Chicago's resident Chaucer expert. Moe drives Taibbi to the park where she arranged a meeting. She takes city streets, staying off highways, interstates, and even parkways. The Honda had vibrated when she briefly hit fifth gear on her way home from her night out with Whistler. It lasted only a moment, but it got her attention. After online research over breakfast, Moe thinks she has a bad engine mount or a clogged fuel filter. Until she gets her paycheck, she can't do anything about it. So she prefers to take it easy.

"I know what you're thinking," Cynthia says to Moe after introductions. "It's scandalous for a woman to teach such bawdy material. What can I say? I'm wild and I refuse to apologize for who I am." When Moe doesn't react, the professor explains, "That's my icebreaker for the first day of class. Freshmen give me that exact reaction: no reaction. It kills with grad students."

"Oh," Moe says. "Jokes."

"If jokes by definition elicit laughter, then it doesn't meet basic criteria." Cynthia has a playful glint in her eye. She slowly smiles and her lips barely move, but her nose crinkles and the corners of her eyes show a subtle spray of fine lines. Moe is immediately charmed.

"Mind if I record for background?" Moe asks.

213

"No. Do you mind if we walk and talk?" Cynthia moves along the meandering path. Moe falls into step next to her. "Thanks for meeting here," Cynthia say. "I'm doing research. Do you know the Newberry?" She indicates the grand building adjacent to the small park.

"I've heard of it," Moe says.

"If you've never been, it's a treat. They don't have an original *Canterbury Tales*, but they do have photographic facsimiles of several of the tales from the Ellesmere manuscript. Including 'The Miller's Tale' and 'The Wife of Bath.' It's so saucy."

Moe smiles her most winning smile. They walk a few paces before she says, "So, you worked closely with Professor Greene?"

"Yes. He was my department mentor. Showed me the ropes. He laughed at my attempts at humor. He deceived me into believing I'm hilarious."

"I'm sure your jokes are wonderful. I might not be your target audience."

"I'm only playing. Jokes that must be explained are the defining characteristic of my comedic repertoire." A comfortable silence follows, filled only by the sounds of their footfalls, the city outside the park's perimeter momentarily made distant.

Moe says, "I read the reports of Greene's accident. There was a student killed in the car with the professor. Kati Gabor. Pregnant at the time. The car that struck them was driven by the professor's wife, Meredith Greene. You see where I'm headed? It certainly has the makings of a love triangle turned violent."

"I want to avoid speculation," Cynthia says seriously.

"I wouldn't want to print anything speculative. But I would like to hear what you know."

"Calvert was a gentleman. Never once got out of line or hit on me. I'm gay. That isn't a secret. But I didn't list it on my CV. He had no reason to assume I was not interested in men. He never gave me reason for concern. There are professors with reputations for chasing skirts. It is a long-standing tradition in higher education. But not Doctor Greene.

The circumstances of the accident did lead to rumors, but never from those that knew him."

"How do you explain Kati Gabor?"

"I don't have an explanation. She was an exchange student. She had no family here. Perhaps he offered to drive her somewhere. To her ob-gyn appointment, for instance."

"That would be weird. If I'm being honest, it stretches the bounds of polite to the border of creepy and inappropriate. I'm willing to be convinced."

"You're right, of course. I would think a girl in a strange land would prefer a female companion on an outing to a lady doctor. However, it's not beyond reason to think she simply felt comfortable with him. Calvert wanted to help. He was giving her a ride. Nothing more. Perhaps he persuaded her it would be easier than public transportation?"

"Would you like such conjecture to be true?"

"Yes. I suppose I'd like that to be how it happened. Something innocent. Something kind."

"Suppose then, the professor's intentions were pure, the fetus Kati carried was not his. Why would the professor's wife T-bone the innocent couple? The photos of the collision tell a story of an intentional crash. Her brakes were functional. She rammed them at speed. No skid marks. Witnesses say she accelerated into the impact."

"Perhaps she misunderstood the situation."

"That's a hell of a misunderstanding," Moe says.

"Agreed."

"Mrs. Greene could only misunderstand if her husband didn't explain the kind thing he was doing for a student," Moe continues. "What man would miss the opportunity to prove what a good guy he is? Why keep it secret? If I've got it right, they were about to celebrate their twenty-first wedding anniversary. That's significant."

"It is," Cynthia agrees.

"Do you have any impression of their relationship?"

"He didn't speak of her often to me. But when he did, it was always fondly. Maybe there was a wistfulness, but that is such a nuanced interpretation as to be meaningless."

"And I'm right that they had no children?" Moe asks.

"No children. Not everyone wants kids. For instance, I don't think I could be selfless enough to be a mother," Cynthia says.

"I feel the same. But I bet few parents feel ready before they have kids."

"Solid point—Moe, isn't it? I'm so bad with names." They have completed their circuit of the park.

"Yes, my name is Moe." She pulls her Vicky helmet on.

"You'll get to the bottom of things. Your determination is written all over your face." Cynthia gives Moe a long, slow appraisal. She meets her eyes through the yellow bubble shield. "I better get back to it. Chaucer won't read itself."

Moe starts Taibbi. Cynthia calls over the engine, "Is Vicky your girlfriend?"

"No"—Moe knocks on the helmet—"came with the bike."

"That's good," the professor says. She crinkles her nose and smiles with her eyes.

"See you around professor," Moe says, but she doesn't leave, only revs her engine.

"You can call me Cyn. All my friends do."

Moe pulls into the city. When she glances back, Cyn is still watching her go.

Partner Bonding

On his drive back from Bug Off, Whistler calls Suzuki.

"You got Zucchini. Shoot."

"Jesus, don't say that. Stand up for yourself or the guys will treat you like a punch line."

"Ah, partner, I didn't know you cared. Admit it, I'm growing on you."

"Like fungus. No. I'm sorry. I want us to act like professionals. Not an inept parody."

"You're full of assumptions. You assume because we don't take things seriously we are not serious. You're wrong. Ever hear of coping mechanisms? You assume they call me Zucchini to ridicule my name, my Japanese heritage. In fact, it's my prominent man-tackle that earned the nickname. I wear them with pride, the nickname and the genitals. Think about it."

"I did and it can't be scoured away fast enough."

"No kidding, there are reasons to keep things light. The work is hard. It eats at you. I have a daughter nearly our victim's age. The only way I can see that mangled throat and keep doing my job is to play it off. You see? People are capable of compartmentalizing for good reason. It's a tool that works for us as a species. We are made for it."

"Maybe. Hey, I didn't know you had a daughter."

"I made that up. But my broader point stands."

"Dick."

"I think you mean Zucchini."

"Did you make any progress on the case?"

"I'll tell you what I found soon enough. But I'm hungry and you owe me."

"Fine. Name the place."

"I'm feeling the need for some soosh. Meet you at Umami. I'll get us a table."

"Dammit. Okay. But I'm going to smuggle in a cheeseburger."

* * *

Umami has a lunch buffet; to Whistler it looks slimy, bright, and mysterious. He has no interest in expanding his palate. He loads up on California rolls with tons of soy sauce, wasabi, and pickled ginger.

Suzuki looks happy. "The sapporo roll is killer, man. If you like tuna soosh, it is the go-to roll." He takes up chopsticks and starts dipping and eating. "The only downside is no sake. But it is BYOB. So let's remember for next time."

Whistler doesn't mind the California roll. The salt punch from the soy sauce covers most of the seaweedy flavor. "Tell me," he says. "What did Schmidt's PO have to say?"

"This guy looked like a power lifter gone to pot. He sat around his desk, not behind it. You know what I mean?"

"Yes."

"He said Allen Schmidt was punctual, never had an infraction. Married with a stable job. Continues to meet the terms of his early release."

"Damn it."

"But get this. I asked the Incredible Bulk—" Suzuki pauses for the laugh that doesn't come. "You are a tough crowd. His bottom line on Schmidt: 'Most people I deal with are career criminals, addicts, institutionalized in one way or another. But Schmidt is rare con that gives me hope for our prison system. Not because he's a good person. He's not.

But prison scared the shit out of him. Fear of incarceration, fear of loss of freedom, fear of being powerless among bigger, meaner convicts; it keeps Schmidt very focused on the straight and narrow. He's a success story.' And you know what?" Suzuki pinches his last morsel with plastic chopsticks, shakes it at Whistler as he says, "He meant it."

New Horizons

Moe finds managing Loni and Dale hugely inconvenient for many reasons, most of which revolve around the pair being young, green, and needy little humans. Moe's biggest issue is that the kids work on their own stories at their own pace, which means Moe can be interrupted anytime, seven days a week, by a twenty-something in the middle of a crisis. It's distracting. Everything is urgent; their stories are vital, their voices are so original they defy edits, and they speak for an underrepresented and misunderstood generation that intends to teach everyone older how it is done, despite their utter lack of life experience for context and apparent inability to write a paragraph without someone applauding them as they type. She's learned her wards aren't terribly active in the mornings. *Little babies get tuckered out after a big day.* Moe is finding a rhythm that involves focusing on her own stories first thing, then heading to the office for a long lunch and counseling session with the whippersnappers. Once she's endured as much as she can, she makes herself scarce and does more of her own reporting.

Whenever she sees Jerome, he's pleased as punch with her predicament. Vivian, for her part, tries to give advice on how to guide the youngsters without crushing their spirit. "You have to keep showing them where the trail lies. They can't see it yet, but if you keep pointing it out, they will find it."

"Tell me I was not like that," Moe said.

"You were not like them at all." Vivian used a lugubrious and obviously patronizing tone, fully enjoying the moment.

"Shit," Moe said. "Starting to think a paycheck isn't worth the torture."

"But you're so good at it," Vivian had replied, as if she hadn't a care in the world.

Now Moe is doing a reverse commute on the Eisenhower Expressway on her way to Berwyn. Taibbi has been behaving, and she doesn't have time to waste. Moe knows in her heart that Chicago's newest hero, Calvert Greene, is not as heroic as the public has been led to believe. He may not be a killer, but he could be. She'd looked into Greene. She found an injunction issued against him by the family of his deceased wife, and a pending wrongful death lawsuit being considered by the family's attorney. Very recently, he'd been escorted from his old apartment after the doorman at his building reported his presence. According to the daily report, he'd cooperated and no charges were filed. Moe wasn't able to speak to cops who filed the report. She left several messages but they hadn't responded. *I would reach nirvana if I could prove the man Sophia publicly dubbed a hero is actually a serial murderer.* Moe grins so wide something pops in her ear, the sound cushioned in her helmet.

Taibbi is cruising along. Moe is at one with her new bike, her body and the bike humming at the same unified frequency as they flash through traffic. *I'm making good time.* The lane opens ahead of her. She twists the gas and feels like she's flying. She cranks the throttle harder. The engine hesitates and sputters. She loses speed. The back wheel fishtails. She brakes hard. The tires try to grab pavement. *I'm gonna crash.* She's jarred by a wicked wobble that threatens to unseat her. She slides back on the seat and mashes her center of gravity lower. Three cars shoot past. A horn blares. Ragged desperation forces her to keep wrestling the bike for control. Taibbi slows. The tires begin tracking. She can feel the road. The engine smooths out and the shimmy subsides. She sits up straighter. "What the actual fuck," she says inside her Vicky helmet.

She tries her hazard lights, can't find the button on the hand control. "Screw Flat Ass Ricky," she says with venom. "And his pathetic handshake too."

She carefully picks her way across the lanes of traffic to take the Austin exit, drives backstreets until she finds the place. According to the website, New Horizons is a residence for people transitioning from long-term immersive therapy to independent living. When she called, she was transferred to a social worker named Abbey. Next to the main building is a doughnut shop, You Can Dough It, staffed by current and former residents. That's where she's supposed to rendezvous with the overly perky social worker.

"I have to say I'm not completely, like, surprised to hear from you. When I saw on the news what Professor Greene had done I felt, like, so proud. He has really come a long way! He's a celebrity around here." Her voice has a ragged edge like she just woke from a long sleep.

Moe's biggest pet peeve is women who talk in passive, unprofessional ways. She's anxious from her near-death mechanical problem, which feels like a betrayal. She's angry. And with each "like" uttered, each vocal fried upspeak, she longs to crawl across the table and beat the stupid from this girl's skull. Instead, she keeps her expression neutral and says, "I'm hoping to do a deeper dive into his story, share his recent challenges. It makes his accomplishments that much more remarkable, don't you think?"

"It, like, really does."

"May I?" Moe asks while pressing the button on her recorder. "So, you worked with him closely?" She's determined to keep this short and move on to the next interview.

"Like, very closely. Each client has a treatment team that meets three days a week. As part of Professor Greene's team, I made sure he got to treatment and provided transportation and basically, like, *lots* of support. I coordinated resources to create a smooth path to independent living. He is a remarkable case. I was, like, so lucky to work with him."

"Because . . ."

"Because his condition is so rare, as I'm sure you know."

"Yes, of course. How bad would you say his condition was when he first arrived?"

"He had, like, a serious brain injury. Normal problems for a damaged frontal lobe: memory loss, diminished language, poor decision-making—or what we call bad executive function. Sometimes people say they feel like they are losing their minds. Well, in some ways Calvert's accident damaged his left-brain functions, leaving him only access to strong feelings with no ability to place them. But, fortunately, his physical condition improved quickly with physical therapy twice a day. But his syndrome became, like, way more prominent."

"Can you pronounce that syndrome for me? I'm not sure how to say it."

"Cotard. Sounds just like it's spelled."

"Okay, thanks. That's so helpful." *Jackpot.* "Now that Professor Greene is away, does that mean he no longer needs treatment?"

"I'm scheduled to make a home visit next week. He's on, like, pretty standard initial treatment for the disease: a regimen of daily anti-psychotics. Counseling is, like, not fruitful because the condition is brought about by the brain lesion. It's not about his understanding. It's about his damaged cerebral physiology. There was some debate among his treatment team. But Doctor Shaw's decision is the final word."

"Disagreement over course of treatment?"

"Yes. But mostly over, like, diagnosis. Kathy Davis, the head counselor, felt the diagnosis of Cotard's was premature. Felt it was possible Professor Greene was using the idea of death as a convenient shelter to allow him to disassociate from the loss of his wife. But Doctor Shaw was convinced. Like, *very* convinced and so excited to document the professor's treatment plan for publication. But the grant fell through."

"This gives me so much to go on." Moe rises from the table, takes her recorder and her helmet with her. "Oh, one more question: What was the grant for?"

"Well, traditionally the only documented cure for Cotard is electro-shock therapy. Doctor Shaw proposed targeted micro-shocks to specifically address the cause of the condition. But I can't give you too many details. HIPAA, you know—patient confidentiality."

"I, like, totally understand."

No Rest for the Wicked

Calvert has an uneaten, room-temperature sandwich resting in his lap. Lunch is his only regular meal since Rosa was hospitalized and Coffee Girl was closed. Though last night he shared a beer with Barney as a kind of temporary send-off for the Far Afield Festival.

He doesn't feel right. Earlier that morning, he'd poured two anti-psychotics into his palm. When he tried to clap them into his mouth, one shot over his shoulder. He leaned down and slurped water from the faucet to swallow half his dose. He crawled around on the sticky floor to find the second pill. Never spotted it. It had vanished. He didn't fish another pill from the bottle; concerned it would upset the stable system of mated pairs. Now he wonders if the delicate balance of his brain chemistry has gone off. His mood is dark and he can't shake it. He hasn't felt so much emotion since finding Rosa. Something structural may have shifted in his head during the Blake Machine incident; *important components may have slipped out of place.*

He watches Allen unpack his food. Allen has a series of mismatched butter tubs of various sizes stacked and secured with a web of rubber bands. He begins rolling the bands from around his assemblage and onto his wrist. Though Calvert is curious about what Allen is up to, he doesn't inquire. He is not speaking to Allen. Allen seems not to have noticed. If Calvert had to name the feeling he's having for Allen, he'd call it "perplexed." Though, if he were more alive, he might call it "anger." Not because Calvert was left alone for the first half of the day to check rooms for evidence of pestilence, with no company other than Daisy. That had become routine. In fact, Calvert prefers working with Daisy to being micro-managed by Allen, whom he has begun to actively dislike.

His feelings arise from three things. The first is Allen's thieving. Today Allen filled an entire five-gallon bucket with tiny bottles of shampoo, conditioner, lotion, mouthwash, and a stack of baby-sized soaps. He also gathered a pair of earrings, a cable for a smartphone, a zippered flipbook that held children's DVDs, a couple small bottles of booze, jars of fancy nuts, a roll of toilet paper, and a hand towel, topping the entire haul with a tightly rolled pillow. Calvert is aware Allen's petty crimes are illegal. Legality is not his concern. What bothers him is that it breaks faith with people that trust Bug Off to do honest work. It feels wrong.

The second of Allen's activities that has begun to fester like the brown spot in Calvert's brain is also about honesty. Allen has taken to prepping select rooms before Calvert enters. The rooms he prepares show evidence of bed bug infestation. The dried husks of dead bugs require Calvert to pull out heaters and blowers, vacuums, and spray bottles. It is a time-consuming process. Calvert doesn't mind the work but suspects it's a scam that Allen, and probably Kaz, play on the hotel to prove the worth of their service. It's also an insult to Calvert, who is not supposed to notice the deceit. *I may be dead but I'm not stupid.* It seems to serve the secondary purpose of buying time for Allen to do what has most upset Calvert.

Earlier, as Calvert finished repacking the equipment on the dolly after a by-the-numbers abatement, he heard a woman in distress. Calvert, his ragged feelings reminded of Rosa, raced down the hall toward the sound, Daisy galloping happily at his side. The sounds got louder at the end of the hall. He ran into the last room and saw the back of Allen. He was wearing only a short blue T-shirt like a pornographic Donald Duck. His dimpled ass was clenching as he thrust his hips into a woman reclining on the bed. She wore running shoes that bobbed in the air, bucking with every motion of Allen's body. She made a strained moan. Allen grunted. In that confused moment, Calvert saw Allen with both hands around the woman's throat, her face red, her hair damp, her eyes pinched tight, and in the ear closest to Calvert, one of the earrings Allen had taken from the Echelon's box of Lost and Found. Calvert was quickly overwhelmed by embarrassment when he understood what was happening. He ran from the room, the noise of his footfalls unnoticed. In the hall, he made a *chick chick* sound to entice Daisy to quit sniffing the carpet and leave the room where Allen was pounding his way through a member of the housekeeping staff.

Now, half an hour later, Daisy, who normally is singularly focused on devouring her well-earned kibble, turns her dusty snout in Allen's direction to watch him unpacking his stack of containers. Her doggie eyes register surprise when one of the butter dishes shoots her direction and hits the thick carpet. She draws back, one forepaw raised, prepared to run for her life. When the dish doesn't advance, she moves forward to nudge it with her nose, smell it. She growls to prove she's not scared. Having made the world safe from aggressive containers, she snorts and returns to her food.

"Silly bitch," Allen says, grabbing his butter tub back. "I call this my hillbilly bento box." Allen is very proud. "After those asshole cops got done casting accusations my way, I bummed a cigarette and walked out front of the station house. Now I didn't need a smoke, but I wanted outside while I waited, and I didn't want anyone to think I was sneaking off. I used smoking as an excuse. See, Professor, I'm smart too." He looks to Calvert for some credit.

"Clever."

"Yep. Clever is the word. Pretty fucking clever. Know what I saw when I was pretend smoking?" He's arranging bowls in a semicircle so each is within arm's reach. "Take a guess."

"A learned cat?" Calvert guesses.

"What the hell is a *learned cat*?"

"I'm not sure. I think Pushkin wrote a fairytale about the learned cat attached to a tree with a golden chain. I don't remember the rest."

"That Pushkin asshole again? You're an insecure son of a bitch, aren't you? I'm tellin' how smart I am and you gotta talk about dead Russians. You can't stop talkin' about how great Russians are." Allen is a bit unhinged. "No. I did not see no fucking learned cat, whatever the fuck a learned cat is. Though I recently spotted a willing pussy. You think that's what Pushkin was talkin' about?"

Calvert plays dumb. He says, "How's your wife?"

"She's great. Gettin' along great."

"Good to hear."

"A food truck is what I seen. It was called Dim Sum Grub. You know Dim Sum?"

"Not that I recall."

"It's a kind of Chinese food. Like steamed tapas served in a bunch of bowls with dipping sauces and weak tea. I found that out when I ordered 'cause it was lunchtime and I was hungry. Thanks to your heroics, my food was stuck in a van miles away. It hit the spot though, those dim sum. Shrimp dumplings, some kind of meatball in a bun, and a sweet glazed thing like a sticky biscuit. The meat was like my Aunt Anus's meatloaf. Which was the best thing she ever cooked. But dim sum cost an arm and a leg, and I'm not made of money. So I got the idea to do it myself, only better." He gestures to his arrangement of bowls.

"The bento box is not Chinese. It's Japanese."

"Well, fuck you, Professor. It's all the same. I was going to share my de-fucking-licious meal. But you can eat your crappy sammich for all I care. Hey, know how to tell if a guy is a Chinaman or Jap?"

"Look at them?" Calvert asks.

"You can't tell that way. No one can tell."

"People can tell."

"Nope. Not a soul."

Calvert says, "Ask them?"

"No, you can't ask. They don't speak English. They only speak ping pong ping pong." Allen is getting loud.

"You can tell if they speak Japanese or Chinese," Calvert says reasonably. He knows the more calmly he answers, the more upset it will make Allen. For reasons he can't fathom, he wants to upset Allen.

"No. No one can tell the difference," Allen says stubbornly.

"I can."

"No one normal. You wanna know or not?"

Calvert doesn't care, but he says, "How?"

"If he tries to give you a business card, he's Japanese."

"What if the person is Korean or Malaysian. What about Vietnamese or Burmese? Taiwanese? Couldn't he be Japanese and not have cards?"

"Are you trying to ruin my joke? You are. I told it wrong. But you are trying to ruin my good-time joke. Why? Why ruin my super funny joke? Men don't ruin other men's jokes. Everyone knows that. Friends play along."

"Were you telling a joke?" Calvert asks innocently.

Allen has had it. "I said it before and I say it again: fuck you." He restacks and re-bands the containers. It takes him a while. He gets the configuration wrong and has to start from the beginning. He doesn't speak to Calvert. When he's done, he carries his improvised bento way down the hall to the room where he had sex earlier.

Calvert is pleased with himself. He wants to ask, *Does your wife know what you do while you're at work? Do the women know you're married? Why cheat on a woman who loves you?* But he knows the answer.

Calvert doesn't want to think of those things. He keeps seeing Rosa. He sees her eyes the last time they were open. He feels how heavy her body is in his dead arms, how hot her flesh is against his abdomen. Not a memory of the event, but the event itself, happening to him right now and every moment. He calls down the abandoned hallway, "Allen."

"What?"

"I should go see Rosa at the hospital."

"I'm eating."

"I didn't mean to frustrate you," he lies.

"Go visit her if you want to. I don't know why not."

"Okay." Calvert takes a bite of his floppy sandwich. He stands as he chews. Daisy is lapping the last of her water, pushing the bowl back and forth across the hall to get every last drop. She looks at him, licking her jowls wetly. She watches him walk to the main elevators. He sees her cock her ears to question his departure, but she doesn't ask.

Unverified Nicknames Production

Nothing is easier than getting a taxi at a high-end Chicago hotel. Calvert walks through the grand lobby and out the revolving door, wearing his Bug Off uniform. The doorman says, "Hello, sir, need a car?"

"Yes, please."

"Where you headed?"

"Rush Medical Center."

The doorman calls, "Syed," and beckons with a twitch of two fingers. His white cotton gloves make Calvert think of sitting on a mall Santa's lap a lifetime ago. The association makes him feel warm toward the doorman. The part of himself that sits back and witnesses his own demise makes an observation: *The fatty myelin that protects the axon of my nerve cells is flaking away, causing thoughts to arc wildly. The organizing structures of my stored experience are breaking down. My card catalog has been upturned.* This failure of linear brain function began with his accident of course. But since being unceremoniously discharged from his treatment program, the rate of decline has been escalating. The confession of past transgressions dragged from him by Christian's art piece completely broke his faith in the value of discursive thought. He's ambivalent about his death. But he does hope to see Rosa before it is finalized. Rosa's genuine smile flashes his way. *Myelin.*

A round-bellied man with a black neck beard and a brimless cap on the crown of his shaved head hops in his taxi and drives past two other cars to park beside Calvert. The man pops out, jogs around the car, and shakes Calvert's hand. "Airport," he suggests hopefully.

"Rush Med," the doorman says.

The driver looks irritated. "Luggage?"

"No," Calvert says.

The driver forces a smile and opens the back door. He waits as Calvert settles in, firmly closes the door, and turns to the doorman. "What is going on today, John? I've only gotten four fares and none to the airport. I said I was sorry."

"Don't be paranoid, Syed. Next one. You come back. I'll get you an airport run."

Calvert listens through the gap at the top of his window. He watches his driver pass around the front of the taxi, slip into the driver's seat, and punch buttons on his rate meter. "Rush Medical Center," the guy says. "Which building?"

"What buildings are there?"

"Med center proper. The Butterfly building they call the new one. Maybe the outpatient building where they do MRIs and such things. The professional building."

Calvert doesn't answer. All he knows is he found Rosa and feared she was dead. He hoped to save her, exactly as he wishes he could retroactively save Mere and Bump and Kati. He knows Rosa is at Rush and that she hasn't woken, that her brain may have been damaged from lack of oxygen. And if she dies, at least they will have that in common.

Syed must see the confusion on Calvert's face. "When I get closer, my friend." Syed says. "You can decide as we drive." He turns the radio up on a song Calvert knows as Gerry Rafferty's "Baker Street." Calvert smiles, but his brain won't fire far enough into his past to tell him why. The cab joins the street traffic. The car turns left at one corner, right at the next, left then right, over and over edging north and west, block by block.

The ID of the driver reads: Syed Sarfraz Badshah. Calvert thinks that "Syed" is a title, something like "Mister," but he may have invented this knowledge. While stopped at a traffic light, Syed turns the radio down and asks, "You like my cab? It's nice isn't it? I call it the Bananafish. Because of the yellow color. You know this story by American author?"

"I used to know it. I like your cab. It is tidy," Calvert says, taking in details: fresh vacuum marks in the carpet, the oily sheen of cleaner on the dash and door panels. He's happy to be out of his head.

"I own this cab. It is my cab. Once Chicago had a great mayor. Do you know Harold Washington? The best mayor for the city. My mayor. I came to Chicago in nineteen and seventy-eight. I was here when Mayor Washington was elected. I was driving for horrible man. He took all my money. But Harold Washington is always mayor in my heart. There was lottery for taxi medallions and I was big winner. Twelve hundred people applied, and I won. It was my American dream to have my own business and work hard. It was worth big money. Maybe two hundred thousand dollars. Did you know a medallion cost so much?"

"I did not."

The more excited the driver becomes, the faster he speaks and the thicker his accent gets. Syed leans his chest into the steering wheel and tucks the cab behind a delivery truck. "John is the doorman," Syed explains. "He assigns cabs. We argued about his president. He thinks the president could be great if the press was fair. I disagree. Now John won't give me airport fares. It's not right." He smacks the dash for emphasis, not particularly hard.

"It sounds unfair," Calvert says.

"It is an abuse of power. Owning my cab is good, but because of ride-sharing apps, my medallion is worth half what it was. I was going to retire on my medallion. Sell it and live on the profits in old age. Now I must keep driving. Things are tight and John is mad because of his president. John is making my life hard, playing his child games. It's racist crapshit. John is a name for toilets and that is what I think of him. Toilet John." Syed turns the radio up to Kenny Loggins' "Danger Zone."

The cab slows as it takes the ramp up to Van Buren and turns left over the interstate. "Martin Van Buren was the eighth president of the United States," Calvert says.

Syed replies, "I memorized all presidents as part of citizenship test."

Calvert barely hears. He's thinking that Van Buren was Vice President under Andrew Jackson and Jackson was nicknamed Swampfox. *Did I ever have a nickname? Bearcat* comes to mind. Calvert knows he created the sham-memory. *I was never a Bearcat.*

Kenny Loggins finishes singing. Syed turns the radio down and says, "I go through rigorous background check to drive a cab. People call me terrorist. But I am safe. They check me thoroughly each time I renew my license. Uber says they check their drivers, but they don't check." Syed follows traffic toward the towering medical campus. "An average fare earns eleven dollars." The driver speaks fast, intent on making his point before the ride ends. "But airport runs make forty an hour." Syed pulls to the curb. He pushes buttons on the meter. "Twelve thirty-six," he says. Calvert passes him a twenty. Syed hands him a business card. "That is number for my taxi. You call me when you need a ride." He takes a long time making change.

"Keep it," Calvert says.

"Thank you, my friend. This is the main building," he gestures toward the looming architecture. "You go in those doors."

Calvert likes the easy way Syed uses the term "friend." What would they do as friends? Would they discuss presidential history over beers at a bar fit for a man nicknamed Bearcat? Would Syed attend his funeral and tell stories about the time they drove to the hospital? Rosa called him a "true good friend." Her smile flashes across his vision. *Myelin.*

He exits the cab and goes straight into the hospital.

Conspirators Conspire

Ruther combs his mustache and smooths his hair. He breaths deep with his eyes closed. His eyes pop open and look from Suzuki to Whistler.

"Detectives, I have called you here to listen to your good news."

Whistler starts to speak.

"Wait," Ruther says. "This is what I want you to say: 'We now have no doubt who the killer is. We have an airtight case. We don't even need a confession or an eyewitness. Don't worry esteemed leader Ruther, you have worked hard to become the revered inspector that you are. You've busted your ass for decades. Now take a load off. We've done our job so you are able to tell the chief of Ds and the mayor's slimy chief of staff they can have their press conference and happily allow the mayor to take credit for the work we've done.' Can you repeat that guys? Can you do that for me? Preferably verbatim and in unison."

Suzuki says, "Well . . ."

"Let me stop you there. I'll make it clear why I need this. That's only fair. I've been cussed up one side and down the other. Our most likely witness is in a coma. The doctor said, 'Her body needs the rest.' Well, no shit. We all need the fucking rest. I need a trip to an island with hula girls. Do they even still have hula girls? Is that still a thing? Have I missed my chance? I digress. The canvas of the neighborhood gave us dick. The tip line was a bust. Calvert Greene may have a suspicious history, but he was locked inside an institution during the Ginny Flores attack. I'm not saying it's a dead end, and I'm not even admitting the Flores case is related. I'm saying if that's the theory of the case we are working, then Greene ain't the guy." Ruther hammers his fist on the case files on his desk. "We have no physical evidence. Unless Diaz's mystery smell and missing headband and lack of high heels counts as physical evidence."

"Hair tie," Whistler pipes up. Ruther's agitated expression makes him regret it.

"In case you're not getting what I'm giving," Ruther says, louder now, "the answer is *no!* A mystery smell is not physical evidence. Speculating about hypothetical evidence is abso-fuckin'-lutely not evidence! You know what is evidence? Evidence! Actual evidence! The press has declared one of our suspects a hero and are now claiming the recent attack constitutes a pattern. Sound familiar, Diaz?" Ruther takes a few deep breaths. "You understand why you need to say the things I've instructed. Please, boys, the floor is yours." He slumps back. "Proceed."

Suzuki looks at his boat shoes.

Whistler loosens his tie.

"Suzuki," Ruther says, "you started to say something. I interrupted. I'm so fucking sorry. Continue."

"The probation officer thinks Allen is too scared of prison to be our man. It's clear Mr. Schmidt has a capacity for violence and ample anger issues."

Whistler says. "Women issues too. You know his record. He broke a woman's neck. He's familiar with the Echelon, was clearly at the Zhang crime scene."

Ruther says, "Give me a plausible theory."

"Schmidt got to the coffee shop early, parked around back, and forced his way in as the owner opened up, attacked her, ran out when Greene showed, hopped in his van, parked out front, and acted shocked when Greene came out carrying the vic. Ginny Flores, who may be connected, Schmidt could have known her. He could have gotten her pregnant. That would connect him to three victims. According to Gladsky at Bug Off, Schmidt was working alone the day of the Harpole attack. And—get this—Gladsky said Schmidt has been known to hook up with staff at these hotels. So it feels like the Ginny Flores shoe fits Schmidt perfectly. And with Harpole he could have left the International, driven to the Echelon, and returned with no one the wiser. The way I see it, he locks the dog in a room, sneaks out the freight elevator. It would be easy."

"Did you hear the part where I said 'airtight case' and 'actual evidence'? A public defender could drive a garbage truck through that reasonable doubt. Speculation does not lead to convictions."

Suzuki speaks up, "We've taken this as far as we can without Mrs. Zhang or a warrant. The crime scenes, the canvas, the bodies, the video evidence is all a bust. If Zhang's brain is vegetable soup, that only leaves one option: fish for evidence in the most likely pond. That's Schmidt's van, Schmidt's house. It's time to twist arms, Inspector. If the chief of Ds is so invested in seeing results, he needs to point to the judge that will give us a warrant."

"So it's on me?" Ruther says. "Is that what you are fucking telling me? This is somehow my problem? I guess that's why I'm a living legend." He fishes a comb from a pocket and gives his mustache a thorough grooming. The comb goes away. He clears his throat. "Diaz, you figure out exactly where Schmidt is at the moment. Suzuki, bet his wife might have feelings about his reputation for hooking up at work. With any luck, she'll blow her top and offer to testify against the prick. Only one way to know. Have her come in. Be persuasive. Diaz, I'm going to use your theoretical scenario to convince a judge this is more than a fishing expedition." He stands. His leather chair bangs his file cabinets. "But you better be fucking right. Now get the fuck out and wait for the bat signal."

Thinning the Soul

The door to Rush Medical Center leads down a hall lined with photos of former hospital administrators, their gilded frames screwed to the wall to prevent theft. At a turn in the hall sits an oversized semicircle of built-in counters, behind which a tired-looking attendant waits.

"May I help you?" The man's curly hair is black at the roots but white on top, as if age has dusted his head with powder. His tag reads "Lucky." Calvert assumes it is a name and not a declaration.

"I'm here to see Rosa." He tries to recall her last name. She told him a story about the father of her son. Chinese name. "Rosa with a Chinese last name."

Lucky gives Calvert a slow, appraising look. "You want a doctor or a patient?" He already sounds exhausted by the exchange.

"Sorry. I was unclear; my brain is disintegrating. A patient. She's very nice, Rosa, in a coma. Does that help? We are true good friends."

"Wait." Lucky holds up his whole hand, suddenly full of energy. He looks hard at Calvert. He takes up his phone and taps away at the screen. He waits, he flicks, he taps. He turns the phone to Calvert. "That's you," he says.

On the screen, Calvert sees an image of himself standing with a microphone in his face. He feels no connection, no sense that he is the person in the man's phone. But it is his likeness. He nods to Lucky.

"I knew it! You came to see the woman. I recognized you, but when you started talking, that's when I knew. You saved her life."

Calvert knows the characterization isn't accurate. He wants to explain that, given his imminent death, walking into danger posed no risk. He was only looking for coffee, perhaps a bagel. His stomach grumbles. He focuses on his current reality and says, "I'm here to see Rosa."

"Oh, cool, man. Can I get a picture? My girl is gonna flip her wig." Lucky moves around the counter and throws an arm over Calvert's shoulder, tucks in close, and holds the phone at arm's length. "Say 'bags of money.' Three, two, one, *bags of money.*"

Calvert does not say "bags of money."

Lucky looks at the image on his phone. "Dope," he says. "You need to walk on down the corridor." He points around the bend in the hall. "You'll find some elevators. Go to the fourth floor. When you get off, turn right. You'll find another desk, and they can tell you where to go. Okay? You tell them you're the one who saved that girl. They'll know where to send you. Okay?"

"This way. Elevator. Fourth floor. Turn right. Ask at desk."

"You got it."

Calvert walks away. He sees through the floor-to-ceiling windows along his right that the hallway runs parallel to the street, and he's moving against the closest lane of traffic. The sun glares in, bounces off the hard white surfaces, and makes his upper lip perspire. He fears his meat will cook before he reaches Rosa. He picks up the pace and steps into the waiting elevator.

Inside, the air is cool, the light dim. His body chemistry stabilizes. He thinks of Lucky taking pictures. *Does capturing a likeness shave off a thin curl of identity? Am I infinitesimally less than I was before the photo?*

Professor Greene once had a layover in Madrid. He ordered gelato from a kiosk and stood watching people pass. A woman in a long floral skirt and a colorful shawl was asking for money. An American businessman said, "Five dollars if you let me take your picture." He pulled money from his pocket. "US dollars," he said, flapping the bill in the air. He took his phone out, preparing to steal an image. His voice was too loud and his behavior abrasive. Professor Greene didn't want to be associated with him. He tried to eat his gelato in a European manner.

"No, no," the woman said, distressed by the loud American aiming the flat back of his phone at her. She had turned her bent back to him and left without the money.

Calvert knows now what Professor Greene once knew: some cultures believe a camera steals a piece of the human soul.

When the elevator opens on the fourth floor, Calvert wonders: *Can a body go on in the absence of a soul? And what of my students with their habitual selfies? Are their souls as thin as tracing paper, ready to rip loose and blow away? And why do they always stick their tongues out?* He remembers the gelato he was eating that day had been smooth and flavored with espresso. The lingering memory of smooth, sweet espresso reminds him of Rosa, and he picks up the pace as he moves down the hall.

At the reception desk, Lucky has called ahead to explain Calvert's needs. The woman leans over the counter to point at the floor under Calvert's feet.

"You see the colored dots? Follow the orange dots to the orange elevators and go to the sixth floor. There's a nurses' station. Someone there will know the number for Mrs. Zhang's room."

Calvert looks between his shoes. He sees yellow dots, green dots, blue dots, and orange. He follows the trail of orange dots with his eyes. They lead across a busy atrium packed with people in white lab coats or pale hospital gowns. There are people with crutches and canes, people in wheelchairs with oxygen plugged into their nostrils, and two people taking wheeled IV stands for a walk. Past the motion of sickly humanity and the shuffle of feet crisscrossing at random angles, Calvert finds the mouth of a hallway, forty yards away, marked by more orange dots.

"I see the dots," he says. He keeps his eyes down, afraid of losing the trail. He follows the dotted line as if seeking treasure on a pirate's map. He imagines Rosa's room marked with an X. He smiles like a kid, so excited to see his friend that he hops from one dot to the next.

Publish or Perish

After their meeting, Abbey escorts Moe to the main building to meet Greene's psychologist, and lets her in through a series of security doors. Now Moe waits at the front desk. She starts composing descriptions in her mind for the article to come.

"You here about that Calvert cat?" the kid on the other side of the security desk asks, interrupting her process.

She takes in his wrinkled uniform, the bill of his cap twisted off center. She says, "I'm doing background for an article. Did you know him?"

"I know when I was trained I was told to keep an eye out for him. He used to hang around and watch people come and go like he was plotting his escape."

"Did he ever actually try to leave?"

The kid stands to shoot the shit, adjusts the brim of his cap to show Moe a fledgling wisp of a mustache. "It was the night shift. The patient rooms are locked so patients can't go for a midnight stroll, right?" Before he can say more, his eyes register something behind Moe. She hears heels clicking her way. The boy says, "You have a nice day," and sits back down.

Moe turns to see a woman with luxurious auburn hair, wearing the hell out of a dark, knee-length wrap dress and chunky heels. Moe's reminded of the woman who bumped her on the train. *It's not her, but definitely a member of the same clan.*

"You are the reporter?"

"Moe Diaz. I appreciate your time."

"Katherine Davis. Why don't we go to my office?"

They walk to a cluster of offices and common rooms at the center of the building, a spot called the Hub. Moe sits and listens patiently to the psychologist give a carefully orchestrated spiel. She shares no information that isn't publicly available. It feels like a waste of time. Still, Moe tries to probe a little.

"Would you say Professor Greene's recovery was unusual? Sounds like he went from nearly brain dead to the toast of Chicago in a short span of time."

"It's gratifying when a patient responds well to a treatment plan. As you can imagine, every brain injury is unique. Some people heal faster than others. Our team has had a lot of success."

It's clear the woman has decided exactly what information she can divulge and is careful to say no more. Ten minutes after meeting Katherine Davis, Moe is escorted back through the building. Moe hoped to ask the security kid some follow-up questions on the sly, but Katherine ushers her out the security doors.

It's a longer ride than it should be as Moe drives to *Text Block*. She's rattled by her near-crash. The harrowing trek was worth it. It's true she learned nothing to definitively prove her suspicions of Calvert Greene. She did happen across more than she'd expected. That is how journalism works. *The more you dig, the more the story changes.* Dig enough and sometimes you find a story you could have never imagined. She decides to tuck that nugget away to share with her cub reporters when the time is ripe.

She's only halfway to *Text Block*, but Taibbi needs gas, so she downshifts and coasts into an automated gas station. She jams her card in the self-pay pump and removes the nozzle. The pump beeps and flashes a message that the card cannot be read, instructs her to insert her card and remove it slowly. "I did remove the card slowly, bitch," she argues. But she's not mad at the pump. She's in too good a mood. She keeps thinking of Cyn Regan and her scrunchy face. She tries her card a second time. She selects a grade of gas and fills the small tank.

"You are kind of a pain in the ass," she says to Taibbi. She adds, "But you're my pain in the ass," and gives the tank a loving pat. "I'm going to get you taken care of soon."

In another twelve minutes, she parks Taibbi in the *Text Block* lot. Loni approaches before Moe shuts the engine down. "Vivian said it's up to you if I write about the little girl that was shot last night?"

Moe sets her helmet on her motorcycle. "What's your angle?"

"A nine-year-old girl, Clarissa, Avalon Park. Walking with a bag of doughnuts in one hand and holding her father's hand with the other. Gunshots pop off, the dad curls around his daughter. His ear gets blown off and the bullet goes through Clarissa's chest. Dead in his arms. The angle is Clarissa goes to school in Lakeview, where the mother lives. She visits her father on weekends in Avalon Park. I want to talk about her experience in the two places. The idea is of traveling between two kinds of Chicago. I'm calling it 'Dangerous Passage.'"

Moe listens closely. Loni is passionate. "Is it being reported elsewhere?"

"Channel 13 gave a mention in the overnight tragedies segment of the morning news, sent someone to take video of the little memorial of flowers and candles."

"Write it up. Keep it tight. Get it to me by three. I won't know until I read it. Be careful. You're a reporter. This is journalism, not an editorial. Keep that in mind."

"Will do." Loni looks like she wants to clap for herself, but she's too cool. She says, "Will do. I will do that," and rushes back in the building.

Moe is at her desk calling Whistler when Dale arrives. "Can you read this?" he asks.

She doesn't allow herself to feel aggravated. "It's what I'm here for," she says flatly.

Dale passes his laptop to Moe. He leans over her shoulder as she reads. He's reporting about a big-time law practice donating all the billable hours of one of its immigration lawyers to help families targeted by the most recent version of US immigration policy. The article is very comprehensive. Too much information about immigration law, the language too detailed.

"It restores my faith in lawyers. What it lacks is a case study. You need to talk about how this lawyer has changed things for a specific person."

"I thought so. I wanted to see if I was on the right track?"

"I wish I had written parts of it."

Dale's smile beams.

"You have gone over the top on the legal language."

"I just want to get it right?"

"That's a good thing. Just remember the first story doesn't have to be the whole story. It needs to be accurate. But it's only a way in. You don't have to say everything. Does that make sense?"

"Yes. Thanks. I get it." He leaves. Moe waits for him to return. Three seconds later, he's back for his laptop.

She smiles.

"Where was I?" she asks the room. She remembers. Dials Whistler.

"Detective Diaz."

"Very official," she says. "Let me give you what I've dug up on Calvert Greene."

"I'm driving. I'm putting you on speaker. My partner is here. Suzuki, my cousin Moe."

"Hi, Whistler's partner," Moe says.

Suzuki starts talking, "What's with this guy's name? Also, why doesn't he like soosh? That's not natural. Everyone likes a good soosh. It comes from the life-giving sea."

"He's an enigma," Moe explains. She's careful how much she lets on about her arrangement with her cousin.

"Hey, cuz. Keep it short. We're about to scoop up Schmidt." Moe takes that as both a warning and the news Whistler is willing to share.

"An arrest?"

"No. Not yet. A more pointed conversation," Whistler says.

"Person of interest," Suzuki adds.

"I see." That counts as confirmation. "I'm not giving up on the professor. You know the accident he was in? It was hinky. His wife crashed her car into Greene while he was with a pregnant student. No father of the unborn child ever materialized. The professor's head trauma was serious. He's on antipsychotics. He's a candidate for fucking electroshock therapy."

"They still do that?" Suzuki asks.

"Apparently it's used with some success for people with this Cotard syndrome. Which is the professor's diagnosis. But if I, like, read between the lines"—she adds the "like" for her own entertainment—"there was some disagreement between the treatment team about the diagnosis. The head psychiatrist may have wanted to believe it was Cotard's Syndrome."

"Why?" Whistler asks.

"It's rare and the doctor smelled a publication. Self-aggrandizement. Freud would have called it ego. Apparently psychiatry outranks psychoanalysis. Big pharma beats talk therapy."

"That's interesting, but Greene isn't the guy," Whistler says. He drives past a line of taxis and parks in front of the five-star hotel. An attendant comes to open his door. Whistler unclips his badge and holds it against the inside of the windshield. The attendant gets the message and goes back to his station.

"I'm not saying he's the guy," Moe admits. "I'm saying he's no hero. I was right to think something was off. He walked away from a catastrophe that left two people dead. Three if you count an unborn child. He knew Rosa Zhang. He's psychotic. He was institutionalized during the first murder at least, but New Horizons is low security. He could have walked away. It's a long shot, but not impossible. The kid at the security desk said he'd hang around like he was planning a break. I couldn't get a completely straight answer, but I think he snuck out at some point, or tried to. I mean the nickname for his condition is walking corpse syndrome. He's as close to a real-life zombie as you can get."

"*Brains!*" Suzuki moans.

"Greene's boss at Bug Off did make him sound unusual." Whistler ignores Suzuki out of habit. "But he didn't stick his neck out to defend Schmidt either."

"What if Schmidt and Greene are in on it together? A classic homicidal team-up," Suzuki asks lightly, perfectly happy to participate in broad conjecture. "A symbiotic thrill kill cult."

"Not helpful," Whistler says.

"I like the way you think, Suzuki," Moe says to razz her cousin.

"Listen, we're headed up to get our man."

"Bye, Moe," Suzuki says and slides out to stretch his legs.

"Bye, Suzuki. Let's do soosh soon." She waits until she hears the door close. "Are we good?"

"Make it quick."

"I might be wrong about Greene," Moe says. "It's a long shot. But I want to check a few more leads. For one thing, I need to talk to this boss of his, get more background. I've got time late this afternoon, and I'm going out there one way or another."

"He'll give you a whole tour. He's very proud of his extermination empire. His wife is pretty easy on the eyes. Kind of controlling. But I wouldn't kick her out of bed for eating nachos. Also very pregnant."

Moe doesn't care. "Is it fair to say officials close to the case confirm they are questioning a person of interest?"

"Yes. But wait until I have something definitive. We might put this away in the next few hours. Ruther claims to be getting a warrant to search Schmidt's home."

"Based on something new?"

"Honestly, hope and intuition. Do not quote me."

"Keep me posted, but I have to publish this story soon."

"Cuz," Whistler adds, "you sound good. Not as pissed off as usual."

"For reasons I'm not ready to divulge, I'm feeling optimistic." She's happy to leave it at that, so she hangs up.

An Invitation to Care

The orange elevator was not literally orange, but this only caused the briefest instance of alarm in Calvert. Neither was Rosa's room marked with a pirate map X. Instead, there was a placard on the wall next to the door with the name "Zhang" written in streaky dry-erase marker.

The nurse at the station sucked her teeth when she spoke. "I know you—*smek*," she said with a kind smile. "Consuela—*smek*—says she prayed for Rosa every night—*smek*—and that you were the answer to her prayers—*smek*."

Standing in front of Rosa's room, Calvert questions the likelihood he is the unwitting agent of a higher power. A different nurse steers a jostling cart of medications down the hall. As he passes behind Calvert, he says, "You can go in."

Calvert goes in.

He sees Rosa. Still, fragile, and small, like a body arranged for viewing. The sides of the bed are up, the mattress raised, pillows propped behind her head pitching her neck forward and bunching her flesh into a second fold of chin. Her dark hair is brushed and arranged carefully. A blanket and sheet are pulled over her chest, her bare arms out, open palms up. Her eyes are closed and her lids are glossy, as if smeared with Vaseline. The sight stops him. He takes a breath and can't let it out.

After his car accident, he was much as Rosa is now, though he doesn't remember. His brain was swollen. He was unconscious. He regrets again that he slept through Mere's memorial. He knows, per her wishes, she was likely cremated. He didn't attend Kati's funeral either, though he guesses her remains were flown to Budapest and placed near family.

He has begun to mourn their passing to the limited extent his emotions will allow. He secretly mourns Bump too.

A quiet *beeping* reminds him where he is and who he's looking at. He steps farther into the room. A head lifts from the far side of the bed, a woman startled from sleep, snorting, rubbing her face. She stares at him.

Calvert is embarrassed, as if he's walked into the women's restroom. He starts to leave.

"Señor Greene! It's you." The woman gets to her feet and advances on Calvert. She's a short, round version of Rosa with a silver swirl of cotton-candy hair. Her hands are hot as she clasps his. "I prayed you would come." She hugs him, places her cheek to his chest. She holds him tightly. He assumes she's listening for a heartbeat, imagines she can't hear a thing, similar to pressing her ear to a bass drum, only air pressure. She lets loose and smiles. It's like Rosa's smile, only sadder. He allows her to tug him down, kiss each cheek and pat his face. "You are an angel." She releases him.

After a moment's hesitation, he ventures, "You are Rosa's mother."

"Yes. Consuela. Come, sit." As he moves past the foot of the bed, he examines Rosa more closely, casting his gaze up her frail body to her face. Her skin looks healthy, her expression one of peaceful slumber. He can see blue bruising turning to green over the bunched skin of her throat, spreading onto her exposed collarbones. "Sit." Consuela clears a chair and pats the cushion. Calvert sits.

Consuela uses her fingers to brushes hair from Rosa's forehead. She cups Rosa's chin and makes a kissing sound. She moves her chair closer to the one she cleared for Calvert and takes a seat.

"The day she was born," she says, "my mother came from Mexico City. The nurse placed Rosa in my arms and said, 'You did a good job. That was hard work. She is perfect.' My mother leaned toward me. I thought she would tell me how beautiful Rosa was, how much hair she had, how strong she looked. Instead, she said, 'I know how difficult that was. Things get easier. The first thirty years are the hardest.' Then she left." Consuela turns to Calvert. "I thought she was being cruel. But she was right. You never stop worrying for your babies, no matter their age." She exhales as if the air is being crushed from her.

"How is she?" Calvert asks.

Before responding, Consuela works her tiny watch around her slender wrist to read it. "She is resting." Consuela sniffles and rubs the tip of her nose with a ball of Kleenex.

Calvert remembers how hot his body had become downstairs, how his sense of smell has deteriorated. He fears he stinks.

Rosa's mother continues, "The scans came back clean. She may have a mild concussion. She is breathing on her own. Her pulse is good. She is healthy. The nurses love her. They take good care of us." She holds her hands as if in prayer, the Kleenex sandwiched between her palms and her eyes turned to heaven. Calvert looks overhead and finds only lights and a silver asterisk that marks an overhead sprinkler.

Consuela says, "Her windpipe was not broken." She sniffles and jangles her watch. "Superficial bruises, the doctors tell me. At first, they worried lack of oxygen may have caused permanent damage. But no. Praise God." Again the prayer gesture. "Her brain is fine. God brought you to save her at just the right instant. It's a miracle." She unrolls the balled Kleenex and honks her nose. Dust motes float in the shaft of light coming in the window and cutting across Rosa's shoulder. Calvert looks for more Kleenex to offer Consuela. He sees none.

"Why is she still asleep?" he asks.

Rosa's mother draws a shuddering breath and sobs. A nurse enters. Not the nurse who sucks her teeth or the one who delivers medicine. "Oh, Sweetie," the new nurse says. She moves fast, produces a box of facial tissues from somewhere along her route and delivers them to the crying woman. The nurse pats Consuela reassuringly. "I know," she says. "I know."

Calvert doesn't understand the secret the women share. *What is the thing known?*

"And who is this?" the nurse asks.

"The man I told you about." Rosa's mother regains control. "Señor Greene, this is Nurse Alicia. She takes care of Rosa." Consuela takes Alicia's hand and holds it.

Nurse Alicia wears dark scrubs and clogs that look like she dipped her feet in marshmallow fluff. She hugs Calvert. Her stethoscope strikes Calvert in the face. It doesn't hurt. "You did a good thing," she says to him. To Consuela she says, "I'll be back. You be strong. It's only a matter of time." She goes as quickly as she arrived, her mallow-feet squelching out the door.

They sit in silence, passing time. Rosa's mother looks at her watch. "They say my girl is in shock. There is no medical reason she isn't awake."

"I see."

"Do you have children, Señor Greene?"

"Call me Calvert." He's proud he thought of the social nicety. *You can teach a dead dog new tricks.*

"Gracias, Calvert. Children? Do you have any? Are you married?"

"No. I have no wife and no child. I am solitary."

Consuela is pensive. She turns her watch up again, rubs her fingers over the crystal. "I have to get Thomas from school. Will you sit with Rosa? The doctors and the nurses say it's good to talk to her. She will not react, but she can hear you. It's good for her brain. Stimulates the nervous system. Maybe you'd like to read to her. I will leave my Bible. Will you stay?"

There's a pleading look on her face. He thinks of how people speak of faith in God when facing death. There's some saying about religion and foxholes. Calvert can't recall, doesn't know what a foxhole is, but he doubts it has to do with foxes. *Myelin.*

He follows the spotlight of sun from the window to where it now shines on half of Rosa's face. *It's logical for people seek the comfort of belief in troubled times,* he reasons. *But what if it works differently? What if faith is a magnet for hardship? Could thinking fatalistically and romanticizing the afterlife encourage tragedy?*

Consuela repeats her question, "Do you have time to stay with Rosa?"

"I would like that," he says.

Consuela's mouth impersonates Rosa's smile again. She gathers her things in her purse and leaves Calvert alone with the unconscious and completely vulnerable Rosa.

Situational Ethics

After Moe hangs up with the woman at Bug Off, she strolls out back of *Text Block* to look for Jerome. She's noticed something: since her new title was foisted on her, she feels less competitive with Jerome, more like they are colleagues. As she knew he would be, he's hunched on the little bench and staring at the toes of his beat shoes, smoking as always. "Hey, Jerry."

"Never call me Jerry. My father is Jerry. I'm Jerome," his voice, even when irritated, rings pleasantly.

He's bothered and Moe enjoys it. She likes to think of herself as mischievous rather than malicious, but she also knows people who'd disagree. "Oh. Sorry. You said that before." She stands back from the swirling cloud of smoke Jerome steeps in like carcinogenic tea.

"Have I?" he asks with a wry twist at the corner of his mouth. He's a shrewd observer, doesn't miss much.

"Sorry." She means it this time. "I owe you. That connection in the professor's English program was helpful. Very. The perfect source." Moe smiles a bright smile.

Jerome can't decipher her subtext, but his expression reveals his suspicions. He sucks down the last of his cigarette and flicks the butt. It arcs into a patch of gravel and scrub.

"I'm going to meet another source for this strangler angle I'm working. I'm supposed to meet him this afternoon. Can you read Loni's story and post it if it's ready? I won't be back in time."

"I can do that. But you owe me big." He brushes ash from his slacks.

"I will be forever indebted." She holds the door open, but he waves another cigarette in the air, preparing to light it.

Inside, Vivian is at her desk, talking on her cell. She gestures for Moe to take a seat and wraps up the conversation. "Moe! I'm glad you're here. You're doing so well with Dale and Loni."

"I may actually enjoy some things about it," Moe admits.

Vivian smiles knowingly. "Walk with me," she says, and she leaves her office. Moe falls into step.

"I just had a talk with Dale," Vivian says. "He had good things to say about your advice. Their stories have been good. Though I did find a typo. Loni wrote food *dessert*, not *desert*. I'd prefer dessert, but I'm watching my figure." She pulls open the freezer and takes out two microwave diet meals.

"I've been focused on content and process. My line edits may have suffered."

"It happens." She digs a fork from the drawer and pops a pattern of holes in the plastic film. The larger woman looks into Moe's face. "I'm happy you're on staff. The extra time it gives me is paying off." She springs the microwave open, pitches in one meal, and slams the door. "Catch me up on your Calvert Greene story." Vivian pushes numbers and starts the microwave.

Moe retrieves her own laptop from her desk and reads from her notes and a few paragraphs of the article she's started writing.

Vivian nods a few times. The microwave beeps. She peels the film back, stirs the food, and returns it to the microwave. When she speaks, her tone is gentle, "The story of the professor's accident is interesting, but it was nearly a year ago. Is it news?" The microwave beeps. She takes out the hot tray and pokes and heats a second meal.

"You think I should drop the story?" Moe asks, half angry.

"You're a journalist so I get why you want to run down this story, but remember you don't have to print everything you find. You've always insisted we don't dabble in tabloid journalism." *Beep beep beep.*

Vivian carefully lifts the meal from the microwave and swings the door shut.

"I know," Moe says, searching her own rationale. "It's a critique of broadcast journalism. It's supposed to show they forced circumstances to fit the story they wanted to sell of Greene as a hero of convenience. He's not the guy they made him out to be."

"Perhaps. But unless he's the killer, he did play a part in saving that woman."

"I suppose."

"Doesn't that make him a hero of sorts?"

"Yes. But—"

"Our emphasis should be to report the right way for the right reasons without constantly comparing ourselves to other outlets."

Moe feels attacked. She's worried what she might say. She seethes silently while Vivian dumps both of her low-fat, low-cal stir-fry meals into one big bowl. She remains quiet as Viv adds a dollop of thick peanut paste from a jar she keeps in the fridge. She doesn't speak while her boss squeezes three plum sauce packets over her bowl and stirs the sloppy mixture.

"I want you to be honest," Vivian says gently. "Do you think your ambition to scoop Sophia might be leading you down a path you usually know to avoid?"

"Yes. You're right. Fuck." She cusses for catharsis. "I hate that you're right. If I tried to deny it, we'd both know I was lying."

Vivian takes up the bowl and carries it to her office. Moe follows, still listening. "I'm probably at fault. I send mixed signals. I encourage you to wage an assault on the establishment, disrupt the system, channel your indignation into your writing. Journalism takes a good story, but it also needs craft, time, and consideration. The model of a story a day from every contributor is a mistake. It was a good way to generate loads of content. But I'm rethinking it."

"You were only encouraging me. You always have."

Vivian stirs her food and lets the fork rest in the bowl while she talks. "You ever been faced with a choice you only had one shot at?"

"I guess so," Moe says, taking a seat.

"When I was a little girl, I went to court and the judge took me aside and asked me to choose which of my parents to live with." Vivian says it and slurps drippy, limp noodles into her mouth.

"You never talk about your family," Moe says.

"Well, I try not to look back." She takes another bite. "Sometimes you're in a situation with no good options, but you have to pick one. I've heard it put like this: free will exists when faced with a hard choice. One of my parents was not inherently better than the other. They were both kind and loving. They cared for me." She opens her desk and pops a Kleenex to wipe a dribble of sauce from her chin.

"Choosing one would be a rejection of the other. I was a third-grader." She forks some chicken and snow peas into her mouth. "But that variety of decision can be an opportunity to define who you are." She takes another bite and chews. "I chose my father. Not because I liked him more, but because my mother could handle the hurt. My father needed me more. In that moment, I became the kind of person who makes decisions in a way that's best for everyone involved. Not just me."

"That's heavy for a kid."

"It was a lot. But kids grow up faster than you think." She eats more chicken and slurps more noodles. "Once I made my choice, I couldn't take it back. Are you with me?"

"Yes."

She waves her wet fork, "Imagine you have a decision like that and you choose wrong. After the fact, you can't accept it, right? It's a colossal tragedy, but it's too late to change. So you snap." She drops her fork in the bowl.

"It's not a stretch," Moe admits.

"Maybe Calvert Greene made a decision he can't find a way to live with, something about his accident. Sometimes the hardest thing is to sit quietly, alone with your thoughts, and live with the things you've done. Because what's done is done. At times like that, most people distract themselves with work or sex or drugs or food or shopping or other people's business."

"Or they tell themselves they aren't living at all."

"Exactly the point I'm making. This Greene was a pretty smart man. Maybe his big brain found the perfect loophole."

"It makes sense," Moe says.

"It's a working theory. There's no proof. Even if you could prove it, it's not a story that needs to be written."

"How can I trust my instincts if I don't find out? I need to at least follow through with Greene's employer."

"I get that," Vivian says. "Do this: take forty-eight hours. Do what you can. Then let it go. Follow the case. Report the news we have. That is my directive as editor-in-chief. Can you handle it?"

Moe slouches, lost in her own emotional doldrums.

Vivian hoists the bowl and slurps the liquid. She *thunks* the bowl down. "That was not in the least bit satisfying," she says.

"I know how you feel," Moe replies.

One-Sided Relationship

After Consuela leaves, the hospital room feels abandoned. Calvert wasn't aware of the energy she gave off, the outsized space her tiny frame managed to occupy. Once he was alone, he felt himself tumbling in the undercurrent of her absence. *A dead man and an unconscious woman can't match the psychic force of one vivacious grandmother.*

He lifts the Bible she left for him. It's heavy, oxblood leather, soft to the touch, gold-stamp lettering. He brushes his fingers along the words. *Gill Sans* pops into his head. It sounds foreign, a language he's forgotten how to speak.

This Bible is larger than the one he had as a child. His had been wrapped in an idyllic scene of Christ seated among a menagerie of kids and animals. In Calvert's memory a children's choir sings a familiar song. *"Jesus loves the little children/All the children of the world/ Red, brown, yellow/ Black and white/ They are precious in his sight."* When he was young, he found the lyrics confusing because the image on his zippered Bible showed only white faces. He leaves the book where he found it and stands.

Rosa's whole face is in the slant light coming through the window. If she were awake, the glare would be unpleasant. He puts his body between the window and Rosa. She is no less radiant in his shadow. Calvert clears his throat. "Your mother seems nice. There's a family resemblance."

Rosa's head is still thrust forward by the pile of pillows, crunching her chin toward her chest. He wants to fix it. He reaches, but hesitates, afraid to jostle her and tempted to touch her in equal proportions. Is he the kind of dead man that caresses an unconscious woman?

He slips one hand behind her head, her hair tangles around his fingers. With the other hand he withdraws a pillow. He looks into her face. Her eyes dance under closed lids. Her lips twitch as if thinking of something funny. *Rosa is more alive unconscious than I am half conscious.*

Rosa's breathing is deep, with a catch at the end of each exhale, as if her body has forgotten to intake the next lungful of oxygen. He imagines she's attempting to starve her red blood cells, her slumber so perfect she longs to postpone waking.

"Your mother, Consuela, wants me to read to you, but I wouldn't know where to start. I'll just talk." Rosa's hair is bunched to one side. He carefully arranges it. The act feels intimate, loving, like bathing a newborn in a kitchen sink.

He coughs into his fist. "People say I saved you, that I'm a hero. I'm the opposite. There's a word for that, but my mind is mushy." Unconscious Rosa listens patiently. He takes her hand. He counts the thin bones in the back of her hand. *Frail like bird bones.*

When Mere died, he hadn't had the chance to apologize or say his goodbyes. He wouldn't share this if Rosa was awake, but this is a chance to be completely honest. The chance he didn't get with Mere.

He clears his throat. Rosa waits. "I was killed in a car accident. I'm waiting for my body to stop moving. I should be permanently dead any day. When I walked in to get coffee, someone was on top of you." He thinks he sees her expression change. The corners of her mouth draw down, but it could be the sun going behind the parking garage across the street. "I couldn't know you were in danger when I went in. Couldn't know he had his hands around your throat." He looks at the dark marks left by strong fingers. "Couldn't have known he was wringing the life from you." Her expression looks pained. He worries about continuing. He tries to lighten the mood, "You're alive but won't wake.

I'm dead but won't stop moving. What are you gonna do?" She doesn't reply. *Why would she? It was pointless.*

He's lost his train of thought. "Consuela asked if I was married and if I had kids. I was not completely forthcoming." He gets back on track. "The truth is, I was married. Mere and I were happy for a time. We wanted to have children, but there were complications. We tried for a decade. We spent a fortune. It never worked. We agreed to stop trying. Mere became distant. She felt our life was lacking. The absence of a child was a fundamental failure of our union. I focused on work and tried to wait it out. Mere couldn't shake it. I met a student, Kati. We had a relationship. I was a needy man. I was lonely.

"When I was home with Mere, I saw how defeated she was. Our life would never be the thing she dreamed of. I couldn't make her happy. She didn't have any interest in sex if it wouldn't yield a baby. She needed time. I knew that. I gave her as much as I could. I gave her years. I gave her space. I needed to feel wanted. You understand?" He thinks Rosa's face shows sympathy.

"There was an unspoken understanding that Meredith's grief gave her permission to foster a deepening depression. In comparison, the loss of my chance at fatherhood didn't merit conversation. My feelings about the distance between us was not worth the air it wasted to mention. I kept my feeling to myself. It was what was expected." He checks to see that Rosa is still listening.

"I didn't plan it. My feelings for Kati. It happened naturally, and I didn't stop it. I was swept away. Kati was all I could think of. She thought I was smart. She made me feel I was worth being loved. Kati got pregnant. She wanted to keep the baby. You're a mother, Rosa. You understand. Like Mere, Kati wanted to be a mother. How could a baby be bad? My heart was overfull. I hadn't been so happy in ages. If that makes me a bad person, you can tell me." Unconscious Rosa reserves judgment.

"Thank you for that," he says. He pats the hand he still holds. "Kati didn't have a car and she was far from her family. She had no close friends. I couldn't abandon her. I was responsible. So I took her to doctor appointments. I went to the ultrasound. I heard the rapid wet pattering of our child's heart. I was going to be a father. We gave the baby a placeholder name: Bump."

He sees Kati watching the monitor while her doctor rolls the ultrasound probe over her swollen abdomen. The probe makes tracks in the blue gel, like a toboggan in fresh snow. The ghost of Calvert past tries a poor joke about finger painting. He's excited. The black and white lava-lamp blobs form the shapes of tiny body parts. "So there is the head and the face. You see the nose, mouth. One ear. And"—the doctor rubs the probe around, presses it into Kati, making a deep dimple in her stomach—"a second ear."

He goes on talking to Rosa. "In the second trimester, Kati started showing. We couldn't hide it any longer. I drove to Kati's apartment and found a spot along the curb. I walked around and touched the swell of her belly. She moved my hand to a hard knot: our child's head or butt. She smiled at me. She kissed me. I helped her into the car. She struggled to fasten the seat belt. I watched, happily waiting to close her door. I heard an engine rev, the warning growl of a predator. Up the hill I saw Mere's car. Saw her gripping the steering wheel. She revved the engine again. She put the car in drive. She was fifty yards away and gaining speed." Calvert's volume increases. "I slammed Kati's door. I ran. I heard the tires of Mere's car grinding loose pavement. Peripherally I saw Kati, desperate, turning her back to the passenger door, screaming, with both arms covering her belly, protecting Bump as best she could. Mere surging toward me, her engine growing louder. I got my car running. I took the gearshift in hand. Put it in drive. I stomped the gas as Mere's car crushed me." He's out of breath. His eyes make water run down his face, and gather at the corners of his mouth before dripping off. *It's okay. I'm dead. Nothing can hurt me.*

"From what I've been told," he continues once he feels nice and dead inside, "Mere's head went through her windscreen, and the steering column crushed all the ribs in her body. Her organs were shredded, and she died from internal trauma. Her family blames me. It's hard to argue it isn't my fault. Mere saw me with a pregnant woman, knew I'd fathered someone else's child.

"I didn't have my seat belt on. Didn't have time. I flew into Kati, crushing her, striking her head with mine. Killing her with my body. Killing Bump. Kati's neck snapped on impact." He's quiet now. Defeated by the raw truth of it.

Finally he says, "My last living memory was a smell: the odor of blood mixing with urine, feces, gasoline, and the sweet scent Kati had spritzed on her neck and cleavage, bright and floral. It was the last flash of sensation before I died. The smell was an ice pick through the olfactory receptors in my brain. I think that's what killed me."

Untethered Epiphany

Calvert is quiet a long time, caught in a serene pause between ending one thing and beginning the next. With no sensations to jumpstart his mind, he's content to linger in the perfect stillness that washes over him the moment he shared his secret with Rosa.

A sound outside the room brings him back. The nurse with the cart of drugs rolls loudly past. Rosa lays next to him, inert. He watches her, can barely detect the rise of her chest. He listens closely. He's wobbly on his dead feet, a swaying disorientation he relates to the strange art happening he'd been subjected to. *Christian's Blake Machine.* He steadies himself by grasping the raised side of the bed. He takes stock of Rosa breathing again. *Is her breathing truly that shallow? Has my story killed her?*

If Rosa's soul is attached to her corporal body through force of habit, isn't it possible his confession struck her badly and has given her less reason to remain tethered to life? The shock of his narrative has set her free, a kite at the apex of flight, cut loose with a pocketknife.

He turns his face to the ceiling, to the throbbing tube lights and sprinkler heads. He thinks of near-death stories, of people leaving their bodies and seeing their deathbeds far below. Could Rosa be somewhere high above, looking down on him now? He fixes the top of his hair.

Nurse Alicia comes in talking. "How's my favorite patient? Good, I bet, with her handsome prince standing guard." She projects optimism. "You been talking to her?"

Calvert is equally puzzled at being called handsome and concerned he's been overheard.

The nurse seems determined to maintain maximum efficiency of movement. "It's good for her, you know. Keep a light tone. Tell her friendly stories. Things that stimulate her. Don't talk about chores or taxes. No politics. Not these days. It's enough to make anyone want to hide under the covers." She moves from one side of the bed to the other and leans around Calvert to touch Rosa's forehead with the back of her hand. She goes back to the far side of the bed. She toggles a button to make the mattress flat. "Rosa's due for a sponge bath, and she needs to be moved on her side. I'll wait till you two are done talking." She shoves the over-bed table farther out of the way. She opens the top drawer of a dresser and takes out a fist-sized ball of colorful cloth.

The thought of Rosa floating overhead is still with Calvert. He glances up and imagines he can feel her there, watching the proficient actions of her capable caregiver. Watching the stiff, awkward posture of her half-dead admirer, his flat face tipped up and searching.

At the end of the bed, Alicia pulls the blankets loose and folds them up, revealing Rosa's stocking feet and legs. She has long white compression socks pulled up to her knees. Alicia peels one down, then the next. Rosa's legs look healthier without the orthopedic casings. Her caramel skin is glossy. Tiny black dots of growing stubble are reassuring, an indication her body systems continue to run.

Nurse Alicia slips a short pair of soft socks on Rosa's feet, as if dressing a child. "Consuela brought her favorite socks," she explains. The novelty socks have a bright pattern of diamond shapes and black text that says "This Meeting Is Bullshit." The nurse wears a digital tablet on a strap across her torso. She pulls it up, removes a stylus, and pokes the flat screen with the rubber nub. For several moments, she works at charting.

Calvert looks at the deep red mark left by the tight band of the compression socks, one depressed stripe under each knee. It looks painful. He wants to knead his thumbs over the offending marks, molding her flesh like clay until it regains shape. But he keeps his hands to himself.

Nurse Alicia swings her digital pad back to her hip. She tugs the sheet over Rosa's lower body, then the blanket. She tucks them in place. "All done. Let them know at the desk when you leave. I'll come finish with Rosa." In the mouth of the door, she says, "Take your time. She likes your company." Nurse Alicia is gone.

He sees himself from Rosa's out-of-body perspective. Big head, pointy chin, feet made small through foreshortening. The marks on her legs remind him of his own scar hidden under his hair: he touches it. He feels Rosa's eyes on him from above the ceiling, hovering over the flat roof of the hospital. How small and inconsequential he must look.

A new thought bubbles to the surface. He has begun to understand that as his brain disintegrates, it gives off sparks of thought as a carbonated soda lets bubbles loose until it's completely flat. It's the memory of a person seen from high above, like Calvert is being watched by Rosa.

"I know who attacked you," he says. "I can prove it."

He bumps into the chair he'd been sitting in. It tumbles over and he goes with it. As he hits the floor, he watches the Bible's pages spread open, hit the ground, crushing and bending the onionskin paper. He gets up and lifts the Bible quickly, worried his marionette musculature has caused damage to the holy book and the trust Consuela put in him. But the book seems fine.

He goes straight to Rosa, leaving the chair where it lies. He sets the Bible in the bed with her. "I have to go now. I know who hurt you. Don't leave. Come back to your body. Thomas needs his momma." He wants to say something true before he goes, something with meaning. He says, "I also need you not to go."

He doesn't wait for Rosa's reply. He leaves the room, letting his body make all the decisions while his mind is elsewhere.

You Get What You Pay For

Having an office with a door she can lock is a new experience for Moe. For the first time in her professional life, she does not pack her laptop, but leaves it on her desk, open to the incomplete draft of her article on Calvert Greene. She also leaves a half-empty cup of unsatisfying tea. She throws her unusually light messenger bag over her shoulder and hangs her Vicky helmet on her forearm as she locks up. She's giving herself plenty of time to ride out to Bug Off.

"It's not even three," Loni complains directly behind Moe, a frantic undertone rising.

"Loni, I've got a time-sensitive lead," she exaggerates. "Gotta go while the source is hot." She starts walking.

"But—" Loni presents her glowing laptop and follows so closely her toes clip Moe's heels.

"Find Jerome. I told him about your story. He's a good editor. Better than me. Don't tell him that. He'll look after you."

"But—" Loni says.

"Don't worry." Moe half turns without slowing her pace. "Trust your instincts. You know what you're doing." That stops Loni. Moe makes her escape.

Five minutes later, Moe's on the street, rolling steadily south. She doesn't want to drive on I-90. She's reluctant to admit Taibbi scares her. The near-wipeout at high speed may have ruined their relationship permanently. She's considering purchasing an actual car, the kind with four wheels. With her raise, she can afford something used. Besides, the motorcycle will be dangerous and miserable in the winter. She'd spent numerous winters completely suited up for bicycling. In truth, she only biked year round because she had no better option. *Besides, the wind generated by motorcycling will cut right through my low-budget gear.* As if to prove her point, a gust hits her chest so hard it challenges her grip on the handlebars.

Her recent choice of a vehicle isn't the only thing she's second-guessing. After talking to Vivian, she's started doubting her story. Is it news or only a vendetta directed at Sophia? Maybe a desire to prove that, although she's not like the girls she grew up with, she's still worth-while. Perhaps she wants acceptance from girls like Sophia, to be found attractive by the same girls she spent her school years rejecting as inau-thentic or dumb or frivolous. Rejected preemptively, so they'd never have the chance to reject her.

She envies Loni because Loni knows enough to write well, but not so much that she questions her own opinions. *Can we ever understand our own motivations?* Moe has developed a complex relationship with the idea of objectivity.

In J-school, the journalism professors taught that objectivity was a primary requirement for a reporter. It was used interchangeably with fairness and factuality. Moe, however, found the theory only held water for white reporters who have a whole spectrum of opinions represented on any given topic.

As a queer woman of color, she found purpose in advocacy journal-ism. It was a way to transparently adopt a perspective aimed at social justice. *Text Block* was a good fit. She picked her stories. She could be rigorously factual, informative, and honest about news she felt needed attention. The truth was key. Truth separates advocacy from propa-ganda. Her published articles, her clips, demonstrate her perspective. If she starts questioning this Greene story, how can she trust her intuition on other stories? Her cheeks are hot in her helmet.

The signal light ahead of her turns red. She clamps down hard on the brakes, is thrown forward, nearly going over her bars. Her hand comes off the clutch, and the engine dies. She rights herself and restarts the engine. The sound it makes seems off. The engine is surging, the idle a touch too low and running a smidgen too lean. She could be imagining it, hypersensitive to Taibbi's every perceived signal that could indicate looming catastrophe. *What the fuck do I know about anything?*

The light turns green. The car behind her honks. She lets the clutch out too quickly and kills the engine again. "Fucking fuck." She waves the cars behind her around. She hits the electric start and listens to the engine turn over and over before finally coming to life. She checks her tiny, shaking mirrors and can't see a thing. She glances over her shoulder, sees the way is clear, and eases down the road.

In light of her torturous and uncharacteristically insecure feelings about her career, perhaps she's been too hard on girls like Sophia. *On Sophia specifically.* Moe had been offended in J-school by Sophia's apparent need to assimilate, to look and act in ways those in power would interpret as desirable, professional, and cookie-cutter. *Whitewashing,* she used to call it. But maybe that is as good a strategy as any: participate fully. Don't stand outside and throw rocks. No one likes a critic. Change things from the inside. Still, Moe's gut has always told her being changed by the system is the more likely outcome.

On South Torrence, maybe ten minutes from her destination, as if her internal chaos is manifesting in reality, Taibbi starts to vibrate at low speed. It's not the radical shaking that rattled her teeth on the interstate. But it scares her. She lugs the engine down a gear and turns on her flashers. *Thank you, YouTube.* The inside of her bubble screen starts to fog. Her hot breath makes her face damp.

She creeps slowly the rest of the way and pulls into the lot at a crawl to park near an open garage door. She knocks down the kickstand and peels off her helmet. The flashers throw splashes of orange against the building until she shuts the engine off. She walks unsteadily around the corner and into the wide cool space of the Bug Off warehouse. There is a crash behind her. She flinches. She ducks and tries to protect her head with her arms. Her higher brain kicks in, and she realizes no danger is imminent. She walks back outside to find Taibbi on his side in the gravel, leaking fluids.

"Shit shit shit." She gets low to heave the Honda into a standing position, gets him on his wheels, sees the kickstand is bent. She shoves the bike to lean it against the building. The tank and fenders are scratched and dented. The peashooter pipes are dimpled, the chrome cracked and flaking. She's never felt so low. "Shit."

"That's too bad," a man says. "I can get that loaded in back of a van and drive you where you need to go. I don't mind." He's tall, with slick white hair and angular features.

"I'm Kaz. You're the reporter? My wife told me you would be here."

"Moe."

"Svetlana's in the office. Have some coffee." He points toward the back of the garage.

The idea of strong coffee is so appealing she wants to weep. For an instant, the thought of the scrunched expression of Professor Cynthia Regan unexpectedly pokes a ray of light through the dark cloud of her life. Looking at her bike, the clouds roll back in.

She finally says, "I wouldn't say no to coffee."

The Full Picture

Calvert's mind is elsewhere when he jogs from Rosa's room. As he passes the nurses' station, he tries to recall what Barney told him about the exhibition.

He takes the orange elevator and exits on the fourth floor. He backtracks through the congested lobby of swaying invalids. An obese man with yellowed feet and a red face is strapped to a gurney parked in Calvert's way. The man pulls on his restraints when Calvert abandons the trail of dots and passes close to his swollen head.

"Trash!" the man yells. "Trash trash trash trash trash. Dirty trashy trash man. Trash trash trash."

Calvert swings wider, startled by the accusation. In the elevator, he tries replaying the exact words Barney had used. It won't come to him. All he can hear is *"Trash trash trash trash."*

Why'd that man call me trash? There's a book about a young prince with epilepsy by an author Calvert once taught. *Dostoyevsky perhaps or Tolstoy. No. Not Tolstoy.* Calvert's tainted mind retrieves the title: *The Idiot.* In the story, the prince's ability to be an acceptable suitor for the high-society ingénue is threatened because of his seizures. The prince becomes increasingly addlebrained and is forced into a sanitarium. Calvert feels for the fictional Russian. Calvert is afflicted by a creeping death that has turned him into an idiot, unsuitable for love. The elevator doors close.

Trash trash trash. The elevator opens, and two doctors walk briskly in.

Calvert pushes his way between them to exit. He's confused. He's on the floor where he started. *Didn't push the button.* He turns to see the elevator doors closing. "Wait," he says. The doctors watch him through the diminishing space as the doors meet. He tries to use his weak arms to pull the doors open, but his simple machines can't generate enough force.

He looks for stairs. There are no stairs. He walks in a circle. He pushes the "Down" button and waits for the elevator. *Trash trash.* It's well documented that mental illness was not treated medically during the Soviet era. Superstition and folklore dominated thinking about such issues. It was commonly held that the insane had been visited by demons or angels. Some thought possession made victims prophetic, their innocent souls touched by powers beyond the mortal realm. *Was Gurney Man channeling a message? An indictment from Mere? Was he touched? Am I?*

The elevator opens. Calvert hurries in. A girl, maybe five, is there. She backs as far from Calvert as possible, wedging into a back corner. She's alone; this bothers Calvert, but he doesn't know what to do. *Trash.* He pushes the button for the first floor. *Is being strapped to a gurney in my future?* He hopes to die before that happens.

His whole life he believed his mind was his greatest asset. Now, almost thoroughly dead, his fickle brain is abandoning him. *Penance.* He leaves the elevator, glances back at the solitary child. She's gone. Calvert doesn't think they stopped at another floor. *Was she ever there? My hard drive is broken.*

Walking along the stretch of hothouse hallway, he slaps the side of his head, first with the flat of one hand, then the other. The hall, he notices, is cooler than when he arrived, less glare with the sun hidden behind buildings. He slaps himself some more. As if he has a short in his wiring, the impact fixes the bad connection, and Barney's voice comes to him: *"Lyla's photos sold well. Did I tell you she took photos for one whole day for the show?"*

"That's it: Lyla the photographer. That's her name," he explains triumphantly to no one in particular, maybe to the girl who was never there. He rounds the turn of the hall.

"What?" Lucky asks. "You say somethin'?" He and a tall man in a similar uniform are in front of the desk, their chat interrupted by Calvert's arrival.

"Talking to myself," Calvert explains. "I need to get home fast."

Lucky points through a solid wall. "Cross over to the outpatient building. Taxis line up along the side. This is my pal, Lex. Can he get a picture with you?"

Calvert gives no reply. He jogs down the hall between portraits of administrators past and shoves his way across the busy sidewalk. He feels his pocket and reaches for his phone. He searches for a number he'd entered from a business card. He dials as he crosses the street.

Message From the Dead

Before starting, Ruther informs Whistler that the judge won't issue a warrant. "But I've got him on speed dial. Get me something convincing, catch Schmidt in a lie, and we'll send him back inside for good. Whistler opens the door, feeling confused and pressured. It goes downhill from there.

If an interrogation is a dance, Schmidt has taken the lead. If it's a boxing match, Whistler hasn't landed a punch. Schmidt has an answer for everything, and they are the same answers as last time. In an honest, natural, human way, Schmidt's story changes slightly, a different emphasis or varied vocabulary, an extra detail he'd previously omitted. But not in a practiced way that feels cautious or contrived. In a convincing way. Which is infuriating.

"There are lots of white vans in Chicago. I bet white is the most common color of work van. I know you don't have my plate number because it wasn't my van. Besides, I was across town at the time.

"Sure, I work at the Echelon now and then. But do you know how many people a place that size employs? A lot, I bet. You should check into that.

"I was there to pick up Cal before work. The professor doesn't remember how to drive. Imagine that. This guy has a PhD and can't drive. He ever tell you about Pushkin? If he hasn't, he will. Trust me. Pushkin is some writer he remembers all about. Doesn't know his cock from a carburetor. But he knows about Pushkin. It's a crazy world.

"Killing my aunt was an accident. God rest her soul. I regret losing my temper. I was a hothead when I was young—horny and angry. I take full responsibility. I did my time. Paid my debt to society. That's how the parole board saw it. I'm a free man. Legal as the day is long. I'd never hurt a woman. I focus on pleasing as many as I can. You have to do what you're good at. Am I right?"

Whistler doesn't answer. He feels like he's on a speed date gone bad. He knows he should start from the top, slow it down. Make Schmidt repeat in detail every moment of the morning Rosa was attacked; repeat every question, rephrase his inquiries until Allen is frustrated and fidgety. Try to trip him up. Get him to punch holes in his own alibi.

The plan to bring Schmidt's wife in had been solid, but Suzuki hadn't been able to locate her. If she'd been observing as Allen bragged about his life's work pleasing women, Whistler might have had leverage. Instead, Whistler is wondering how it's possible for this gross ex-con to be attractive to anyone. It gets under his skin. He glances up surreptitiously. *I can't even find a date.*

A vision of the hot TV reporter, Sophia Garcia, suggestively handling her microphone, passes through his mind. His face flushes. He shakes it off, clears his throat, tries to focus on the case file he's pretending to look at, attempts to come up with a new approach. It's unclear what will work. Schmidt has hexed him with some kind of prison voodoo.

"What if I told you we have your wife watching right now? Listening to everything you say? How do you think she's taking you bragging about other women?" Whistler takes a stab at it but doesn't try to sell it.

Schmidt smiles. "My wife is in Atlanta for the next week to visit her mother. I doubt she'd agree to the interruption. She's a saint. I'm not. She knows the score. She tries to save me from my wayward behavior, and I try my damnedest to keep my place in hell. It's our thing. Don't get me wrong—she'd be disappointed. But that would only make her more determined to rehabilitate me."

Whistler realizes the ex-con has spent far more time being interrogated than Whistler has spent interrogating. Schmidt knows how to act cooperative while giving nothing, knows the legal system better than the overworked public defenders. Whistler is playing checkers; Schmidt is playing chess. The worst part, Whistler is being persuaded of Schmidt's innocence. He glances from the file to the suspect again. Schmidt has hard eyes as he grins his teeth at Whistler. He's smug. He didn't ask for a lawyer. *He hardly needs one.*

Schmidt clears his throat and drops his hands into his lap. Whistler says, "Please keep your hands where I can see them."

"It's your game boss. I'm just playin' it."

Whistler has one move left: sliding the photo of the potential first victim under Schmidt's nose. The trick is, he isn't likely to get a spontaneous confession. All he can hope for is a telling reaction when he sees dead Ginny Flores. If the look is there, Whistler will know. He won't have proof. But he'll know. Schmidt will know he knows. That could rattle Schmidt. A rattled Schmidt could make mistakes. Whistler would find rattling Schmidt deeply gratifying. He grips the glossy edge of the crime scene image, ready to reveal it dramatically.

There's a knock on the door. Whistler is relieved. "Stay put. I'll be back," he says. Giving orders makes him feel even better.

"You got it, boss," Schmidt says, unperturbed.

Whistler is nearly giddy to slip into the hall. He finds Ruther holding a cell phone. Whistler hopes the judge has reconsidered the search warrant. "I've got a call from Greene. He says he needs to speak with you." Ruther passes him the phone.

Whistler's reflexes take over. "Hello."

"I'm headed to my apartment. I know who attacked Rosa. I think I can prove it. Can you come?"

Whistler's heart races. Greene's information is in a file on his desk. He asks the address anyway. He tries to commit it to memory. He can't concentrate.

Ruther sees his excitement. His mustache flutters expectantly.

Whistler says, "What is it? Who is it? What proof do you have? Just tell me." He worries the wisp of hope will blow away.

Greene says, "I'm leaving the hospital. I was with Rosa. It will be easiest to show you. Can you meet me?"

"Is she awake? Did she tell you something? They said they'd call. They haven't called."

"No. She's still unconscious. Can you come to my place?"

"I'll meet you," Whistler says. The call ends. He wanted something concrete. He wanted to ask if it's Schmidt. He didn't have the chance, didn't think quickly enough. Still, he caught a break. "I'm heading to the professor's place. He has some kind of proof."

"Proof of fucking what exactly?" Ruther asks.

"Proof of who attacked Rosa Zhang. He didn't say what. He sounded agitated, and I was worried about pushing him. I think I need to do it on his terms."

Ruther is skeptical. "An addled twitch with documented brain injuries thinks he cracked the case, and you run off to witness his delusion in person? Fine. He called you, You can make the decision. What about the ex-con?"

"Kick him. I'm getting nowhere. Let him stew for a while. Maybe I shook his cage. Tell him not to leave town. I'll scoop him up when I need to. Oh—don't let him leave without the dog. She's with Suzuki."

"Will do," Ruther says.

Whistler grabs a folder from his desk and is through the squad room before he appreciates the minimal grief Ruther gave him. The thought warms his heart.

Creative Problem-Solving

Calvert pounds up the flight of steps to his apartment. His quick-time footfalls make hollow, rapid-fire sounds like a double bass drum. His mind tumbles to the name Ginger Baker. He doesn't attempt to unpack the reference. His chaotic memory is losing his interest. He's focused on the task at hand.

He hits the landing, passes his apartment door, and bangs on the Fluxus Flotsam Artist's Studio. No one comes to the door. He's panting. He turns his wrist up, doesn't have his watch. His taxi ride was fast. Still, he believes Detective Diaz should arrive any moment. *Why isn't Barney home? Barney is never not home.*

He slaps the meat of his left palm to his left temple. *Think.* He thinks of the classic rock power trio Cream. *Myelin.* He gives his skull a forceful punch. Pinpoints of static burst like floaters in a dropped snow globe. He remembers: Far Afield Festival. The apartment is abandoned because Barney and the others have gone to the art festival. He bashes his body into the studio door. The hard fibers that hold his left arm in his shoulder joint pop and ping as if coming apart. *Everything is unraveling.* He collapses like his strings have been cut, falls in a lifeless tangle of limbs.

"That's it," he says, defeated. "I can't keep moving this carcass around. I'm ready to be fully dead, please." The universe does not respond directly. But new thoughts begin to boil to the top of his fevered brain.

This body, known previously as Professor Greene, once put emphasis on logical problem-solving. Now his brain won't string facts together. All he can manage is a loose pile of misshapen artifacts. Since the Age of Enlightenment, empirical thinking has been held in the highest regard in the Academy. He'd become a professional within that structure. He was an evangelist for the power of education and linear knowledge. But with limited access to the things he once knew, he has to find a new way.

Perhaps I've been wrong. People are not successful animals due to logical thought. The ability to imagine a possibility and then bend reality is where human advantage lies. Being human is a creative act. Humanity demands invention to evolve more than logic. The reptilian and mammalian brain combined form the limbic system. Those primitive components allow people to live instinctively, to feel their way as much as utilizing the higher functions of cold reason. The ego has convinced the fat fleshy frontal lobe that it is the most vital part. But the brain evolved to serve the needs of the body. Not the other way around.

Calvert may not be dying, but evolving. He may require less of the expansive complexity of a Tolstoy and instead more of the fantastical playfulness of a Soviet satellite writer such as Kafka or Pushkin. He allows his nimble diagonal rationale to reach back to his first visit to this building. He recalls his curiosity as to what one might raise on a Megan Ranch.

"Please let me know if your neighbor gives you any trouble," she had whispered. "We'd like to get him out of there. If you see anything illegal going on, let me know. I'll make it worth your while."

"What things?" he'd asked.

"Drugs, deviant behavior, any kind of business being run from the premises, anyone not on the lease living in the space." She'd slipped a business card into his hand. He'd entered that number into his phone.

He stands back on his feet as if hoisted from above. *Deus ex machina.* He ignores the dead language and rushes into his apartment while rifling his pockets, finds his phone, and dials the number.

"Megan Ranch."

"This is Calvert Greene. Apartment two oh one and a half."

"Mr. Greene. I'm running late for hot yoga. If there's a problem, please call the handyman I provided."

"The neighbor has been giving me trouble," he says. Through the phone, he feels her attention turn his way.

"Go on," she says.

"I suspect illegal drugs in use, deviant behavior occurring, a business being run from the premises, and people living there who aren't on the lease. Also, they are gone, and they locked property of mine inside. Could you let me in?"

"I'll be right there," she says.

Calvert hangs up, feeling like a new man.

Nearly Definitive Proof

Whistler has trouble finding the door to Greene's place. He asks a woman with an empty cat carrier, and she points behind him. "You're welcome," she says as he tugs the door and storms up. Before he can knock, Greene is already pulling the door open.

Whistler walks a circle around the kitchen table, takes in the details of the room. It's sad and tiny. He leans back against the sink, arms crossed. "I'm here. Tell me what you know. What you think you know." The light fixture over his head flutters as if it's considering if it wants to go on. He looks up at it, watches it settle into a steady cold glow. He stares back at Greene, a little less intently.

"I will show you," Greene says with no urgency.

"Good. Do it. Let's go."

"When Ms. Ranch . . ." He stops speaking mid-explanation. The city noise rises with the opening of the street door. Whistler watches Calvert pivot his head in a stiff way, as if orienting his auditory receptors. Whistler listens too. "Wind ever open the door?" he asks.

In response, Calvert puts one finger to his lips. There is a promising squeak on the staircase. They tip their heads in unison, listening. A woman rounds the corner and enters the apartment like she owns the place, which, perhaps she does. Whistler straightens up.

The woman is wearing a yellow monochrome athletic top, matching soft shoes, and black yoga pants patterned with clusters of small white flowers adorned with yellow centers and curling green tendrils. Her hair is tied in a bouncing sprig on top. Her left hand is a fist around a clutch of keys. She has an ecstatic energy, but the presence of mind to introduce herself: "Megan Ranch."

"Detective Diaz."

Megan looks at the badge on his hip and nods, businesslike. Without missing a beat she asks, "You want in?" She dips her head in the direction of the neighbor's apartment.

"If you'd let us in, it would be a big help," Whistler replies. "There may be evidence pertaining to a crime."

Megan doesn't pause to consider the privacy of her tenants. "Let's go," she says. She leads the way. Whistler admires her floral pants.

Megan is fast; she has the door unlocked in a rattle of keys before Whistler reaches the landing. "Let's see what we see," she says. She gives a cursory knock on the open door as she walks in. "Hello?" she calls as an afterthought. No one responds. "I'm going to take a look around." She moves down the hall into what looks like a kitchen and disappears around a corner on the right. Greene is there beside him now. "She seems to know what she's doing. Where's this evidence?"

"This way." Greene leads Whistler into a sparse room with a red couch, three ratty dress forms rolled into a corner, and the remnants of a tension mount lamp in pieces on the floor. The walls are bare and freshly painted. The professor's body stiffens. He looks flummoxed. "This is where they should be."

"Where what should be?"

Greene ignores his question and meticulously walks the perimeter of the room. He runs a hand over the walls.

"Well?" Diaz asks.

Greene is feeling a place on the wall.

Whistler walks over to see exactly what he's doing. "Well?" He's getting tired of the weirdo's wall stroking.

Greene turns, "I'm not crazy!" He grins like an imbecile. The expression does not inspire confidence.

"I could charge you with obstruction of justice for wasting my time," Whistler says. But he doesn't leave. He tucks his thumbs in his belt, willing to be convinced, but nearly out of patience.

Calvert shows Diaz the wall. He rubs at a rough place. "Feel," he says.

Whistler pulls a skeptical face, but he touches the wall. "So?"

"This is where the picture was hanging. They painted and patched. The photo was here. Right, here." Greene pats the wall.

Whistler can feel something. He imagines trying to explain this to Ruther. He says, "This," as he smacks the wall. "This does me no good. Photo of what? Where did it go?"

"I don't know. But the rough patch is proof the photo was here. It's a real thing that exists. We only have to find it."

Megan Ranch silently glides into the room and starts speaking. "You said they were giving you trouble. You said drugs and misbehavior. This place is clean. Tidy even. Only one bed and no proof of people squatting or running a business. I didn't even find a bong. I have a bong, for Christ's sake. Everyone has a bong." She glares at the Whistler. "It's legal now."

"I didn't say anything."

"The toilet was not flushed," she goes on. "That was disgusting! I had plans. I am supposed to be sweating now. Then a quick shower and"— Whistler attempts to show no interest in Megan's shower plans—"then a pedicure while reclining in a massage chair. A good massage chair. With Riesling." She waggles her finger at Greene. Whistler is glad she's not lecturing him. "The chair is called the Dream Weaver. What the hell?" She seems to run out of words.

"My mistake," Greene offers as explanation.

"And the trouble Barney is giving you?"

"Sometimes he plays music that is not to my tastes," Greene replies flatly. "At a volume that is intrusive. He always turns it down if asked. Otherwise I couldn't ask for a nicer neighbor."

Whistler has the distinct impression the professor is enjoying himself.

The angry woman turns in a huff and stomps, nearly silently, from the room. There's a rattle of keys being taken from the dead bolt. She calls from the front hall, "Lock the doorknob when you go. And don't ask me for any favors. You can expect your rent to go up next year."

Greene is unperturbed. He walks out of the room. "Detective," he says. "The pictures."

Whistler hustles over. On a long table made of old doors, under a chandelier of oversized headlights, are six stacks of framed photos.

"This is what you want to show me? This is the proof?"

"I think so. If it wasn't sold."

"What does that mean?"

"There was a photo. It was displayed in there. On that wall with the covered-up nail holes. There was an open house. Some of the photos sold. It may be gone."

"Photos? Photos of what? Photos of who?"

"I'll show you."

"Goddamnit. Just find it."

Greene examines the top image, carefully sets it aside, checks the next image. He stacks the second image carefully on the first before moving on through the pile.

Whistler jams his hands in his pockets and jangles some change around to keep himself from knocking Greene down and sweeping all the pictures onto the floor. He watches Greene put the first pile back in its original order. "Oh my God," he blurts. "Let me help. What are we looking for?"

"No. I'll do it. This is Lyla's art. We have to be respectful."

Whistler looks at the top of one of the stacks: a color image, an overhead shot of people on the sidewalk taken out the window of the apartment. His eyes go to a man standing apart with hunched shoulders, wearing a backpack, hands cupped in front of his mouth, lighting a cigarette while shielding his lighter from the wind. His brain starts churning. "We're close to Coffee Girl?"

"A block away," Greene confirms. He removes a photo from the top of the next stack.

"These images are from the day Rosa Zhang was attacked?"

"Lyla took pictures all day." Calvert nods at one of the wide windows.

Whistler goes and looks out the window. "The photographer was set up at this window, close to the attack, on the day of the attack?"

"Yes," the professor says. He has replaced the second pile and is moving through the third. "One of the shots is a photo of the killer."

"Who?" Whistler asks. His tone isn't angry. Greene is screwy and infuriating. But he may have something. Whistler can feel it.

His phone rattles in his coat. It nearly gives him a stroke. He fumbles the phone out. It displays a text from Ruther: *CALL ME.*

He calls Ruther. "What's up, Inspector? Did you take a run at Schmidt? Did he crack? You got the warrant? You found evidence in the van?"

"Shut up a second."

Whistler shuts up.

"Where are you now?"

"With Greene."

"Forget that twit. The hospital called. Zhang woke up. She's back asleep already, but not in a coma. She spoke briefly, asked about her kid. Get over there and sit until she's ready to talk. She may know who we're looking for. Doctor what's-her-face said it was fine for her to give a statement when she's awake. Keep it short." Ruther hangs up.

It's only a matter of time before Schmidt is in cuffs, Whistler thinks. He watches Calvert going through the images. The photo is probably gone. *Who cares?* The pressure that's had him ready to blow is bleeding away. *Rosa Zhang will be an eyewitness. I will close my first case.* He feels foolish for doubting himself. He remembers what he promised Moe. Given his pending victory, he feels generous. *Why not spread the love?* Mostly he wants to brag to someone who might care. "Give me a second," Whistler tells Greene. He sends his cousin a quick text: *Rosa*

Zhang is out of the coma. I'm heading there soon to get a statement. Don't print anything yet. I promise you can have an exclusive.

Greene inhales sharply.

Whistler slips his phone away. "Did you find it? *This day gets better and better.*"

Calvert holds up a framed photo. The photo is dark, but there's a bright flash of hair.

"Who is it?" Whistler asks. *Schmidt has light hair.*

"My boss," Greene says. "Kaz Gladsky."

Muppets to Blame

Whistler rushes around to take the framed photo Greene is holding. He eyes the figure captured in the predawn light. The man's head and face lit by a streetlight. *It's Gladsky. He had knowledge of the crime scene north of the river, a white van, opportunity. He was the older man who impregnated Ginny Flores, who followed her home and left her dead in an alley.* He looks at the picture. *He fed me leads about Schmidt and Greene to keep me distracted.* Whistler is irritated. *Gladsky was so obvious.* He lets the photo fall away, overcome with momentary frustration at his gullibility; he pulls the image back to take a harder look. *It's Gladsky. Is the image good enough? Is there a time stamp? Will the photographer testify? Am I seeing what I want to see? Could this be any man with blond hair? Could the image be refined? Is there a memory card somewhere?*

He turns to Calvert, "Did Gladsky know Rosa?"

"I recommended her cortado to him. It's very good."

"Hot damn," Whistler says. *Kaz Gladsky is the killer. Not that creepy Schmidt motherfucker. Not this weirdo professor.* Whistler wants nothing more than to put Gladsky in cuffs, to prove he knows what the hell he's doing. He wants to get some respect. *It's all coming together. Moe and I were both wrong.* "Moe," he says. "Shit, Moe." Whistler shoves the framed photo into Calvert's hands. "Keep that safe. Lock it up. I gotta go. My cousin is meeting with Gladsky right now."

He starts moving, going for his phone. As he slips it from his pocket, he's reminded of Ruther's news, of his orders to sit with Rosa.

"Rosa woke up," he tells Calvert. "I have to go to my cousin. Will you wait with Rosa? Call me the moment she wakes. I'll have my partner meet you there."

The professor's pallid skin goes almost lifelike. "Rosa is awake?"

"Yes. Well, she's sleeping again. I guess comas are tiring."

The professor doesn't restack Lyla's images. He absconds with the photo that proves his boss is a killer. Whistler follows Greene to confirm the evidence gets safely to the professor's apartment. Then he trots down the steps and fast-dials Moe. It goes to voicemail. He stops walking to speak. "Moe. If you aren't at your meeting with Gladsky, don't go. If you're already there, make an excuse and get the hell out. It's him. He's the killer. I have the proof. We were off base. It's Gladsky. I'm heading there to make the arrest."

He starts moving again, scrolling for Suzuki's number, and steps onto the busy sidewalk. A woman is there with two snuffling French bulldogs, fat as dumplings. They scatter when he stomps into their midst. The woman tugs on their leashes. "It's okay. It's okay, Bert. Calm down, Ernie. It's okay."

Whistler realizes too late what he's blundered into. The dogs weave around his legs. He's snared in a cat's cradle. He clutches his phone, trying to protect it as he tumbles sideways. He lands on one of the dogs. The impact is hard on both of them. Whistler grunts loudly. His phone flies from his hand, hits the sidewalk and skitters off the curb and under a parked car. The dog yelps and runs from under him, which causes Whistler to hit the sidewalk. His ribs flex. Something pops in his clavicle. He has weak clavicles.

Whistler tries to stand. He nearly falls again.

"Oh my God, you okay?" the woman asks.

"I'm fine." He notices two things. First, Woman-with-Dogs was not speaking to him but to the dog Whistler landed on. Second, the woman is every kind of attractive. His feet work themselves free.

"Is Bert okay?" he asks. She's very near him, patting the dog that seems physically uninjured, but deeply insulted, grunting and snorting and wiggling and blowing bubbles of snot from his nostrils.

"Ernie," she says, to correct Whistler, as if it's obvious which dog is Ernie. As if to say, *Does he really look like a Bert? Asshole.* The silent "asshole" is emphatically communicated.

"Is Ernie okay?" The other dog, Bert, wanders in a circuit around the group, nearly tripping Whistler again. He hops over the trailed leash. His sudden movement startles Bert, and the dog shits on the sidewalk.

"Why don't you watch where you're going?"

This isn't going the way he'd like. He says, "I'm on police business. It's an emergency. If you and your dogs are fine, I need to go." He begins to macho-jog to his car with great urgency and purpose. He makes it thirty feet before he remembers his phone and has to jog back, less macho.

The woman watches his return. "Big emergency, huh?" She demonstrates her vast capacity for facetiousness while unbraiding the tangle of leashes.

He goes down on his belly and reaches around under the car. He gets a hand on his phone, pulls it out and shows it to the woman as proof. "My phone."

She smiles and says, "Your screen."

He looks at his phone. The screen is fractured with jagged chunks missing.

"City issue," he says real cool. Projecting he's a laid-back guy.

"Our tax dollars at work." She takes her mutts down the street, baby-talking to them as she goes. He thinks he hears her say "Keystone cop," but he might have imagined it.

"Shit," Whistler says. He runs for his car.

Something to Lose

Calvert takes Lyla's photo into his apartment and closes the door behind him. He looks for a secure place, slips it under the foot of his mattress.

Before he found Rosa unconscious, as he walked into the dark volume of space that was Coffee Girl, fine hairs on the back of neck had stood on end; a basic animal warning from his evolutionary past. He felt, briefly, as if he had entered a mausoleum. *Did I know Rosa was being choked to death? That Kaz was bending his lean face over Rosa to watch the light leave her eyes, panting his breath onto her cheek?* Had he known he was in a room where a murderer was murdering? Could some dormant corner of his lizard brain have engaged and rather than flee, he had chosen to press forward into danger? *Was I brave?*

The thought of Kaz, his severely tidy hair, sharp features, and vise-like fingers, causes Calvert to snap the dead bolt on his apartment. He wants to preserve himself so he can see Rosa one more time. Locking his door is a tacit admission he has something to live for, that he'd prefer to be a living person rather than a near-dead golem.

He takes Syed's card from his pocket and taps his phone.

"American Taxi."

"Syed. This is Calvert Greene. We drove to the hospital. Can you drive me there again?"

"Yes. Visiting your friend again already?"

"Yes."

"A woman?"

"Yes, a woman."

"Such good news. A man should have a family. Where are you?" Calvert gives the address.

"The veterinary hospital?" Syed asks.

"I live upstairs."

"Ah. I know it. I know it. My wife gets her cat's teeth cleaned there. She loves her cat more than me. Matina the cat. Matina, Matina, all day Matina. Fifteen minutes, Mr. Greene. I'll meet you at the curb." He ends the call.

Calvert leans against the table and kicks off his shoes. He unzips his Bug Off coveralls and lets them bunch in a pile around his feet. He breathes deeply through his nose and thinks he can smell soap, a sour smell from his garbage under the sink, and a musky odor coming from his body.

He digs his phone and wallet out of the pile and sets them on the table. He picks up his watch; it reads 6:12. *Fifteen minutes*, he tells himself. He tugs off his socks, feels a chill as his sticky feet press into the gritty floor. He quickly gets the shower going and lets the water run as he prepares to shaves and brush his teeth.

Through the bathroom window, the light has a bright, warm quality. *A forceful orange. Can color have intention? I'm undermedicated.* He scans the floor's darker corners for the fugitive pill. It doesn't materialize. New feelings, or old feelings he's having anew, ping brightly across his mind. *This is your brain on Pop Rocks.* He gets back to preparing to see Rosa.

Ten minutes later, he's clean, standing in fresh underwear with his hair combed, applying deodorant. He dresses in dark jeans and the T-shirt he printed with Barney. He tops it with an optimistic mint-green button-down. He finds the slip-on shoes issued by New Horizons. He straps the watch to his wrist and grabs his phone and wallet. *Time to go.*

The Worst Realization

Despite her desire for coffee, Moe hesitates. She never liked letting people do things for her. Hated to feel indebted. To anyone. But especially a source.

Gladsky, apparently taking her inaction as insecurity, approaches Moe and offers his arm, as if they are a paired couple in a wedding party. Like she is his prom date. She finds it amusing, maybe even sweet. If she weren't so exhausted, she'd take issue with it. But in this case, she allows him to escort her to the office.

He introduces Moe to his wife and explains, "She rides a motorbike to us and it breaks. You will take care of her, yes? I go to empty the van."

Pregnant Svetlana smiles at Moe like a very fertile Florence Nightingale. "Of course. Leave her to me."

Gladsky takes his leave.

"I'm happy to meet you, Moe, of course. But I regret your troubles." Svetlana is poised, tall and fair, despite her condition. *She's the anti-Moe.*

"It's good to put a face to the voice on the phone. Thank you for letting me speak to your husband for my story. I'm sorry to have caused your husband work," Moe says.

"It's nothing." Svetlana walks away for a moment and returns with two small plates. She sets one in front of Moe, the other on a nearby desk.

Moe looks at the pastry on her plate.

"*Placek*," Svetlana says slowly.

"*Plazek*," Moe repeats.

"No. *Placek*," Svetlana enunciates.

"What is it?" Moe asks to avoid the language lesson.

"Is Polish coffee cake. Very delicious." She pinches a bit and pops it in her mouth. "Delicious." She gestures for Moe to try.

Moe tastes hers and has to agree. "Delicious."

"I put water on to boil. Should be ready. I make you Inka or Polish coffee? Do you know Inka?"

"Isn't it instant coffee? Like Sanka?"

"No. You stir it in hot water. Polish grains, very nutritious."

"Sounds interesting. Coffee would be heaven." Moe never says things like "Coffee would be heaven." *I must be in shock.*

Moe watches Svetlana scoop grounds straight into a mug and pour scalding water over it. She carries the pungent brew over and places it in front of Moe.

"Now," Svetlana says, "we wait."

After drinking the gritty Polish coffee with no dairy, Moe thanks Svetlana. She does feel better. Calm and warm and capable of dealing with the mechanical money pit Taibbi seems to have become. *Maybe it was the coffee cake that helped.*

Svetlana says, "Now you have tour by my husband." It was more of an order than an invitation. Svetlana calls Gladsky into the office and speaks to him in harsh Polish. He bends his head under the instructions.

"Come," Gladsky says.

As they walk around the warehouse, Gladsky pointing out details he thinks are most significant, she notices his gold chains and wristwatch. She isn't a good judge of authenticity, but if they are real, he dropped some cash and wants people to know it. *New money syndrome,* she thinks.

When the warehouse tour is over, Moe asks, "Mind if I use my recorder when I ask questions?"

"Not at all." He seems flattered.

"Allen Schmidt and Calvert Greene both work for you?"

"Yes."

"They were both at the scene of the attack at the coffee shop. Mr. Greene reportedly ran off the attacker. Does that seem like something he would do?"

Gladsky smiles at the question. "To me, this Greene is not a man that could run off anyone. He is barely a man at all." It seems like a strange reply. Moe guesses his attitude lost something in translation. She asks more questions, but Gladsky doesn't have much to offer. Her heart really isn't into this line of inquiry after her conversation with Vivian. She turns off her recorder and tucks it away.

Interview over, she waits while Gladsky drags a long, heavy board to use as a makeshift ramp to get the Honda into the back of his van. He takes the handlebars of her bike and shoves Taibbi over, puts the front wheel to the plank, and asks Moe to give him a hand.

She stands at the back of the bike. "I can't thank you enough. You and your wife have been so gracious. I've been nothing but trouble."

"My pleasure," he says. "I—"

Moe's bleating phone cuts him off. "Sorry. Give me a second. I keep the volume high when I ride. Probably my boss." She twists her bag and digs out the phone. It stops ringing. "Missed it."

"If it's important, he'll leave a message," Gladsky says.

Moe notes the hardwired misogyny. The phone pings loudly. She sees the message is from Whistler. "Must be important." Moe makes an apologetic smile and puts the phone to her ear. Gladsky holds Taibbi while she listens:

Moe. If you aren't at your meeting with Gladsky, don't go. If you're already there, make an excuse and get the hell out. It's him. He's the killer. I have the proof. We were off base. It's Gladsky. I'm heading there to make the arrest.

The message is loud. Moe feels like she's been doused in ice water. Gladsky's back is to her. Under his shirt, his shoulder blades slide closer to his spine. She can't tell if he's preparing to shove the bike or if he's tensing because he overheard the message. She can't gauge how far Whistler's voice traveled.

"Ready?" Gladsky asks. His tone gives nothing away.

"Almost." Her brain starts to work. "I need to send a text." She turns her volume down and thumbs a message to Whistler: *I'm with Gladsky. My bike died. I can't leave. Hurry.* When she puts her phone away, she reaches around her bag for some kind of weapon. She wants to clench her keys in her fist, like a makeshift gouge. But they're dangling from Taibbi's ignition switch next to Gladsky. She grabs the only thing she can find and tucks it in the front pocket of her jeans.

"Ready?" Gladsky asks again.

"Ready as I'll ever be." She considers running, doubts she'd get far on her short legs and clunky boots. All she can think to do is stall. Her hands find something solid to shove at the ass-end of her ruined bike.

"Let's get this over with," she says.

The two of them force the bike up the ramp and into the tight interior of the van.

Mad Dash

Before leaving for Syed's American Taxi, Calvert digs under the sink for a roll of garbage bags and tears one free. He carries it to his bed and pulls Lyla's incriminating photo from under his mattress. He puts it in the bag and leaves, locking the door behind him.

On the sidewalk, he hops over a pile of dog shit on his way to the back seat of Syed's taxi.

Syed turns down the music. "Hello, my friend."

"Hello, Mr. Syed. Rush Med Center, quick as you can."

"You look nice, my friend. She will be impressed. Very handsome."

Calvert buckles himself. Syed turns up "Satisfaction" by the Rolling Stones and drives.

The ride isn't bad. The taxi finds green lights and steadily flowing traffic until they near the University of Illinois at Chicago. "Roller Derby. Very popular. Big rivalry. One of my fares said it's the national flat track championship. So sorry. We must go around."

Calvert nods. Anxiety blooms in his chest. He interprets the sensation as impending denouement, the nature of which he can't fathom. He looks at his watch, at the numbered ring and the mysterious buttons. He twists the ring counterclockwise, willing it to give him the time he needs.

The detour takes less than ten minutes. They come at Rush from west on Harrison. Syed parks and points to a stairwell outside the parking garage. "You take the stairs and cross the glass foot bridge at level four. It's the best way."

Calvert gives Syed all his cash and goes straight for the stairwell. It's getting dark out.

"Goodbye, my friend," Syed calls.

Calvert bangs the rusty exterior door open. The smell of urine is overpowering. He leaps the offending puddle and jogs eight switchback half-flights to exit at the door with the foot-tall numeral four. He finds a corridor to the glass bridge. The red taillights of the American Taxi hover a block to the east, waiting for the signal to change.

A brief snippet of a dream journey to an intersection with an unchanging traffic light comes to mind, an imagined trek during a sudden storm. A blues man named Robert Johnson met the Devil at a crossroads. Looking at the dark cityscape, Calvert recalls Johnson died mysteriously without ever making it to Chicago. Then Calvert is over the footbridge. The automatic doors open as he approaches the abandoned atrium where a man on a gurney called him "trash" only hours ago. The space is vast, hard surfaces and high ceilings. He finds the orange dots and follows them to the correct bank of elevators.

Two floors up, the hallway is dim. Hospitals have visiting hours, and he's past the preferred time. He walks without making noise, thankful he changed footwear. He moves past the empty nurses' station and ducks into Rosa's room. No one is there except Rosa. *Didn't Detective Diaz promise to send his partner? I must have made good time.*

He moves to her bedside. Rosa snores softly. He slips his hand under hers, cradles the weight of her warmth in his palm. She doesn't stir at his touch. Her face is lovely, restful. *She's not unconscious, only resting.*

He doesn't know what the big hurry was. He feels the heat coming off his body, his heart pounding, and his jaw clenched. He exhales, lets his teeth unclamp.

When his breathing slows he whispers, "I'm here with you."

A Weak Serpico Moment

Whistler's car has no flashing lights to help him cut through traffic; it has no radio to call dispatch. Stopped at a traffic snarl, he tries to make his phone work. The touch screen is ruined. He can read the first line of a pop-up text from Moe: *I'm with Gladsky now.* He tries to read more of the text with no luck. Traffic moves. He pitches the phone aside. Low sunlight coming across the lake forces him to narrow his eyes until he turns south.

* * *

In the back of the van, Moe watches Gladsky use a ratchet strap to secure the front of the bike. He passes her a strap. She hooks it to a tie-down and starts to fish it through the frame.

"Not like that," Gladsky says. "Run it over the seat and hand me the other end." *Not as cordial as earlier.* He has an edge; maybe he's impatient because she doesn't know his system. *Or something else.*

"I'm going to fish it through the frame." She's trying to waste time and sound casual.

"No talking. Only listen. Hand me the end."

She passes the strap to him. He hooks it and works the ratchet to squeeze the play out of the shocks. Moe looks around. She sees a box of black rubber gloves.

"There," he says, tugging on the bike. "Things are better when you listen." He hunches to get around the bike and steps out the open side door. Moe climbs out the back.

Gladsky is next to her. He has a floral smell.

"What is that scent?" she asks lightly. But she recalls Whistler talking about a phantom smell. She feels the blood leaving her face.

Gladsky smells the back of his hand, his eyes on hers. "The spray we use for Cimex lectularius remediation. I mix it myself. Lavender oil is natural repellent. Svetlana gets it from Washington Island. Do you know Washington Island?"

"I've never been. But I'd like to. Tell me about it. I hear it's nice."

"We talk about island on the drive. I take you home now."

"Sure," she says. "It's been a long day."

"It'll be over soon." All warmth has left his voice.

"Let me just run to the little girls' room." She starts moving, breaks into a jog, is nearly pulled off her feet. He has a hand around her messenger bag. She slides out of the strap and runs. She hears him pick up speed.

She makes it to the bathroom and slams the door closed. Gladsky rams himself into the door. She puts all her strength into keeping him out, uses her low center of gravity and powerful legs to shove the door. He wedges an arm and shoulder through, starts to force his muzzle in the widening gap. She knows he will overpower her, tackle her, and choke the life out of her.

Those dead girls feel less abstract now. She's standing among them. They felt this desperate, this loss of control. They were overpowered, despite their best efforts. They had no recourse. Helpless. *No. Fight. Do something. Try something.* Her feet slip on the cement. She turns her back to the door, pushes with all her weight, all her strength. Her no-slip soles grip.

"Little pig, little pig, let me in." His mouth is near her ear. He edges his body deeper into the gap. He reaches a hand around and caresses her hip. She wants to pull away but can't. The skin on her arms goes to goose flesh. She finds the dull half-pencil she'd shoved in her front pocket. She clutches it, folds her thumb over the eraser end, draws it back and drives it as hard as she can into the meat of Gladsky's shoulder.

*   *   *

Whistler races his Civic across the gravel and skids to a stop near the van parked in the mouth of the open garage. Moe's bike is in the back, her helmet off to one side. No sign of her.

He steps out, draws his gun. "Moe!"

He listens. *Nothing.*

He moves forward, crosses yards of cement, keeping his eyes peeled, gun up. "Moe," he calls. His voice echoes around the hard space. He sees Moe's bag on the floor, walks to it. "Moe?" he yells again.

"Whistler." He zeros in on Moe's voice. It's coming from a closed door.

"I'm here."

When he's nearly to the door, Gladsky walks around the corner with a hammer in one hand and his other arm bloody at the shoulder. Whistler trains his gun at the center of Gladsky's chest, blurts the Pacino line, "Freeze, you fuckface." Gladsky freezes. "I'm here, Moe," Whistler says. "Drop the hammer." He gestures with the pistol, closing the gap between him and the killer. Gladsky looks at the hammer he holds, seems to be considering his options. "Don't think about it. I'll shoot you dead. Drop the fucking hammer and get your hands up."

Gladsky drops the hammer. It strikes the floor with a crack. Gladsky puts his uninjured arm straight up and the injured one as high as he's able. He winces. "You got me, Detective." He smiles a sharp smile.

Whistler is forming a sentence. Before he can utter his next command he's struck in the back of the head. He hits the ground hard, eyes unable to focus, gun out of his hand. He sees the legs of a woman straddling him. She sets a fire extinguisher next to his head, starts scolding Gladsky in Polish. Whistler doesn't need to understand the words to know Svetlana is not happy. Whistler looks up at her body, her round abdomen directly above him. Her belly button is distended against her tight shirt.

He thinks of Moe, how he has let her down. His eyes close.

He inhales sweet lavender and something sharp and chemical. The scent is a harsh shock, like a paper cut to his sinuses. *I know that smell.* But it doesn't feel important anymore.

A Final Tender Act

Calvert moves around the far side of the hospital bed. He knows the nurses will disapprove if they find him. The plastic bag with the framed photo bumps against his knee. The chairs have been arranged near the windows. He places one silently closer to Rosa's bed, hidden from the door. He wedges the photo in the seat by his hip for safekeeping.

He checks his watch. The detective should arrive soon. He wonders if Detective Diaz told his partner to expect Calvert. He imagines the detective walking in, finding him next to Rosa. "It's okay. Detective Diaz sent me. Official police business." He practices what he might say. His voice is soft. When he was teaching, he knew how to get students to listen. He was comfortable in front of students, in his own skin. His heart aches to belong somewhere. He misses having students, misses his kids.

"One of my kids dropped by my office to ask if I'd recommend her for—" Calvert remembers starting to say once.

"Why do you do that?" Mere interrupted.

"Do what?"

"Call them 'my kids.' They aren't yours and they aren't kids. You are a professor. They are your students."

He realized, not for the first time, she harbored jealousy over his academic family: sixty surrogate children each semester. She was angry, not only with him but at the world, life, God, and the universe of chance occurrences that led to their inability to have a child of their own. She was bitter in ways he'd never imagined her capable of. He replied, "I'm sorry. You're right. They aren't my kids."

"What were you saying? Something about a student?" she asked, to make amends.

That was when he'd first realized he enjoyed his time with his students more than he liked time spent with his wife. On campus he was admired. At home. . . "Never mind," he had said. "It's not important."

The chair is comfortable. Calvert feels wrung out. Again he checks his watch.

"It's okay," he says again, trying to put on a smile, "official police business." The smile makes his tone more easygoing. The smile turns into a chuckle. He barks a full-on laugh. He covers his mouth and rises to see if he disturbed Rosa. Her chest lifts as it fills with air, and settles as the air leaves. He sits, still smiling. *I'm happy.* His happiness is remarkable. *I haven't felt happy since . . .. right before I died.* He thinks of Kati, the pain he'd caused, the lives he'd ruined, and his smile evaporates. *I'm a monster. I'd nearly forgotten.*

He doesn't know how other men feel when they're unfaithful. Do they consider the people they're betraying? Are they tortured with guilt? Do they justify their actions in various ways? *I deserve happiness. I need to be loved. If my wife would only smile, act excited, touch me. If only Mere would have sex with me, hold me, hold my hand.* So often he's overheard women talk about the fragile male ego. *"Men are little boys,"* they say. *"It's like having another child to raise."*

His reverie is invaded by an unwelcome image of Allen's bare ass, clenched and dimpled as he humps the woman at the hotel. He's still mad at Allen. But what about this woman? Why would Allen's wife marry a man in prison? Did she expect him to be a good man? Was she faithful? He knows his anger at Allen is at its root self-loathing. All the death that followed his affair with Kati is due to his capitulation to basic human longings. *Can I be blamed? Yes. But is it forgivable?* He doesn't know.

To Rosa he whispers, "I can't be trusted. Not because I would hurt you. That's the last thing I want. But this feeling I have, this love, it's a new love. Young love, if an old man can feel such a thing. It won't last. Life will wear it away. All I know is if you give me the chance I'll try not to fail you like I failed Mere. Like I failed myself. If you will have me, it would make me as happy as I can be. I could be some kind of father to Thomas. A good kind of father. I'd like to have the chance." He's too scared of the disappointment that accompanies such hope to say more, even to a sleeping woman.

He watches Rosa for some indication. She gives none. If Rosa has feelings for him, if they have any chance of building a life, he'll have to repeat the same monologue when she's awake. The sinking feeling this gives him is buoyed by the thought of the future conversation taking place over tasty cortados. The two of them, warm cups cradled in their fingers, face-to-face over a café table. He sees it coming into view, like the line of the shore after a long evening swim.

He hears voices from the nurses' station. For the third time he checks his watch. *The detective will be here any moment.*

The chair eases his tired bones. *If this is how it feels to live, I'm not sure it's for me.* He listens to Rosa's breathing. He closes his eyes to rest them. Only for a moment.

What You Wish For

Some subtle change brings Calvert's slumbering mind back to life. What he immediately perceives: the hospital bed, Rosa sleeping, and an undefined thing that woke him.

His pupils spread to draw light. The night is cloudy, the stars and moon dulled, gray slashes of subdued light passing through the slatted blinds stripe the room in two-tone gunmetal. Instinctively he stays still, hidden behind the hospital bed. He tries to work out what woke him. *The creak of the door?*

He remembers the line he practiced, *"Official police business."* He finds no humor in it now. If his ears were capable, they would cup to gather more sound. He senses someone. *A nurse? Not likely.* In his experience, nurses are not concerned with being considerate of sleeping patients. It could be Detective Diaz's partner. *Of course it's the detective.* Calvert doesn't remember falling asleep, but he might have dreamed the whole thing; the sound and the suffocating presence are an emotional hangover from another guilty dream. The thought relaxes him. The tension in his bunched muscles wicks away. He hadn't been aware how tightly he was squeezing his ass, but he sinks an inch as his rump unclenches. His hip moves away from the sharp frame in the plastic bag, making him aware of a sore spot from pressing against the hard edge for too long.

Rosa's profile looks serene, her mouth hanging loose in complete surrender. Her chest seems still. He has a split second of alarm that she stopped breathing. Tightness coils in his legs to push his body into action. Before he can move, the blanket across her chest rises, holds at the apex, and settles back, followed by a ragged snore. *That was it. Her snoring startled me.*

He breathes in as he watches Rosa's next inhalation. A scent fills his head, floral and softly sweet. His sense of smell firing fully after a long absence grabs his attention. His eyes fill with tears. *I'm back from the dead.*

He'd been so certain he was dead. There was no question. Not only does he now know he's alive, but he's happy about it. He's excited to breathe in unison with Rosa, to watch her sleep and hear her snore. Thrilled by the smell of her perfume. He lets the scent fill his head again. It's oversweet. Too brash for Rosa—oily and industrial. It's a wrong smell.

A dark figure looms over Rosa.

Calvert moves, clutching the thin plastic bag. In the time it takes to stand, his intention evolves. Initially, he wanted to explain his presence. By the time he's on his feet, he knows it's a killer standing over Rosa, death personified.

Kaz Gladsky's pale hair gives off its own light. He isn't startled when Calvert appears across the bed. Kaz puts a finger to his lips and makes a calming, shushing sound. He smiles down at Rosa, leans toward her as if to kiss her forehead, and wraps both his gloved hands around her throat. He squeezes firmly. Rosa's eyes go wide; her mouth opens, and her hands claw at Kaz's grip, gouge at his face.

For a brief second, Calvert is hypnotized by the slow speed of Kaz's action. But when Rosa starts thrashing, Calvert's body heats up, his face goes red, and he lets out an anguished "Noooo!" He swings the plastic bag, smashing the frame and glass into the side of Kaz's skull. Kaz recoils.

The moon breaks through the clouds. Light cuts into the scene. Shattered glass tumbles, flashing brightly as the bag rips and debris falls onto the hospital bed, onto Rosa's body. She curls against the head-board, as far from Kaz as she can get.

Calvert rushes around the bed, takes two steps and jumps before Kaz can recover. Even filled with adrenaline and momentum, it's clear as soon as his small body collides with the larger man that his strategy was a bad one.

Kaz catches Calvert and twists as they fall. Calvert lands hard underneath the larger man's mass. The wind is smashed from Calvert's lungs, his back flattened to the floor. He sucks air. He tussles around. Calvert can't get Kaz off him, no matter how he bucks. Gloved fingers constrict Calvert's throat. Kaz's left thumb probes Calvert's Adam's apple and pushes. There's a pop as the ring of cartilage flexes.

Calvert is a crazed beast. He tries to pry his attacker's fingers back, punch his face, bend his powerful arms, tries to knee him, and scratch his eyes. He cuts a red line in Kaz's angular cheek. Kaz applies more pressure and leans his face away, his expression easy. He rides the fight from Calvert, knows it's only a matter of time. Calvert quits struggling. Lyla's photo slips off the bed and drifts like a leaf to settle on the floor. Calvert watches Kaz gaze at it, sees his eyes register the proof that could convict him. Kaz's smile shows the sharp tips of his canines.

Calvert's eyes bulge and roll back in his skull, fluttering at the infinite void of his mind.

He sees beautiful Kati crushed as his skull strikes her.

Mere is a crumpled mass of meat and blood lying on the hood of her car.

At the end of his life, he doesn't watch a highlight reel, but is faced with a few unresolved regrets tied tight around his neck and allowed to drag him into a cold, deep pit. He knows now how cruel God is, how he was tricked back to life, only to be killed again. *It's what I deserve. To die badly. To die and to die again.*

He brought Kaz a gift: Lyla's photo. Without the photo as evidence, Kaz will go free, once he chokes Calvert and kills Rosa.

Rosa.

The pressure in Calvert's body stops. Air rushes in. His throat pops into shape. Kaz's deadweight falls across him. Calvert's eyes slip into their sockets and roll down so he can see.

Rosa.

Rosa stands over Calvert. The heavy chair he'd been sleeping in clutched in her hands. Knuckles white. The back legs of the chair are missing, broken across the shoulders of their assailant. Her gossamer hospital gown comes loose at the back and slips down one shoulder. Her hair is a frantic halo aglow in a circle of pure moonlight.

The lights come on.

Calvert closes his eyes, too tired to hold them open. People are filling the room.

In that moment, he could have died happy.

Good for the Soul

Sitting in the back of an ambulance, Whistler takes his stitches like a man. Which means he tries not to shriek as the curved needle pokes through his scalp. Despite the attempt to numb the site, he feels the pop of his epidermis as it's punctured, the surgical thread grabbing at nerve endings not used to stimulation, and the pressure as the two sides of the wound are drawn together and knotted in place.

Moe grins at his discomfort, tosses his car keys in the air and catches them.

His hair is crispy with dried blood; it crackles when the EMT tips his laceration into the light. "Almost done," she says.

He wants to shower and change.

"That about does it," the EMT finally says. She moves into his line of vision, which he enjoys. "I'm obligated to inform you untreated concussions are a cause of dementia in old age. If you refuse to go to the hospital for a CT, you increase the risk of issues in your retirement years." She punctuates the warning with a breathtaking smile.

"At this rate, I'll be lucky to reach retirement." He feels steady enough to get on his feet.

"You really ought to have it checked. You could have a mild concussion."

"This is my case. I'm going to see it over the finish line."

"Wow," Moe pipes up. "You must be very sporty to use that metaphor." She's anxious to go.

"Stop it," he says.

"At least take some ibuprofen. It will help with pain and swelling. You're going to have one hell of a headache."

"This man will not be sidelined," Moe declares. "He's no bench-warmer! He's a vital part of a winning team, I tell you!"

"Please stop," Whistler says. "Thanks again," he calls to the EMT as she packs to go.

The cousins walk to his car and have a half-hearted debate about who should drive.

He drops her at *Text Block*. "Call me," she says.

"I said I'd call you." He guns it before she gets another word in. He drives to the station as fast as he can. Inside, Wendell gives him a nod. Whistler takes the elevator, not wanting to jostle his tender head on the stairs.

After swallowing some pills with lukewarm coffee from his "Crafty Ass Bitch" mug, he settles heavily in the audiovisual closet to watch the monitor.

Ruther stops in. "You feeling better?"

"I'm good."

Ruther hands Whistler a water bottle. "That's not for you. I'll be back for it in ten minutes. Keep it safe. Watch and learn, young Padawan. Hit 'Record' on that camera."

A minute later, Whistler watches Ruther on the monitor in front of him. "Mrs. Gladsky. Sorry to keep you waiting. Are you comfortable?"

"I'm fine. There has been a misunderstanding."

"I think you're right. Detective Suzuki can get a little overzealous. You know. But still. It's good that you're here. Your husband's in a lot of trouble. I was hoping you could help us out. Answer some questions. You know. Then we can get you on your way."

"I can't believe this is happening."

"No. Of course not. The wife never knows in cases like this. What's that saying?" He looks up and to the left, pretending he's trying to remember something. He gives a quick wink to the camera. He snaps

308

his fingers, his mustache flairs as if to say *Eureka!* "'Love is blind'. That's it. It's a cliché for a reason. Trust me. I see it all the time." Ruther slips out his comb and fixes his mustache, smooths it with his fingers. He manages to look sheepish, as if preening for the much younger and very attractive woman. He sets a chair next to Svetlana's. She visibly relaxes. *Smart,* Whistler thinks. *Making her think she's in control, and that they're on the same side.*

Ruther places a folder in front of her. Before opening it, he says, "Oh. I should get the legal formalities out of the way. Detective Suzuki read you your rights?"

"Yes."

"And you understand your rights?"

"Yes."

"Just because you waived your right to an attorney, that doesn't mean you can't ask for one at any time. You know that."

"Yes."

"But you don't need an attorney. Correct?"

"I want to be helpful. I need to get home and rest." She touches her pregnant belly as explanation.

"Of course. You have nothing to hide. We really appreciate your help. Honestly, the way I see it, you are a victim in all this. But that's over now. You're safe here. You need a pillow for your back? You want to put your feet up maybe? I can get another chair."

"No, thank you."

"Well, I'll get these questions out of the way fast as I can and get you on your way." Ruther's mustache is calm. He opens the folder in front of Svetlana, like sweetly displaying the first spread of a picture book for a cherished child. It's a photo of Ginny Flores next to a dumpster. Ruther explains, "I'm sorry to tell you this. This is Ginny Flores. Have you ever heard that name?"

"Never."

"I didn't think so." He kindly pats her hand where it rests on the table. "Ginny was pregnant. She was choked to death. Your husband met her where she worked in the laundry of the International. He gave

309

her gifts. Expensive gifts. Jewelry and more intimate things like lingerie. The kinds of gifts one would give a lover. Gifts designed to impress a young girl in love for the first time. They started an affair." He pauses, flips to a close-up photo of Ginny's brutalized throat. "According to Ginny's mother, the relationship lasted several months." He turns to Svetlana, who has gone still. "I'm sorry to do this. I know it must be difficult. I hate to spring this on you, to put you through this. But we need to get a complete picture before we charge your husband, Kaz."

"I understand," she says. "It's such a shock." She makes sniffling sounds.

Ruther produces what looks like a crisply ironed handkerchief from the pocket of his blazer.

"Thank you." She bends into it, makes more sniffling sounds.

Ruther glances at the camera while patting her shoulder gently. "I'm so sorry to upset you, especially in your state. Moments like these, they make me want to quit this job. Making good people face horrible things makes me feel like a bad person," he says. His voice drips with need, desperate to be forgiven and understood.

"No," she says. She sits up, a determined look on her face, giving a convincing rendition of an innocent person's attempt to be strong. "It is not your fault. You have to do your job. Kaz is the one." She holds the handkerchief over her face. The move looks comically melodramatic through the monitor. *She's overconfident,* Whistler thinks. Trying to play Ruther. She declares resolutely, "I must be strong for Ginny. She never had a chance to be strong for herself. I will not let him hurt anyone anymore. Including me." She squeezes the handkerchief in her fist to demonstrate the strength of her commitment.

"So brave," Ruther says. "Thank you." He turns his attention back to the case of Ginny Flores. "This much seems clear. She got pregnant and intended to keep the baby. We think that may be why he killed her, the thing that triggered him. He had two women pregnant at the same time. But only one was his wife. You see?" Ruther places his hand over the crime scene photo as if to shield Svetlana from so much harsh truth. He leans a bit closer. "Had she lived, Ginny's baby would have been your unborn child's sibling."

"Half sibling," Svetlana corrects him.

"Of course. Half." He moves the photo aside to reveal the next victim. "This is Anna Beth Harpole, in town from California for a conference. Went for a morning walk. Kaz spotted her and attacked her and left her body next to a dumpster. Same as Ginny." He lets her sit and stare at the photo. She passes the wad of handkerchief from one hand to the other. "We have video evidence of his van."

Whistler appreciates how Ruther wields partial truths.

Svetlana rocks in her chair, folding her arms over her belly. Either buying time or genuinely bothered. It's hard to tell over the monitor. Whistler sips a bit of coffee. The stitches in his scalp pull.

Svetlana says, "Was she pregnant also?" She doesn't look at Ruther. Whistler wishes he could see her downcast eyes. He has a flicker of regret at the way the job is shaping his worldview. But it slips away as he focuses back on the monitor.

Ruther says earnestly, "She was not pregnant. Thank god for that."

"Yes," Svetlana solemnly agrees.

Ruther taps the photo of Anna Beth. A photo Whistler took himself with the digital tablet. Whistler can almost smell the rotten dumpster and sweet flowers. He sets his coffee aside. Ruther redirects. "Did you have any indication your husband could be so violent? Any hint this kind of thing was going on?"

The reply is not immediate. "Yes," Svetlana says. Whistler can see her wheels turning. She's clearly feeling comfortable enough to improvise. "Kaz was sweet when we met. He bought me gifts. The kinds of gifts you say he bought for the girl Ginny. These earrings." She brushes her hair aside to show a dainty silver hoop. "I was in love. He was charming, you see? And I am much younger than him. He insisted we marry right away. I was happy. I got pregnant. My father died suddenly. Kaz took over the business. That's when things started to change, slowly at first. Kaz would yell about the house being dirty. He would get so mad. Grabbing me hard, leaving bruises. Bruises on my wrists. Finger marks on my arms. Once he nearly crushed my throat. His grip was hard." She touches her neck.

"You're safe here," Ruther reminds her.

Svetlana starts to cry, gasping for breath.

Ruther says, "We should stop. It's okay. You can come back tomorrow. " But he doesn't close the folder or give her space. He hovers and waits. In the AV closet, Whistler waits too. He can feel the turn coming.

"It's just. Looking at these pictures," Svetlana says. "I knew he was capable of violence. I never dreamed it could be this bad. Not murder. I married a nightmare. He deceived me. Looking back, it makes sense." She sobs and cradles her belly. "He could have killed me, killed my baby. Like these poor women, like Ginny's baby." She honks her nose wetly.

"You need water?"

"No." She stops crying. "I'm sorry."

"You have nothing to apologize for. You've had so much to contend with: your first pregnancy, your father's passing, running a business, and a manipulative husband. I remember when my wife was pregnant, her hormones went out of control. She couldn't think straight. She cried watching a Hamburger Helper commercial. Once she went a little crazy at a restaurant because the pepperoni on her slice wasn't evenly distributed. 'Why can't people be more careful?' she wanted to know. Was it like that for you?" Ruther places a hand on Svetlana's shoulder again.

"Yes." She rattles her head. "I didn't know what he was up to. How could I? Because of the pregnancy." She turns slightly to present her belly. Strokes it in circles like polishing a bowling ball,

"You sure you don't want some water? Let me get you some. It's no problem. I want to help."

"Yes," she acquiesces.

Whistler watches Ruther leave the room. There is a rap of knuckles on the door. Ruther opens it and snatches the bottle of water.

"You taking notes?" he asks. He winks, thoroughly enjoying himself. He closes the door before Whistler can respond.

On the monitor, Svetlana is not crying. She looks relaxed, in control. There is a knock on the door. She brings the handkerchief to her nose and blows loudly.

Ruther walks in. He drags his chair to the opposite side of the table. He plunks the water bottle down. She's taken aback. He says, "So you were so confused that you attacked one of my detectives? Knocked him clean out, split the back of his head open?"

"He didn't identify himself. He had a gun on the father of my child."

"But you had met him before? Right?"

"His back was turned."

"Yes, I see. That makes perfect sense. When you saw who he was, after he fell, you must have been in shock? Yes?"

"Yes. I was shocked."

"Of course. And is the shock why you didn't call an ambulance? Is it why you left him to bleed out without calling anyone for help?" Her mouth moves with no sound, trying to form a response. Before she can start to lie, he says, "After leaving him wounded, you drove home to pack a bag, ten thousand dollars cash, and your passport, because you were confused?"

"Yes. Very confused."

"So confused you ransacked the journalist's bag and found her phone, saw the text about Rosa Zhang being out of her coma? How confused do you have to be for that to happen?"

"I'm pregnant, with hormones."

"My wife was pretty loopy, but she never committed the attempted murder of a Chicago detective, conspired to commit the murder of a witness to a crime, or try to flee the country to avoid prosecution. I've heard of hormones but that is a serious case of hormones. She did get worked up about that pizza, though."

Svetlana knows she's been played and gives a defiant look.

"So," Ruther goes on, "when your husband told me you directed him to go to the hospital and kill the only living witness?"

"It's a lie. It was him. I knew nothing. I was confused. So pregnant. So scared." She rubs her belly to remind him of her vulnerable state. But she knows it's too late. Whistler can see it in her face.

"I suppose you didn't nail Moe Diaz in that bathroom so you could make your escape? She's lying about that?" Svetlana starts to speak, maybe to lawyer up. "Wait right there," Ruther says, and leaves before she gets the chance.

Fifteen seconds later, he bangs into the AV closet. He burns a DVD. His mustache is in total control. He smiles at Whistler, toggles a switch to change monitors to a view of Kaz Gladsky. "Watch and learn," he says again. Then he wheels a TV out of the room. A minute later, Whistler sees him arrive in the room where Kaz is waiting.

Ruther says, "Women. Can't live with them, can't get away with choking them to death." Then he plays the DVD of Svetlana claiming her innocence, blaming Kaz for the whole thing. Whistler watches Gladsky's face droop as he realizes Svetlana is hanging him out to dry.

"Fucking bitch," Kaz says.

Ruther says, "You are under arrest for the murders of Ginny Flores and Anna Beth Harpole, and the attempted murder of Rosa Zhang, Moe Diaz, and Calvert Greene."

"I want a lawyer," Kaz says.

"You're going to need a good one."

Hot Shrimps

Two nights after the arrests, Whistler explains it to Moe over a big plate of hot shrimps.

"Ruther sat me in front of a monitor in the AV closet. 'Watch and learn, young Padawan,' he said."

"What's a Padawan? A nerd thing?" Moe asks, her fingers orange with spicy sauce.

"From *Star Wars*. A Padawan is a Jedi in training. It's common knowledge."

"Like I said, nerd thing."

"I knew what he meant."

"Exactly, a nerd thing. Got it. Proceed, young Padawan."

"I watched the monitor as Ruther interviewed Svetlana."

"Sociopathic bitch."

Whistler rubs the line of prickly suture ends along the back of his skull. "You plan to keep interrupting?" He swigs beer to cool his mouth.

"You plan to make a point soon?"

"You're sassy. Can I assume your love interest agreed to a date?"

Moe smiles a smile he remembers from their shared childhood, genuine and a bit bashful. It looks right on her. "Get on with it," she says.

"Ruther was masterful. The way he worked those two. I learned a lot."

"He got a confession?"

"They implicated one another. The lawyers will sort it out. With the evidence we have—it's a matter of sentencing. See who the jury thinks deserves how much time. Convictions look very likely. They may take plea bargains. But it won't save them from decades in prison. Though Svetlana will have that baby soon. I feel bad about that part. The baby didn't do anything. You know. Svetlana is trying to leverage it for sympathy. But I doubt it will save her."

Moe knows a hair tie with Anna Beth's DNA had been found over the gearshift of Kaz's van, a grim memento. Along with one taken from Rosa.

"Can I quote you? On any of this?" she asked.

"It's mostly educated guessing about how it will play out. It is out of my hands mostly. Except for testifying in court." He swigs the last of his beer. "What the hell. If I say anything newsworthy, you can call me an unnamed department source. Let me read it before you post it."

"Of course." She licks her fingertips one after the other, enjoying her life. She finishes her beer and waves the empty in the air so the server will bring another.

"So listen," Whistler says, "I met this girl. But she's like half a foot taller than me. Blonde. You think I have any shot?"

"You want me to be honest?"

"It's always dangerous to open that door. But go for it." Cold beers are placed on the table.

Moe smiles at her cousin. "She'd be lucky to have you. You could always use a step stool."

He shakes his head. They knock their beers together and drink, not saying much but happy to be together.

"Here's a funny thing: I'm actually enjoying my editing duties. It forces me to consider what I do deeply enough to teach it to others. You see what I mean?"

"I think so. Sounds like a good thing."

"I was talking to Dale a while back. Gave him some advice. I told him the first story isn't the whole story. That got me thinking about Precious Sharp and Maria Reyes. Remember them?"

"Sure. What about them?"

"I made pretty quick assessments of their deaths without a lot to go on. Mostly my gut. I decided they weren't related to the Anna Beth Harpole murder, and I moved on."

Whistler gets a sly look. "Same thing you accused the cops of doing."

"I know. So because the first story isn't the whole story, I'm going to take another look."

"That's good. I may have learned a lesson from Ruther about interrogation."

"What's that?"

"After he played Kaz and Svetlana against each other and they asked for separate lawyers, he told me something that made a lot of sense. He goes something like, 'I realized a long time ago I have a face people are unimpressed with. People who think they're smart figure I must be dumb. People who think they're hard assume I'm soft. On and on. It's my gift. I project an unimpressive mediocrity, and that gives everyone I interview the idea they are in control. It gives me an unbelievable advantage. I know exactly who I am, but no one else does.' What do you think of that?"

"That is deeper than I expected," Moe admits.

"Which proves his point."

"I guess so," she says.

They drink their beers and pay their bills. Outside Moe says, "I've been thinking about what Ruther said about projecting mediocrity. Maybe you have the same gift, Whistler."

"I'd tell you to fuck off, but I've been thinking the same thing."

317

Diaz Family Reunion

Three weeks later, at her dad's insistence, Moe organized a barbecue. She invited Whistler and his coworkers, her uncle Sebastian, Vivian, Jerome, and the ankle-biters. She also invited Cyn.

Now Moe parks her new used Jeep Renegade and grabs the ice her dad insisted they needed right after she introduced him to Cynthia Regan. She knew the ice was a ruse; Francis wanted a chance to get to know the woman she was dating. Cyn seemed comfortable with the arrangement and had even blown Moe a kiss as she left.

Moe uses her foot to knock open the gate and waddles across the yard, a twenty-pound bag gripped in each hand. Cynthia is cranking an umbrella open over one of the tables. Francis holds his hand above the grill to test the heat. Moe feels like celebrating. She has spent much of the last several weeks researching and interviewing and writing. She's not clear on all the angles, but from her cousin's and her own digging, she knows new details of the case—by far the biggest story she has ever broken.

It started with Ginny Flores. When Svetlana discovered Kaz was having an affair and that Ginny was pregnant with his child, she convinced him to end it in the most permanent way possible. Then Svetlana got the idea that her husband should kill another random girl, someone who could never be connected with him, in the same way as Ginny. "She thought it would make him less likely to be suspected," Whistler told Moe. They agreed it was a crazy kind of logic. But Kaz had found he enjoyed stalking new victims and planning attacks. A psychosis was born: he kept killing and began collecting mementoes.

Kaz had confirmed, as part of his plea deal, that his second victim was Maria Reyes. He'd seen her crossing the playground on her way to get her piccolo; when she came out, he called out to ask her for directions. She wanted to be helpful. He'd passed Precious Sharp in the aisle of a corner market, followed her home, gotten to know her routine; he'd drawn the process out a good long while. Moe had been wrong about Precious's boyfriend, wrong about the school custodian too. But her second look at the murders had put them on Whistler's radar. Whistler had tipped the DA, who offered Kaz some minor concessions for coming clean. So Moe got it right in the end. She was glad their stories had been told and their killer found. Mostly she was relieved that Loretta Sharpe had a little peace. Mr. Reyes, however, had seemed as tortured by his unexpressed grief as the first time she'd spoken to him. She liked to think it was a good thing she had done. One other thing she'd been able to pull off was to push the instrument rental store to write off the loss of the stolen piccolo and cancel the debt.

Her articles had brought public pressure. The mayor weighed in, like a crime fighter in an impeccably tailored suit. Had anything changed? Maybe not. Moe knew some victims would get far less attention and effort than they should. But she could keep writing. And her cousin, the police detective, would keep detecting.

To her boss Vivian's delight, Moe's coverage was reposted widely. Vivian started selling ads to national accounts. Money was coming in and Moe was getting a bonus.

Moe finishes forcing the ice into the already full coolers. She watches Francis at the grill, tongs in one hand and a beer in the other. He chats easily with Cynthia, sharing his closely guarded grilling secret of lump charcoal from a specific combination of hardwoods. Cyn looks beautiful in a floppy hat, sundress, and a lot of exposed skin. Moe feels foolish at her initial reluctance to invite her.

"I'd love to meet your family," Cyn had said. "What's the big deal?"

"My father, he is . . . traditional."

"It's not a secret you're gay? I don't have relationships with people who aren't out."

"I'm out. He knows. But I've never introduced him to people I've dated. My personal life has always been . . . partitioned."

"It's a lot easier to be your whole self all the time. Being a different Moe for different people must be exhausting."

"It's how I've always done it."

"Consider this an opportunity to simplify. Besides, fathers love me," Cyn had told her.

"Hey, cousin," Whistler calls. Moe didn't know he'd arrived. "Your girlfriend is nice. Smart too. And white. She may be the whitest woman ever in this yard." He carries a big tray covered in aluminum foil. "Clear a spot, would ya? This thing is hot."

Moe makes room and Whistler sets the load down fast. "Oh man. Hand me a beer." She reaches in the cooler, digs through far too much ice, and passes him a bottle. He rolls it over his forehead and the back of his neck. Moe can see the place where hair is growing over the fresh scar.

"Where's Uncle Sebastian?" Moe asks.

"He stopped for fresh tortillas. He sent me with the tamales. He'll be here." He twists the cap off his beer. Moe knocks her bottle against his and they drink.

"What about that tall blonde you were going to invite?"

"She's engaged to an actuary."

"Hmm. Too bad. What's an actuary?"

"I think it's the study of the cost of risk. Something like that. He's a numbers guy for an insurance company. He's boring, but he's tall."

"Too bad. Oh. I bought you something." She produces a circular box. "Because you're a detective and that's a big deal. And you closed your first case."

"That's what the hot shrimps were for."

"No, that was because you tried to save me. As if I need saving. And because we survived."

"I see." Whistler pulls the top off the box. Inside, the most beautiful short-brimmed, upturned fedora he has ever seen. He lifts it carefully, puts it on his head. "How's it look?"

"Like it was made for you," she says. "Because it was. There's a Cuban guy in Albany Park. I told him to make it look tough."

"I love it."

"It's your signature look," she says.

The back gate opens and a petite Asian woman steps in and waits. Moe admires the way she's put together. *I wish I were a dress girl.* Someone joins the woman in the dress; he stands exactly the same height, and is dressed like he's misplaced his golf bag.

Whistler barks, "Zucchini."

"Partner!" Suzuki calls. He and his wife come over. Introductions are made. They talk lightly and swig beers. Cynthia joins them and holds Moe's hand, introduces herself. The back gate opens again. Jerome holds it for his suburban fiancé. Dale and Loni walk in moments later. Jerome and his date take the momentary commotion as a chance to wander away and smoke a few cigarettes.

"Food's ready," Francis says. He proudly carries a platter piled with meat.

"You didn't have to throw this party for me," Suzuki jokes. "I know I arrested the strangler, rushed to his house, and arrested his wife before she could escape. I retrieved my partner's firearm and still had energy to get lucky when I got home." Suzuki pats his wife on the ass.

Everyone's side conversations stop, not so subtly anticipating Mrs. Suzuki's reaction.

"He wishes," she says. "He fell asleep on the couch watching *The Great British Bake Off*. Like he does every night."

Everyone laughs. Moe watches Cyn's brow crinkle in that special way. She glances around to all the smiling faces, with the exception of Suzuki. Apparently he hadn't enjoyed his wife joking at his expense.

Reopening

The grand reopening of Coffee Girl takes place on a Monday. Calvert, having lost his job at approximately the moment Rosa broke a chair over Gladsky, has been helping out part-time. It's twenty minutes to six, and he's brewing coffee for the morning rush while Rosa makes them each a cortado. They move in a comfortable waltz within the narrow space behind the counter.

Either Calvert is no longer dead, or he never was. He's still deciding how best to frame the entire episode. His memory continues to improve. With his recent resurrection came the knowledge that Rosa is a young, beautiful woman, and he is a man in his fifties. On the face of it, they are a poor match, only marginally better a paring than he and Kati had been. Furthermore, Rosa's affection for him does not reach a romantic level. He's learning to live with that. However, the realization has allowed him to avoid the embarrassing confession he'd intended to make. Since she is not his love match, he has license to keep his secrets.

"When I'm done with the coffee, I'll put out the baked goods," Calvert says. While Rosa was recovering, she enlisted her mother as official baker for Coffee Girl. Each morning Rosa drops Thomas with Consuela and picks up an order of flavored conchas, bow-tie Danish, and cream cheese–filled bear claws.

Rosa says, "I left them in back."

He's taken inspiration from Barney, his neighbor. He committed himself to a life of celibacy. *'Committed' may be too strong a word.* He's also begun learning the craft of letterpress printing. In Barney's studio, and with his friend's help, he's begun to print small posters on tan chipboard. His first print had been a quote from Nikolai Gogol: *"Whatever you may say, the body depends on the soul."*

"That's a good print," Barney said. "What's next?"

"I'd like to hand-set my obituary."

"That's twisted," Barney had said. "I like it."

Calvert pushes the door to the storeroom, and Daisy sits up in her dog bed.

Allen and Jackson, the two remaining employees of Bug Off, had pooled resources and purchased the extermination company for a fraction of the value. The new Bug Off would maintain existing contracts. The two of them, along with Jackson's dog, Buddy, will continue checking a block of rooms five days a week on a rotating schedule for good money.

Allen had stopped by Coffee Girl the previous week. "Jackson told me to take this bitch to the pound 'cause we only need one dog," Allen explained. "But I thought, *That crazy professor might like to have her.* So I brought her by. What do you think?"

"It depends what Daisy wants," Calvert said. Hearing her name, Daisy walked over to flop on Calvert's feet.

"That settles it," Allen said. "Good luck, Professor. Stay crazy."

"Do I have a choice? You be good, Allen."

"Where's the fun in that?" He had turned and walked away.

Now Calvert says, "Daisy, stay," and she settles back down. He pats her side a few times. "Who's the best guard dog?"

He washes his hands over the sink and takes the baked goods to the pastry case, where he arranges them for maximum appeal.

"Come sit," Rosa says.

Calvert checks the time. *Ten more minutes.* He's anxious for the day to go well. He sits across from Rosa. "I'll take Daisy to the park for a minute before we open." The park has become one of his favorite spots. It has cast cement benches with raised backward letters as if set for letterpress printing. The benches rest at perfect angles for watching Daisy play and sniff her dog friends.

Rosa lifts her cortado.

He lifts his. He loves how easy it is to be in her presence. In truth, he hopes that somehow, with the passage of time, she may begin to have stronger feelings for him than she does now. He taps the bottom of his tumbler on the top of hers. "To starting over."

"To new beginnings," she responds.

He tips the coffee to his lips. It's silky and rich. The aroma surpasses words; it speaks to the structures of his brain that predate language and logic; it nurtures his very soul. He takes a tiny sip while looking into Rosa's face, catching the soft smile at the corners of her mouth, at the edges of her eyes. It's not the smile she first showed him, the one that brought her whole face alive. It's quieter, guarded, and betrays a cautious worldview. But it's honest and speaks to the toll life takes if you live long enough. And she chooses to share it with him.

He sets the coffee down between sips, to make it last as long as possible.

Acknowledgments

Thanks to my creative co-conspirators Audrey, Jamie, Benjamin, Tinameri, Bob, Ben, Melissa, Caroline, Sprout, Joseph, Jean, Meredith, Wayne, Stephen, Brad, Marialena, Deron, Bryan, Chris, Heidi, Shawn, Jay, Dana, Mike, and Stash; plus, the entire community of writers, artists, printers, and collectors associated with Artists Book House. Without your warmth, help, and inspiration, it may never have happened.

Always and forever, Declan and Eliza.

My gratitude goes to Paula Munier, Matt Martz, Ben LeRoy, Sara J. Henry, and a small army of professionals at Crooked Lane Books who made this book better each time they touched it. We should do this again sometime.

A special thanks to Milo and Celeste.